The Best Laid Plans

ALSO BY CAMERON LUND

Heartbreakers and Fakers

The Best Laid Plans

CAMERON LUND

RAZORBILL

RAZORBILL

An imprint of Penguin Random House LLC, New York

This book is a work of fiction. Any references to historical events, real people,
or real places are used fictitiously. Other names, characters, places, and events
are products of the author's imagination, and any resemblance to actual events
or places or persons, living or dead, is entirely coincidental.

To anyone who isn't ready or feels like they're falling behind.

Remember, it's not a race.

The Best Laid Plans

ONE

THE FIRST THING I see when I open the door is Chase Brosner's bare ass, flashing at me from the bed like some neon Vegas billboard. Then I see the girl underneath him, hands gripping his back, and when I see the fingernails, I know it's Danielle. I was with her when she painted them, *black*, she said, to match her heart.

They're completely wrapped up in each other on the bed—Andrew's *parents'* bed—and I can't move, my hand frozen on the doorknob. This is not what I expected when I wandered upstairs, trying to get away from all the people who don't even remember it's my birthday, who are only at this stupid party because they know Andrew's parents are away on a ski trip and there's free beer. But now, as I take in the image of Chase's ass, of Danielle's fingernails clutching his skin, her dark hair spread out on the pillow, I realize this is so much worse than the party.

It only takes about three seconds for Danielle to notice me—

though it feels like three thousand—and then she screams. I scream too and drop my beer, which splashes onto my feet. We lock eyes as she scrambles for the sheet, pulling it up to cover her naked body. Chase tumbles onto the floor, wrapping himself up in the comforter like a human burrito.

"I'm so sorry," I say, bending down to pick up my cup, wiping up what I can with the sleeve of my sweatshirt before it does damage to the floorboards. "I didn't know there was anyone in here."

"Get out!" she shrieks, and I do, slamming the door shut behind me.

And I know it sounds crazy, but as I stand blinking on the other side of the door, all I can think about is this: What if this is *it* for me? What if this is officially the first and last ass I'll ever see for the rest of my life? When I shut my eyes I can still see it, bright and white, like when you stare too long at the sun, and I'm afraid it's going to be seared there forever. It's not a *bad*-looking ass, I guess, although I don't have anything to compare it to. It's just attached to a guy who I don't even like—a guy who makes dumb jokes about his farts, who cares way too much about basketball, and has an unhealthy obsession with the word *dude*. But there are certainly no other naked guys on my horizon, not with the way high school has gone so far.

I'm still there when the door opens again and Chase and Danielle step out of the bedroom. They're finishing pulling on their clothes, and I wince as Chase zips up his fly.

"Keely," Danielle says, her voice breathy. Her arms are wrapped around his bicep, and I can smell the candy sweetness of her perfume. She's got lipstick smudged across her cheeks, her dark hair messy like an unmade bed. I need to stop thinking of messy beds. *Ugh.*

"Hey, dude." Chase lifts his arm into the universal bro-gesture to fist-bump, then brings it back down to his side, presumably remembering I'm not, in fact, a dude. Easy mistake.

"I'm so sorry," I say again, backing away from them.

"Whatever." Chase shrugs like it's no big deal.

"Actually, can we talk?" Danielle motions her head toward the hall bathroom to my left. "Alone?"

"Sure," I say, but my chest feels tight.

To everyone else it probably looks like Danielle and I are friends—which I guess, according to the rules of high school, we are. We're in the same group and sit at the same lunch table, but we don't really ever talk one-on-one. Looks like things change when you accidentally see someone naked.

"I'll meet you downstairs." Chase kisses Danielle in a way I feel uncomfortable watching, his hand just on the side of her boob, about to squeeze. She giggles and he pulls away, nodding at me. "Later, Keely." Then he lumbers down the staircase. I can smell the stale beer on him as he passes.

Once he's gone, Danielle pulls me into the bathroom. She shuts the door and locks it, then turns to the mirror, speaking to me while looking at herself. I don't blame her—if I looked like Danielle Oliver I'd probably stare at myself all the time too. Her pale skin is luminous, her cheekbones model sharp, and she's got big brown eyes that turn up at the corner, like a cat's.

"You have to promise not to tell."

"I won't."

"Good." Some of the tension drains out of her. "I'm still playing hard to get."

CAMERON LUND

I bite the side of my cheek so I won't laugh. Danielle and Chase aren't dating yet, but they make sense: they're the beautiful people, the ones you'd read about in the tabloids if high school were like Hollywood. It was only a matter of time before they got together. So I'm not sure why Danielle is so intent on keeping this a secret. It's not like she was discreet earlier when she was laughing and chasing him in a circle around the kitchen, trying to draw on his face with her red lipstick.

"Didn't he just . . . get you?" Hopefully she won't kill me for the question. But here's the thing—it's pretty well known around Prescott that Danielle Oliver is—*was*—a virgin, and it's not because she's openly circulated the fact. That's just how things work around here. Our nowhere Vermont town is so small that even if you're barely friends with someone, you probably still know everything about them. I mean, we've been together—all sixty of us in the senior class—since elementary school, so secrets tend to hop from student to student like a twisted game of telephone. And the fact that Danielle has managed to stay a virgin for so long is probably Prescott's top news story.

I'm a virgin too, but this isn't surprising enough to be news.

I can see the moment right when she decides to tell me. She smiles and it spills over her face like light filling up a dark room, and she's so stunning I feel it in my chest. Her eyes are sparkling as she turns to me. I can see the secret brimming in her, like bubbles in a glass of champagne.

"Okay, so maybe he got me," she says. "Guess who's finally a woman."

"Wow." I'm suddenly unable to find the right words. "That's . . . congrats. Way to go!" I don't know why I've turned into a cheesy

4

greeting card instead of a real, functioning human. *Wishing you all the best on your journey. Reach for the stars!* She must not find it too weird because she continues talking like I haven't said anything.

"It didn't even hurt that much. Ava told me she passed out her first time, so I guess I was expecting it to be a little more extreme." She licks her pointer finger and runs it under her eyes to fix her mascara. "Ava is *so* dramatic." If Ava Adams were in this bathroom right now instead of me, she'd know exactly what to say. Ava is Danielle's favorite. I'm just the one Danielle tolerates.

"Do you like him?" I ask, swishing the now-mostly-empty beer around in my cup.

She doesn't answer for a few seconds, probably deciding whether it's worth telling me the truth. Then she shrugs. "It was time. I can't believe I was a virgin for this long. So embarrassing."

My cheeks burn at the casual dig. Being a virgin shouldn't be a big deal—*I know that*—but the fact that Danielle shared the label with me always made me feel a little better. If Danielle Oliver does something, it automatically shaves five million points off the embarrassment scale.

Ava was the first girl in our class to lose her virginity. She and Jason Ryder did it middle school grad night on the playground behind the big slide. I was horrified back then when I first heard about it. Sex was still something foreign to me, something people did in movies—and not even in the movies I watched. Then other girls started doing it too—Molly Moye lost it to one of her older brother's best friends, Jessica Rogers to a girl she met over winter break in Vancouver. My friend

Hannah lost hers junior year to her boyfriend Charlie. They spent the night at his lake house, lit a bunch of candles, and played her favorite album. Turns out, even Morrissey couldn't save them.

When we first heard these stories, the rest of us were eager with questions. What did sex feel like? Did it hurt? How did you know what to do? And now Danielle has joined them. Now we're seniors and the questions are drying up.

Now I'm the only one left.

I can hear the low thumping sound of music downstairs, a high female screech and peal of laughter, a crash as something falls to the floor—a water glass maybe, or a table lamp. I wince, hoping Andrew's mom won't kill us, because even though it's his house and his party, she'll know I was here. I'm always here.

Danielle grabs a hand towel and scrubs the smudged lipstick from her cheeks. I want to reach out a hand to stop her—Andrew's mom will flip out about a stained towel, especially after the broken *something* downstairs—but it doesn't seem like the time. She leans closer to the mirror and stares. And I swear, her expression is of someone wise—someone who will never again wonder if a boy likes her back, never again get a huge pimple in the middle of her face. Danielle has always been confident, but now she looks unstoppable.

Next to her I still look like I'm twelve years old, even though as of today I'm officially eighteen. I've always been ridiculously short, but now I look even smaller because Danielle is wearing these black chunky heels and I'm in my socks; I took my snowy boots off at the door like we were supposed to. I touch my hair—darker blond than usual because I didn't wash it—cursing myself for thinking some dry shampoo and a ponytail were proper party attire. It's like I'm setting myself up for failure.

Danielle purses her lips. "Do you think I look older now?" She moves her head back and forth to check out her reflection from all angles. "Now that I'm a woman I really feel older."

I don't want to admit to her what I've just been thinking, so I cross my eyes, throwing back her question. "Do I look older?" I know birthdays don't magically change you from one day to the next. Still, there's a part of me that wants to feel the way Danielle is feeling—I want to be unstoppable too.

She looks at me blankly. "Why would you look older?" *Of course* she doesn't remember, even though Hannah brought cupcakes to school today to celebrate and Danielle said the recipe was too *eggy*. Even though this party is supposed to be for me.

"It's my birthday."

She wrenches her gaze away from the mirror and turns to me. "Oops, I totally forgot." Her hand catches on a tangle in her hair. "Chase was so sweet tonight. He knew it was my first time, so he didn't rush it." So we're back to Chase. I guess I can't blame her. If I had just lost my virginity, maybe I wouldn't want to stop talking about it either.

"I'm glad it was just how you imagined," I say. "There are a lot of jerks at this school. It's good you found a nice one."

"I know," she says, "Chase Brosner." She grabs my hand and pulls me to the door, unlocking it and yanking it open. "Remember," she says. "This never happened."

We leave the bathroom together and head downstairs. The air is warm, despite the snow falling outside, and it smells like sweat. We're almost at the bottom of the stairs when it starts.

The applause.

It's quiet at first, over the din of the party, over the flow of the Kendrick song playing through the speakers from somebody's phone. But then as more people notice us, it picks up. People stop talking, stop dancing, pause their games of beer pong mid-throw, and join in, hooting and hollering and cheering. Somebody grabs the phone, and Madonna's "Like a Virgin" blasts through the living room.

Danielle stiffens beside me on the staircase.

Across the room from us, Chase is sprawled out on the couch with Jason Ryder and Simon Terst, a sleepy smile on his face.

Simon leans forward, practically twitching with excitement. "Not bad, Brosner!"

Jason Ryder takes a long swig of his beer and then pats Chase on the back, hard enough it probably hurts. "Guess she's not *unfuckable* after all," Ryder says, his words slurring together.

Danielle is still frozen in place, one heel hovering over the next step.

"Danielle," I whisper, clutching her arm, trying to steady her, trying to steady myself. "Are you okay?"

How has everyone found out so fast? We can't have been in the bathroom for more than ten minutes. Did Chase announce it the second he came down the stairs? Maybe he told Jason Ryder and Ryder opened his big dumb mouth.

"I'm fine," she hisses. But her hand grabs on to mine and she squeezes for just a second before she pulls away. She takes a deep breath and reaches a shaky hand up to smooth down her hair. And then she bows.

The crowd goes wild.

TWO

DANIELLE STRAIGHTENS back up, smiling like she's Chase at a home game and we're all holding signs with her name on them. It's like the Madonna song is just her entrance music. I follow behind her the rest of the way down the stairs, hoping that nobody has made the connection between the song and *me*, how it's my entrance music too.

At the bottom of the stairs, Ava barrels over to us, grabbing Danielle possessively by the arm. Ava is tiny—more boobs than body—with pale freckly skin she keeps perfectly tanned even in winter, due to a passion for tinted coconut body lotion. Her hair was red once upon a time, but last year she started dyeing it different colors to match the holidays. Right now it's a faded pink from Valentine's Day, and it looks just like the cotton candy they make down by the lake in the summer. She's wearing the same bright red lipstick as Danielle, her ears decked in the same silver studs, and in her hand is the same matching purple phone case. It's a uniform that makes things clear: even if we're technically friends, I'll never be able to penetrate their two-person club. Sometimes I think she and Danielle are so used to being exactly the same that dyeing her hair is the only way Ava can think of to stand apart: her one tiny rebellion.

"Did you seriously just hook up with Chase?" Ava tugs on Danielle's arm. "Everyone says you slept with him."

"Everyone says," Danielle repeats, her mouth twisted. "So it must be true."

Ava tugs harder. "I've got it from here," she says to me. And then they walk away, whispering to each other in low voices I can't hear. Suddenly I'm overwhelmed again by the need to hide. I take a hesitant sip of what's left of my beer, just for something to do. It tastes like warm pee.

Parties have always been Andrew's thing, not mine, and I don't know how he's so good at convincing me to come to them, not when I'd rather be ten hours deep in a Netflix binge. I scan the room for him, or for Hannah, or *somebody*, but I'm too short to see over the crowd.

I'm going to kill Andrew for throwing me a birthday party and then leaving me to fend for myself.

C'mon, Collins, he whined earlier when I insisted it was a bad idea. *We've spent all your birthdays together. Can't stop now.* It's true— Andrew was there the day I was born. Before, actually. Our moms became friends in Lamaze class, so we've been stuck with each other forever. Andrew's birthday was last week, and his parents took us out for dinner at Giovanni's. Not really the birthday adventure he had in mind. So now that they're out of town, I'm stuck with this.

I walk into the kitchen, narrowly avoiding Jarrod Price, who's puking into the trash can. There are cups and dirty plates scattered all over the Formica counter. Andrew promised to get me pizza if I agreed to the party, and now the boxes litter the kitchen, covered in stray crusts and congealed cheese.

I gather up the dishes and put them in the sink, lathering up the sponge with soap and water.

"Please tell me you're not cleaning right now." Andrew slings an arm around my shoulder and pulls me into a quick hug. He's always reminded me a little of a golden retriever—a smiling, floppy mess of sandy hair and freckles. Sometimes I swear I can see him wagging his tail.

"I just thought I'd get a head start." I pick up a red plastic cup and run it under the faucet. Andrew whacks it out of my hand, splashing us both. His flannel shirt is already so rumpled it's like he's been rolling around in it. Which he probably has, with some girl or other. *Gross.*

"No cleaning on your birthday," he says. "House rules. Besides, this is a red Solo cup. It's disposable."

"Don't let it hear you say that. You might hurt its feelings." I glance across the room to where Danielle is standing, surrounded by a gaggle of junior girls. "Do you think she'll be okay?"

Andrew follows my gaze. "She's Danielle Oliver. She thrives off attention. Things couldn't have worked out better for her if she'd planned it."

I think about my conversation with her upstairs, how she made me promise not to tell. "I just feel bad. If it were me—"

"She's not you." He loops an arm around my back again. "Thank God. You think I would have stuck around her for eighteen years?" I let him lead me over to the fridge. "I got you those stupid watermelon drinks you like. Did you see them?" He pulls out a pink frosted glass bottle and I grab it from him with joy.

"And you're only telling me now? I've been trying to drink this stale pee all night." I motion to the keg, sitting on a pile of dirty beach towels in the corner, thanks to Andrew's cousin who turned twenty-one a few years ago and has been supplying our booze ever since.

"I'm just trying to toughen you up a little," he says. "Someday you're going to find yourself out in the wild, maybe at a party with a host who isn't so charming or thoughtful, and there won't be any stupid watermelon drinks and you'll think to yourself, *Thank God Andrew Reed taught me how to drink beer.*" He motions toward the keg. "But you're right, this tastes like pee."

Still, he reaches over and pours himself a cup. That's when one of the juniors peels away from Danielle and comes up to us, touching Andrew lightly on the shoulder. Cecilia Brooks is always lightly touching people's shoulders. It's like she's mastered some sort of secret code. I know for a fact Tim Schneider always does her trig homework when she asks, which is the kind of powerful I wish I could be.

"Hi, Drew." She tucks a strand of curly blond hair behind one ear and smiles, revealing two rows of perfectly white teeth. Cecilia's parents are dentists.

"Hey, Cecilia," he says. "I've been looking for you!" His usual line. Party Andrew has a different personality than regular Andrew. He always gets way cheesier when he's around girls, and somehow it works. Andrew upgrades girlfriends like he's upgrading iPhones.

"No you haven't!" She laughs and slaps him lightly on the chest. "You're such a liar."

"He's been talking about you all night," I improvise, trying to help him out. "I can't get him to shut up about it."

Andrew steps down on my foot, indicating perhaps I've gone a bit overboard.

Cecilia turns reluctantly to me. "Oh, hi, Keely." Then her eyes go wide. "Oh my gosh, is that a watermelon Breezer?" Her hand comes up to rest once more on Andrew's shoulder. "I love those!"

I want Andrew to be above it. But no straight boy, it seems, is immune to the magical touch of Cecilia Brooks—especially not Party Andrew.

"Yeah, do you want one? I bought plenty."

"Really? You are so sweet!" *Shoulder touch.*

I'm glaring at him, clutching my watermelon Breezer with two hands, as if somehow his pathetic pandering will cause it to slip from my grasp, sprout little wings, and fly into hers. He grabs a frosted pink bottle from the fridge and cracks it open, handing it to her. She takes a sip, glossy lips resting in just the right way on the mouth of the bottle.

"So, Drew, I came here with Susie, right?" Cecilia says. "But she might be too drunk to drive. She's had like way too many shots of raspberry Smirnoff. Do you think . . . are people staying over here tonight? Do you think we could crash here?" *Shoulder touch.*

"You can definitely sleep here," Andrew says, and Cecilia beams at him. I can practically see the hearts in her eyes.

I know he's lost to me for the night, along with the rest of the watermelon Breezers, so I finish my drink and set it down on the counter, ready for the next move. We've been here before and I know my lines. "I'm gonna go find Hannah. I'll see you guys later." I wave and walk into the dining room.

Andrew chases after me, leaving Cecilia behind. "Hey, you can take my bed tonight, okay?"

"Aren't you two going to need it?"

"It's your birthday. You're not couching it." He grins. "Besides, we can take the guest room. Or the shower."

"Please don't put gruesome images in my head," I say, hitting him on the shoulder in a not-so-delicate way.

"C'mon, there's nothing gruesome about a shower. This isn't *Psycho*."

We discovered Hitchcock when we were twelve, stumbling upon a DVD of *Strangers on a Train* at the local video store. We watched it on the fuzzy TV in his basement, bringing down our sleeping bags to spend the night and pretending we weren't scared. This led to a slew of basement movie marathons and the infamous time I peed my pants during *The Birds*. Now, whenever we see seagulls at the beach, or flocks of geese in the sky, he always says something infuriating about the air smelling like pee.

Andrew breaks into an impish smile, the corner of his mouth going crooked. He motions back toward Cecilia, his voice low. "Tonight, we'll be Strangers on a Drain."

"Oh, stop."

"I can't wait to check out her Rear Window, if you know what I mean."

"I've got some birds for you." I laugh, flipping both my middle fingers at him.

Andrew waggles his eyebrows. "Tonight I'm gonna show her my Hitchco—"

"My favorites!" Hannah crashes into us then, pulling both of us into a tight hug. "Are you guys seriously doing Hitchcock puns? If I didn't love you both so much I would hate you right now." Hannah's grip is surprisingly strong because she's been playing field hockey since sixth grade and has the muscles to prove it. A hug that almost hurts is a Hannah Choi specialty.

"Oh no," Andrew says, pulling out of her grasp. "If *you* don't think we're funny, then who will?"

"That's why you have each other," she says, laughing and brushing the long bangs out of her eyes. Hannah has shampoo-commercial hair—black and thick and bouncy. She's gorgeous, which doesn't do me any favors considering I spend most of my time standing next to her.

"Actually, he's ditching me." I lower my voice, nodding my head back toward the kitchen. Cecilia is still there, whispering now with Susie Palmer, her arms folded.

Hannah flashes Andrew a wicked smile. "Oh, are you and Cecilia Brooks going to do each other?"

"Yeah, probably in the shower," I say with a grimace. "I just heard way too much about it."

Hannah laughs. "If anyone can handle all the gory details, it's you."

"We're not going to *do each other*, as you so beautifully put it," Andrew says, all faux-offended. "Besides, it's your birthday, Collins, so if you want to hang out instead . . ."

He trails off, and I can tell he's waiting for me to give him permission to ditch me. I should be annoyed, but it's not like I didn't know this would happen before the party even started.

"Don't let me hold you back from love."

He scratches his nose. "You sure? Hannah and I wrote you this birthday rap and we haven't gotten a chance to—"

"That sounds excruciating." I laugh, practically shoving him away from me. "Just go. If you keep ignoring her and talking to us, you'll miss your chance." I can feel Cecilia's glare from here like it's a physical touch. "I have Hannah. And leftover pizza."

"Okay, cool," Andrew says. "And I'm not ignoring her, you know. I'm giving her time to miss me." He turns back to Cecilia then, flashing his stupid Party Andrew smile, and like always, it works. She comes into the dining room, sliding an arm through the crook of his elbow.

"So, Andrew, I need a partner for beer pong. Want to play?"

She begins to pull him as if he's already answered her question, and he lets her drag him away. "I'll see you two later, okay?"

"Have fun, kids!" I wave, and he calls back to me.

"My sheets have birds on them, Collins, so try not to wet the bed!"

I flip him off again and hear his laugh as he leaves the room.

"He's disgustingly good at that," Hannah says. "I don't know why we're friends with him."

"We're enablers," I agree.

I know Andrew appreciates our help with girls, and if I asked for his help with guys, he would do the same for me; it just hasn't ever happened. Guys don't come up to me at parties and magically touch my shoulder. Before I can help it, an image flashes through my mind of Danielle and Chase naked and tangled together on the bed and I feel a little sick. I look around the party and try to imagine who I would approach if I could, who I would let lead me into the master bedroom like Danielle did. It occurs to me suddenly that I could do it, I could try to lose my virginity tonight, right now, on my eighteenth birthday, and then it would be over.

But there's nobody here I want that way. Not Chase, who knows he's the best-looking guy in our class and acts like it. Not Jason Ryder, who acts even worse. Not Edwin Chang, who everyone knows is in love with Molly Moye, or Jarrod Price, who is pretty much always high. Definitely not Andrew, who is basically my brother and is currently wrapped around Cecilia like a winter scarf, whispering into her ear as she wriggles in his arms.

I've known them all for too long—since they used to pick their noses, have farting competitions, eat melted crayons and glue. It's hard to look past that now. I think for the millionth time about how college will be different, once I'm out of nowhere Vermont, once I get to the city and can walk down the street and be surrounded by strangers for the first time in my life—people who don't all look and act exactly the same, who won't know my parents or what I was like when I was ten, won't think of me as Andrew's best friend, as the girl Danielle tolerates—the least cool one allowed at the lunch table.

I shake my head and loop my arm through Hannah's. "Andrew said I've got dibs on his bed. Want to share the room with me?"

"Yes. Thank God. I've been trying to find a spot to sleep for a while, but everyone's claiming them. I tried to take the couch in the office and Sophie practically murdered me."

Here's the thing about parties in the middle of nowhere. There's no such thing as Uber, and you'd be an idiot to drive drunk—especially with the snow—so everyone spends the night. It's like one giant alcohol-infused sleepover.

Hannah and I head up the stairs, passing a wall of framed pictures from Andrew's childhood, pictures I've seen a million times and am mostly in—Andrew and me on Halloween dressed as Ghostbusters, fistfuls of candy in our tiny hands; Andrew and me in middle school, blond and skinny with braces and acne, the height of our awkward phase. Hannah taps her finger on one as we pass—Andrew's tenth birthday, when he and I got in a mud fight. We're smiling at the camera, completely splattered.

She grins. "Think everyone has already seen these, or is there still time to hide them?"

"It's too late."

"I can't even tell which kid you are." I know she's joking, but she's got a point; I look exactly like a boy here. But there's no use hiding the past. If I can remember everyone picking their noses, chances are everyone remembers me like this too.

I spent all of elementary school with Andrew. I didn't see the need to make any other friends, not when Andrew and I biked at the same pace and could quote all the *Star Wars* movies by heart—even the prequels. My mom warned me of the dreaded "cootie" phase—of the day Andrew would change and decide he couldn't be my friend. But it didn't happen. Puberty hit and we somehow stayed friends.

There were uncomfortable years, sure. I remember being the only girl at Andrew's thirteenth birthday pool party and being terrified to strip down to my bathing suit, wanting desperately to join in the cannonball contest but worrying my suit would fly off or my period would start. I remember posing for pictures with him at family gatherings, our parents casually telling us to "get close together" and me not being able to breathe from the awkwardness of it. I remember the time Andrew invited me over in seventh grade and I showed up in my pajamas, not expecting a bunch of other boys to be there—*cute* boys from our class—and I was so mad he hadn't warned me that I didn't speak to him for three days.

And then there was Andrew's first kiss, with Sophie Piznarski at the eighth-grade dance. He pulled me outside the cafeteria to tell me, his face a confusing mixture of excitement and embarrassment. *Was this kind of conversation okay? Could we talk about these things? Was it too weird?*

During those turbulent, traumatic years of frizzy hair and braces, when Andrew and I were still testing the waters, trying to figure out how to relate to each other; when he was always surrounded by other boys, and every time I tried to talk to another boy it felt like I had clay in my mouth, it was a mercy I met Hannah. She was cooler than I was, and friends with Danielle and Ava—girls who, at thirteen years old, already looked like Instagram models. She invited me to sit with her at lunch, rescuing me from tomboy obscurity and the vulgar conversations of middle school boys.

I was worried my new group of friends would make things different with Andrew—that he'd feel weird or left out that I had a new best friend besides him, but I should have known better. The first time I hung out with both Andrew and Hannah, they bonded over a mutual obsession with Harry Potter, and soon the three of us were inseparable. They're both Gryffindors, of course, and even though I'm a Hufflepuff, they say they love me anyway.

At the top of the stairs we see Molly Moye making out with Edwin Chang, the two of them leaning against the door to the hall closet like they might try to climb inside. Edwin still has a bottle of beer in his hand, and it's seriously close to spilling because he's trying to hold it steady and grope Molly's ass at the same time. Hannah is friends with Molly from field hockey, so we've hung out enough times for me to know that Edwin and Molly getting together like this is a momentous occasion, but for some reason I don't feel like celebrating.

"Is everyone in this house in heat?" I mutter under my breath, walking over to take the bottle out of Edwin's hand and setting it down on the hall table, on top of a magazine so it won't leave a ring. He barely even notices, just gives me a quick thumbs-up, which I return, because I'm trying to act like I'm cool with everything. We edge by them into Andrew's room, and once the door closes, I relax. The place is a mess, but it's a mess I can clean up. The floor is strewn with laundry, and the bedsheets—green with flying ducks—are unmade and rumpled. Against one wall is the old couch I usually sleep on when I stay over. Hannah plops down on it while I sit on the bed, throwing her an extra blanket.

"So what happened?" she asks. "I was in the basement and I heard everyone cheering."

So I tell her about Danielle and the crowd and the Madonna song, the word *unfuckable* loud over everything else, as sharp as a blade.

"It's just so typical." I take off my woolly socks and flop back on the bed. "This place sucks." I'm going to USC for college, in California, which everyone thinks is crazy, but I need to be somewhere completely new. I'm sick of Prescott—the snow, the ice, the wind so cold sometimes it feels like it's actually eating you. All I know is I want to make movies, and Vermont is pretty bleak on that front. All we have are writers, snowboarders, and serial killers.

Hannah is going to NYU to study art, and Andrew is going to Johns Hopkins because even though he hides it well, he's freakishly smart. Johns Hopkins is in Baltimore, which is 2,646 miles from Los Angeles, which is 2,777 miles from New York. I've looked it up. Next year, we'll just be three distant dots on a map. That's the scariest part. I'm ready to get the hell out of Prescott, but I'll never be ready to leave them.

So we need to make the next few months count. All that's left

20

are the *moments*—the big memories we'll look back on, the ones that will matter when we talk about high school twenty years from now. When school ends in June, the three of us have a plan to blast "Free Bird" from Andrew's truck speakers and point our middle fingers to the sky as we zoom out of the parking lot— one final *fuck you* to everyone and everything else. I already have it planned out in my head, can picture the rest of the school year like the frames of a movie.

"Next year everything will finally be different," Hannah says. "I can't wait to get out of here." Hannah is Korean—one of only three Asian kids in the entire school—and I know it's part of the reason she's excited to move to New York. Her parents actually met at NYU and then moved here from the city when she was five, and she's been talking about going back ever since, living in some bohemian artist loft. I mean, I get it. New York is vibrant and exciting and diverse. Vermont is one big bowl of crunchy white granola.

"Prescott is the most depressing place on Earth," I say. "But I'm glad you're stuck here with me."

"I'm so happy you were born, birthday girl," Hannah says. "And I'm happy Andrew exists too. He's one of the good ones. He gave us this room."

I laugh. "I've just been using him for his bed this whole time."

"I actually don't think Andrew would mind you using him for his bed," Hannah says, waggling her eyebrows.

"You're disgusting." I make a fake gagging noise like I'm in kindergarten. Hannah has been joking about Andrew and me getting together since middle school, but it's never going to happen.

"You know"—Hannah frowns—"I really thought Chase was

a good guy too. I bet he didn't mean to tell everyone about Danielle. You know how Ryder is. He probably punched it out of him or something."

I'm not sure if she actually believes what she's saying or if she's only trying to convince herself. Hannah has always tried to see the best in people, even when they don't deserve it.

I pull back Andrew's sheets and climb under them, not bothering to change. Hannah tucks herself in under her blanket. We lie still for a few seconds, looking up at the glow-in-the-dark stars on the ceiling, and then I hear Hannah's voice, soft and muffled.

"It kinda reminds me of Charlie."

I roll over to face her, propping my chin up on my hand. Cheating-Asshole-Charlie, as he's more commonly called, broke up with Hannah mere days after they first slept together. Turns out he was also sleeping with Julie Spencer the whole time. I know being in Andrew's room sometimes makes Hannah think about Charlie because this is where we spent the night after they broke up. Andrew looked up how to play all the best power breakup songs on his guitar, and we scream-sang along to them off-pitch and at the top of our lungs. *You're a Gryffindor and he's a Squib*, Andrew told her. *You remember that.*

He's not a Squib, Hannah said. *He's a fucking Death Eater.*

"What Chase did is bad, but it's not the same," I say now, needing to believe it for Danielle's sake. "She'll get over it. She'll be okay because she doesn't . . ." I trail off, but Hannah finishes the sentence for me.

". . . love him?"

"Yeah."

"Sex and love are supposed to go together," she says. "But anyone who falls in love is screwed." She reaches up to switch off the light. "Falling in love with a high school boy is the single stupidest thing you can do."

I wake up a little later when I feel a weight press down on the mattress beside me. Turning toward it, I crack open an eye and see Andrew sitting on the edge of the bed, his hair sticking up in all directions. He's got my purse in his hand, and when he sees me he drops it, the contents spilling out at his feet.

"Sorry," he says. "I tripped on it." He reaches down to stuff everything back in, then lies down next to me.

"What time is it?" I whisper, my voice hoarse from sleep. He glances at his phone, the light from the screen bright in the dark room.

"Four thirty."

"Where's Cecilia?"

"Basement. We were trying to sleep on the couch down there, but there wasn't enough space. I kept sliding onto the floor. I bruised my elbow." He holds it out for me to see.

"So you just left her?"

"It's your birthday," he says, like this is an explanation.

"You're an asshole."

"No way." He slings a heavy arm over me. "I'm the best."

"No, get off." I roll away from him so that I'm practically falling off the other side of the bed. There's a noise from the couch and Hannah turns away from us, snuggling deeper into the cushions.

"Shhhhhhhhh," Andrew says loudly, slinging his arm back over me.

"No. You've got Cecilia all over you!"

"We showered, remember? I'm clean as a whistle." He lets out a soft whistle, as if this somehow proves his point. I sigh but let him keep his arm on me, too tired to give any real protest. His phone buzzes and he lifts it back off the pillow, the light of the screen blinding us both when he clicks it on.

"Love poem from Cecilia?" I whisper. "'O Dearest Andrew. O Captain my Captain. Why did you leave me all alone on the couch in the basement?'" I can't see his face very well but can practically feel him rolling his eyes.

"She'll be fine, Collins."

He reaches into his pocket and pulls out a pair of tortoiseshell glasses with big thick frames, glasses I've always thought make him look sort of like someone's grandpa. He always keeps them tucked away in his pocket, only putting them on when it's extremely necessary, like he finds them embarrassing. I scoot closer so I can read the text with him. It's not from Cecilia after all, but from Susie Palmer, Cecilia's friend—the one who had *like way too many shots* and couldn't drive.

Are you asleep? I'm alone in the guest room if you want to find me

"She realizes you just did her best friend, right?" I ask.

"I'm not gonna answer her." He clicks the phone off so the screen goes black. My eyes take a second to adjust to the dark, and for a moment I can't make out the shape of his face next to me on the bed. Then slowly his glasses come into focus.

"Really?"

"You sound surprised," he says, voice soft. "I'm not that big of an asshole."

"Or you just have a massive crush on Cecilia and you don't want to mess it up," I say, grinning. "I get it."

"It's because her *conversation* is so stimulating." He smiles, and I shove him, rolling away and closing my eyes. I'm used to this side of Andrew now, Party Andrew, who hooks up with girls like it's no big deal, joking about taking coed showers like it's something we all do.

In comic books, superheroes have this big moment—a spider bite or a puddle of radioactive goo—that turns them from someone normal into something extraordinary. But Andrew changed from Peter Parker into Spider-Man slowly—so slowly I didn't notice while it was happening—the years morphing him from the gangly kid, all hands and feet and freckles, into someone girls find *cute*, someone with power over girls like Cecilia Brooks and Susie Palmer. And with great power comes great responsibility, so I try my best to keep him in check—to keep him from becoming SuperDouche.

Still, I can't help thinking about how he's so much farther along than I am. It's like everyone else in school is competing to beat each other's high scores and I'm still trying to put the batteries in my controller.

"G'night, Drewchebag," I say into the dark. But he's already asleep and he answers me with a loud drunken snore.

THREE

"NOW THAT I'M a woman, I'm going to order an espresso," Danielle says from the driver's seat on our way to Dunkin' Donuts the next afternoon. "That's the little one without any milk and sugar, right?"

"Yeah, and it tastes like gasoline," Ava answers from shotgun. "Besides, you've put five Splendas in your coffee since seventh grade. I don't think one magical night can change that."

We've just spent all morning helping clean Andrew's house—scrubbing down counters, mopping the floors, shoveling the driveway so everyone's footprints and tire tracks are gone. Andrew's mom is a bit intense about the house—she refers to her bedroom as "the sanctuary" and spends so much time at Crate and Barrel she probably gets the employee discount. So we know she'll notice if something is out of place. The morning after a party is always a several-hour ordeal if you're nice enough to stick around. Guys like Jason Ryder never do.

I have this idea in my head that things will be different once I get to California, that the kids there are classy and drink wine with their pinkies out, that the guys don't get drunk on Keystone Light and then try to smoke weed out of the empty can. But maybe people are the same everywhere.

We've been sent on a dumpster drive, so the car is piled with bags of trash we're supposed to drop—empty bottles and cans that we couldn't leave as evidence inside the house. I'm in the back seat with Hannah, who looks a little green, probably from the smell wafting out of the trash bags. Unfortunately for all of us, Ava loves musical theater, so we're currently listening to a song from *Wicked* that's about three octaves too high for the day after a party.

"For the love of God, can we turn this off?" Danielle reaches for the stereo, but Ava slaps her hand away.

"No! 'Defying Gravity' is literally the best song of all time. Are you telling me this doesn't make you feel something?"

"Yeah," Danielle says. "It makes me feel like I want to die."

"Careful," Ava says. "I could put on *Cats* instead. *Cats* is terrifying."

Ava has been the star of every school musical since freshman year. She'll be at NYU next year with Hannah, and although their majors are different, the image of the two of them exploring New York City together makes my heart hurt if I think about it for too long.

"Is there a musical where all the songs are just relaxing ocean sounds? Let's listen to that," Hannah says, leaning her head against the window.

We're on a curvy back road lined on either side with pine

trees. Prescott is full of roads like these, carving through the middle of nowhere. Downtown is only a four-block strip lined with shops and restaurants. In the summer, the nearby lake draws tons of tourists: families with inner tubes and giant tubs of sunscreen, or hikers with backpacks and dreadlocks passing through on the Appalachian Trail. Fall brings the leaf-peepers, city people from New York or Boston who drive so slowly on the roads they're a hazard to traffic. But in early March, we're a ghost town.

As we pull onto a busier street, Dunkin' Donuts appears on our left, a glorious pink and orange beacon of all things good in the world. Danielle drives right past it.

"What are you doing?" Ava shrieks. "I need caffeine! I have a headache!" This is hard to believe from the decibel of her voice. Ava always projects like she's trying to reach the back of an auditorium. Sometimes people get on her about being too theater kid, but I kinda like that about her. She always feels everything totally and completely. One time in ninth-grade English she cried while reading this poem out loud to the class and she wasn't even embarrassed about it.

"We're going to the one on Base Hill instead." Danielle rolls her eyes as if this should be obvious. Dunkin' Donuts locations dot our state like confetti. There are three in our county alone, even though we don't even have a movie theater and have to drive almost an hour to get to a mall. "They just put one in right next to that gym where all the EVmU guys work out."

Eastern Vermont University, our local college, is known for its herbology department, if you know what I mean. Lots of kids from Prescott go there on the weekends to crash parties, but I've never wanted to put myself through that; a college party sounds like literal torture.

"What, now that you're a woman you only want college boys?" I ask Danielle, grinning.

"We've given high school boys too many chances," she says.

"I hate that expression by the way," Hannah says. "The concept that you have to get penetrated by a peen in order to become a woman. Like, why are we giving guys so much power?"

"And what about lesbians?" I add.

"Yes!" Ava says. "Chase Brosner does *not* have a magical penis."

"Thank God," Danielle says. "His ego is already big enough."

"No guy has a magical penis," I say, laughing. "They all just think they do."

"Have you talked to Chase?" Hannah asks. "You know . . . since?"

Danielle pulls the car sharply into a turn, ignoring a yield sign. "We both got what we wanted. He's an idiot if he thinks it's ever going to happen again after that show last night."

"He's such an asshole." Ava nods in agreement. "It's like Charlie all over again." She glances back at Hannah. "They act like they care about you, but it's all a big joke, isn't it? They only care about you until they cum."

"There's already a bag of trash sitting next to me," Hannah says. "Do we really have to talk about Charlie?"

"I'm just being honest," Ava says, her voice rising. "Isn't it depressing that none of us is still with the guy we lost our virginity to? When you care too much, it just hurts you." She turns around in her seat, eyeing me pointedly. "Keely, you're lucky you're still a virgin."

"Whatever. I don't regret it." Danielle pulls into the parking lot and stops the car in front of the gym, shifting a little too forcefully into park. We watch as a beefy guy in his midtwenties pushes open the gym door, holding it for a girl behind him. She walks through into the cold air, wrapping her arms around his waist like she belongs there.

"It's only going to get worse in college," Danielle says. "You're supposed to be done with the awkward part, right? You're supposed to get that out of the way in high school." She looks right at me. "Being a virgin in college is like having a disease."

Ava was right about the espresso, of course. Penetration did nothing to change Danielle's taste buds, and after one sip, she orders something that's mostly whipped cream. While she and Ava wait at the counter for her second drink, Hannah and I walk our coffees back to a table in the corner.

"Danielle's just putting on a show, you know," Hannah says, taking a hesitant sip of her latte. "She's pretending she doesn't care, because Chase literally screwed her over. That thing she just said about having a disease is such an unhealthy mind-set." She fiddles with the lid of her cup. "Honestly, virginity shouldn't even be that big of a deal. We only make it a big thing because we put all this pressure on it. You shouldn't worry about being a virgin. Everybody thinks it's fine."

"That's the problem though." I set down my coffee. "Everybody knows. Everybody shouldn't think it's fine, because everybody shouldn't know."

I went with Hannah to *The Rocky Horror Picture Show* last Halloween, dressed up in wigs and corsets. When we first arrived, the show's emcee took a tube of bright red lipstick and drew a big V on each of our foreheads to let the rest of the audience know we were "Rocky Virgins" and this was our first time seeing the show. This is how I feel every day in the halls of Prescott—like everyone in school can still see that big red V on my forehead, like I never washed it off.

My parents have always been really open with me about sex. They very willingly gave me the "birds and the bees" talk in fourth grade, going into way more detail than was absolutely necessary at the time. The phrase "clitoral stimulation" will probably be seared into my brain for the rest of eternity.

We aren't a town of churchgoers for the most part, at least not in the way you'd think. It's not uncommon here to identify as "spiritual" instead of "religious"—to believe in an energy in the trees or to look for guidance from the stars. My family celebrates Christmas, but it's always been more about presents than anything else. Danielle has always described herself as *Jew-ish*; she never bothered with a bat mitzvah and usually cheats during Passover, saying she could never last more than a day without a bagel.

I know in some other parts of the world, in cultures different from ours, religion plays a much bigger role in shaping ideas of sex and purity. For some people, sex comes with marriage. It's not embarrassing to wait, it's expected. Sex is a demonstration of love, something sacred.

But then, Hannah thought her first time was sacred. She loved Charlie, and he claimed to love her back. She waited for the moment it felt right. When he suggested they spend the night at his lake house, she knew what was implied. It was romantic, special—perfect. Until the next week, when he dumped her for Julie Spencer.

I'm not waiting for marriage. I'm not even really waiting for *love*. What I want is respect and trust. I want to know that whoever I have sex with will make me feel safe, that they won't leave me for a junior in their French class, or never talk to me again, or tell everyone at the party in a matter of minutes. I don't think I could handle a public humiliation as well as Danielle did. For that matter, I don't think I should have to.

Wait until you're ready, people always say. But how are you supposed to know when you're ready? Do you wake up one day and suddenly feel more grown-up, more like an adult? I don't feel like an adult at all. If having sex means opening yourself up to heartbreak, or ridicule, or pain, I don't know if I'll ever be ready.

"If it's this bad now, how's it going to be next year?" I ask miserably. "We're going to college in the two biggest cities in the country. There probably haven't been any virgins in LA since the eighties."

"We have six months until college," Hannah offers. "You still have time. And next year is our fresh start, remember?"

The little bell above the door jingles and a cold gust of air swoops into the store, blowing a guy inside with it. He looks college-aged, probably an EVmU student coming from the gym next door. I watch as he puffs into a pair of fingerless gloves, rubbing his hands together. He's all dark hair and clean lines, with warm chocolate eyes and hard cheekbones tinged pink from the cold. And I swear—he's the best-looking guy I've ever seen in real life. Hannah and I gape at him, pausing mid-conversation.

"He looks like James Dean," she whispers, slack-jawed. Hannah knows this because I've had a *Rebel Without a Cause* poster tacked to my wall since fifth grade. It's one of my favorites.

Our eyes trail him as he approaches the counter, coming up behind Danielle and Ava. He's wearing a leather jacket that covers his butt, and I inwardly curse the cold weather. I can tell the moment Danielle notices him. She nudges Ava, who stands up straighter, hands reaching up to smooth her pink hair. They both turn to face him at the same time.

"You're up," Danielle says. Then she licks a dollop of whipped cream from the top of her drink, staring at him like she's licking something else. Danielle's stare is a powerful thing; she uses eye contact like a weapon.

"Uh, thanks," he says. His voice is like warm, hot fudge.

The girls rush back to the table.

"Did you see that guy?" Ava hisses, probably not as quietly as she should.

Danielle takes a long frozen sip of her drink. When she pulls her mouth away, there's a red lipstick mark on the straw. Before Danielle, I always associated lipstick with old ladies, the smell of powder perfumes and hairspray that always hovered around my grandma. But lipstick is Danielle's signature.

"I should go back and talk to him." She glances over her shoulder.

"Yeah you definitely should!" Ava nods vigorously.

Danielle looks back at him and shrugs, then walks to the door instead. "Whatever, he's not worth it."

It's not like Danielle at all to shy away from a guy, especially one as good-looking as James Dean, and I wonder if Chase has messed her up more than she's letting on.

I glance back once more as we leave, just to get another look at James Dean, and feel myself flush with excited embarrassment when he looks right at me. Then he lifts a tiny cup of espresso to his mouth and takes a long sip.

FOUR

WE'RE DRIVING AGAIN when my phone beeps. I pull it out of my pocket to find a cryptic text from Andrew.

> Help!

I suck in a sharp breath, then text back.

> Don't scare me. This better be something serious. Are you dying?

I wait a moment and my phone beeps again.

> We're in so much trouble

I feel my chest clench, like something heavy has been dropped there. My phone begins ringing, playing a tinny, canned version of "Eleanor Rigby." I pick up even before the violins can start.

"What's going on?"

"Is that Andrew?" Hannah mouths from the seat next to me.

"My parents found the condom," Andrew says.

"What condom?" I'm caught off guard by his words. The car swerves, and Danielle reaches up to turn off the music.

"Chase and Danielle's condom," he says. "They found the wrapper on the nightstand next to the bed."

I can't help it. I laugh. "Seriously? They didn't throw out the wrapper?"

Danielle swears softly from the front seat, and I can tell she's caught on, even if she can't hear Andrew's voice on the other end of the line.

"Your mom's gonna kill you," I say.

"Yeah, and she's gonna kill you too."

"What did I do?"

"Your parents are here."

I sigh, the weight on my chest increasing. "I didn't have a party!"

"Yeah, but it was your birthday. Obviously you were here."

"Fine," I answer. "I'll get dropped off."

I hang up the phone and turn to Danielle. "You left the condom wrapper on the nightstand?" I can't tell whether I'm angry or whether I want to laugh.

She purses her lips. "At least we used protection."

Andrew's house looks spotless. When we pull up to the front, it's easy to forget that last night even happened at all, that we spent the morning lugging trash bags across the slushy ground.

"Tell Andrew I'm sorry," Danielle says as I jump out of the car. "His parents won't kill him?" She actually looks worried. I want to tell her Andrew will be fine. He's used to getting into trouble.

I'm the one she should be apologizing to. But she's craning her head out the window and looking toward the house, and she doesn't focus her worried gaze in my direction at all.

"Don't worry about it," I say instead. I shut the door and walk toward the house, my boots crunching in the snow. The car peels out of the driveway, the smoke from the exhaust leaving little puffs in the cold air. I can hear *Wicked* come back on from all the way down the street.

My mom must have spotted me coming up the driveway, because she bursts through the front door and onto the porch. Like usual, her white-blond hair is wild around her head, curling out like wisps of smoke. When I was little, I used to think my mom was a beautiful witch in a fairy story, with her long colorful skirts and the gemstone rings stacked on her fingers. But then I realized she's just from Vermont.

Right now she's wrapped in a purple pashmina to keep out the cold, and it whips behind her in the wind like a flag. I shrink back slightly when I see her, preparing for a lecture, angry words to match the angry whip of the pashmina.

"Honey, it's freezing! Where is your coat?"

The soft tone of her voice catches me off guard.

"I'm fine."

She grabs ahold of me as I get up the steps and ushers me inside. The house smells like garlic now instead of the stale beer stink from last night, and there's classical music playing—I recognize Debussy from when I used to take piano lessons.

There are bags of ski gear dumped in the front hallway, boots dripping melted snow onto the tile floor. Andrew's parents always close out the ski season in Canada for their anniversary weekend, and usually Andrew stays with my family while they're away, but this year they said they trusted him on his own. I'm struck suddenly with the fear that if they're talking to us before they've fully unpacked, this must be serious.

When we get into the living room, Andrew's parents are sitting on the couch by the window, my dad on the love seat next to them. Andrew is perched on the coffee table, half off it like he's prepared to flee. They're all holding steaming mugs in their hands.

"Keely, sweetie, would you like some yerba maté?" Andrew's mom asks, getting up from the couch and heading into the kitchen, long skirts billowing behind her. There's a reason our moms bonded so quickly when they met—they're the same kind of hippie artist weirdos. "Robert picked some up from the health food store on our way home." She rummages through the cabinets and pulls out another mug. I smile when I see it's one Hannah made—she sometimes sells mugs at our local craft fair.

"Your mom brought us over some homemade bruschetta," she continues. Our parents are all vegans, so they're always cooking up new recipes. Andrew's mom places a few tomato-and-onion-covered toasts onto a little plate for me. "You have to try some."

I'm trying to get a grasp on the situation, but I can't. Andrew made it seem like we were in trouble when he texted, but my mom's concern, the smell of the garlic, and the tinkling piano music makes this feel like some friendly lunch instead. But maybe this is the punishment—being forced to drink yerba maté and hang out when we'd rather be literally anywhere else.

I look to Andrew for help, but he seems just as confused.

"So we talked about what we wanted to say to you," my mom starts, "how we wanted to . . . well, how we wanted to bring this up—if we even wanted to bring it up at all." My dad puts his hand on her shoulder to show they're a Parental Unit and he agrees with her no matter what.

"We know these things happen," he says, running a hand through his beard. My dad has had the same beard my whole life, and sometimes I think it's his proudest accomplishment.

"A part of me has been preparing for it," Andrew's mom says. "I mean, really, we've always known this might happen, even hoped for it a little bit. We've certainly joked about it a lot."

"You guys are all grown up now," my mom says. "It's hard for us. You were our babies. But this is normal, of course. And you were being safe."

"We're certainly glad you used protection," my dad agrees. "We raised you right."

I choke on my tea, spitting it back into my mug as everything clicks together. They aren't mad about a party. They don't even know about the party.

"But did you really have to do it in our bed when there are so many other places available?" Andrew's mom adds. "You know our room is off-limits." She pauses. "Is that why you went in there? Was it some sort of *kink*?"

"God, Mom, stop!" Andrew jumps up, banging his knee on the edge of the couch. "That wasn't our condom, okay?"

The room suddenly feels hot and cramped. Hearing Andrew use the words *our condom* makes my stomach flop uncomfortably. It's just messed up.

"Well, who else's could it be?" his mom asks, and I swear she sounds a little disappointed.

"Are you saying you two aren't using protection?" my mom jumps in. "Because if that's the case, we have a lot more to worry about than—"

"We're not having sex!" I shout, jerking suddenly and spilling my plate of bruschetta. The toasts scatter all over the carpet. I bend down and scoop the tomatoes up with my fingers, trying to clean, trying to hide my face, to keep busy, to focus on anything other than the conversation around me. I can't look at my parents, can't make eye contact with anyone—especially Andrew.

He bends down to help me, grabbing some bruschetta into his napkin, and I stare intently at the floor. His shoulder is an inch from mine, and I can feel the energy radiating off him, can feel the heat of our parents' gazes as they read too much into the situation.

"I've got it," I say.

"It's okay, I can help."

"No, seriously. Stop." I pull the napkin from his hands. He stands up, arms raised in surrender. Everyone is staring at me. I place the trashed plate back onto the coffee table while everybody watches. I've never felt so uncomfortable in my life.

"So if it's not yours, how did a condom wrapper end up on our bedside table?" his dad asks. "Did it fly in through the window?"

"We had some people over for Keely's birthday, okay?" Andrew says, sitting back down on the coffee table.

"Some people? Like a party?" his mom asks.

"No, like a casual get-together with some friends. What did you guys expect, leaving us alone on her birthday weekend?"

"A casual get-together with some sexually active friends, it seems," his dad adds.

"This isn't a big deal," Andrew says. "You're blowing this all out of proportion."

"Oh, am I?" his mom asks. "I haven't even gotten started."

• • • • • •

"We probably should have just let them believe it," Andrew says later. We're slumped in the hammock in his backyard, cocooned in a pile of coats to keep warm. It's still a little too cold to be outside, but the thought of being in the same house with our parents after everything that's just happened is too unpleasant. "They didn't even seem mad when they thought it was ours." He pushes his leg against the ground so that the hammock begins to swing. "If I knew they were gonna flip about the party, I would have just gone with it, you know?"

So our parents are making us get part-time jobs through the rest of the year. They're disappointed we're not being, in their words, trustworthy or dependable, and they think getting jobs will help teach us discipline. Which is messed up. It's not like I've never worked. I spent my last two miserable summers bagging groceries at the local market, making awkward chitchat with all my parents' friends when they came by the register. Andrew is the one who's reckless, who acts impulsively, who jumps off cliffs with his eyes closed. I'm the one who's always waiting at the bottom with the safety net.

This is the last semester of senior year. Last year when I was stressed about homework and the SATs, freaking out about getting into college, I was always so envious of the seniors who got to goof off, joking with teachers and skipping class like it didn't matter. But I was just waiting for my turn. I knew one day I'd be able to float through the hallways too like I'd already finished. Now our parents are taking that away.

Not to mention these are my last few months with Andrew and Hannah.

"I can't believe I'm in trouble too when it wasn't even my party." I pull a coat tighter around me to stay warm.

"Your birthday, your party," he answers. "Besides, you're an accessory to the crime. When you see a crime being committed and say nothing, that makes you responsible."

"I'm not responsible, remember? I'm untrustworthy and undisciplined."

"Yeah, you're pretty terrible," he agrees.

The sky is a bright gray, giving the illusion that we're in a cloud. The bare branches of the trees above us stretch out like fingers. Inside the house, the windows are lit up by warm light. I can see Andrew's mom emptying the dishwasher in the kitchen.

"That was weird earlier," I say. "I can't believe they thought we were . . . we . . ." I can't say it, can't get my mouth to wrap around the words. Instead, I laugh, shoving him slightly with my shoulder under the pile of coats. "Your mom clearly hasn't met Party Andrew."

"Let's hope my mom never meets Party Andrew," he says, shoving me back.

"Party Andrew eats bacon," I say. "She'd be horrified."

"Yeah. *That's* the part that would make her the maddest." He laughs, snuggling into my shoulder like a cat. "C'mon, Collins, you wouldn't date me?"

"Oh, are you done with Cecilia?" I ask, pursing my lips. "And Susie Palmer? And Sophie Piznarski? And—"

"All right," he says. "Point made."

"It's a moot point really." I give us another push with my foot so the hammock keeps swinging. "We all know you're gonna make little blond babies with Cecilia. Little Sally and Bobby."

"You named them?"

42

"*You* named them, Andrew. In the future. I'm just reporting back. Sally loves manicures, lip gloss, and binge drinking, by the way. Just like her mother."

"You're so weird."

"She's an adorable kid."

He laughs and soon I'm laughing too, our shoulders shaking so hard the hammock shakes too. I take a deep, gulping breath, trying to regain control, and suddenly I snort. Andrew hears and loses it.

"No, really," he says between choked laughter. "You're the adorable one. The sounds that come from your body are just so cute."

"You know what's cute?" I snort again before I can stop myself. "Hearing you say the word *condom* in front of our parents. I think that'll be seared into my brain forever."

"Really?" he asks. "I could have called it a 'rubber' and that would have been worse."

"A little raincoat," I say.

"Hey—a *big* raincoat," he says back, and we both burst out laughing again. It strikes me somewhere in the back of my mind that this is the first time it's ever occurred to me that Andrew has a penis—that it's there, not even a foot away from me— only hidden by a few pieces of fabric. It's a weird, uncomfortable thought, one that sticks out at an awkward angle. I shove it quickly away, and then I'm laughing again and it's gone like it never even happened at all.

FIVE

WE'RE SITTING IN Greek mythology Monday morning when Danielle gets the note.

It's an easy class, one of the ones basically designed for spring seniors, where you're always breaking into little discussion groups and everyone just talks about the weekend. Danielle and Ava usually sit next to Chase and some of the other basketball guys so they get maximum flirt time, but today they're with me. Danielle has been weirdly nice since the party—she brought me an iced coffee and a Ziploc bag of homemade cheddar scones before class and then sat down next to me like it was totally normal.

Making food for people is kinda Danielle's *thing*, and she's surprisingly great at it. She'll probably have her own TV show someday. One time sophomore year we were all watching *Kitchen Nightmares* at Hannah's house and Gordon Ramsay made some poor guy burst into tears, and Danielle said, *I think I'd be good at that.*

Cooking? Hannah asked.

Well, yeah, Danielle said. *And making people cry.*

I'm sure some part of her is using the scones as an excuse to ignore Chase, but maybe some other part of her feels bad.

Now, when she taps my desk, it makes me jump.

"Did you see who sent this?" She has a little scrap of white paper clenched in her hands. I take the paper from her and unfold it. It has five words scrawled across it, written in blue ink:

DANIELLE OLIVER IS A SLUT

I crumple the paper and let go like it's burned me. "I wasn't looking. Sorry."

I glance around the room for a guilty face, for someone who might be paying us a little too much attention. Chase is slumped in his desk on the opposite side of the room. I note the pencil he's chewing on and then look back at the blue ink on the paper. There's a chance he used a different writing implement and then slipped it back in his bag, but I really doubt Chase could be that sneaky.

"Where did you get it?" I whisper.

Ava leans past Danielle to whisper back. "We just found it. It's like it came out of nowhere."

We all turn toward Chase, and he must feel the heat of our stares, because he looks up and locks eyes with Danielle. He stops chewing on his pencil and cocks his head, the expression on his face unreadable.

"I don't see how anyone thinks they can get away with this," Danielle says at lunch, popping a grape tomato from her salad into her mouth. "It's like treason."

We're in the senior section, by the windows where the tables get the most sunlight. Prescott is small enough that everyone has lunch at the same time, but it means we're always fighting over the best tables, like we're vying for spots in a lifeboat. People used to care a lot about who they sat with, but now that we're seniors, we've all gotten over ourselves, and stuff that used to matter doesn't anymore.

Right now though, it's just Danielle, Ava, Hannah, and me because Danielle is keeping the note a secret. Before this weekend, I don't think she would have even let me see it. I know it's probably because I was there with her at the party. I'm fully in this now.

She lays the note down on the table, smoothing out the edges with a black-polished fingernail.

"Whoever did it probably doesn't think they'll get caught," Ava says, flipping her hair—bright green now for Saint Patrick's Day—behind one shoulder.

"Does the handwriting look familiar?" Hannah leans over the note and studies it. The letters are a mix of upper- and lowercase, some big and some small. Like someone was trying to make sure they wouldn't be recognized. Ava is always watching these true crime documentaries on Netflix, and sometimes she texts us articles. This note kinda reminds me of that—like someone is asking for a ransom.

"Don't worry," Danielle says. "I'll find out who did it." She smiles, then eats another tomato. I can hear it burst between her teeth.

"Hey." Andrew sits down in the chair next to mine, and Danielle snatches the note off the table, putting it away before he can see. Then she leans toward him, tucking a strand of dark hair behind one ear, revealing a row of silver studs.

"Drew, I'm sorry about this weekend. The, you know . . . wrapper." Her face turns pink. "I should have said something sooner. I can't believe he didn't throw it out." She reaches across the table and pats his arm.

"It's no big deal," he says, taking a casual bite of his sandwich. But the tips of his ears turn pink to match her cheeks.

"If you could just . . ." She clears her throat. "Could you not tell anyone about it?"

"Everybody already knows about it," Ava says, biting into a baby carrot with a loud crunch. "Clearly."

"Yeah, but they don't know every little detail." Danielle reaches over and grabs another baby carrot, flicking it with two fingers so it spins back across the table, landing in Ava's lap.

"Ouch!" Ava says, even though the flying carrot definitely didn't hurt.

"Hey, Danielle," a voice calls out from behind me. Chase is making his way over to our table, a backpack slung low over his shoulder. "Hey, guys." He nods to us. "Dani, can I talk to you?" He rests a hand on her shoulder but withdraws it quickly when she turns to look at him, her gaze icy.

"She doesn't want to talk to you," Ava says in a clipped tone.

"Ava," Danielle hisses. "Seriously. We're not in seventh grade anymore. I can speak for myself."

"Fine," Ava says, standing up. "I was just trying to help." She grabs her food and walks to the busing counter, slamming down the tray just a little too hard.

Whenever Danielle and Ava fight like this, Ava usually storms off and spends the next few hours with her theater friends, who she ironically likes to say are "less drama." But I know she'll probably be back with Danielle by the end of the day.

"I'll talk to her," Hannah says. She gets up and follows Ava out of the cafeteria.

"Sorry about that." Danielle turns to Chase. "What's up? Do you want to sit down?"

Chase rearranges the dirty Red Sox cap on his head, putting it back slightly askew. "Well, actually, do you want to go for a walk or something? I kind of wanted to talk."

"We can talk here." Danielle motions toward Andrew and me. "They're harmless."

"We can go." Andrew starts to get up from his chair. "You guys can ha—"

"Don't be silly." Danielle reaches a hand out to touch his shoulder. Her voice is sweet, but her back is straight, her movements stiff. It strikes me that she knows what's coming. Her armor is on, laced up tight. Does she want us here for moral support? It feels wrong—Danielle needing anyone's help for anything.

Chase slumps into the chair next to her.

"Okay." He seems caught off guard at having an audience. "So this weekend was really fun." He looks at Andrew for a second. "Nice party, dude." Andrew nods that special guy-nod back. "It's just—" he begins again, but Danielle interrupts.

"Here's the thing. I don't think you really understand what this weekend was for me. I just don't *like you* like that, Chase. No hard feelings."

"That's not what I—" he tries to butt in, but she keeps talking.

"I just kind of want to explore other options, and I really don't want to be locked down with one guy. It's not a good time. We can be friends though, right?" She pats his hand and looks at him, her eyes big.

Chase darts a quick glance at Andrew, as if he's trying to figure out what to say, as if he needs help. "What the hell, Danielle?" This is probably the first time a girl has ever spoken to him like this—Chase Brosner, star of the basketball team, the hockey team, *and* the lacrosse team. He's been everyone's crush since sixth grade.

"What?" Danielle asks, bringing a hand up to examine her cuticles.

"You're being crazy."

"I'm not being crazy," she says. "I'm just saying something you don't like."

"Fine," he says, his tone sharp. "We can be friends. I'm looking forward to it."

"Good, I'm so glad you understand."

"Cool." He shakes his head and pulls his backpack up over his shoulder, and then lumbers out of the cafeteria. When he's out of sight, her gaze hardens. Andrew turns to Danielle, looking at her like she's a puzzle he's trying to solve.

"But I thought you liked him."

"He was clearly about to screw me over, and I'm not going to let him get away with that twice. So I did it first."

"You couldn't have done that in private?" I ask.

"I needed witnesses," she says. "Now he can't make up a story. I dropped *him* and you both saw it." She takes another bite of salad and sighs. "I win."

SIX

HANNAH AND I meet in the student parking lot after school. She's agreed to take me job hunting, per my parents' notion that teaching me responsibility will make me stop attending any of Andrew's parties; as if he would ever let me.

"Ready to face your punishment?" she asks. "Firing squad or electric chair?"

"Definitely poison," I say.

"That's how the cowards do it."

We walk together across the parking lot to Hannah's Jeep. She got it used for her sixteenth birthday, and at this point, I've ridden in it almost as many times as she has. It's stopped snowing now, but there's still a light dusting on the ground. The sun is out and the parking lot is white and glittering. For the first time in months, it almost feels like I don't need a coat.

I take off my woolly mittens—a gift from Hannah—and stuff them into my pocket. She knitted us each a pair for the holidays this year, and mine are scratchy and lumpy and I love them.

"So, where am I taking you?" she asks. "Do you know any places hiring? Would they hire you back at Green Mountain Grocery?"

"I'm not working at Green Mountain again," I say, narrowing my eyes. "Those were dark days in my life."

"Where's Andrew gonna work? He's in this too, right?"

She pulls open the driver's-side door and I climb in on the other side, knocking the snow off my boots. As usual, the floor by my feet is littered with trash—dirty plastic coffee cups stuffed with napkins, old school folders and binders, papers spilling from the sides. Knowing Hannah, there are probably some essays from sophomore year down there, forgotten and disintegrating. I've learned to ignore the trash problem, which is saying a lot, for me.

"Yeah," I answer, shrugging. "You know how his uncle works at the fire department? He's gonna help there."

She starts the engine and turns on the fan. "Wait, as a fireman? Are we okay with him doing that?"

"Just in the office," I say. "Are you kidding? I would kill him if he got anywhere near a fire."

"Does he get to wear a uniform?" She side-eyes me, grinning.

"Hannah, no. We're not in a porno." This is a new low, even for her.

"Fiiiine," she says, stretching out the word with a sigh. "Can't you help? His uncle is basically your uncle too, right?"

"Apparently it only takes one person to make coffee and sort mail."

Andrew and I loved Uncle Leroy when we were kids because he'd sometimes let us climb up into his fire truck. But one time, I ate too much fried dough and threw up on the front seat. I'm not sure I've ever been forgiven for that.

"That sucks," Hannah says. "Andrew throws a party and gets a glamorous job out of it, and you get stuck with the electric chair."

"Poison," I correct.

She pulls the Jeep out of the parking lot, tires spraying slush onto the sidewalk, and heads in the direction of the university. As we drive closer to campus, cresting the hill on Woodhaven, the same bright Dunkin' Donuts sign from yesterday comes into view.

"Here are some stores that have employees," Hannah says, her voice deadpan. "If you're lucky, they might need some more."

She turns into the lot and slides the Jeep into a parking spot. I look at the stores spread out in front of us, feeling depressed at the thought of working at any of them. At the end of the lot is an old sad Chinese restaurant, aptly named "Chinese Food Restaurant," the once bright letters of the sign faded to a sickly yellow. It's the mecca for Prescott stoners because the all-you-can-eat buffet is only $5.99. I went there once with Andrew and Hannah in tenth grade, and we all got food poisoning and spent the rest of the night sprawled out on the floor of Andrew's room in pain, taking turns running to the bathroom.

Another reason I can't wait to get out of Prescott: better food. Last year, I went with Hannah and her parents to New York City to check out NYU. We all already knew she was going to apply— her parents pretty much never stop talking about it—but we wanted to see the campus for ourselves. We ate at so many cool places—breakfast burritos at a corner bodega, lunch at her mom's favorite secret ramen spot, and dinner at this amazing

Indian restaurant with food so spicy it made me sweat. That's what I want more of. Green Mountain Grocery doesn't even sell hot sauce.

Next to Chinese Food Restaurant is an old video store Andrew and I used to love when we were kids. I'm actually kinda surprised to see it's still in business. A while back, it started stocking textbooks to sell to students and then opened a cafe in the front of the store. I guess coffee and cookie sales have kept it afloat, but the new Dunkin' Donuts will probably put an end to that.

"I'm leaning toward prostitution," I say.

"Look! The video place is hiring." Hannah grins. I think at first that she's kidding, but sure enough, when I squint my eyes I can just make out the red hiring sign tacked to the front of the store.

"No."

"Let's at least go check it out." She pulls open her door. "This could be the start of your glorious film career."

"I'm not getting out of the car."

And then we see him—the guy from yesterday, with the eyes like melted chocolate and the windblown brown hair. *James Dean.* He emerges from inside the video store holding a big square chalkboard and then props it up on the sidewalk. Crouching down in front of it, he pulls a piece of chalk out of his pocket and begins to write. I squint but can't make out what it says.

"Okay, maybe I'll get out of the car."

Hannah turns to me with sparkling eyes. "Do you think he works there?"

"Unless he's vandalizing the storefront."

James Dean turns in our direction, and we both instinctively back away from the window. He rubs his hands together and blows into his fingerless gloves, little puffs of steam rising in the air. I can just barely see his shirt from here, black, SCORSESE written across the front in block letters. It's amazing.

I pull down the passenger-side visor and study myself in the little mirror. My hair is falling out of its braid, and it looks a bit like I've just gone for a run. But maybe James Dean will think I'm athletic. Probably not.

"Do I look okay?"

"You are a beautiful unicorn princess," Hannah says. "Now let's go." And before I have a chance to object, she jumps out of the car, yellow boots crunching into the snow. By the time I climb out after her, she's already halfway across the parking lot, easily maneuvering over the slick patches of ice.

"Hannah, wait!" I call out, trying to catch up. The ground is slippery beneath my feet, and I'm trying to go as fast as I can while remaining upright. She's almost at the sidewalk now, and turns once she's hopped up onto the curb. James Dean turns too, and from this distance, I can see that his cheeks and the tip of his nose are flushed pink from the cold. It's adorable.

And then my boot catches on a thin patch of ice and I slip, falling backward into a wet pile of slush. My elbow is throbbing when it hits, and I can already sense the bruise forming on my tailbone. I can feel the cold seeping through my pants—snow finding its way into places snow has no business being—but the heat spreading across my face is worse. This is not the kind of grand entrance I wanted to make. I lie back for a second, letting the embarrassment wash over me, avoiding the moment I'll have to face James Dean. Maybe he didn't see me fall. Maybe he turned back to the chalkboard at just the right moment, and

I can still get up and scramble away and come back tomorrow shiny and new.

"Keely!" Hannah's voice calls, high and sharp. I sit up, dizzy, turning in her direction, and then I see it—a bright red car is sliding right at me over the ice. The driver blasts on the horn and I scramble to my feet. As the car turns sharply, slush sprays in all directions, and I career myself toward the sidewalk. I land hard on my hip, bruised but out of the way.

The car skids around me, finally coming to a stop. The driver rolls down his window, his face blotchy and purple.

"This is a parking lot, you dumb bitch! What are you doing? Making snow angels?"

"Hey!" says a deep male voice behind me. James Dean is waving a piece of chalk at the driver. "She fell. Give her a break!"

"I almost ran her over!"

"Exactly! Maybe you should slow down."

"Whatever," the driver huffs. "You're lucky I'm not calling the cops."

"Yeah? Let's call them." James Dean's voice is firm and steady. "You almost killed this girl."

"Go to hell!" The driver clucks his tongue and backs away, slush spraying out from under his tires. And then he's gone. The calm of the parking lot falls over us, and we stand for a moment too long in silence. My heart is thudding like crazy and my mouth feels dry, adrenaline coursing through me.

"Are you okay?" James Dean puts a hand on my shoulder and I jump at the contact, still dazed.

"Keely, you almost died!" Hannah grabs on to my other arm. Her eyes are watery.

"I'm fine," I try to say, but the words get caught. I clear my throat and try again. "I'm fine."

"That started out pretty funny, but now I feel bad for laughing," James Dean says with a slight grin, showing off a set of perfect dimples. "You should come inside. You want some tea? Coffee? Whiskey? We have it all."

I let him steer me into the store. My thoughts are still fuzzy, whether from the shock or from the heat of his hand on my shoulder, I can't tell. A little bell jingles over the door as he pushes it open. Walking by, I glance down at the chalkboard and see that it reads:

I SPEAK SIGN LANGUAGE

The store looks just like I remember, but maybe a little more bleak—the floor is made of peeling linoleum and illuminated by dim fluorescent lights. In front of us is a curved glass counter filled with pastries and bagels, and behind that the wall is lined with textbooks. The rest of the space is filled with DVD cases, covering the walls and piled onto rolling racks. Andrew and I used to love exploring those racks when we were kids. We'd pool our allowance together and ride our bikes here in the summer. Even though we could probably find whatever we wanted online if we tried, this place felt like more of an adventure. But then we grew up and stopped coming. Seems like we're not the only ones. There are no customers or other employees around; we're the only people inside.

"Is it usually this empty?" Hannah asks.

"We do better in the morning when people want coffee," James Dean says. "Now is kind of a slow time. Hardly anyone's bought a DVD for like twenty years. Mostly collectors. Vintage types. Actually, there's a regular who looks like a vampire. *Blade.* Not *Twilight.*" He steps up to a set of barstools by the counter and opens a little gate, taking his place behind the register. "I'm Dean." He runs a hand absently through his mussed hair.

No way. I look over at Hannah and see her eyebrows rise and her mouth open. She begins to laugh and brings her arm up to fake a coughing fit. *What are the chances?*

"Your name is Dean?" I ask stupidly.

"Um, yeah," he answers. "Why?"

"It's nothing."

Dean motions to the bar stools for me to sit. I look down at my wet clothes. My coat is actually dripping onto the floor, a puddle forming on the tiles beneath me.

"I'm kind of soggy," I say. "I don't think I should—"

"Please, these stools are a hundred years old, they've seen worse."

"Actually, I should go," Hannah says, turning to me. "Now that I know you're okay. You're okay?"

I nod.

"Great."

"You just got here," he protests. "Stay for a drink."

She laughs. "This is supposed to be a job interview, actually. So I'm basically intruding. It's not very professional." She backs away, toward the door.

"Job interview?" he asks. "You want to work here?"

I shrug. "I saw your sign."

"But you two have fun!" Hannah calls. "I'll be in the car! Bye, *Dean!*" The little bell jingles as she pushes open the door, and then she's gone. I clear my throat awkwardly and sit down on one of the bar stools. My wet pants feel cold on my legs. He begins rummaging through the cabinets under the sink and pulls out two glasses, setting them down on the counter. Then he pulls out a bottle of whiskey.

"So, what was your name again? Kelly?"

"Um, it's Keely." I pull at a loose thread on my coat, eager to have something to focus on besides my embarrassment and cold butt. Will I leave a wet mark on the stool when I stand up?

He unscrews the top of the bottle. "Would you like some whiskey, Keely?"

I glance behind me instinctively, like someone might be watching.

"I'm not allowed to have whiskey."

"Not allowed?" He pours two glasses of amber liquid and then screws the cap back on. "Says who? If you're not in control of your own body, who is?"

I feel a blush spread up my cheeks. "No, I mean, I've had whiskey before."

I don't know why I'm lying. I've definitely never tried whiskey. The only time I've even been tipsy is from drinking watermelon Breezers, which taste like Popsicles. Whiskey makes me think of Irish fishermen or old-timey cowboys—someone weathered and grizzled and clouded by pipe smoke, not someone like Dean with twinkling eyes and adorable dimples. The smell of the cup in front of me makes me slightly nauseated, but I lean toward him hesitantly.

"It's just . . . I'm not allowed. I'm not twenty-one." I bite my lip. "I'm still in high school." My voice instinctively lowers, like I'm admitting something shameful.

"Cool. I'm twenty." He shrugs. "But that's just arbitrary, isn't it? It's your body. So why does someone else get to say what goes into it?" He picks up the glass nearest him and holds it up. "If you want to drink whiskey, drink whiskey. If you don't, don't. It's as simple as that. So would you like some whiskey?"

He holds his gaze on mine, a smile in his eyes. I pick up the glass in front of me and clink it with his, then take a sip. He grins and takes a sip of his own.

It's horrible—sharp and sweet at the same time, like old medicine. My throat is burning and my eyes begin to water, but I force myself to swallow. As I do, a warm feeling spreads across my chest.

"Better?" His face is cool and easy, like the whiskey hasn't affected him in any way.

I cough a little. "I guess."

"It should warm you up. I think I have a dry sweatshirt, actually, if you want to put that on. You look a little . . . damp." He grabs a backpack, pulls a black EVmU sweatshirt out of it, and tosses it to me. Somehow, I catch it without spilling whiskey all over the counter.

"You go to EVmU?" I peel off my wet coat and pull the sweatshirt over my head. It's soft and warm and smells like boy, in a good way. I have a flickering hope that maybe he'll let me keep it, and I push the thought away before it can fully take root. I'm being ridiculous.

"I do," he says. "Junior. Film theory." He motions to the rows of movies behind him. "That's why I work in this fine temple of the arts."

I laugh, taking another hesitant sip of my whiskey. It still burns my throat, but a fluttery feeling is forming in my stomach.

"Seriously," he says, grabbing a DVD off the nearest shelf.

"This right here is a relic of the past." He lays it down on the counter in front of me and taps its case with his index finger. "We're in a museum of the obsolete. We're about to fall away to time. Just by being here, you're a part of history."

"Aren't I always a part of history?" I ask. "I mean, everything we do becomes part of the past the second we've done it."

He grins. "Touché." Then he clinks his glass against mine and swallows the last of his drink. When he sets the empty glass down on the counter, he rests his chin in his hands and leans toward me conspiratorially, like he wants to share a secret.

"Did you know that in the first movie theater, the first time anyone saw a film on-screen—it was this clip of a train pulling into a station, and the audience had never seen anything like it. They freaked out—ran screaming, panicking, out of the theater, because they thought the train was real; thought they were about to get run over, flattened, by this train. That was only a little over a hundred years ago. And now here we are: IMAX, 3-D, virtual reality, and these little guys are another part of film history. Like that train." A lock of brown hair falls across his forehead, and I resist the urge to reach out and smooth it away.

"You really love this place," I say.

"Sarah quit last week because she got hired at the Bagelry on campus. Said there'd be better tips there, which is probably true. We get a coffee rush in the morning, but it's not great." He shrugs. "You have to really love this place to work here. You have to really love movies. Sarah didn't have the passion." He lowers his voice to a theatrical whisper. "She was a *bio major.*"

I tell him about how I'm going to Los Angeles next year to study film. "I love Hitchcock," I say, brightening. "My best friend and I, we've seen them all. We can quote every line from *Vertigo* start to finish."

"The girl staring at us from inside that car out there?" He nods toward the window. Hannah's Jeep is still parked where we left it, and I can just make out the outline of her hair.

"No. Well, Hannah's my best friend, but she's not who I . . ." I trail off, not wanting to tell him about Andrew in case he gets the wrong idea, like everyone else. "It doesn't matter." I begin fiddling with the end of my braid. "I don't know why she didn't just stay here."

"Because this is a job interview," he says. "Which you're acing, by the way. Have you ever worked anywhere before? I guess I should ask that."

"At Green Mountain Grocery, the past two summers. It was horrible."

"Great! I'll have to run you by Mr. Roth. He's the owner. But you should be golden."

"Don't you . . . I mean, I don't want to hurt my chances or anything, but don't you need my résumé or, like, references or something?" I take another hesitant sip of my whiskey.

"Nah, I can already tell you're perfect."

I swallow and the whiskey spreads like fire through my chest.

SEVEN

FRIDAY NIGHT AND we're sprawled out on the couch in Andrew's basement watching *Saving Private Ryan*. I've told him about the video store and the job, but not about Dean, because it's way too embarrassing.

We have bags of McDonald's takeout dumped on the coffee table in front of us (a secret from the vegans) and I'm trying to focus my energy on the delicious fat clogging my arteries instead of on the color of Dean's eyes, but it's harder than it should be. I've never felt this way about any of the guys at school. Maybe it's just because Dean is new and different and interesting, and I didn't watch him pick his nose in kindergarten.

Andrew reaches over and steals a fry out of the bag in my lap.

"I don't know how you can eat at a time like this," I say, handing him the bag. I haven't touched the fries since the invasion of Normandy, and now they're cold and soggy. It's late now— maybe past midnight—and the darkness of the basement is making the movie even more intense.

Andrew's phone beeps and he jumps, picking it up to read the text.

"Anyone interesting?" I ask, and he shrugs.

"Cecilia."

"Still Cecilia? It's been like a whole week."

He grabs a handful of fries and brings his fist up to his mouth. Andrew is always grabbing handfuls of things and it drives me crazy.

"I've dated girls for more than a week," he says, licking the salt off his fingers. "I think you have this idea that I'm a lot shittier than I really am." He says it with a smile, his voice easy, so I know he's not mad.

"So you and Cecilia are dating, then?"

"Okay, so *dating* isn't the right word."

I roll my eyes and then we both get distracted by the TV, because there's a huge explosion and the sounds of soldiers dying. Before I can help it, I wonder if James Dean likes *Saving Private Ryan*, if he's seen it before or if he only watches abstract film school movies. Do they even call them movies in film school? I need to learn before next year.

"Do you . . . think about her a lot?" I ask, and then I feel my cheeks get hot, because it's a weird question. "Like, do you find your mind wandering to Cecilia at random times?"

"Not really," he says. "Only at night. Or in the shower." He grins.

"That's not . . . never mind," I say. And then I can't let it go. "I mean, does she give you that stomach flip? Like when you drive over a big hill?"

He picks up the remote and pauses the movie.

"I know the stomach flip. Believe me." He reaches a hand up

to fiddle with his hair, the floppy part on his forehead. He's got his glasses on so he can see the movie, and he takes them off, tapping them against his palm. "Are you . . . have you . . . um . . . do you like someone?"

"I don't know," I say. "No." For some reason, I feel like I have to deny it. "I guess I'm just wondering what you get out of it. Is it just sex?"

Now he looks really uncomfortable. His face is probably even redder than mine, and I don't know why I said anything.

He scratches his chin. There's stubble growing in there, just barely. "No," he says. "It's not sex . . . just sex."

"Was Sophie different?"

Andrew dated Sophie Piznarski for six months our freshman year, back before Party Andrew existed. I hung out with them sometimes, just the three of us, me sitting awkwardly on one end of the couch playing games on my phone while they cuddled together on the other.

"Sophie was a long time ago," he says. "It's different now. I'm different."

"No kidding," I say.

"It's just easier this way."

"Cecilia's easy?"

"That's not what I'm saying. I mean, *I'm* easy. I like things to be relaxed and . . . I don't know. Feelings suck. No feelings, no stress."

"C'mon, if you're not feeling anything, what's the point?"

"I feel lots of things," he says, and I can sense that he's getting agitated. "You have no fucking idea." The curse word takes me by surprise. He was all jokes and smiles a few seconds ago, but I must have struck a nerve. His hands are in his hair, scrunching and pulling, and he probably doesn't notice he's doing it. I reach a hand up and rest it on his, trying to stop him.

"All right, I believe you."

He pulls his hand away. It's as if all the parts of Andrew have been mixed up and he's trying to set them right again, get them back in their proper places.

"Sorry, Collins." He takes a deep breath and then smiles, back to normal. "Don't mind my weird shit."

"Hey," I say. "I'll listen to your weird shit whenever, okay? I'm here for your weird shit anytime you need me."

He puts his glasses back on, adjusting them until they're straight. "Thanks."

"You're allowed to have feelings, you know."

"Thanks for the tip, doc," he says.

"I mean it. I'm your best friend. You can talk to me about real stuff."

"A little confident, don't you think?" he says, grinning. "Just proclaiming yourself my best friend."

"Oh, shut up," I say. "I think I'm allowed to proclaim myself whatever I want after eighteen years with you."

"Actually, I've been getting really close with Jason Ryder lately," he says, a mischievous smile on his face. "He might be taking your spot. He told a hilarious joke recently about women and sandwiches, and I think it might make him best-friend material. He's—"

I shove him before he can finish and he falls off the couch.

It's my first day of work after school on Tuesday, and when it comes I'm a nervous wreck. Every class seems to be about five seconds long, like I've spent the whole day stuck in hyperspace.

Andrew, Hannah, and I have ceramics together last period, which is usually my favorite class, but today I can't stop checking the time. We're sitting at a big wooden table lined in paper, trying to paint our mugs with colored glaze. Mine looks less like a mug and more like a monster from the deep.

"Excited for today?" Hannah asks me from across the table. She dips her brush into the blue and paints a perfect swirl.

"What's today?" Andrew asks. His mug broke in the kiln, so he's just been watching us glaze.

"Keely's big first day," she says. "Our little baby's all grown up."

"Video store?" he asks. He has a thin stripe of purple paint on his left cheek and I wonder how it got there, considering he hasn't touched the paint all class.

I nod, feeling the swooping rush of nerves in my stomach. I glance up at the clock and see that the class period is almost over. Suddenly I want to throw up.

I tried to dress up a little bit today. I wore black pants—real pants instead of leggings—and the new sweater my mom got me for my birthday. She keeps complaining that I haven't worn it, but that's because it's too small and bunches around my boobs. Usually I try to keep attention away from that zone, but today I thought I'd try something new for James Dean's sake.

"Are you nervous?" Hannah flutters her eyelashes in a way that means she's talking about James Dean and not the job.

"You're an animal, Collins," Andrew says. "You'll kill it." He reaches down and digs around inside his backpack, pulling out a bag of potato chips. I don't know how he can stomach them right now—the room smells like clay and turpentine—but I'm not surprised. As he's mid-chew, a girl comes up to our table.

She's walking with quiet hesitant steps, like a deer in a forest worried it's going to be shot. She's thin and dainty like a deer too, with big eyes and a pointy nose. Her name's Madison Jones. Sophomore.

"Um, sorry," she says. "Excuse me. Sorry." Madison says *sorry* a lot in class, like she's apologizing for existing. She taps Andrew on the shoulder. "Sorry. Are you done with the blue glaze?"

She's focused only on Andrew, directing her question at him, even though he's clearly eating potato chips and not painting.

"Oh, yeah." He turns to me. "Collins, you done?"

She glances quickly back to her table, a group of sophomore girls, and their heads are all bent together, whispering and giggling.

I slide the jar of blue glaze over to her. "Yeah, whatever. This mug is hopeless anyway."

"It's not hopeless," Hannah says, ever reassuring. "You have a lot of potential."

"Oh, sorry," Madison says, flicking her eyes to me and then back to Andrew. "I didn't know your girlfriend was still using it."

I feel myself turn red, but it's more because of the fact that she won't look at me directly, that she won't address me by name, than the accidental use of the word *girlfriend*. It's not like that's new. Andrew is red too, his freckles bright, and he puts the bag of chips down.

"She's not . . . I mean—"

"Actually, yeah, I'm still using it." I slide the jar back in my direction.

Andrew looks flustered, and I roll my eyes at him, because he should be used to this by now—it's only happened to us once a day since the start of high school. But for some reason it still ruffles his feathers. He always has to correct whoever makes the mistake: *She's not my girlfriend.* Because God forbid somebody keep thinking I'm a real, datable girl.

Hannah looks flustered too, her eyes darting back and forth between Madison and me. I know she hates conflict and she's horrified I won't share.

"Oh, okay, sorry," Madison says. She fiddles with the hem of her shirt, brings the tip of her braid into her mouth.

"We're not together," Andrew says again, as if Madison is dense and needs extra clarification.

"Not anymore," I say, smiling sweetly at Madison. "I dumped him last year after the incident with the cheese."

"The what?" asks Madison.

"Collins," Andrew says, a warning in his voice.

"Never mind." I pick up the jar of glaze and hold it out in her direction. "Take the blue."

"Sorry, are you sure?" She's still chewing on her braid.

"Yes," I say. If she apologizes one more time, I might lose it. "Just take the stupid jar."

I slide it toward her, but it's too forceful, my arm is too tense, and before I can stop it, the jar is flying through the air. It lands with a crash on the tile floor, and blue glaze sprays everywhere— all over Madison, all over my nice birthday sweater.

She shrieks, the braid falling out of her mouth. Hannah runs to the sink to grab some towels. Miss Blanchard, our art teacher, runs over in a panic. Andrew is laughing deep belly laughs, and then I'm laughing too, because his laughter is contagious. I look down at my ruined sweater and realize I've forgotten to be nervous about James Dean. For a while I wasn't even thinking about him at all.

• • • • • •

That disappears the second Hannah drops me off in front of the store.

"You'll do great," she says. "Now off you go."

She practically shoves me out of the car. I'm wearing my coat so my ruined sweater is hidden, but I know I'm going to have to take it off at some point. I didn't wear anything underneath the sweater, and I'm definitely regretting that decision now.

Hannah drives away, and I stand for a moment outside the door, trying to psych myself up. Then I push it open. My nerves calm down when I get inside because James Dean isn't there. Instead it's a heavyset, balding white guy behind the counter—probably the owner, Mr. Roth.

"Welcome," he says when he sees me, breaking out into a smile. "How can I help you?"

I raise my hand up to awkwardly wave. "I'm Keely. Your new—"

"Ah!" he interrupts. "My new recruit. Come in, come in!" I'm already in, but I guess he means to come farther into the store toward him. He claps his hands together, as if I've done something worthy of applause. He might be the jolliest person I've ever met. "Come get settled in. Today should be relatively easy. I just have some paperwork for you to fill out. Want me to hang your coat?" He reaches out a helpful hand, but I pull my coat tighter around me.

"I'm okay, thanks."

"Let me just see if Dean has your papers," he says, turning toward the back of the store where there appears to be a break room. The name sends a burst of nervous energy through me. "Dean!" he calls, and then there he is.

He looks just as perfect as I remember him—better maybe—in a black T-shirt just like the other day, except this one says HERZOG. I guess directors are his Thing. His hair is combed back in a style perfectly mimicking that of the real James Dean.

"Hey," he says casually, leaning against the door frame to the break room, arms folded. "We meet again."

"Hey," I say back, trying to be just as casual.

"All righty." Mr. Roth claps his hands again. "I've got to go. Dean here has you covered. Tim should be in around five o'clock—he's our other cashier—and then I'm sure the three of you can get everything sorted." He bustles around the store, straightening and moving bits and pieces around. "I'll see you all tomorrow!"

Then he's out the door, and it's just the two of us. Alone again.

"He's . . . very jolly," I say.

"Practically jovial," Dean agrees. He's still leaning against the door frame like he's waiting for somebody to take his picture.

"Should I . . ." I begin, trailing off, not sure what I'm about to ask. It's hot in the store and I want to take my coat off, but I hug it tightly to my chest. My hands feel clammy.

"Right," he says, pushing off from the wall. "Paperwork."

He walks over to the counter and riffles through some drawers, then pulls out a stack of forms. I take a seat again on one of the stools. The coat situation is getting bad—I'm starting to sweat in earnest now. I decide to cut my losses and take it off. Dean raises an eyebrow when he sees my sweater.

"What happened to you?"

I motion to the stains. "There was a . . . blue paint incident at school."

"Clearly."

His eyes flicker to my chest, to where the sweater is pulled tight, and his gaze lingers for a moment too long. My whole face burns.

"I'm not good at ceramics," I say, which makes sense in my head, but I realize Dean might not see the connection.

"Well, let's hope you're better at working a cash register."

"I am," I say. "Promise."

"Promises are dangerous," he says. "You should never make a promise unless you mean it."

"I mean it."

"Good," he says. "Me too."

"Good," I say, though I'm not really sure what he means or what he's promising, if he's promising anything at all.

We spend the next hour going over everything in the store—how the movies are organized in the computer, how to fill up the coffeepots and open the cash register (this last one involves lots of elbows because it always jams). Apparently the cookies and pastries are just from Le Soleil bakery down the street—Dean picks up a bag of them each morning and drops them off with Mr. Roth on the way to his 8:00 a.m. lecture.

"So why do people come here instead of just getting them right from the source?" I ask, examining the various flavors lined up neatly in the glass display case. There are little action figures surrounding the cookies—a tiny Iron Man and Black Panther, a slightly less tiny Hulk.

"Because I work here," Dean says, breaking into a grin. "I'm charming." I look up at him and immediately blush and look back down at the counter. Do girls actually come here to talk to Dean? Is that why he thinks *I'm* here?

He must see my confusion or panic, because he shrugs. "I'm

totally kidding." At this, I flush even redder, but he continues on, thankfully ignoring the state of my face. "We're like four blocks closer to campus, so that's probably the main reason. But people come here for the vibe too. Where else can you get a little plastic Avenger with your cookie?"

Dean has a point. I do love the vibe in here. I don't know why I ever stopped coming. This store is part of the reason I fell in love with movies in the first place.

"I feel kinda sad for Mr. Roth," I say. "I mean, there's that new Dunkin' Donuts—"

"See that poster behind you?" Dean interrupts. "The *Blues Brothers* one?" I turn and see the classic poster, Dan Aykroyd and John Belushi in sunglasses, slightly faded from the sun. "That's been taped to the wall since the eighties. Roth could probably sell it on eBay or something if he wanted, but he never will. Same with *Raiders of the Lost Ark*," he says, nodding his head to another wall, "and *Shawshank*. If you like movies? This place is magic."

"I *love* them," I say, the words like a sigh. I love *him*. All I want is for him to think I'm as cool as he is, because he is *so* cool, and beautiful, and terrifying. James Dean is magic.

"You okay?" He waves a hand in front of my face and I blink a few times. *Was I staring at him?* If I was staring at him, I might actually die.

"Yup," I say. "I'm great. I'm good. Are you good?"

"I'm good too." He smiles. "You know, I think this is the beginning of a beautiful friendship."

• • • • • •

HANNAH

How was your first day??

ME

I have good news and bad news. Good news: I think James Dean and I are friends? Bad news: I think James Dean and I are friends

HANNAH

That's a good step! 🖤

ME

Pretty sure he was quoting Casablanca though, so not sure if it counts?

HANNAH

A random old movie quote! He's perfect for you. Was it in like a professional co-worker way or a flirty way?

ME

I mean figuring out if something is flirty is not one of my skill sets

HANNAH

Ok like did he touch you or make eye contact? That movie is romantic, right?

ME

I need an expert

• • • • • •

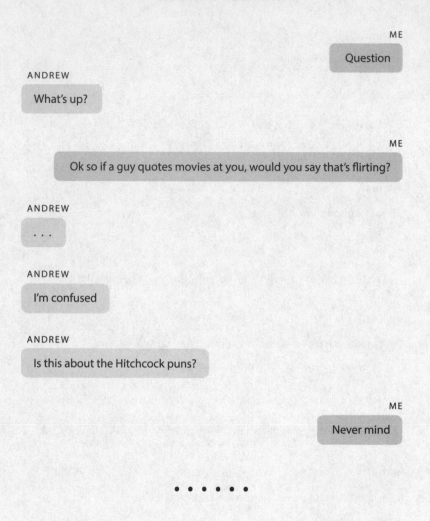

ME

Question

ANDREW

What's up?

ME

Ok so if a guy quotes movies at you, would you say that's flirting?

ANDREW

. . .

ANDREW

I'm confused

ANDREW

Is this about the Hitchcock puns?

ME

Never mind

• • • • • •

We watch *Casablanca* that night because I am the world's biggest overanalyzer, and I need to decode it for clues.

Hannah can never just watch a movie—she says they're boring, which I ignore for the good of our friendship—so she's having Andrew and me simultaneously help her with an art project, painting colorful patterns onto leaves she collected from her backyard last fall. She says she's going to hang them on her wall once we're done, but if the ones I paint mysteriously fall beneath her bed, I won't be offended.

I still haven't told Andrew about James Dean. Not that there's anything to tell. But still, admitting I have a crush to Andrew makes the stakes feel higher. If Andrew knows, it'll be more embarrassing when this goes absolutely nowhere.

But Hannah is not the subtlest.

"Okay, so this movie is clearly romantic," she says. "All the kissing and the sad music. If I were into a girl I would reference this movie to get in her pants."

"Yeah, Collins." Andrew looks up from his leaf. "I'm surprised you picked this one."

"It's a best picture winner!" I say. "Arguably one of the best movies of all time."

"Yeah, but *Gladiator* won best picture. We could have watched that. You're just not usually the kissing type."

"I am too the kissing type! I like kissing. I kiss people!" Okay, so maybe not *exactly* the truth, but I would definitely kiss James Dean if I could.

Andrew is bright red. "I didn't mean . . . in real life. I meant the movies you watch."

Hannah is laughing at us so hard she knocks over a jar of yellow paint and it spills onto her rug. "Oh my god, why does this keep happening?" We all jump up and look for some towels to clean it up, and luckily some of the weirdness dissipates, the tension broken. "We have to stop spilling paint," Hannah says. "I swear this never happens unless you fools are around."

"We're bad luck," I say, thinking of my ruined sweater. Except—James Dean didn't seem to mind the stain at all. My cheeks flush at the memory of his eyes on me.

In the movie on Hannah's laptop, Rick puts Ilsa on the plane to escape the Nazis, sending the woman he loves away with her husband in order to save her life. *We'll always have Paris*, Rick tells her as they say goodbye. They might not be together in the end, but they'll always have their memories.

Except that's not the quote James Dean used. If he liked me, he would have said something about Paris, not something about friendship. I think he's probably just into movies, not into *me*.

"Hey, guys, next year when we're all flying to different places," Andrew says, "at least we'll always have Paris."

"We'll always have Prescott," I say.

"Let's go with Paris," Hannah says, dabbing at the rug with a bath towel. "I'd much rather have that."

EIGHT

ON WEDNESDAY, Chase tries again with Danielle. We're walking to chemistry together when he comes up behind us and swings his arm casually over her shoulder. She smiles until she turns and sees who it is, and then her smile twists into a snarl.

"Hey, Dani," he says.

She ducks out from under his arm. "Don't call me that."

"Come on." His grin is easy, like he's used to getting what he wants.

"What do you want?" she asks instead.

"Just want to talk," he says. "Just a conversation. We're friends now, right?"

"We're not the kind of friends who have conversations," she says.

"Collins," he says to me, like I can help him in some way.

And then Jason Ryder makes it worse, lumbering down the hall like he owns it. He breaks out into a wide grin when he sees us, sees Danielle and Chase standing together. He pats Chase roughly on the back.

"Hey, look," he says. "It's Slutty and the Beast, back together."

"Dude," says Chase.

"Aw, Jason," Danielle says, her voice sweet. "It's cute when you try to make jokes. You'll get it right someday." She pulls her bag higher on her shoulder and turns to me. "We're late." Then she sets off down the hall. I scamper after her.

"The part that makes me maddest," she hisses when we're out of earshot, "is how Chase and I were both equals in this bullshit. We had sex with each other. Together. But for some reason, I'm a slut. I'm a slut because I've had sex one time with one person." She walks faster, not looking at me.

"You're not a slut," I say, because I feel like I need to say something.

"Well, obviously," she snaps, turning her head to me. "That's the whole fucking point."

Andrew's parents are having a date night in Burlington, so he's decided to have a guys' night—something with tacos, because guys seem to have an inexplicable obsession with them. It's too risky to have a party, so tacos are a safe compromise. Cheese and ground beef aren't illegal, even if they horrify our vegan parents to their core.

"I'm not coming," I tell him when he invites me, but we both know I'll end up there anyway. Still, I tell Andrew I'll help him shop for supplies, so we find ourselves at Costco, piling gargantuan ingredients into our cart—whale-sized tubs of guacamole and sour cream and a jar of hot sauce that would outlast the apocalypse. The bag of shredded cheese we buy is legitimately bigger than I am. Andrew stands it up next to me to take a picture.

"Why did you invite Ryder?" I ask, jumping onto the front of the cart. I know Andrew hates Ryder as much as I do, and yet he always seems to be everywhere.

"Chase invited him," Andrew says, pushing me and the bag of cheese down the aisle. "And I can't just tell Ryder not to show up. Hey, ready for warp speed?" He starts running, pushing the cart faster, building momentum as we go. The aisles at Costco are about the size of city blocks, so there's plenty of room. As we gain speed, he jumps onto the back. I scream and put a foot down to brake us before we crash into a ceiling-high stack of Chips Ahoy! cookies.

Once we've slowed down to a steady roll, I jump off the cart and move around to the back so I'm the one pushing. He jumps off and walks beside me.

"You were downstairs that night, right?" I say as we turn into the refrigerated aisle. We pause in front of the juice.

"What night?"

"My birthday."

"Oh. Yeah."

"What happened when Danielle and I were still upstairs?" I don't know why I haven't thought to ask him before. "How did everybody find out about it? Chase must have said something, right?"

"Somebody could've seen Chase and Danielle go into the room together," he offers.

"But then how did everybody know so fast?"

"Chase isn't a bad guy," he says. "If he said something, it was probably because he was excited, not because he was trying to embarrass her."

I think again of the note Danielle got the other day, someone actually calling her a slut for losing her virginity to a guy she was into. Could Chase have written the note? It doesn't seem like something he would do. Andrew is right—Chase might be dumb sometimes, but I don't think he's the kind of evil to shame a girl he slept with. The note could definitely be from Ryder. But why would Ryder go through the effort of disguising his handwriting if he was going to call her names today in person?

"Ryder called Danielle a slut today," I tell Andrew. "To her face. How is that okay?"

He stops the cart so fast I bump into it. "It's not okay. Fucking Ryder."

"Yeah, but how does he always get away with shit like that?"

"Just wait until next year," he says. "If someone acts like an asshole in college you can just stop hanging out with them. We just have to get out of high school and it'll be better." It's the mantra we've been repeating to ourselves since high school began. I just hope it's true.

"Hey, Collins, what does this look like to you?" Ryder lifts his taco in my direction.

"It looks like a taco," I say, sprinkling some cheese onto my own and trying to ignore him. We're standing at the kitchen counter, the spread of toppings laid out in front of us in various containers. Andrew is on the stool next to me, and Chase is across the counter with Edwin Chang and Ryder's sidekick, Simon Terst, who might be even worse because he actually looks up to Ryder like he's some kind of hero.

"Exactly," Ryder says. "A taco. A muffin. A tuna sandwich." He waggles his brows. "Get it?"

"No," I say, my voice flat and sarcastic. "Explain it to me."

Ryder tilts his head to the side, a smile frozen on his face, and I can see the cogs turning behind his eyes as he tries to figure out if I'm serious.

"She's got it," Andrew says.

"Hey, Terst." Ryder ignores Andrew and turns toward Simon, holding his taco up to Simon's nose. "Bet you've never been this close to a taco. How's it smell?"

"Fuck you." Simon swats Ryder's hand away. "My life is an all-you-can-eat taco buffet."

Ryder starts laughing at this, and not in the nice way. Simon is small and twitchy and is almost blind without his wire-rimmed glasses. Danielle started referring to him as the Rabbit back in sixth grade, and the nickname kinda stuck.

"Sure, man," Chase says. "You're drowning in tacos."

Simon's face is red and blotchy. It occurs to me he's probably a virgin too. This awkward label is something we share. I bite into my taco and chew, trying to distract myself.

"I'm a one taco kind of guy," Edwin says. He and Molly Moye have been inseparable ever since my birthday. "Molly or nothing."

"Seriously?" Ryder asks. He raises his hand up to imitate cracking a whip, making sounds with his tongue pressed against his front teeth. "Someone's whipped."

"Not whipped," Edwin says. "Smart. I'll never do better than Molly. She's amazing."

"When you have a girlfriend you can get it whenever you want," Chase says. "One girl who knows what she's doing."

"How about ten girls who know what they're doing?" Ryder breaks into a wide smile. He turns to Andrew. "Right, Reed?"

Andrew rubs the back of his neck. "Yeah. I mean, not at once, but variety is nice."

Andrew talking about girls as if we're some sampler platter he'd like to try is so gross that I pick up a handful of shredded cheese and throw it at him. The shreds flutter down into his lap and he brushes them off, unbothered. "Whatever, Drewchebag," I say. "You don't even like variety. You like blonds."

He stops brushing the cheese out of his lap and looks up at me. "What?"

"You seriously need me to point this out? Cecilia and Sophie and Susie Palmer all look pretty much the same. You definitely have a type."

"I've never noticed," he says. "It's not on purpose." The tips of his ears are bright pink.

"Susie Palm-job," Ryder says. "Worst handy of my life."

"Worst handy," Chase says. "Kinda redundant. I mean, any hand job is pointless, isn't it? Like, I've been touching my junk for eighteen years. I know what I'm doing. Any chick that tries is set up for failure."

Sometimes hearing the guys talk like this makes my anxiety spike. It's like they think a girl is expected to be a pro the first time she ever sees a penis. I hate that I'm not brave enough to tell them they're being idiots.

"But this was worse," Ryder says. "Like she was squeezing out a washcloth. She has sandpaper hands."

"A sand job," Edwin adds.

"Aren't we past the age of hand jobs anyway?" Chase says. "Hand jobs were cool in middle school. Like, in eighth grade, I was super stoked if a girl went anywhere near there. But at this point, I'm over it. I'd rather just do it myself."

"Mouth or nothing," Simon says, like he has any right to decide.

"I'd use my own mouth if I could reach," Chase says. "DIY."

"All right, David Blowie," Andrew says. "Keep the details to yourself."

"Would you rather," Edwin says, "get a sand job or blow yourself?"

"Depends who the sand job is from." Chase grins. "I'd take a sand job from Danielle."

"Agreed," Andrew says, and I look at him, surprised. I didn't know he saw Danielle that way.

"I'd cut off an arm for a sand job from Danielle," Ryder says.

"Forget that," Simon counters. "I'd cut off an arm to see Ava's tits."

"Seen 'em," Ryder says. "Worth it."

"Can you guys stop?" I interrupt. "You're talking about my friends. You don't think I'll tell them all of this?"

"So?" Ryder shrugs. "We're complimenting them."

I'm about to throw the giant tub of guacamole at Ryder's face, but luckily for him, there's a knock at the door. Everyone stops talking.

"Who else is coming?" I get up to answer it, like it's my house. It basically is.

"Oh, it's probably Cecilia." Andrew gets up too.

I stop walking. "Cecilia?"

"Yeah," he says, like it's normal for her to be showing up here.

"No girls at taco night!" Ryder calls out to us, and I whirl around to face him.

"What the hell do you think I am?"

"You don't count." He crunches into his taco and smiles, his teeth full of beans. I think again that this is why—*this is why*—

83

I'm still a virgin. Why would I ever be attracted to any of them when I've heard these conversations? This is why James Dean matters so much; he's a chance at a fresh start.

Andrew beats me to the door and opens it, and there she is: Cecilia Brooks. She's as lovely as ever, wisps of blond hair curling around her face, apple cheeks pink and glowing. When she takes off her coat, she's wearing a V-neck sweater, soft baby pink and tight around her chest, low-cut so that both our pairs of eyes—mine and Andrew's—are drawn there, trying not to stare.

"Hi, Drew." She gives him a quick hug, then turns to me and waves, keeping one arm securely on his shoulder as if he might float away if she lets him go. "Hey, Keely."

"Hey," I say, walking back into the kitchen. They follow behind me, and when I turn to glance back, her hand has slid down from his shoulder and is now wrapped around his waist.

The kitchen looks cleaner when we come back. The guys have wiped up the spilled taco fillings that were strewn about the counter and have thrown away their old napkins. They're all sitting a little bit straighter.

"Hi, everyone!" Cecilia says.

"You want a taco?" Chase asks, getting up from his stool.

"I can make you one." Andrew peels away from her and opens one of the kitchen cabinets to grab a plate.

"It's okay," she says. "I'm not hungry." He puts the plate back.

"Here," Edwin says, getting up from his stool. "You can take my seat. I was getting tired of sitting anyway."

"Oh, thanks, Edwin," she says, touching his shoulder lightly as she sits down.

There's silence as we all look at one another, unsure of what to say. She's like a disturbance in the airwaves, a ripple in the water. The room smells different—fresh and flowery. She must be wearing perfume strong enough to overpower the smell of beans.

"You look nice," Andrew says. "I like your sweater."

She looks down at it and then back up at all of us, a bright smile on her perfectly symmetrical face. "Thanks. It was on sale."

"Nice," Andrew says. "You look good in pink."

Out of the corner of my eye, I can see Chase bringing his hand up to cover a yawn, which makes me yawn in response. And there's a small part of me—a part I'm not particularly proud of—that's suddenly relieved I get to see what's behind the curtain. Not just because I see the truth that Cecilia doesn't, but because I get them without all the bullshit. I get the real Andrew—the one who is funny and lively and sometimes makes me snort milk out of my nose, but who at other times makes me so frustrated I want to shake him. The truth is a little scary. How can I ever trust a guy around his friends when I know so well how guys act around their friends?

But as I watch Andrew tap his fingers quietly on the surface of the counter, the ticking of the clock loud in the now silent room, I realize maybe a tiny bit of me is glad I don't count.

NINE

IT SNOWS THROUGH the rest of March, and then finally it's April, and everything melts under a warming sun. The store gets slightly busier as people come out of hibernation, and I settle easily into the work. Mr. Roth is hardly ever there, and so I spend most of my days with either Dean or this older guy Tim, who can spend an entire shift analyzing a single episode of *Star Trek*. Obviously I've tried to tell him *Star Wars* is better, but he won't listen.

It's Thursday evening and the store has been empty for nearly an hour. I'm up front organizing the rows of sticky pastries into a precarious pyramid formation I've been mentally referring to as "Sugar Mountain," when Dean pops his head out from behind a row of DVD cases at the back of the store.

"So you said you like Hitchcock, right?"

"Yeah, why?" I call back to him, placing a croissant neatly on top of Sugar Mountain, a pile of flaky crumbs raining down onto the counter.

He emerges from behind the stacks and comes to join me at the front of the store, a DVD case clutched in his hands. "So what's your take on horror, then? Are you just into old-school, suspenseful stuff? Or have you explored the genre a bit?" His eyes are sparkling in excitement, little crinkles at the corners. "How about monsters and zombies?" He raises his brows. "Gore?"

Dean places the movie down in front of me. It's called *Mayhem in the Monastery* and features a terrified nun in the grasp of a giant bloody hand. The scream on her face is almost funny.

"This is horror?" I ask skeptically. "Not comedy?"

He grins for a second, then goes stone-faced. "This is terrifying. C'mon." He snatches the case off the counter and, without waiting for me to follow, turns and heads to the back of the store.

"C'mon where?" I glance at the front door. Through the clear glass I can see that the parking lot is empty, Dean's motorcycle the only vehicle in sight. Yes, Dean drives a motorcycle, because *of course he does*. The chalkboard out front reads:

DAD, WHAT'S A VIDEO?

I sigh and put down the pastry I'm holding, abandoning Sugar Mountain to follow him into the break room. There's an old couch against one wall that probably has things growing in it, and across from that, a small TV. The walls are covered in more old movie posters, which I kind of love, and in the corner there's a life-sized cutout of Legolas from *The Lord of the Rings*, which has probably been there for years. I guess somebody put a Santa hat on his head around Christmas and it's still there.

Dean is inserting *Mayhem in the Monastery* into the DVD player.

"We can't watch now." I pause halfway through the door. "What if we have customers?"

"We never have customers," he says dryly. The menu pops up and scary, dramatic violin music fills the room.

"We do have customers," I protest weakly. "That woman came in earlier for a coffee. And what about that vampire guy?"

The truth is, I don't want to sit next to Dean on the small couch almost as badly as I do want to sit next to him. Sitting next to him means not knowing where to put my hands and having to keep my body rigid, because if I relax, what if I lean toward him and our shoulders touch? He probably wouldn't want our shoulders to touch because he's used to his shoulder touching prettier, older girls—sophisticated college girls who study film and smoke clove cigarettes and talk about how art makes them feel.

"There's a bell over the door," he says. "Remember? If anyone comes in we can go back up front." I know he's right. In the three weeks I've been here, we've had more time alone than we've had with customers—it's just we usually don't spend it actually hanging out. This is the first time he's paid this much attention to me, and I am practically glowing. He presses PLAY on the remote. "It'll be fine. I promise." There he goes again with the promises.

"Mean it?" I ask.

"Every time."

He flops down on the couch and I sit hesitantly next to him. The screen goes dark, then opens on a scene of a mountain, swirling fog licking the top of the peak. A woman's scream fills the room and the title card flips into view: *Mayhem in the Monastery.*

Dean's leg is relaxed, his knee leaning toward mine. He shifts and the edge of his knee makes contact. I can't tell if it's on purpose. The touch is so light he may not have even noticed, though to me, the spot is burning, spreading heat up my leg and through my body, warming my chest and cheeks.

I can't focus on what's happening on the screen. His presence is too distracting. Why did he pull me back here? Why is he suddenly paying me this attention? Is it just because he wants to watch a stupid movie? Is it because he's bored? Or did he want to sit here next to me, want to let his knee touch mine? I can hear my breath, distractingly loud in my ears, so I close my mouth and try to breathe from my nose, but that only makes me dizzy.

"What do you think?" He turns to me, shifting so his knee loses contact. I feel a rush of relief and suddenly I can breathe again.

"I can't tell if you actually like this movie or if it's a joke."

"But you look scared," he says. "You're so tense you're practically running from the room."

"I'm not scared!"

"It's okay if you're scared. The nuns are very scary." And then he reaches over and takes my hand, squeezing it gently in his.

I've held hands before, but not like this. His hands are rough and slightly calloused, but I don't mind. His fingers are dancing in mine, a light feathery touch. I let them trace the center of my palm, then move up my wrist. They flutter on the sensitive skin there, then move back down as he takes a light hold onto each of my fingers, playing with them one by one.

As we let our hands slide along each other, my breath catches in my throat. I want to speak, but I don't know what to say or how to say it. I don't know if I'll ever be able to speak again. All I can focus on is the feel of his skin on mine and the roaring rush of blood in my ears as the world fades away to just soft, moving hands.

The little bell jingles at the front of the store and I jump, the bright light of the break room crashing back into focus. I blink at the screen as a woman in a nun's habit runs screaming through a dark forest, the exaggerated image so out of place with my mood. Dean pulls back his hand and picks up the remote, pausing the movie.

"Duty calls."

"Right."

He stands up and walks toward the door. "I can get it if you want to keep watching. There's a really good part coming up."

"You don't think it's Mr. Roth?" I feel disoriented, like I've woken up from a nap.

"Nope, older lady. She's seriously eyeing your tower of pastries."

"Don't let her eat my mountain!"

"I'm on it. Keep watching. There's a scene coming up where a zombie gets his head cut off by a shovel. Sorry. Spoiler alert."

"Sounds lovely."

He moves to walk back into the store, but then pauses and turns back to me. "I'm glad you're into this kind of stuff." He motions toward the TV. "Sarah, who used to work here, only wanted to watch, like, really basic movies. I could never get her to watch anything weird. You're pretty cool."

He grins and then leaves me alone in the break room. His words flow through me like warm light.

TEN

DANIELLE OLIVER SUCKS IN BED ;)

DANIELLE FOUND THE note taped to her locker Friday morning, right after first period. Now it's laid out in front of us on her bedroom rug and we're gathered around it, sprawled out on the floor. It's early on a Saturday night and we're planning on sleeping over, already in our sweats and surrounded by boxes of Chinese takeout (a risky order from Chinese Food Restaurant).

"It's actually kind of pathetic," Danielle says. "Like, if someone has a problem with me, they should say it to my face." She picks up the note and rips it cleanly in two, throwing the severed pieces into the trash. "Whoever wrote this is a fucking coward." She scoops up a piece of broccoli with her chopsticks.

"Well, maybe they're jealous," Ava says. She pulls a box of nail polish out from under Danielle's bed and begins rummaging through it. "Maybe it's someone who loves Chase and she's mad you got there first. Now that you've slept with him, nobody else is going to measure up."

It's just the kind of compliment Danielle needs, and I wonder if Ava is just trying to be a good friend or if it's something she truly believes.

"That doesn't narrow it down," Danielle says. "Everyone loves Chase."

I can tell she's a little proud when she says it.

"Maybe Chase wrote it," Ava says, and it's like her compliment has been revoked. Sometimes I think it must be hard for Ava to have a best friend who will always be slightly meaner, braver, and better at getting in the last word. I understand the temptation to poke the bear, but I never would. Maybe my survival instincts are stronger. Or maybe I'm just scared.

"The winky face is the worst part," I say, trying to deflect. "It's kinda . . . sinister."

Ava cracks open a bottle of nail polish and Danielle wrinkles her nose. "Are you seriously painting your nails right now? We're eating."

"I'm done." Ava shrugs, beginning to paint her thumb green, the same color as her faded Saint Patrick's Day hair.

"Your hands are covered in chicken, and that nail polish smell makes me want to gag." Danielle closes the box of broccoli and sets it aside a little too forcefully, letting her anger out on the takeout instead of Ava. But we all know Ava's getting off easy— Danielle can bite much harder than this.

Just then, my phone vibrates in my pocket and I pull it out. There's a text from an unknown number.

Hey work buddy

I feel my face flush, hope flooding through my chest. I never gave Dean my number, but maybe he got it from my paperwork.

Who is this?

I type back slowly, then set my phone down on the rug in front of me so I can see the screen, my heart thudding so loud I'm surprised the other girls can't hear it. I put aside the carton of orange chicken I've been picking through, my hunger gone. An answer comes back almost immediately.

Who do you want it to be?

My cheeks redden and I feel my breath quicken. I pick up the phone and wait, unsure what to say. He writes again.

So how does Keely spend her Saturday nights?

There's a pause and I stare at the ". . ." on the screen that means he's still typing, trying to calm my racing heart. I save his number into my contacts as James Dean, grinning stupidly. He texts again.

I bet you're on a date

"Who are you texting?" Hannah asks from next to me. "You're so red right now." She reaches over and grabs the phone from my hands, which are too sweaty to hold on. "Oh my god, James Dean. He finally texted you? This is amazing!" She sits up, folding her legs under her and tucking a lock of black hair behind her ear.

Danielle and Ava sit up too.

"Wait, who is that?" Ava asks. "A guy from your work?"

Hannah shows them the texts.

"Dude, he's really into you." Danielle reaches over to take the phone.

"No he isn't," I answer automatically, shoving the idea away before I can latch on to it. I can't let my hopes rise like that. It's easier not to care.

"No, seriously," she says, scrolling up. "He texted you three times in a row."

"What do I say?" I ask, my face somehow getting even redder.

"What guy is this?" Ava asks. "There are rules to these things. You have to wait at least ten minutes. And no exclamation points. Ever. Enthusiasm is way too desperate."

"You know who he is, actually," Hannah answers. "We saw him at Dunkin' Donuts. The morning after, well." She clears her throat and looks at Danielle before continuing. "After Andrew's party."

"I REMEMBER HIM!" Ava shrieks, almost spilling the bottle of nail polish in her hand. "Cheekbones for days."

"He went to EVmU, right?" Danielle asks.

"Yeah, he's a junior," I answer.

"Oh," she says. "Interesting." She hands the phone back to me with a blank expression.

"What?" I grab for it, relieved to have his messages back in my possession. "Do you know him or something?" I think about how she almost approached him but then changed her mind at the last second.

"No, it's nothing." She shrugs and rummages through the box of nail polish.

"What?" I ask again. "Just say it."

She grabs a little bottle of black nail polish and then looks up at me.

"It's just . . . well . . . he's in college and he's probably been with his fair share of girls. I mean, he looks like a model."

"What, are you saying I'm not good enough for him?"

"Keely, you're beautif—" Hannah begins to say, but Danielle speaks over her.

"You're a virgin. That matters." She shrugs. "He doesn't know, obviously, so he's probably trying to sleep with you and turn you into a steady hookup. But if you tell him you're a virgin, it could only go two ways: he'll be weirded out and lose interest, or he'll take your virginity and never speak to you again. Neither of those are good scenarios." It's blunt, but it sounds true, and it's completely discouraging. "I just doubt he wants to teach you how to have sex. He's got too many options to be interested in that."

"You don't know him," I say sharply. "What if he actually likes me? What if he wants to do things the old-fashioned way?" Three faces stare back at me blankly. Danielle begins to laugh.

"You're saying this hot college guy, who probably has his pick of every girl on campus, suddenly starts texting you, and wants to take you out for a nice steak dinner? Do you want him to give you a promise ring? Maybe you guys can hold hands and then after you can write about it in your diary." She's still holding the unopened bottle of black nail polish in her hands and she shakes it as she speaks, the *click click click* emphasizing every word. "Sorry, Collins, it has nothing to do with you. You're totally datable. It's just—a guy like James Dean doesn't want to *date* anyone."

I sigh and look down at my phone. "Well, I need to answer him. It's been too long."

Ava clicks her tongue. "The longer you make him wait, the more he'll sweat."

"Give me the phone." Danielle sets the nail polish aside, her hands still dry. Then she holds her palm out to me.

"Wait, what are you going to say?" I drop the phone into her hand, hesitant.

"You just have to come across as more experienced," she says, typing something onto the screen and then turning it to me.

> I'm on a date, but it's kinda boring

She presses SEND and we all inhale at the same time, staring at the phone. Danielle puts it down on the rug in the middle of us and we don't speak, willing it to vibrate. After three tense minutes, it does, and we all lunge for it. Danielle reaches it first.

"Let me have it!" I say.

"What does it say?" Ava says, her hands wet with nail polish. "Someone show me!"

> We're having a party tonight. You should come by when you're done.
> I promise not to be boring ☺

We let out a collective shriek. I feel a nervous excitement bubbling up inside of me. There's no mistaking the tone of this text. Some part of him is interested in me. Maybe he felt the same energy I did the other day in the break room. Maybe his knee on mine was on purpose after all.

"You have to go to the party," Danielle says.

"I can't go to a college party," I say immediately. "I don't even like high school parties." I feel like a pent-up ball of energy—like I need to jump or scream or run around the room.

"Your parents already think you're sleeping over at my house, so you have no excuse." Danielle types a response.

> Maybe. I don't know how late I'll be. What's the address?

He answers almost immediately.

> 415 Maplewood Ave. Don't bring your date. I want you all to myself

"And that's how it's done." Danielle drops the phone onto the rug. "Let's get ready." She stands up and begins rummaging through her closet. "I know I have something perfect in here for all of us."

"Wait, all of us?" I ask, a sinking feeling creeping into my stomach.

Danielle turns back to me and rolls her eyes. "You don't think I'm going to let you go to this party by yourself, do you? You'll get eaten alive."

"College party!" Ava squeals, running over to the closet, her boobs bouncing with every jump. I feel my stomach flip in a way that has nothing to do with the Chinese food.

ELEVEN

DANIELLE LIVES RIGHT by the west end of campus, only a few blocks away from the EVmU pool and track. When we look up Dean's address and find out it's walking distance, it feels like it's meant to be. And yet the walk is not easy or pleasant because Danielle has dressed us all in heels—sparkling, sequined, five-inch monsters.

Ava has put on two bras—a sports bra over her everyday push-up bra, so her boobs are hoisted to her chin, her tiny frame overpowered by cleavage. I refused to wear a short skirt like the others, and Danielle eventually relented and let me wear my jeans on the condition that I borrow one of her bras and lacy black crop tops. My stomach is more exposed than it's ever been, and the air feels chilly against my skin. Still, the cold stomach is nothing compared to the feet. My feet are a half size smaller than Danielle's, so they're slipping and sliding in the torture shoes and rubbing in all the worst ways.

"This is what everyone wears," Danielle hisses when I complain. "I've been going to frat parties since birth. Deal with it."

"Yeah, everybody calm down," Ava says, even though her complaints about being cold have been our steady soundtrack for the last twenty minutes.

Hannah did my makeup tonight for the party, keeping it simple like I requested—just eyeliner, mascara, and a touch of lip gloss, which feels sticky and tastes like cotton candy. My hair is in soft waves, curling down my back. I have to admit I feel . . . pretty. Pretty, but not myself.

We turn down Maplewood Ave. and pass some grad student housing, a convenience store, and a few fraternity houses, their yards scattered with the debris of old parties—red cups, destroyed cardboard beer cases, a Slip 'N Slide that looks frozen solid. There are a few guys outside in the yard, and I automatically fold my arms over my stomach, trying to hide myself. Someone whistles as we walk by, and Danielle flips her hair over her shoulder, looking back at the frat guys with a smile.

We stop at the end of the street and I check the address.

"I think this is it. 415 Maplewood."

The house is white and slightly run-down, peeling paint and scattered trash. There's a faint thump of music coming from inside and a murmur of voices, too quiet to understand.

"Were we supposed to bring something?" I ask no one in particular, an overwhelming sense of anxiety filling me.

"Like what?" Hannah asks.

"I don't know." I tap my phone against my palm. "Like a ham?"

"No one brings a ham to a party."

"No," I say, "I mean, like, a housewarming gift. Something to eat. Cheese and crackers?"

"This is why you have us." Danielle pats my shoulder.

"Should I text him?" I look back down at my phone. What's the proper protocol for attending a party where you only know one person?

"Let's just go in," Ava says, walking purposefully across the lawn and up the front steps. She pulls on the door handle but it doesn't move. "It's locked."

I take a deep breath and type a quick text.

I'm outside

We wait just a moment. There's a clicking sound as the lock slides over and the door opens, and then Dean is illuminated in the door frame. Tonight's shirt says SPIELBERG. He's smiling in a relaxed, easy way, and I can tell he's been drinking. He looks both surprised and happy to see me.

"You made it!" He brings me into a hug, and I die a little bit at the contact. He holds on a moment too long to be casual, before pulling back and finally noticing the others. "Oh, there are more of you!"

"Yeah, sorry. I brought friends," I say, feeling my cheeks warm. "I hope that's okay." Why didn't it occur to me to ask?

"Yeah, it's cool. Come in." He ushers us into the hallway, where it's bright and warm. There's a pile of sneakers by the door and I start taking off my heels, thankful I can finally be rid of them, but Danielle gives me a sharp look and continues down the hall, so I leave them on. It smells faintly like stale beer and marijuana smoke, something earthy and rotten, and as we walk, my heels stick to the floor.

"So I live here with my buddy Cody," Dean says, turning back to me. "We were in the dorms together freshman year." He leads us into the living room to where a group of about twenty people are gathered. I realize immediately that we're wearing the wrong thing. It's all sweaters, sweatpants, and flannel shirts, like everyone is trying so hard to look like they don't care. I can see the contempt in their shadowy eyes, pierced lips puckered like something tastes sour. I fold my arms, feeling exposed, wishing I brought a sweater to cover my bare back and shoulders.

"*I thought this is what everybody wears at frat parties,*" Hannah hisses under her breath. She's in a crop top too, showing off her toned stomach.

"*Yeah, well, this isn't a frat party, is it?*" Danielle hisses back. Dean motions us toward a skinny black guy on the couch, who's rolling a joint on the cover of a *History of Film* textbook. He has thick horn-rimmed glasses and a knit beanie.

"Hey, Cody, this is the girl I told you about from work."

I feel myself flush, pleased to be referred to in such a way. *The girl I told you about.*

"Hey, dude!" Cody says, nodding his head. Dean motions to the girls behind me.

"And this is . . . well." He notices Hannah and his eyes brighten. "I know you. You came into the store."

"Hannah," she says, giving a little curtsy. Ava plops down on the couch next to Cody, her skirt riding up as she crosses her legs.

"I'm Ava. You're cute."

Cody lets out a surprised gust of air, smiling wide to show his teeth.

"Oh, really? I like you." He looks back at Dean. "I like her."

Danielle grabs Ava's arm, pulling her back up off the couch. "Don't be so obvious. Let's go get a drink. Dean, right?" Danielle gives Dean a glittery smile. "Do you have anything to drink?" It makes me nervous. She's the one guys are supposed to stare at. Why would Dean want me if he could have her?

"Yeah, sure," he says. "Follow me."

"Hold up!" Cody puts a finger in the air to pause us, then lifts the joint off the table, rolling it between his fingers. "I'm coming with."

Dean walks toward the kitchen and we all follow. He grabs four cans of Bud Light out of the fridge, handing them to each of us. Then he grabs a fifth can and throws it to Cody, who catches it one-handed and cracks open the top with one fluid motion.

I open my own can and take a hesitant sip, trying not to crinkle my nose at the taste. Like always, it tastes like pee. I wish I'd taken Andrew more seriously when he tried to teach me to drink beer. I wish Andrew were here with me now. I'd definitely be freaking out a lot less.

Dean turns to me, leaning forward to speak in a soft voice.

"I have something special for you." His voice fills me with warmth.

"Really?"

He pulls back from my ear and smiles. "Yeah, come to my room for a sec." Before I can answer, he turns away from the kitchen and heads down the hall. I follow, throwing a glance back to my friends, who are all grinning stupidly. Ava gives me a thumbs-up. Danielle pulls her phone out of her purse and texts something. I feel my phone buzz in my pocket a moment later and glance at it.

Cool, confident, and experienced, remember? Don't blow it . . .
Or maybe do ☺

Dean walks through his bedroom door and I follow him in, pocketing my phone before he can see it. His room is pretty bare, just a worn dresser and a bed in one corner, sheets unmade and rumpled. There's a framed poster of *The Bicycle Thief* on one wall and a Pink Floyd poster on the other, the one with the row of naked women's backs. A laundry basket sits in the corner, clothes piling out of it and onto the floor. He walks over to a cabinet in his closet and pulls out a bottle of whiskey. It has a seal of red wax at the top.

He holds it up for me. "I know you like whiskey."

"Oh," I say, surprised. I clear my throat. "Yeah, I do." Danielle's text is etched into my mind: cool, confident, and experienced.

"This is Maker's Mark. Each individual bottle is sealed with wax by hand, so they're all unique." He moves a finger down the red wax at the top of the bottle. "Pretty cool, huh?"

"Yeah."

"You wanna break it open?"

He hands me the bottle and I hold it gingerly, afraid I'll drop it. I have no idea how to break open the wax seal. I reach into the purse hanging from my shoulder and dig around for my house key. Pulling it out, I run the jagged edge down the side of the wax. Dean takes the bottle from me, folding my fingers forward so the key is closed in my palm.

"There's a tab," he explains. "You just pull it." He grabs ahold of the tab and the wax peels away, exposing a normal bottle top underneath. "That was a diligent effort though." I feel my cheeks warm and stuff the key back into my bag. He brings the bottle up to his lips and takes a sip, then hands it back over to me. "Cheers, work buddy."

I hold my breath and take a small sip. When I breathe out I feel a rush of heat flood my chest. The taste is just as bad as I remember it—sweet and chemical at the same time. Do people actually like the taste of whiskey or is everyone just pretending?

"So how was your date?" Dean asks once I swallow.

"My date?" I ask, and then remember the text Danielle sent. "Right, my date." I take another sip of whiskey just to stall. "I mean, like I said before, it was boring." I'm trying to think of something to say, but of course I've drawn a huge blank. For a second my mind flashes to Andrew, the silly comment I made to him in art class, and then the worst possible answer falls out of my mouth. "He wouldn't stop talking about . . . cheese."

"Cheese," Dean says, the corner of his mouth turned up. "Really?"

"Yup. He lives on a cheese farm. I mean . . . dairy farm. I mean, cows. You know how it is around here with all the cows." *Oh my god.* My brain is actually malfunctioning. Dean's eyes are twinkling with amusement and I know he's enjoying witnessing my slow death. I point at his chest, trying to change the subject. "So what's the deal with your shirts?"

He looks down. "They're all movie directors."

"Well, obviously," I say, glad we've moved past my conversational glitch. "I mean, do you make them?"

"Dress for the job you want, not the job you have," he answers, which isn't really an answer at all. But I get what he means.

"You should make a *Hitchcock* one," I say, filled with an overwhelming desire to touch him in some way.

"He's your favorite, right?"

"I mean, he's kinda messed up. But brilliant." I take another sip. It doesn't taste as bad this time, like my senses have been dulled. "Are any of them women? I just realized you don't wear any women."

"Wearing women. Sounds a bit *Silence of the Lambs*, don't you think?"

"I'm serious."

"I only wear my favorites."

I want to say something about that, but he's standing so close to me that I can see the freshly shaved stubble on his jaw, can almost feel his warm breath. I don't want to challenge him and ruin the fizzling magic of this moment.

"Okay, how about *Collins*?"

"You're a director?" He raises his eyebrows, an expression I hope means he's impressed.

"I might be," I say. "Someday. And then you can put me on your shirt."

"Well, let me know when the time comes," he says, leaning toward me, his voice low. "Because you'll definitely be one of my favorites."

"Okay." I can tell I'm smiling like crazy, but I can't help it. I feel clumsy, alight from his words. I put the bottle down on top of the dresser and notice a pile of photographs, in disarray as if someone has carelessly dropped them there. "What are these?"

I pick up the first picture in the pile and look at it before it can cross my mind that it might be personal. It's a woman, slim and beautiful, with long dark hair and a wide smile. She looks like someone you'd want to tell secrets to over a steaming mug of tea.

"Oh, that's my mom," he says, scratching the stubble on his face.

"Sorry." I put the photograph back down on the dresser. "Are these private? I didn't mean to look. I just—"

"It's no big deal," he says, picking it back up. He smiles, running a finger down the side of her glossy face. "I took these when I was home over Christmas break. I don't get to see her much, so it's kind of nice to have these." He picks up another photograph, this one a German shepherd, tongue flopping out the side of its mouth. "They're like tiny stand-ins for my family. Sometimes when I'm, like . . . lonely or stressed or whatever, I'll talk to them. Is that corny? Sorry, that's pretty corny." His face turns an adorable red color. "I've clearly had too much whiskey if I'm telling you these things."

"It's not corny," I say. "It's sweet." I want to reach a hand up and run it through his tousled hair, but I keep my arms firmly by my sides.

"To be honest, I miss Charlie the most." He grins. "He's the dog."

"That's my friend's ex-boyfriend's name, actually. Charlie. He's a Death Eater." I press my lips together as soon as I've said it because *oh my god* Dean is going to think I'm idiotic. He doesn't seem like the type to appreciate a Harry Potter reference.

Luckily he laughs. "Really? Hmm, well, this Charlie is more of a shoe eater. And a furniture eater. And sometimes even his own shit."

"Glad Hannah's ex didn't do that," I say. I have to get us back on track. How do I keep leading us into the least sexy conversations of all time? I look back at the pictures. "What's your mom like?" I just want to know everything about him, wrap myself up in the details of his life like a blanket.

"She's a badass," he says. "Raised my brother and me on her own."

"I like her." I pick up her picture, standing it vertically on the dresser as if it has little legs. "Hi, Dean," I say in a high-pitched voice, wiggling the picture to make it talk. "You should clean your room. It's a mess." I'm surprising myself, acting silly like this. I've been so reserved in front of Dean so far, so *nervous*, like every interaction between us is a test I need to pass. Maybe it's the sips of whiskey working their way through me, warming me from my chest to my toes. Maybe it's the change in location. I'm so very aware of his bed only a few feet away from us. We've never been truly alone before, not like this. I wonder briefly if he locked the door when we came in. I didn't notice.

"I shouldn't be drinking in front of my mom," he says, picking up the bottle of Maker's Mark. "She wouldn't approve." He takes a sip anyway and then hands it over to me.

"Well, then I probably shouldn't drink either. I want to make a good impression on her."

He puts a hand over her face, shielding her eyes. "Coast is clear."

I giggle, feeling light and airy. Then, horribly, I snort. I feel heat flood through me. Snorting in front of my friends is one thing, but this is James Dean. I have always tried so hard to limit my awkward bodily noises in front of boys.

"Did you just snort?"

"Nope," I say, and then take a drink from the bottle. "So what do you say when you talk to them? The pictures."

"If you don't snort, then I don't talk to pictures," he answers, grinning. He runs a hand through his dark mess of hair and I watch it enviously.

"Fine," I say. "I may have snorted. What do you say?"

"Give me another drink first."

I hand him the bottle and he takes a sip, smacking his lips dramatically when he's done. Then he puts it back on the dresser and picks up the picture of his mom. He clears his throat and then winks at me. Winking is usually something people do in cheesy movies, but seeing James Dean, a normal, cute, definitely-not-cheesy guy, wink at me makes it feel new, like he's the one who invented it.

He grins, looking at me and then down at the picture of his mom. For a moment—just a flash—I'm filled with embarrassment that I asked him to do something so silly, so awkward and personal. Why did I think this was a good idea? Then he begins to speak and my anxiety melts away at the warm, easy tone in his voice. He isn't embarrassed. Of course he isn't.

"Mom, how's it going?" he says to the picture. "You're looking fantastic, really sepia-toned. Please don't judge my behavior at the moment." He glances away from the photo to look at me, his gaze locking on to mine. "Because I am drinking, and I have a pretty girl in my room, and I might kiss her."

"Are you drunk?" I ask suddenly, leaning closer to him—so close I can see a fleck of gold in one of his eyes.

"Probably," he says. "A little." He smiles at me in an easy, relaxed way, and I feel myself drawn to him, smiling to match his.

"I think I might be," I say.

And then he kisses me. I've only been kissed once before, at summer camp when I was fifteen. This kiss is nothing like that one—a kiss I now know, with certainty, didn't count. Dean's tongue rubs against my lips, begging permission, and so I open them and let him in, the feel of it new and wonderful. He moves his hand from my neck down my arm and then takes hold of my hand, intertwining our fingers. He tugs me over to the bed, never breaking contact. I sit down with a *thunk*, the bed lower than I expected it to be, and start to giggle, the tension and energy between us too much. Dean pulls away to place a light kiss on the top of my nose.

"You're cute."

He gently pushes me back so I'm lying on the bed, and then lies over me, his body covering mine, touching mine in all the right places. His hands roam through my hair and down the side of my waist to touch the bare skin between my jeans and top. He pulls his lips from mine and begins to press light kisses down my neck, and I tighten my grasp on his shirt. His smell is intoxicating, aftershave mixed faintly with tobacco smoke, and something about it feels so grown up. He smells like a *man* somehow, not like some boy from high school, and it's terrifying and exhilarating all at once.

I don't know how long we stay like that, entwined together on the bed. It could be hours, days, years. I'm in a daze, my only thoughts on the feel of him.

"You should stay over," he says, breathing huskily into my ear. His voice is a rough whisper and as he speaks, his lips brush the soft skin of my earlobe.

"What about my friends?" I ask, pulling away slightly.

"They'll be fine." He brushes a strand of hair behind my ear. "They can stay over too, on the couch. Or they can go home. Whatever."

"I should just check," I say, pulling out of his grasp to find my phone. I have no idea what time it is. How long have we been in his room? I press the button to light up the screen, and see it's already after midnight. I have a bunch of texts.

HANNAH

Don't do anything I wouldn't do!

DANIELLE

Are you still a virgin?

AVA

have you seeen Deany's wieney?

HANNAH

Ava is dancing on the coffee table. We might need to take her home soon

AVA

🍆🍆🍆🍆🍆🍆🍆🍆🍆

DANIELLE

Ava is singing show tunes! We're taking her home. It's for her own good. Stay here and get laid

HANNAH

Do you want to come with us?

AVA

Keely god liuck u luve yo!

"I think they might have left," I say. I know I should be upset they ditched me, but a part of me is glad I have an excuse to stay. I type a group message back.

> I'm going to stay here. See you guys tomorrow

As soon as the message sends I feel the impact of what the words mean, my stomach flipping uneasily. I'm staying the night. In a boy's bed.

"Good," he says. He flips off the light on his bedside table and then he pulls me back down, a smile in his kiss. His lips brush my cheek, then my chin, then down my neck, giving me shivers. He pulls away and then brings his shirt up over his head, revealing a toned chest. I reach a hand up to his shoulder and then brush my fingertips softly down his bare arm, reveling in the feeling of his warm skin.

"Your turn," he says, his voice raspy. He holds on to the bottom of my top, and then slowly pulls the fabric up over my head. I don't stop him, but I suck in a deep breath when he leans back to look at me, and I'm thankful the room is dark.

I'm in Danielle's bra—a black lacy one from Victoria's Secret, and it's a little too big for me. She noticed my old sports bra when we were getting ready earlier and insisted I borrow one of hers, a "real bra," just in case. Now I'm glad I did.

"You're so hot," he says.

"Really?" I ask before realizing it's the wrong thing to say.

"Damn right," he says, pulling me toward him. He settles down into the mattress and I settle onto him. We stay like that for a while longer, though it's hard to judge how long. I feel like we're separate from time—like the world is going on around us, but we aren't a part of it. We're in our own galaxy, just lips and warm breath and soft hands. I feel like I'm honey dripping slowly from a spoon.

And then he pulls his face from mine and whispers the words that snap me back into focus.

"Should I get a condom?"

"What?" I whisper back, though I heard him perfectly. I don't know what else to say. He tucks a strand of hair behind my ear and says it again, his voice scratchy from lack of use.

"Should I get a condom?"

Yes. Isn't that the obvious answer? Isn't this what I was hoping would happen when I came to his house, when I went alone to his room? I think of Danielle's warning from earlier in the night, an uneasy feeling churning in my stomach. *If you tell him you're a virgin, it could only go two ways: he'll be weirded out and lose interest, or he'll take your virginity and never speak to you again. I just doubt he wants to teach you how to have sex.*

It's a catch-22. I don't want to be a virgin anymore, but I don't want to scare Dean away by letting him take my virginity. What if he freaks out at my inexperience? Or maybe worse—what if he never talks to me again afterward, because he's gotten what he wanted? I wish there was some way to just get it over with, some way to have already had sex. I don't want Dean to have to teach me. I want to already know what I'm doing. I want this not to be a BIG DEAL.

Maybe Dean doesn't have to know I'm a virgin. I know the basics. I could probably fake it. But what if it hurts? Hannah told me the first time she had sex with Charlie, it hurt so much she cried. They lay on top of a bath towel just in case, and she bled all over it. I can't imagine the humiliation I'd feel if I bled all over

Dean's sheets. He would have to wash them right away, would have to take them into the living room where Cody might see them, and they'd both laugh and call me disgusting, and that would become my label: the disgusting high school girl who ruined Dean's sheets. The lying virgin caught red-handed. I'd be an embarrassing blip on Dean's timeline, a regretful mistake.

"Keely?" He sits up and leans over to his bedside table, rummaging through it in the dark. Then there it is in his hand—a condom, wrapped in a shiny square package. I've seen condoms before in health class. They're passed around in a basket several times a year while everyone giggles and self-consciously grabs a few, like some twisted grown-up version of trick-or-treat. Still, condoms are novel to me. The fact that Dean keeps them in his bedside table, that he uses them enough to have them on hand, feels strange. To Dean, are condoms just as ordinary as hand sanitizer or Advil?

"It's okay," I say, though it doesn't mean anything. I feel like I'm speaking into a tunnel.

"What's okay?" He reaches down toward his belt, undoing the buckle with deft fingers.

"No, I mean, we don't have to."

"You're cool with no condom?" he asks, flicking it away. He pulls the belt off.

"No," I say, shaking my head. "We don't have to have sex."

He grins at me, his teeth still visible in the dark room. "Of course we don't *have* to." He kisses me, pulling me back toward him, back into our galaxy. "But we want to." His hand reaches toward the button of my pants.

I remember with horror that I'm wearing an old pair of underwear, cotton with polar bears I've had since middle school.

Danielle didn't offer to let me borrow any "real underwear," and I didn't ask because that would have been too weird. I feel clammy, my breath shallow, like I've had too much whiskey, even though we stopped drinking ages ago.

"Wait."

"You okay?" He draws back his hand.

"I think we should wait."

"Oh." He sounds disappointed. Sitting up, he pulls away from me. "Oh. Okay."

"I want to," I say, stupidly upset I've let him down. "I want to. Just not yet."

"Are you sure? It's not a big deal." He kisses me again, as if he knows the magic he holds in his kisses, the spell he casts over me with his lips and tongue. But I'm stuck, my virginity an invisible wall between us. I'll make a decision later. This isn't my only chance with Dean. It can't be.

"Another time, okay?"

"You promise?"

"I promise." I take his hand in mine and squeeze, the thought hitting me that promising is sort of like making a decision after all.

"You know how I feel about promises." He kisses the tip of my nose and then sits up and gets out of bed. "I'm gonna go take a shower. I won't be able to sleep until this goes away." He motions casually toward his pants, unembarrassed.

"Oh, sure." I'm trying to sound casual but I can't breathe.

"See you later, work buddy." Grabbing a towel out of the hamper, he slings it over his shoulder, whistling as he leaves the room.

When he comes back fifteen minutes later, I pretend to be

asleep. It feels easier to lie next to him with my eyes closed than to have to come up with new things to say. I can be cool, confident, and experienced again in the morning. He climbs into bed next to me and curls himself around me, tangling his legs with mine.

I don't sleep a wink.

TWELVE

IN THE MORNING I'm still lying stiffly beside Dean, who's snoring softly, little puffs of air tickling my ear. His arm is slung over me, holding me still. I sit up as much as I can, trying to reach for my phone without waking him.

When I get ahold of it, I click it on and check the time: 7:30. I have to get back to Danielle's soon, before her parents notice I'm missing. Is it too early to wake Dean? I study his face for a minute, thankful for the opportunity to stare at him unnoticed. He looks younger when he sleeps, and less intimidating. He has a dark freckle next to his left eye and a little scar on his forehead I can just barely see through a part in his messy hair.

I'm worried that once he wakes up the easy way things were last night will be gone, that everything between us was only a result of the whiskey. Talking to him now might ruin it. I don't want him to see the morning crusts in my eyes. What if he tries to kiss me and I have morning breath? Or worse, what if he doesn't try to kiss me at all?

I have to get out from under his arm.

I shift slightly to the right, trying to wiggle over to the side of the bed as quietly as I can. He moves and the arm tightens, pulling me closer into his chest. I lie still for a minute, enjoying the feel of it. With his body against mine it's easy to imagine just staying here forever.

But then I think again of my greasy face and the mascara that's probably smudged under my eyes. No, definitely better to sneak out. I pause for a moment, sinking into him and closing my eyes, trying to remember exactly how it feels to be wrapped up in him, in case it's the last time. And then I lift his arm just enough to squeeze under and climb out of the bed, trying to gather up my scattered clothes.

As I put my top on, I feel a lot more exposed in the morning light than I did last night. I glance over at the pair of sparkling torture shoes lying by the door. I really don't want to strap them back on.

To get to Danielle's, I'll have to retrace our steps from last night past the rows of frat houses, around the grad housing, and then through downtown. And it'll be busy. On Sundays in the spring, they block off a bunch of streets for the craft fair, so people can sell handmade candles and mittens and other wholesome things.

I can't do it.

I sit back on the mattress and text the girls.

> Is anyone awake? Can someone come get me?

After waiting a minute with no answer, I scoop up my heels and tiptoe out of Dean's room, praying no one else is awake in the house. The floor feels even stickier on my bare feet than it did with shoes, but I'm afraid the heels will make too much noise if I put them on.

Finally I get outside and shut the door quietly behind me. The sidewalk in front of me is still empty, and I contemplate just sucking it up and making the walk. Maybe no one will be out after all. But then, down the street in the direction I need to head, a girl comes around the corner. She's wearing a tight red dress and holding a pair of gold heels in one hand, walking fast with her head down. She passes one of the frat houses on the corner, and a voice rings out from the front porch, amplified by a megaphone.

"Hey! We've got a Walk of Shame!"

The girl's head whips up and she walks a little faster. I duck, trying to hide, hoping the guys across the street will be too distracted by the other girl to notice me.

"Was it worth it?" the megaphone voice calls out. Another voice joins in, beginning to sing: "Lady in reeeeeeeeeed."

There's a clump of trees behind Dean's house, and I run toward them, taking cover. Then I call Hannah. It's cold for April, colder than it was the night before, and I'm shuffling my feet trying to stay warm. The phone keeps ringing and then, Hannah's voicemail greeting. I end the call and try Ava and Danielle. There's no answer. They're probably all still in recovery from last night.

I wait a few more minutes, and then decide to call Andrew. I don't want him to see me in these stupid clothes. I know he'll tease me about it for the rest of eternity. Still, desperate times call for desperate calls.

• • • • • •

His truck pulls up fifteen minutes later.

Rolling down the window, he calls out to me. "What can I get for twenty bucks?"

I scramble out from the trees and hop in the truck as quickly as I can. "How about a punch in the face?" I fold my arms self-consciously over my chest, trying to block it from view. "Can we go?"

"I'm just kidding," he says, shrugging and glancing over at me. "You look nice, actually." He pulls out onto the empty street. "It's just weird to see you dressed like a girl. Where did you get those clothes? I know they're not yours because they don't have sleeves."

"They're Danielle's."

"Right. I should have known."

We drive past the frat house and I breathe out a sigh of relief, thankful the megaphone guys never noticed me. "Thanks for coming to get me. I know it's early."

"I was up already."

We drive by Main Street where the craft fair is getting set up, zipping right past the turn to Danielle's house.

"Wait." I say. "You were supposed to turn back there. I have to get back to Danielle's before my mom comes to pick me up."

He turns to me and raises an eyebrow, a smile spreading across his face. "Collins." He reaches over to pat my knee. "Do you really think I'm just gonna pick you up from a mysterious place on campus dressed like a *girl* and drop you off at Danielle's, no questions asked? I'm gonna need some dirt."

"Drew, I have to—"

"Let's go get breakfast. Jan's?"

Jan's is where we go to get our cheese and meat fix—it's a tiny little diner downtown with sticky counters, plastic booths, and the best bacon in the entire world. Andrew and I go there way too often, usually on mornings after the vegans have served us leaves for dinner.

He turns the truck onto Pinewood, and we see a collection of tents being set up, strung with woolen mittens and colorful baubles. There are people milling about, signs advertising local beer and hot cider. "Look, the craft fair!" Andrew says, leaning over to get a better look. He pulls into an empty parking spot on the side of the road.

"Drew, the whole point of you coming to get me was to avoid the craft fair." I pull my phone out of my bag and check the time again. It's 8:24 already. "I really have to go back to Danielle's."

He clicks off his seat belt. "Just tell your mom we're together. She won't be mad."

I glare at him. He glares back, mirroring my expression. Then he picks his phone up and starts typing in a number, bringing it up to his ear.

"No talking on the phone while you're driving," I say, reaching a hand out to grab it from him.

"We're parked."

"So?" I don't care if he talks to my mom. I just care about being seen in this outfit. I'm trying to avoid the general public until I can find a less ridiculous pair of shoes. I lean back in my seat and fold my arms over my chest, narrowing my eyes as he talks.

"Hey, Karen," he says into the phone, his voice all cheery smiles. "Everything's great . . . I'm with her right now actually . . . Yup, earliest she's ever woken up I think. A new record. We're just getting some breakfast . . . Yeah, no problem. See you later!"

He ends the call and turns to me. "See? She loves me." He opens the car door. "Let's go."

I grab his arm to stop him. "Wait! I can't go out there dressed like this. It's obscene."

"You're being dramatic," he says. "You look normal. Like, my aunt Mildred would wear what you're wearing to church."

"You don't have an aunt Mildred," I say.

"Fine," he says, relenting. "I have a sweatshirt in the back." He reaches behind me and rummages around, pulling out a navy blue Prescott hoodie. It smells like campfire. I grab it from him and pull it on eagerly, covering up my stomach.

"Okay, now can we go?"

"Just Jan's," I say. "No craft fair."

"Just Jan's."

He jumps out of the car for real this time, and I follow him out, stumbling a little in the sequined heels. Just as I right myself, I feel my phone vibrate. There's a text from Dean.

Why'd you sneak out?

I feel warmth flood through me, relieved he's contacted me. I pause for a minute, trying to think of something to say in response. What would Danielle say?

Had to be somewhere

There. Appropriately aloof. He texts back a minute later.

Nice. See you at work. Last night was fun

Andrew waits impatiently as I put away my phone. I feel a goofy smile spread across my face, and I can see him trying to figure it out.

We head down the sidewalk toward Jan's, me about five paces behind him because his legs are so much longer than mine, and he's wearing sensible footwear. Once we get there, I scamper inside as quickly as possible, and he rolls his eyes at me.

It's not until I have a big pile of steaming pancakes in front of me that Andrew finally breaks down and asks.

"Okay, so what the hell?"

"What?" I feign innocence and reach over to grab a piece of his bacon. He swats my hand away and the bacon drops back onto his plate.

"Why were you hiding in the woods dressed like my aunt Mildred?"

I take a bite of pancakes to stall for time, and they burn the roof of my mouth. "There's a guy," I say finally, feeling my face get hot.

Andrew takes a long sip of his coffee and then puts it down on the table, running a finger absently around the rim. "Who is he?"

"We call him James Dean." I lower my voice so that hopefully he can't hear me. He does.

"We do?" he asks, leaning forward. "Is he a rebel without a cause? Does he have a motorcycle?" He takes a bite of bacon.

"Yeah," I say. "He does."

He puts the bacon back down. "Oh."

"He works with me at the store. He had a party last night and invited me, so we all went." I can see the information clicking into place in his head.

"So he goes to EVmU then?"

"Yeah, he's a junior."

"Hmm," he says. Then he takes a bite of his own pancakes, chewing them for a while. I wait for him to continue, but he doesn't say anything more.

"What does 'hmm' mean?"

He runs a hand through his hair and leans forward, putting his elbows onto the table. "Just . . . be careful, okay?"

"What are you saying?" I know what he's saying. It's the same thing Danielle told me, the same thing I was worrying about last night.

"I know how guys think," he says. "I just don't want you to get hurt."

"We didn't, like . . . have sex or anything," I say, my voice coming out strangely high-pitched. After I say it, Andrew's face turns red.

"Okay," he says. "But he wants to."

"How do you know what he wants?"

He gives me a pointed look. "He wants to."

I'm feeling combative for some reason. Of course I know he wants to; he told me so last night, condom in hand. I swirl a spoon in a circle around my cup of coffee. I can't look at Andrew. I take a deep breath and speak, my voice quiet.

"I've never . . ."

"I know," he says. I look up at him then and the expression in his eyes is kind, the familiarity of it comforting.

"I haven't told you, because, I don't know, it's sort of embarrassing to talk about. And you're clearly, like, really experienced, and so is everyone else, and I'm pretty much the only one left." The words all come pouring out before I can stop them.

"You're—" he starts, but then the waitress comes back over, holding up a jug of coffee.

"How you guys doing? Anyone want a refill?" We both jump, turning to her with guilty faces.

"We're fine," I say, my voice catching. "Thanks."

"No prob! I'll come back in a little while with the check."

We turn back to each other and I struggle to find something to say.

"You don't have to tell me about it," he says finally. He toys with the rest of the pancakes on his plate, using his fork to cut them up into fluffy little pieces.

"It's okay," I say. "It's actually kinda nice to talk about. I've wanted to tell you about Dean forever, but it seemed weird. I didn't know what you'd say."

He puts his fork down on the plate and folds his hands in front of him on the table. "Just be careful with this guy, okay?" he says again. "Does he know? That you're a . . . um . . . that you've never . . ." He trails off.

I shake my head. "I haven't told him yet." I add the "yet" for Andrew's sake. I'm not sure if I'm ever going to tell Dean, but that feels too complicated to express to Andrew.

"You shouldn't dress like someone you're not for his sake," Andrew says. He taps his shoe against my sparkly heel under the table.

"You said I looked nice."

"You do look nice," he says. "But you just don't look like you. This guy's not worth that."

"You don't know him."

"No guy is worth that." He takes another bite of bacon and then pushes the plate toward me. "Want the rest?" I reach out and pick up the last piece, biting into it. "Next time you should just order your own."

"Why would I order my own when I can have yours?" I smile, finishing the piece and licking the grease off my fingers. "You're always too full to finish it."

"Or do I pretend to be too full so you can have some?" He raises an eyebrow at me. "It's like the chicken and the egg."

"How appropriately breakfasty a puzzle this is. Eggs and chickens and bacon," I say.

I'm glad things seem to be back to normal, but I know we're both faking it a little bit, trying just a little too hard.

THIRTEEN

"**YOU DID THE** right thing," Ava says Monday morning at school. "You can't sleep with him right away, because then he'll lose interest."

We're all gathered in the lounge, a "seniors-only" room with wall-to-wall lockers and a bunch of fluffy couches. It's like Prescott's version of the VIP section at a concert, and as freshmen, we were dying to get a glimpse inside. Now that we're finally seniors, the excitement has worn off. It kinda smells like old milk.

We're on the ancient blue couch by the window—Hannah, Danielle, Ava, and me—recapping the events of the weekend. There are only five minutes left until first bell, so the lounge is bustling with students, the noise blocking out our conversation. Ava looks around and lowers her voice. "He can't know you're a virgin because then he'll think of you *only* as a virgin. Suddenly that's what it'll be about. He'll just want to take it.

Your virginity won't be *yours*, it'll be *his*."

"Guys are experts at making everything about them," Hannah says. She has our French textbook propped open in her lap, and she's scribbling last-minute notes before class, the paper torn and wrinkled because it's probably lived in her car for a week with the gum wrappers and takeout bags.

"What do you know about being a virgin?" Danielle says to Ava. "You haven't been one since you were fourteen."

Ava crumples a bit at Danielle's comment, and I keep talking, trying to pretend I didn't hear it. "You can't lump all guys together though." If what they're saying is true, it's all just too depressing. "Not all guys are bad. Maybe he won't care I'm a virgin. Maybe it's not a big deal."

"I'm sure there are great guys out there," Hannah says. "We just haven't met them." She sighs, closing her textbook and stuffing it back into her backpack. "Like, take Charlie."

Hannah hasn't brought up Charlie to anyone besides me for a while. He turned her into a crying, insecure, puffy-eyed mess, and we were all thankful when he graduated at the end of last year and moved away for college. Now he's probably some poor girl's problem in South Carolina.

"Charlie knew I was a virgin. He was my first relationship, obviously, and he knew that. And he was wonderful about everything. He said he loved me. We waited six months before we finally had sex, and I thought it was special. Turns out . . ." She doesn't need to finish the story.

I look at the empty spot on Hannah's neck where there was once a delicate chain, a silver "H" that Charlie gave her for Christmas. She used to fiddle with it constantly, probably liking the reminder of him every time she touched it. We threw it in the lake when he dumped her, but still her hands sometimes absently reach up toward her neck out of habit.

"Charlie was a Death Eater," I say. "That's a special case."

"Okay, well, Chase then," Danielle says, glancing around the room to make sure he's not around. "Chase told everybody we did it like five seconds after he got his dick back in his pants. How's that for special?" She pauses to let the words sink in and then we all burst out laughing.

It does seem like we're surrounded by a special breed of assholes, but maybe that's just guys in general. Even the good guys like Andrew still sometimes treat girls like shit, and I know it won't be long before he gets tired of Cecilia.

I don't want to be that girl, the one someone throws away. Danielle is right. I can't let Dean find out the truth.

On Wednesday I have work again with Dean after school, and when the bell rings at the end of the day, I feel a little like I'm going to throw up. I still haven't seen him since the night of his party, or more accurately, since the morning after, when I tiptoed out of his bedroom. Will he act differently when he sees me? Will he try to kiss me hello? I've never kissed anyone hello before, and the prospect of it floods me with anxious energy. How will I know which way to turn my head? How long should the kiss last? Will there be tongues involved? Or even worse—what if I only think he's trying to kiss me hello but he's actually just going in for a hug and I end up with his ear in my mouth?

There are a million ways this could go wrong.

Hannah's field hockey practice has started back up after school, which means she's unavailable for emotional support, so I have to ask Andrew for a ride to work instead.

"When are you getting your own car?" he asks on our way over.

"Soon," I say, even though we both know I'm lying.

"I'm keeping a tally, you know. You owe me so many rides now, you better drive back and forth from California to Maryland every single weekend next year."

"Hmm," I say, trying to listen to him but still thinking about the probability of the ear-in-the-mouth situation. I'm wringing my hands so tightly my knuckles have turned white.

"You're nervous," he says; not a question but a statement, because he can likely see it on my face. "That guy from this weekend."

"Dean," I say.

"James Dean," he corrects, with an exaggerated eye roll that shows how silly he thinks it is. He motions to my outfit—a pair of black leggings and a gray Prescott hoodie. "At least you look like you again."

"That's probably not a good thing." I reach up to pull down the visor and look at myself in the little mirror. I turn to him. "Do I look okay?"

"You always look okay," he says, flicking on his blinker and turning the truck into the parking lot of the video store. The compliment takes me by surprise.

"Really?"

"Come on, Collins. You know you're beautiful."

Beautiful. The word catches me off guard. It's not a casual word, something easy like *hot* or *cute*, words I've heard Andrew use a million times.

"Oh." My face is so warm you could probably bake cookies on it. I don't really believe him. I know he's just trying to be nice.

"Thanks," I say, not looking at him.

"It's whatever," he says. I glance over at him quickly and he's not looking at me either. I wonder if he's embarrassed he said anything. He parks the truck and reaches over to unlock my door, leaving the gas running.

"Be careful, okay?"

"It's just work," I say. "Not a big deal."

He narrows his eyes at me and doesn't need to say anything back, because I can hear him telepathically: *I can see through all of your bullshit, Collins.*

I turn toward the store, smiling when I see the chalkboard out front, recognizing Dean's handwriting.

VIDEOS: GET 'EM WHILE THEY'RE HOT!

But the smile is bittersweet, because this means he hasn't called out sick or mysteriously died, but is in fact right on the other side of the glass door in front of me. Andrew honks and I turn back around, raising an arm up to wave goodbye. He waves back and then drives away. I take a deep breath, trying to calm myself. Then I push the door open and walk in.

And there is he, behind the register, resting his adorable head on his adorable hand. I only get a flash of him before I whip my head down to stare at the ground, because suddenly my eyes don't know how to work properly. I barely notice Tim is behind the counter too—*Star Trek* Tim, who's smiling and waving at me like he has no idea I'm in complete anxiety hell. It's actually good that Tim is here, really. No alone time with James Dean means I won't have to deal with the whole trying-to-go-in-for-a-kiss-but-ending-up-with-his-ear-in-my-mouth problem.

"Hey, Keely," Tim calls out as I take off my jacket and walk over to the register.

"Hey, Tim," I say, making eye contact with the floor. I can't look up on the chance Dean might walk into my eyeline. I know I'm being awkward and probably ruining everything, but this is the first time I've ever dealt with seeing a cute guy after a hookup and it's excruciating. I'm even more impressed now with how calm Danielle was when she saw Chase in school after the whole condom incident.

It's getting weird now, so I force myself to look up at Dean. Our eyes lock. I feel a shot of electricity at the contact, almost as if it were a physical touch. He smiles and raises his hand to his forehead in a quick army salute. His hair is rumpled and I can't help but flash back to when I was running my hands through it. All I want is to run my hands through it again and again.

"Hey," I say, raising an arm up to army salute him back. My voice comes out scratchy and I have to clear my throat. Somehow I don't sound like me.

"Long time no see." He breaks out into a full smile, and his dimples melt me into a puddle on the floor. I wonder if Tim can see me down there, if he can tell I'm no longer solid but pure liquid.

"Store is closed today," Dean says. "Roth wanted us all in to do some spring cleaning. Heavy overhaul. We're supposed to have it all cleaned and ready to open back up tomorrow."

I groan, heading back to the break room to dump my bag. The room is in disarray. The guys have pulled the couch away from the wall for better cleaning access, and the linoleum floor is covered in dust. There's a mop and a broom leaning against the cutout of Legolas, placed in such a way that it looks like he's holding them both.

"Is Legolas helping us?" I call out to the front of the store.

"Yeah. He's got the break room covered," Dean calls back.

"I hope he knows what he's doing," I say, placing my stuff down on the lumpy old couch. "This place is a disaster."

"He's thousands of years old." Dean's voice is suddenly right behind me and I jump. "I'm sure he's cleaned the elf kingdom a time or two."

"Mirkwood," I say automatically, and then want to die.

"What?"

"Huh? Nothing." I turn and see him leaning casually against the door frame. "Hey," I say again, flustered, feeling like an idiot.

"Hey," he says, full grin.

Then he walks toward me and wraps a hand gently around my lower back. The other slides through my hair, curling around the back of my neck, and suddenly he's kissing me; kissing me like we aren't at work, like Tim isn't a few steps away in the other room, like he isn't scared of being interrupted. No, he's kissing me like we're back in our galaxy, the only two people in a sea of stars. It doesn't matter that we're in the dirty break room, surrounded by dust bunnies. Nothing matters but James Dean.

He pulls back from me, smiling.

"Wow," I whisper before I can help it. I don't know why I was ever nervous.

He lets go of me. "I just needed to do that. Now let's get back to work." He winks and then turns around and walks back out of the break room like he hasn't just kissed me into oblivion. I realize that I'm smiling. My face feels stuck that way.

FOURTEEN

IT BECOMES A regular thing, making out with Dean. We claim the old green couch as our own, turning Legolas around so he won't witness our sins. We kiss sometimes out in the store too, when we're feeling daring, when customers are scarce; me sitting up on the counter with my legs wrapped around him so we're eye to eye. I dream about coming to work, wishing it were more than two days a week, wishing I could live here, could inject it into my veins, let it fill me up from the inside. My heartbeat has a rhythm, has a name: *James Dean James Dean James Dean.*

"So what are you guys?" Hannah asks, the inevitable question, the question no high school girl can ever resist because we crave labels, need to keep organized when we feel like pieces of ourselves are flying apart.

"Who says we have to be anything?"

We're in study hall and we're supposed to be doing French

homework, but I have work after school today, so obviously the topic has turned to Dean.

"Well, do you want it to be something?" she asks.

"He hasn't asked me to hang out again." I lower my voice to a whisper, like it's embarrassing to admit to her. "We only ever make out in the store."

"If he asked you on a date, would you go?"

Truthfully, I'm not sure. A date feels too *real*. What if he asks me about past relationships? I can't admit to him I've never had a boyfriend, and I obviously can't tell him I've never had sex. Making out in the break room is perfect because we can never go all the way, not at work—it's wonderful and easy and safe.

Until one day it's not. We're on the green couch, my back pressed into the cushions, his body over mine. His hand is tangled in my hair and he nips at my ear, at my neck, at my lips, and then pulls back to look at me.

"I can get used to working like this," he says, his voice husky.

"Me too," I say.

There hasn't been a customer for about fifteen minutes, so we've been taking advantage of the extra time in the best way we know how. Thank God for the bell above the door.

He leans in to kiss me again and I melt into it, feeling his body sink into mine on the couch as he settles all of his weight on me. He runs a hand through my hair and then trails it down the side of my face, down my neck, and rests it on my chest. Then he moves it lower, running his fingertips lightly over the skin at my waist, and then his hands are undoing his belt and snapping open the button of his pants. I hear the sound of a zipper and am shocked out of my stupor. I push him away, looking around frantically. He jumps off me and raises his arms up as if in surrender. I notice his unzipped pants, half hanging off his hips.

"We can't do that here." My voice sounds shrill.

"What difference does it make?" he asks. "We're already breaking the rules."

"Someone could come in!"

"C'mon, it'll be fun. We won't get caught."

It doesn't sound fun to me, having sex here where someone might walk in. He's probably used to adventurous girls, girls who get off on having sex in public, who do it in their cars, on the beach, in bathrooms at the back of a bar. I've never even been in a bar.

I'm such a kid.

"I don't want to lose my job," I say, which is true, but is actually about number 5 on my list of worries behind (1) I can't have sex for the first time on the gross green couch in the break room, (2) I hope Dean likes me, (3) If he wants to have sex on the gross green couch though, he probably doesn't *like* me—just wants to have sex with me, (4) I wish I knew what the hell I was doing.

"Just touch me." His voice is achingly low. I can feel its vibration in my stomach, can feel excitement and anxiety pooling there and spreading across my chest. He's still standing in front of me with his pants unzipped, and he pulls them down so he's just in his boxers. "You've never even touched me."

I can't help thinking about taco night, when the guys at school were so casually complaining about handjobs. *Mouth or nothing*, Simon had said, like he had any right to insist on anything. Is that what Dean wants? If I use my hands, will he be disappointed? Will he complain about it to his friends later the way Ryder did?

But I push those worries aside. James Dean is standing in front of me in his boxers and I want to touch him, want to see the expression on his face when I do.

"Okay." My voice is barely a whisper. I reach my hand out toward his boxers, my fingers shaking. I've never touched a penis before and I don't know what to expect. What does it feel like? How tight do you hold it?

And then I hear the jingle of the little bell. I scream, which is probably the worst thing to do, and jump away from Dean, scrambling to the other side of the room. He rushes to find his pants, tripping as he pulls them back up and over his hips. He's smoothing out his shirt and fixing his hair, and he nods to me. "Your hair, Keely."

There's no mirror back here, but I run and check my reflection in the microwave and I can sort of see that my hair is sticking up everywhere. I run my hands through it to smooth it down as Dean leaves the break room and walks back out into the store, like nothing ever happened.

"Sorry," I hear him say. "We were dealing with something in the back."

"Was anyone watching the register?" It's a deep gravelly voice I recognize—Mr. Roth! I feel a swirling in my stomach like I might throw up. I brush my hair to the side with my fingers, hoping I look presentable—that my lips aren't too puffy or my clothes too rumpled so Mr. Roth won't know what we were up to. What if he had walked into the break room? What if I had actually reached out my hand all the way, put it into Dean's boxers, and Mr. Roth had seen? The thought is horrible and humiliating. I can't believe I was so reckless.

"I was just gone for a second," Dean says. "Nobody came in the store."

"Someone should always be up front by the register," says Mr. Roth. "I'm tired of this."

I take a deep breath and walk out of the break room into the main room of the store, rolling my shoulders back and trying to stand up tall.

"Hey, Mr. Roth," I say, my voice breaking and giving me away. "I was just taking a bathroom break. What's up?"

Mr. Roth launches into a speech about a shipment of new books we'll be getting later in the week, but I can barely listen to him. All I can imagine over and over again is the look he'd have on his face if he had walked in on us. Dean and I have to stop messing around in the store.

When Mr. Roth finally leaves, after what feels like an eternity, Dean pulls me close to his side, whispering into my ear.

"Come over after work tonight." I can feel his lips against my skin. "I don't want to be interrupted."

"I can't tonight." The words cause a physical ache in my chest. "I have a history test tomorrow." I'm torn, because a part of me wants to be close to him, wants to spend every possible second with him that I can, but another part of me is scared to be alone with him. The test is just a convenient way to stall.

"If not tonight, when?" he asks, pulling back to look me in the eyes.

"I promise," I say, which isn't a real answer.

"Didn't realize you were so into playing games," he says with a laugh.

"I'm not playing games." I feel a prickling sensation in the bridge of my nose like I might be about to cry. He tilts his head to the side, studying me.

"Are you a virgin?"

My breath catches in my throat. His voice is low and I can't read his tone, can't tell how seriously he's taking the question, which way he wants me to answer.

"I'm not," I say, the words rushing out of me before I can stop them. "I swear. I really have a history test tomorrow."

He smiles. "Good."

Then he kisses me again and pulls away.

All I can think about is the stupid lie I just told. Now I'm stuck with it. There's no backtracking from this. I'll just have to pretend I know what I'm doing, and hopefully I'll have enough natural talent that Dean won't suspect me. I'm such an idiot.

"I lied to Dean about being a virgin," I say to Hannah the next day, pulling her into the bathroom at school the moment I see her, the handicapped single stall on the first floor so I know we're alone.

"What?" she asks, her eyes bulging.

"I didn't mean to. It just came out before I had a chance to think about it, and then I'd already said it so I couldn't take it back."

"Slow down," she says, putting her hands on my shoulders as if the weight of them will hold me down to earth. "What did you say?"

"He asked me if I was a virgin. I was put on the spot."

"You should have told him the truth," she says. "If you're contemplating having sex with someone, you should be able to be honest. If you can't be honest, then you're not ready."

Easy for her to say. She can look at the problem from a distance and act rationally. But when I'm around Dean, nothing feels easy or rational—my head is a mess.

"I know," I snap at her, and then I feel bad. She's just trying to help.

"Not everything Danielle says is right." Her voice is soft. "I get that she told you Dean wouldn't like you anymore if he found out, but that's not necessarily true. If he likes you, he'll wait."

"When I lied to him, he seemed so relieved," I say, looking up at her and then covering my face with my hands.

"He'll understand if you tell him you lied," she says. "And if he doesn't understand, is that really someone you want to be with?"

"Yes!" I say, pulling my hands away. "I like him so much. He's smart, and interesting, and way too cool for me, and I just don't want to mess this up. You don't get it, because it's always been easy for you. You've always had guys who liked you. If you stop being interested in someone, it doesn't matter, because you have a million other guys who can step up and take their place. That doesn't happen with me. This is my only chance."

Hannah's chewing on her bottom lip as she studies me. "Do you really think that?"

"I don't know why Dean likes me in the first place," I say. "It's like this crazy fluke and that's why I don't want to ruin it."

"Do you really think it's been so easy for me?" Hannah brings her hand up to fiddle with the skin on her collarbone, the place where her necklace used to lie. "Do you think Charlie was easy?"

"That's not what I meant." I realize I'm kind of going off the rails—this whole situation has made me a bit crazy. "Of course Charlie wasn't easy."

"What are you going to do?" she asks, her eyes softening.

I can't give her an answer. I don't have one.

FIFTEEN

ANDREW AND CECILIA are slowly making me want to gouge my eyes out with my fork. We're sitting in study hall together and she's feeding him—actually feeding him—making airplane noises with her spoon as she brings it to his mouth. I'm pretty sure Andrew knows how to feed himself. He's been doing it pretty successfully for like eighteen years.

"He's not a baby," I say, looking away as Cecilia takes the spoon out of his mouth and drops it back into the container of strawberry yogurt. She ignores me.

"Do you like Tootsie Pops?" she asks him, reaching into her backpack. "Mr. Savoy was giving them out in Spanish earlier."

"Hell yeah," he says, and she pulls out two.

"Grape or watermelon?"

"Watermelon," he says, and she hands it to him.

"I like Tootsie Pops too," I say, just for fun, because I know she's not going to give one to me.

"You want some?" Andrew asks, pulling it out of his mouth and offering it in my direction.

I make a face. "Gross, no, put that back in your mouth."

"I want some," Cecilia says, and she leans forward and wraps her lips gently around the top of the lollipop, sucking it in a way that makes me wish I were blind.

Luckily, they're interrupted as Ava barrels over and crashes down into a seat at the table, her eyes wild, purple Easter hair flying in all directions. "They put up the posters for prom!" she squeals, like this is the greatest news she's ever heard in her entire life.

At the word *prom*, Cecilia sits up straighter in her chair.

Ava turns to her, pressing her hands down flat on the table, like she's trying not to float away. "The theme is *Under the Sea*, which is not very creative, but I bet they'll have a bubble machine, which is all I've ever really wanted out of life."

"When is it?" I ask, and they turn to me like I've just said a bad word.

"You don't know?" Ava narrows her eyes.

"It's right after you guys get out," Cecilia answers, finally acknowledging my existence.

The seniors usually get to leave for summer a few weeks before the rest of the school, and this year we had so many snow days that Cecilia will be stuck here without us until almost July.

"It's on June twelfth!" Ava throws her arms up into the air, flailing around on her chair. "We only have like two months to find dates!"

I've seriously never seen her this excited, and that's saying something with Ava. She's moving around like she's having an exorcism; I wouldn't be surprised if her head started to spin in a circle. Andrew and I make eye contact across the table, and I start laughing, because I know from the tilt of his head and the twitching of his lips that he's probably picturing the same thing.

"If there's a bubble machine, I'll be there," he says.

"Are we supposed to wear costumes?" I ask, picturing the matching mermaid dresses and coconut bras that are sure to haunt our prom pictures for the next decade.

"I'm going as a lobster," he says.

"No, you have to wear something nice." Cecilia turns to him and lays a hand on his shoulder. He tenses right as she says it, and she lifts her hand and looks away. His face has gone slightly pale, and I can tell he feels uncomfortable because he knows she thinks he's going to ask her. I know he won't, because two months is a long way off. He could never stay with someone that long.

"Who are you going with?" Hannah asks at lunch. I immediately think of Dean and then try to wipe the idea from my mind. I've never been into school dances because of all the awkward small talk and double-sided tape and the not wearing comfortable shoes, but now that there's a potential guy involved—for the first time in my life—even I'm a little excited about the idea. I don't know what's happened to me. I'm a monster.

"She's going with James Dean, obviously," Ava says, taking a sip of her smoothie. At least, she claims it's a smoothie—it looks like brown sludge and is so thick she's struggling to suck it up the straw.

"I never thought you'd find something you couldn't suck," Danielle says dryly, her eyes on Ava.

Ava pulls the straw out of her mouth. "You'd know. You're the expert on sucking!"

Danielle's lips quirk up into a smile. "So I've been told."

"What are you drinking?" I ask, pointing at the sludge. Some of the liquid has started to separate, spreading into two colors like a test tube experiment.

"It's coca-kale-a," she says, as if it's obvious. "It's made from diet kale."

"I'm sorry, did you just say diet kale?" Hannah asks. "Isn't all kale diet kale?"

"This stuff is better." Ava tips the drink toward us. The smell wafts pungently across the table. "They strip out all of the calories from the kale before they puree it. All that's left are kaleories. I heard Beyoncé drinks one before every show."

"I bet." Danielle wrinkles her nose for a moment at the drink and then turns to me, her eyes sparkling. "So, James Dean then?"

"I don't know," I say, picking through my Caesar salad with a plastic fork. I bought it from the school cafeteria, so the lettuce looks brown and wilted, and I'm only eating the croutons. "He just doesn't seem like the . . . prom type." Plus, I'm pretty sure we're just hooking up and not dating and people definitely don't take their hookups to their high school prom.

Danielle shrugs. "Do you have any other prospects?"

"She's the only one of us with any prospects at all," Ava says, setting her drink down on the table. The liquid inside doesn't even jiggle—it's congealed into a solid. She turns to Danielle. "Who do you want to go with?"

"No one," Danielle says. "Our class is pathetic. Chase is out, obviously, and I'm not touching Ryder after he called me a slut.

Besides, we all know Ava's gonna fuck him again."

A small, strangled sound comes from Ava's mouth and her eyes go wide. Sometimes it's hard to tell if Danielle is trying to be funny or if she's just mean. And lately, the mean has gotten a lot meaner.

"I'm not going with Ryder to any more dances," Ava says.

"That's what you said last year," Danielle says, tilting her head. "But then . . . wait, tell me again about the fall ball?" She takes a bite of her salad and smiles.

Ava looks stung. "Well, maybe I'll go with Chase this year if you're not."

Danielle laughs. "Do you actually think he'd ask you?"

Ava clenches her smoothie and backs away from the table. Her mouth opens and closes a few times like she has something to say, but then she sighs and turns around, storming away from the table.

"Lighten up," Danielle says, "I was just kidding." She sighs and stands, following Ava out of the cafeteria. I hate watching them act like this, but I don't know what I could do to make anything better. Danielle wouldn't listen to me.

"Promise me you'll always be nice to me," Hannah says once they're gone.

"No matter what," I say.

She swirls her straw in her drink. "So you really don't think you're going to ask him?" We're back on James Dean. "You don't have to tell him anything you don't want to."

"I don't know." I bite into a crouton, picturing Dean in a tux, and it's kinda beautiful. But then I remember the relief that flashed across his face when I told him I wasn't a virgin, and the image pops.

"You'll be fine. Beautiful unicorn princess, remember?"

"I'm a lying, idiot princess."

"Well, at least you're still a princess," she answers. "That counts for something. Just ask him, okay?"

We get let out of French early because Madame Deschenes has a headache, so Hannah and I take our time in the bathroom after class and then head to the senior lounge. It's mostly empty, except for some of the guys in our French class. When we walk in, Andrew and Edwin are huddled over by the window with Ryder and Simon Terst. I say *bonjour* to them, but no one answers me. They're all focused on something on the wall I can't see, pointing and whispering in a way that can only mean something bad.

"What does it say?" Simon asks from the outside the circle, trying to break through. Ryder is blocking his view of whatever they're looking at because he's practically seven feet tall.

"It's so gross, man," he says to Simon by way of explanation.

"What's going on?" I ask. Andrew steps aside so I can see. Someone has taken a Sharpie to the wall and written a message in thick black ink.

DANIELLE OLIVER TASTES LIKE
ROTTEN FISH

The letters are messy, like someone scrawled them there in a hurry. I feel my stomach clench. Hannah takes a sharp breath next to me.

"Who wrote this?" I ask, feeling slightly queasy. This is so much worse than a few hidden notes stuffed into a bag or a locker. This is public. Who would do something so messed up?

"I don't know," Andrew says. "It was there when we got here."

"What the hell." Hannah turns to the huddle of guys. "Hey, asshats!" They stop talking and look at her in surprise. "Who wrote this?"

Ryder steps back, holding his long arms out in surrender. "Whoa, Choi. Calm down. Are you on your period?"

Hannah reddens at his remark.

"It was on the wall when we came in," Edwin says. "There wasn't anyone in here."

"We should clean it." I scan the room for something I can use to scrub the wall. "We should get rid of it before anyone else sees."

"No way!" Ryder moves slightly to block me. "It's hilarious." He pulls out his phone and snaps a quick picture.

Simon pulls out his phone, imitating Ryder. "Good call, dude."

"Delete those pictures," I say, my voice rising in alarm.

"Hey, man. That's not cool." Andrew takes a step toward Ryder and Simon.

"You telling me what to do?" Ryder asks, stepping forward. "You got a problem?" Despite Andrew's sizable height, Ryder still towers over him. Edwin takes a step closer too, rearranging himself so he and Andrew are shoulder to shoulder. Andrew looks at Ryder and narrows his eyes.

"If you think this"—he motions toward the writing on the wall—"is funny, then I've got a problem."

"You guys are seriously mean," Hannah says, spitting the words at Ryder and Simon. She pulls a water bottle and some napkins out of her bag, using them to scrub the wall. The marker doesn't budge, the words dark and angry as ever.

"Looks like it's permanent." Ryder smirks.

"Did you write this?" I ask him, taking a step forward. He's so much taller than me that it's almost comical. But *fuck him* if he thinks something like this is funny.

"I wish I wrote it," Ryder answers.

"I'm getting some soap," Hannah says, running out toward the bathroom down the hall.

"You sure about that, man?" Andrew nods at Ryder as more people start pouring into the lounge. The other classes must have been let out. Hannah still isn't back with the soap and towels, and now everyone is going to see.

And then Danielle walks in, arm in arm with Sophie Piznarski. They're laughing about something, oblivious to the tension in the room. I suck in a breath, glancing over at Andrew, hoping he has an idea. He leans awkwardly against the wall, trying to keep the words hidden from view.

Then Chase lumbers in behind Danielle, messy brown hair tucked in under his usual Red Sox cap. He's whistling, head-phones in, and he fist-bumps the group of guys beside me— Ryder, Simon, Edwin, and then Andrew, who raises an arm awkwardly, trying to keep the words covered. If Chase notices Andrew's strange position or the tension among the group of guys, he doesn't say anything, just continues to his locker.

Hannah runs back into the room with the towels, and her face crumples when she notices Danielle and then Chase. Her eyes dart quickly back and forth between the two and she tucks the towels behind her back, trying to be discreet.

I know it's hopeless, no matter how hard we try to hide the ugly words from Danielle. Now that there are pictures, the whole school will know in seconds. Still, I don't want it to become a spectacle, especially in front of Chase. If he's the one who wrote it, I don't want him to get the satisfaction of a reaction. And if he didn't write it, then I don't want him to know it even exists.

But then, over the clamoring chatter of students, I hear Ryder call out, his voice deep and loud.

"Hey, Danielle. Is it true?"

She pulls her arm away from Sophie's and opens her locker, glancing back over her shoulder at him. "What?"

"Shut up, Jason," Hannah says through clenched teeth, glaring at him. I hold an arm up as he finishes the question, as if the slight movement might help change his mind. It doesn't. He barrels on without concern.

"That you taste like rotten fish?"

The room goes quiet, conversation decreasing to whispers. Chase pulls off his headphones and puts his phone away, cocking his head in confusion at the scene unfolding. Simon reaches a hand up in a high-five motion and Ryder slaps it.

Danielle slowly turns to face them. "What did you just say to me?"

"I'm just reading what it says on the wall," Ryder answers, shrugging innocently. He looks over at Andrew. "Hey, man, show her what it says."

Andrew folds his arms and doesn't budge. His voice is calm and steady. "I don't know what you're talking about."

"You're no fun," says Simon. "It says you taste like rotten fish. Right over there on the wall." He twitches excitedly, likely surprised and delighted he's gotten the words out.

Danielle slams her locker door shut. "Excuse me, Rabbit?"

He pales slightly, moving back and forth from foot to foot, jumpy. If he's a rabbit, Danielle is a fox, and she stalks toward him, eyes narrowed for the kill.

"I said . . ." he stammers, trailing off.

She folds her arms and taps her foot impatiently. "Say it again, Terst. Say it to my face."

"I didn't write it!" Simon's cheeks flood with color.

"That's what I thought." Danielle turns toward Andrew and sighs. "You might as well show me."

"We tried to clean it up," he says, then takes a step to the side.

Danielle looks at the words for a long moment, the quiet in the room palpable. Everyone waits for her reaction, waits to see what will happen next. A few people pull out their phones, holding them up to record the action. The bell rings over the loudspeakers, signaling the start of the next class period. Nobody moves.

Danielle closes her eyes for a second and takes a deep breath, the calm, pretty expression on her face almost eerie. Then her eyes whip open and she turns to Simon, pointing her finger in his face like a blade.

"First of all, let's get one thing straight, Rabbit. You'll never know what I taste like. If you ever even touched me, it would be the single most thrilling moment of your sorry, pathetic existence."

Simon is bright red, a thin film of sweat forming on his forehead.

"That's not true!" he sputters. "That's—"

Danielle cuts him off and turns on Ryder, raising her hand higher so it matches his height.

"And who do you think you are? Nobody thinks you're funny. I'm surprised you even know what this says." She motions toward the phrase on the wall. "Did somebody have to read it to you?"

She whirls on Chase, who's watching the scene with wide eyes. "And if I find out you had anything to do with this, I will castrate you."

He lifts his arms up in surrender, but doesn't say anything back. It almost looks like he's smiling.

SIXTEEN

"DANIELLE IS SO scary," Andrew says the next day at lunch, taking a huge bite of his peanut butter sandwich. With his mouth full of food, it comes out more like "Thanieth is tho sthwy," but I understand what he means.

Danielle got to leave early yesterday after the teachers saw the wall, and Ava—who burst into tears when she heard what happened—went with her. The tears are likely a direct result of the fact that Ava has been living mainly on kaleories for the past week. They're both out sick today, which I know means they're probably together.

We're sitting outside at the picnic tables because it's actually sort of warm out. Hannah is across from us, wrinkling her nose in distaste as she watches Andrew chewing.

"She's really nice underneath everything," Hannah says in typical Hannah fashion. "She just has a tough shell. She's like a turtle."

"That girl is not a turtle." Andrew raises his eyebrows. "If you're going to compare her to an animal, at least make it something carnivorous. Like a flesh-eating piranha or a tyrannosaurus rex."

Hannah sighs. "Okay, well, maybe she's a snail."

Andrew laughs. "Now you're just being ridiculous. If you're looking for something with a shell, how about a hand grenade?"

"What animal am I?" Hannah asks.

Andrew doesn't hesitate. "You're a bird. Something colorful and artsy."

"With strong claws," I add.

"Careful around this one though." Andrew nods toward me and grins. "You know how she gets around birds."

"You're hilarious," I say, sarcastic.

Hannah laughs. "Okay, what animal is Keely?"

Andrew turns to me and bites his lip, thinking for a minute. "You're a giraffe."

"What, why?" I ask. "I'm so short."

"I know," he says. "But giraffes are my favorite." He smiles at me, his mouth full of peanut butter. I smile back, oddly flattered by the compliment.

Hannah sighs and looks down at her hands, her face serious. "I guess Danielle's the best one of us for this to happen to. If someone had written that about me, I'd probably cry."

"People suck," I say. This is why I'm terrified to have sex with anyone—it's because of what could happen after.

"Shit, I have to go." Andrew checks the time on his phone. "I have a study date."

"Cecilia?" I ask.

He crumples up his sandwich bag and stuffs it into his backpack. "Cecilia and I are done."

"Hey, Andrew?" The voice comes from behind us, soft and melodic. It's a junior named Abby Feliciano, pretty and small with straight black hair. I feel a sudden pang of sympathy for Cecilia. For the millionth time, I wish that Andrew wasn't so careless with people's feelings.

"Hey, Abby," Andrew says, standing up.

She holds out a notebook. "I copied down some notes for you if you want. If you don't have time, we can go over them tonight."

"No, it's fine. I'll see you guys later, okay? Abby and I have some studying to do."

"He's *such* a good tutor," Abby says, and her voice is so full of admiration it makes me a little sick.

Once they're gone, I grimace. "Why is it so easy for him? Is he trying to go through the whole junior class before graduation?"

Hannah shrugs, taking a bite of her sandwich. "He got hot. Girls noticed. Especially, it seems, the juniors."

"It's like everything I'm anxious about is no big deal to him."

When Andrew lost his virginity, the last thing he was probably thinking about was whether or not the girl would respect him in the morning. People don't write horrible things on the wall about guys who've had sex.

"He just doesn't realize how good he has it," I say.

"Well, maybe he could teach you," Hannah says, shrugging. She crumples up her empty sandwich wrapper and throws it into the trash, then pulls out a bottle of iced tea. The lid twists off with a satisfying pop.

"Yeah, I'll just have him tutor me," I say, laughing. I flutter my eyelashes in imitation of Abby Feliciano. "He's such a good tutor."

"That's seriously not a bad idea," Hannah says, offering me a sip of the tea. I take it from her, still laughing.

"What?"

"He could tutor you. If you're worried about what you said to James Dean, Andrew could give you a few pointers. He obviously knows what he's doing."

"I guess I could ask him for some advice," I say, feeling my ears get hot. I take a sip of tea and hand it back to her. Now that Andrew and I have started talking about my sex life, maybe it isn't so weird anymore. We got through that conversation in the diner in one piece. Hannah has a point: Andrew could probably tell me some pretty helpful things if I'm brave enough to ask him.

"You could ask him for some advice, sure," she says, shrugging. "Or you could just have sex with him." Her tone is casual, like she's suggesting something completely normal. I snort, hitting her on the arm.

"Yeah, totally," I say. "Brilliant idea. Inspired!"

"Keely, I'm not kidding," she says, and I feel the color drain from my face.

"Hannah, no." I lower my voice to a whisper and look around, worried someone might have heard. Nobody's paying us any attention. I laugh awkwardly, making a strangled sound as the laugh catches in my throat.

"Think about it," she continues. "Obviously he cares about you and respects you. And he clearly knows what he's doing if the junior girls are any indication, so he could get you ready for James Dean. It could be like . . . warm-up sex. A practice round before it really matters." She leans toward me, getting more excited as the idea takes form. Her eyes are practically sparkling. "Would you show up to the major leagues having never once played the game? Having never even touched a bat? No, you'd get a coach and you'd practice, and you'd suck at first, but then you'd get better. Practice makes perfect." She claps her hands together, squealing in a way that rivals Ava. "Besides," she adds. "Then your lie won't matter. You *won't* be a virgin anymore."

"It's not that easy," I say. "We've been friends for too long. Friends don't just . . . have sex with each other." Even saying the words out loud makes me uncomfortable. Despite the breezy spring air, I feel hot and clammy, my mouth dry.

"Friends totally have sex with each other," she says, as if I'm being ridiculous. "What about Ron and Hermione?"

"Ron and Hermione didn't sleep together," I say.

"They definitely slept together! They had kids, remember? You know they got it on down in her Chamber of Secrets."

I laugh. "Okay, sure. But they liked each other. Which Andrew and I do not."

"Good point!" she says. "But friends with benefits is a thing, isn't it? People definitely do that. And it's not like there's any risk of you guys liking each other, because you like James Dean and Andrew likes the entire junior class."

"I can't believe we're even discussing this," I say.

"It can't be *that* outlandish that you guys would sleep together. Your parents thought you had, remember? If parents aren't even shocked by something, then you know it's pretty tame."

"Even if I did think this was a good idea, which I don't, because it makes no sense, there's no way I could possibly ask him. What would I say? It would completely freak him out." She's making me nervous; the *idea* is making me nervous.

"He's a guy. Straight guys don't turn down opportunities to sleep with hot girls."

"Now you're just trying to butter me up with compliments," I say, and she smiles.

"I only speak the truth."

"You're a horrible person."

The bell rings to signal the end of lunch.

"I know, but I'm *your* horrible person, remember?" She pats my knee. "Good, I'm glad that's settled."

"Wait, nothing is settled." My heart is in my throat.

She stands and picks up her backpack. "Aren't you glad you have me here to solve all your problems?"

Later that night, I can't sleep. Every time I feel like I'm starting to drift off, Hannah's words slam into me, jerking me back to miserable consciousness. When I close my eyes, images of Andrew float in front of me—memories of the times I've seen him with girls, seen him pressing them into the walls at parties, lips fused together, hands tangled in hair. I try to imagine him kissing me instead, just testing out the idea, and my eyes shoot open, an embarrassed feeling washing over me like somehow, in his own bed a few blocks away, he can tell what I'm thinking. I hate that Hannah has planted the seed there, but her words are like a wriggling worm in my brain.

The suggestion seems so typical Hannah—like all those comments she's made about Andrew and me since middle school.

But he's cute! she said, in eighth grade, the first time I'd gone over to her house.

I pretended to barf. *He's cute in the way you're cute.* It was hard to explain. *Like, I know you're pretty, but I'm not into girls.*

But you are *into boys.*

But I'm not into Andrews, I said, rolling my eyes. *If you think he's so cute, why don't you date him?*

Because he's yours, she said, like it was obvious.

I've gotten used to these conversations, her pointed jokes about his bed or his stupid job at the fire station. But something about this idea feels different. This isn't just Hannah trying to get me with Andrew. This is Hannah trying to help me with Dean.

I sigh, flipping over onto my stomach. I can't believe I'm even considering it. In the most likely scenario, Andrew would say *no* and then things between us would be awkward and weird. And would it be any better if he said *yes?*

Still, as much as I don't want to admit it, Hannah has a point. It's the perfect solution to my problem. I want to lose my virginity to someone I can trust unconditionally, to someone I know won't stop talking to me after, won't judge me for being nervous, or clumsy, or scared. If I bleed too much and ruin Andrew's sheets—it's okay. I've already peed my pants in front of him. Multiple times. He's seen me at my weakest, my grossest, my sweatiest, and he's stuck by me.

If I have sex with Andrew, I can get the uncomfortable, painful, awkward first time out of the way. I can learn the basics can practice until I feel comfortable, until I know what to do and how to do it. And then sleeping with Dean will be easy. I won't have to worry about my lie.

But it's too strange. Despite all the good puberty has done him—and the confidence and the girls it brought with it— he's still my gangly childhood friend with the freckles and the messy hair. He's still the boy who used to burp the alphabet in my face, who once pretended to be a dinosaur for a week straight, answering all of my questions with a toothy roar. I can't reconcile those memories with the boy he is now, can't see him the way Hannah sees him.

My phone beeps and I roll over to reach for it. There's a text from Dean. A rush of adrenaline spreads through me, thoughts of Andrew temporarily and mercifully pushed away.

> What are you doing?

I squint at the time on the screen. It's 2:00 a.m. on a school night. What does he think I'm doing? I wonder if I'm supposed to be out somewhere. Is he out somewhere?

> Can't sleep

A few minutes later, he texts back.

> Want to not sleep at my place? :)

My heart is thudding wildly in my chest. What am I supposed to say? It's a lot harder without Danielle here to instruct me.

> I can't. It's Tuesday

There's no way I can sneak out of the house and be back in the morning before my parents find out. Besides, I'm already wearing my retainer. My phone beeps.

> That's cute

I type back.

> What's cute?

He takes a few minutes to respond, and I stare agonizingly at my phone screen. Finally, it beeps.

> You are. Sure you won't come over?

And somehow that's all it takes. Somehow I find myself crawling out of bed, pulling on a sweatshirt, and heading over to the bathroom to wash my face and get ready. There's an excited flutter in my chest at the thought of sneaking out—not just breaking the rules, but breaking the rules for a *boy*. When someone like James Dean calls you cute, that's worth any consequence.

> Just for a minute, ok? You'll have to come pick me up

● ● ● ● ● ●

I climb into Dean's car down the end of the block, far enough away so the running motor won't wake my parents. He's looking sleepy in a maroon EVmU sweatshirt, his hair sticking up to one side. I'm reminded of when I woke up next to him in bed, how cute he looked all rumpled and asleep, and I feel myself getting flustered all over again at the memory.

I'm nervous—not just about getting caught, but about seeing him again outside of work. There are so many ways this night could go. Suddenly the whole Andrew debate seems meaningless. I feel electric.

"Were you in bed?" I ask as I get in, making sure to close the door as quietly as possible. Our neighbors have a pair of loud dogs that will bark at the smallest sounds.

"No, Cody and I had some people over but they all went home."

"On a Tuesday?" I ask, and he grins at me.

"You've got a lot to learn about college."

I blush, thankful it's dark and he can't see it.

"I thought you drove a motorcycle." I motion at the patched interior of the Honda. It smells a little bit like old French fries.

"This is Cody's car. I thought the bike might be too loud." He leans toward me, bringing a hand behind my head and threading his fingers through my hair. Then he pulls me toward him and kisses me, his tongue teasing my lips, entering my mouth in a way that feels practiced now, and natural. His tongue slides against mine and the sensation of it raises goose bumps on my whole body.

He pulls away from me slightly so our faces are a few inches apart. "Plus," he says, his whisper laced with a smile, "it's kinda hard to do this on a bike." He clicks off his seat belt and moves closer to me, lifting his body so he's almost on top of me in the passenger seat.

I pull away from him. "Do what, exactly?"

"You know what I mean." He laughs and tries to kiss me again.

"Dean." I move my head to the side so he's forced to kiss the soft skin of my neck. I shiver at the contact and turn my head, giving in for just a second. But then I force myself to pull away. "Dean, we're in a car."

I don't know what to say or what to do. How can I explain to him that I don't want my first time to be here in this car without admitting it's my first time?

"That's okay," he says. "No one will see us."

"That's not the point. I want to be with you," I say, wishing I didn't sound so much like I was begging. "I do, just not here. Not tonight. It's Tuesday, it's not . . ."

"I want to be with you too," he says. "When is it going to be the right time?"

"At prom!" The words tumble out of me before I've had time to process them.

He tilts his head to the side, a grin spreading across his face. "At prom?"

"Yeah. My school is having a prom, June twelfth. It's kind of stupid but it might be really nice, you know, for us to go." My voice is shaking. I'm kind of horrified that I've asked him, but also kind of thrilled. Going to prom with Dean might actually make prom exciting. An image flashes into my mind suddenly—Dean and me on the dance floor, his arms around my waist in front of everyone—and it sends a rush of adrenaline through me.

"So you want me to be your prom date." He's smiling openly now. "You're one of those girls."

"What girls?"

"You're a romantic." He reaches his pointer finger up to tap me gently on the nose. "You're a *Bridget Jones* girl. You're an *Affair to Remember*. You're an Audrey, not a Marilyn."

"What does that mean?" I've seen the movies he's referencing, but I've never particularly liked any of them. There's not enough blood. Dean is the one who quotes *Casablanca*.

"You want the top of the Empire State Building, crying into your ice cream because you can't face your feelings, love can cure cancer kind of thing," he says. "I had you all wrong."

"I don't want to cry into anything."

"Don't worry," he says, reaching over and taking my hand. His fingers are rough and warm. "I think it's adorable. Let's go to prom."

"Okay," I say, feeling an excited fluttering of nerves in my chest, the deadline of June twelfth looming only two months away. Because I know what this really means; what he's really asking me, what I'm really agreeing to. Prom like *promise*.

"I should get inside," I say. "It's late."

"I'm sorry," Dean says, and I'm pleased by the sincerity in his tone. "I wasn't trying to push you earlier into anything. Everything's cool, right? We're groovy?"

I'm laughing, rolling my eyes at his use of the word *groovy*, like he's trying to be some cool dude from the '70s. He sounds like my dad.

"Everything's groovy," I say, and I lean in to kiss him one more time before opening the car door and stepping quietly out into the street.

"Bye, Prom Date," he says, reaching an arm up to wave.

"Bye, Prom Date," I echo, the words sending an anticipatory thrill through me.

He starts the car and pulls away, and I watch as he disappears around the corner.

That's what I don't want to risk: the feel of his fingers in mine, the twinkle in his eye when he makes a stupid joke just for me, the fact that I'm allowed to lean in and kiss him whenever I want. The two months before prom suddenly feel like freedom—now I can kiss him without any added pressure. My decision has been made for me, the date set. And a prom night with James Dean is as close to perfect as I'll ever get.

But then the reality of the situation crashes down on me—the excitement churning to anxiety in my stomach. I have a quick vision of the two of us in bed—the moment I've finally agreed to give him. Why would I risk messing things up when there's a guaranteed way to make that moment perfect?

Before I know what I'm really doing, before I have a chance to change my mind, before my brain has time to process what my fingers are typing, I pull out my phone and send a quick message to Andrew.

> Are you free tomorrow after school? There's something really important I need to ask you

SEVENTEEN

I WAKE UP in a panic. I scramble for my phone, wishing I could erase what I sent. What the hell have I done?

There's a response from Andrew that must have come through after I fell asleep.

> Are you ok?

And then, marked a few minutes later:

> Collins? Jan's before school tomorrow? Picking you up at 6:30

I glance at the time. 6:15. I have fifteen minutes to come up with a lie, to make up something reasonable, an excuse for what I texted. I scroll up on the message thread and reread what I sent.

> Are you free tomorrow after school? There's something
> really important I need to ask you

Okay. It's not so bad. It's not as if I sent him: *I want to have sex with you. Plz respond.* I can come back from this. But what important thing can I make up? Andrew has an uncanny sensor to my bullshit. He's known me for too long—has seen me try to weasel my way out of situations since childhood.

I run to the bathroom and splash cold water on my face. There's no time to shower. The bathroom clock ticking away the minutes has a grip on my thoughts, the pressure wiping my mind completely blank.

I groan and throw my phone down on my bedspread. There's a poster over my bed of a baby polar bear—something I outgrew years ago but never bothered to take down. Andrew once drew round glasses and a lightning bolt scar on the bear's face in Sharpie, the words "Beary Potter" scrawled in messy letters over the white fur. Now the poster seems to be mocking me, the memory of that moment reminding me of everything I'm set to lose.

There's a honk outside—Andrew's truck—and I jump. I grab a pair of jeans off the floor, sniffing them to check if they're wearable, and pull them on. Then I yank open my dresser drawers and pull on the first shirt I see, something I tie-dyed at camp however many summers ago. My phone beeps at the same time I hear my mom's voice call up the stairs.

"Keely, honey, Andrew's outside. Are you awake?"

Her footsteps make their way toward my room.

"Yeah, Mom!" I call back, clicking open the screen on my phone. There are three texts from Andrew.

Wake up!

You better order your own bacon today

oink oink

I throw open my bedroom door and barrel out, almost colliding with my mom, who's standing on the other side, a steaming mug in her hands. She jumps back, somehow managing not to spill anything.

"Whoa, honey, slow down!" She's still in her pajamas, a silk robe she picked up on a trip to Japan, with bright butterflies and flowers etched around the collar. She holds out an arm to stop me.

"Are you okay?"

"Yeah, I'm fine," I say, trying to get past. She reaches up to smooth my hair back from my face and looks at me for a moment, her hand on my cheek.

"You would tell me if you weren't okay. Right?"

"Yes," I pull away. "I'm late for breakfast."

She hands me the mug. It feels warm and comforting in my hands.

"Here, take this with you."

I take a sip, expecting coffee, and choke when a hot leafy sludge hits my lips.

"Mom! What is this?"

"It's coca-kale-a," she says. "It's a wonderful, cleansing drink. Apparently Beyoncé drinks one before every show."

• • •

I grab my backpack at the door, mug still in my hands, and run down the front steps to Andrew's truck. The morning is cold and foggy, typical for April. Warm, muggy mornings won't start for another few weeks, when one day, without warning, summer will arrive in a sweltering haze.

Climbing into the truck, I grunt hello, handing him the mug and watching as he takes a sip, waiting for the inevitable expression of disgust. Instead, he raises his eyebrows.

"This is interesting. What is this?" And then he throws back the mug, slurping down the rest in a few gulps. "Very salad-y. Not sure I would recommend it for breakfast, but thanks." I should have learned by now that Andrew's like a human garbage disposal. He hands me back the empty mug, and I take it, careful not to let our fingers touch. I slump down on the seat, reaching to fiddle with the radio, anything to distract myself from the mess I've gotten into. I'm mad at myself for being aware of his fingers at all.

He's rumpled, his hair sticking up in a way that makes it clear he only recently lifted his head from his pillow. His glasses are on, and they're bent slightly, like he probably just sat on them for the hundredth time. I feel hollow in my stomach as I look at him, and before I can help it, a brief flash pops into my head of what it would be like to kiss him. I begin giggling uncomfortably, feeling my face grow clammy and hot.

Hannah has ruined me.

"So what's up?" he asks, and then stops when he sees my expression. I haven't thought of a cover-up lie, a simple innocuous question to ask him instead, and now it's too late. He fiddles with his glasses, taking them off and then putting them right back on. "Do you want to talk about it now or wait for bacon?"

"Bacon," I say, still caught in a wave of giggles. He turns the keys in the ignition and the truck rumbles as the engine starts.

"Should I be worried?" he asks, checking behind him before pulling out of the driveway. "You said it was important."

I take a deep breath, trying to calm myself, letting the giggles subside. "It was nothing." I clear my throat, trying to remain serious. "Just pretend I never texted you." And then, before I can help it, I burst out into another fit of giggles, this time worse than before.

Andrew drives us to Jan's, mercifully letting my odd behavior slide. He pulls into a spot out front and we climb out of the truck.

The diner is empty except for another group of Prescott students huddled together in a corner booth. It's not uncommon for kids to smoke weed before school and come to Jan's for their early-morning munchies. I've never been an early riser and have always marveled that anyone could love smoking enough to set their alarm for it. These guys are a group of sophomores whose names I don't know, and they're sitting silently, shoveling pancakes into their mouths with glassy eyes.

I steer Andrew toward the booth in the opposite corner, wanting to sit as far away as possible, for privacy. It's unlikely they'd be able to listen to our conversation at all in their state, but I'm feeling paranoid and jumpy.

The waitress comes over to take our order: two small stacks of pancakes with strawberries, two coffees, and two sides of bacon. When she walks away, things fall quiet and I remember why we're here.

"So I'm guessing you have something embarrassing to ask me," he says, "because you sent me that cryptic text and now you're acting like a weirdo." He takes a sip of his water. "Thank God we're already friends, because I probably would have dropped you by now if I didn't know you so well. You've been a complete disaster all morning." He smiles to show me he isn't serious.

"I told you to forget that text."

The waitress comes back with our coffees and sets them down on the table in front of us. Andrew pulls his coffee toward him and grabs three packets of sugar, tearing them open and pouring them in one by one.

I wrinkle my nose at him, taking a sip of my own coffee. "I didn't mean to send it."

He frowns. "You can trust me, Collins. Remember what you told me before? You're here for my weird shit? Well, I'm here for your weird shit too. You're my little weirdo."

"I know." I pick up one of the empty sugar packets in front of him and begin tearing the paper into little pieces—something to keep me distracted.

"We all need someone to talk to about embarrassing things." He takes the sugar packet out of my hands and pushes the little pile of paper away from me. "Remember that time you slept over in first grade and when we woke up in the morning, you had wet the bed?" He grins.

"That was you," I say, laughing despite myself. "You were the one who wet the bed."

"But we can't prove that, can we?" He raises his eyebrows. "Anyway, this can't be worse than that."

"It's worse," I say glumly.

He takes a sip of his coffee, and then his eyes light up. "Okay, what about the time in seventh grade when you got your"—he pauses, tripping over the word—"um, period at school and you had to borrow my sweatshirt for the rest of the day?"

I remember the horror of that day clearly. I stood up at the end of math class and noticed a small red stain on the chair. It felt like all the air had been sucked out of the room and I couldn't breathe, couldn't move. I wasn't friends with the girls yet and didn't have anyone to ask but Andrew. I held my backpack awkwardly over my butt and pulled him to the side of the room, my face burning as I coughed out the words. He let me tie his sweatshirt around my waist for the rest of the day, and we never once brought it up again. It was one of the first times I felt a strange kind of distance from him—when I began to realize I was a girl and he was a boy, and our experiences were going to branch off into different directions.

"I can't believe you're bringing that up," I say, feeling my face heat.

"I'm just saying, this can't be more embarrassing than that." He takes another sip of his coffee and then sets the mug down on the table and leans back in the booth, waiting for me to speak. I don't.

"Okay, I'll ask you questions then," he says, leaning forward again and clasping his hands in front of him on the table. "Is this *similar* to the great period incident of seventh grade?"

I shake my head no.

"Okay, what else is embarrassing? Hmmm. Does this have to do with . . . bodily functions? Bathrooms? Toilets?"

I laugh, shaking my head again. "No toilets."

"Thank God." He thinks for a moment. "Does this have to do with Hannah? Is that why you can't ask her?"

I sigh, shaking my head again. "I can't ask her because she's a girl. I mean, I *could* I guess, but I'm . . . um, straight."

"Hmm. Does it have to do with James Dean?"

I nod, tapping my nose like in charades.

"Did he do something?" He leans forward, frowning. "Do I need to kill him?"

"No. Nothing like that," I say, and he relaxes.

"Is this a sex question?" He leans forward in the booth. "That's why you can't stop giggling. It's because you're five years old."

"Hey!" I say, but tap my nose anyway. He's getting too close and I'm not sure I want to keep playing the game. If I ask him, there's no turning back. There's no guarantee things won't be ruined between us forever. This is worse than the great period incident of seventh grade. Much worse.

"I just want some advice," I say finally. "And you seem to know what you're doing. I mean, I've seen you hooking up with a lot of girls, obviously, and so you must be able to help me out a little."

The waitress comes back with our food and I jump as she interrupts. She sets our pancakes down and I force a smile.

"Careful. The plates are hot," she says in a cheery voice as she walks away. "Enjoy!"

I pick up my fork and begin to tap it against the table, not touching my breakfast. Andrew takes a big bite of his pancakes. Apparently nothing is awkward enough to dampen his hunger. I take a deep breath and the words tumble out of me.

"I want to have sex with James Dean at prom but I don't know what I'm doing. He's clearly pretty experienced, like, he's in college, right? So he doesn't know I'm a virgin. But I don't know if I really want him to know I'm a virgin because that might scare him away. I want him to like me, you know? And I'm just nervous, because I have absolutely no clue how to . . . um . . ." I trail off. "And you could probably help me. It was Hannah's idea, so it's totally fine if you're not into it. Don't feel pressured."

He swallows his pancakes. "Um, okay. I can give you some tips, I guess." He runs a hand over his forehead, scrunching his eyebrows with his thumb and pointer finger, then looks back at me, taking another bite of pancakes. "Why would I feel pressured?"

"Oh," I say, realizing I haven't actually gotten to the crux of it, haven't actually said the part that's the most important. "Oh. That's not what I meant." I clear my throat again and take a sip of coffee, but it's tepid and bitter. I force myself to swallow and then push my mug aside. I lower my voice to a whisper, glancing behind me at the table of stoner sophomores. They're not paying attention to us.

"Collins?" he asks. "Keely?"

I choke out a whisper. "I'm just sick of being a virgin. And I trust you. You would never spread rumors about me or anything like that. I just thought, maybe, we could"—I cough a little—"maybe we could have sex. Like, you could teach me. We could practice."

He makes a choking sound and knocks over his mug of coffee with his elbow. It rushes across the table toward me, liquid spilling into my lap. I jump up, grabbing for a pile of napkins.

"Sorry." He jumps up too, out of the booth, before realizing the coffee isn't rushing in his direction. He sits back down, then stands up again, reaching for some napkins to help.

"I'm sorry," I say. "Forget I said it, okay?"

It's so humiliating. I can't believe I worked myself up, convinced myself to ask him. How could I have possibly thought it was a good idea? I turn to leave, gathering up my backpack.

"No, hey," he says softly. "Sit back down."

I feel tears stinging the corners of my eyes and I try to hold them back, already embarrassed enough as it is.

"Keely," he says, and I sit back down in the booth, my eyes fixed on the pile of soiled napkins on the table. He's silent for a moment, thinking, and then his voice comes out low and strained. "I haven't . . . we haven't . . ." He pauses. "You're so important to me, and this isn't how I—"

"You're important to me too," I say. "That's the whole point."

He pushes his pancakes away, putting his napkins down on top of his plate.

"I don't like you like I like Dean, so there's no pressure," I continue.

"If you like Dean, why don't you just sleep with him?"

"Everyone says the first time hurts when you're a girl," I say, my voice wavering. "I'd rather just get that over with. It's different for guys. Your first time is . . . well, you don't have to worry about pain, or bleeding, or getting called a slut. You saw what happened to Danielle. At least she can handle it. I'd die if someone started writing things about me." I tap the fork against the table.

"And you think Dean would do that?"

"No." I sigh. "I don't know, not really. But being a virgin makes things complicated. I just want to be able to sleep with him without the added significance. I don't want it to have to mean *everything*." I set the fork down. "But it doesn't matter. I'm sorry I ruined everything."

I dig through my backpack and find my wallet, setting a twenty-dollar bill down on the table. "Breakfast is on me today, okay? I'll see you at school."

"No, wait," he says, holding out an arm to stop me. The expression on his face is unreadable. His eyes are crinkled at the corners under his glasses, and his mouth is pressed into a firm line. "Ah, fuck it," he says, sighing and running a hand through his hair. "Okay. Okay, sure."

My eyes widen and my breath catches in my throat. "Really?" I don't know how to feel, whether to be relieved or excited or horrified. "Okay," I say, sitting back down in the booth.

"Okay," he says back, a goofy grin spreading across his face. "Um, when do you want to?"

"Oh," I say. "Right." I think for a moment. "Well, your house is probably better. We've slept in your bed more, so it might not be as weird."

"I think my parents are going out with yours on Friday," he says. "The symphony or something boring."

"That could work," I answer. "The symphony is like three hours, isn't it? Will that be enough time?"

He laughs softly. "That'll be enough time." A devilish grin crosses his face. "Should we do it in my parents' bed and leave the condom wrapper behind?"

I smack his arm, relieved he can joke at a time like this. Maybe I haven't ruined things after all.

EIGHTEEN

THE RIDE WITH Andrew from Jan's to school is jumpy and strange. We're both trying to act normal, but there's a weird current under all of our interactions, a buzzing secret buried beneath everything we say. If I was acting weird before about touching him, it's even worse now. We both reach for the radio at the same time, our hands brush, and I immediately burst out into uncomfortable laughter, pulling my hand back as if I've been burned.

"Are you going to be like this forever?" he asks. "Because then I take it back."

"No, not forever," I say. "Just let me freak out for the rest of this car ride and then I'll be back to normal. I promise. I'm just . . . I'm still processing."

He smiles at me. "You've had lots of time to process. I should be the one freaking out here."

"Yeah, but I have lots of emotions," I say, my voice stuck in a higher pitch than usual. He reaches over and grabs my hand. I try to pull away, but he holds on, linking his fingers with mine.

"See?" he says, lifting up our joined hands. "We're touching and the world hasn't ended."

"Right," I say, calming down a bit. It's true—his touch feels comfortable and familiar and normal. I've been holding his hand for years. He has a scar on his palm from when he fell off his skateboard in fifth grade, and his right thumb is calloused from playing the guitar.

He rests our hands on my knee and bounces them along to the beat of the song on the radio. It's an old song from the Arctic Monkeys, one of my favorites. I smile, feeling myself relax.

When we get to school, we part ways, going to our separate classes. I text him from Greek mythology, feeling light and goofy.

> Plan set in motion. T-minus 3 days till completion. Over & out

He texts back, and I discreetly check the message, trying to hide my phone from Ms. Galloway, who has a reputation of throwing kids' phones out the window onto the lawn, even though her classroom is on the third floor.

> I've heard the Virgin Islands are nice this time of year

I smile, typing back under the desk. Soon we're going back and forth fast enough I forget I'm in class.

ME

> They are very nice indeed. Lots of fun activities

ANDREW

I've heard the spelunking is excellent

ME

spelunking?

ANDREW

cave exploration

I snort, and then look up at Ms. Galloway guiltily, trying to keep my phone hidden. Ava looks over at me curiously.

"James Dean?" she mouths, pointing toward the screen.

"Ladies, phones away or they will be confiscated." Ms. Galloway stops writing on the board and crosses her arms. "And the sprinklers are on right now in the field, so you really don't want your property out there."

I throw the phone into my backpack, looking back at her with perfect innocence.

It turns out it's fun sharing a secret with Andrew. It feels like it did when we were kids and used to organize secret missions against our parents. Mission: Steal a piece of cake out of the fridge without getting caught. Mission: Crawl under Mom's desk while she's on the phone and steal one of her shoes. Mission: Take Keely's virginity.

I haven't told Hannah yet about the Plan—which has become such a monumental deal in my panicking brain I've started thinking of it with a capital letter—and I'm not sure I will. A part of me likes the fact it's just between Andrew and me. It's our secret. And even though it was Hannah's idea to begin with, I'm a little embarrassed to tell her that I've decided to go through with it. That I'm too scared to tell Dean the truth.

I've gone a little wild with the research. I want to make sure we're extra careful—I've seen enough stupid reality shows about teen pregnancy to know it's a bad idea. I'm curious about sex tips too. I know the internet is exploding with information, but I don't know how to find any of those websites, and I'm terrified that if I look up porn on my phone, my parents will see it on the bill. Do they list websites you look at on the phone bill? I think about googling it to be sure, but what if they list that on the bill too?

I decide that books are safe. Books are full of useful information, and they can't be too graphic if someone decided to print them and put them in a bookstore where even grandmas and kids can see them. I pick up three, paying cash just in case: a huge textbook called *Sexual Bodies Explained*, an illustrated guide called *The Art of Love*—which features a cartoon couple engaged in hundreds of different freaky positions—and *Wings of Passion*, a paperback romance novel I grab at the last second, hoping it might give me emotional insight.

I start reading *The Art of Love* late at night under the covers, trying to learn as much as I can. There are chapters on kissing I'm dying to try out with Dean, and heat floods through me as I look at the illustrations and imagine they're the two of us instead of the cartoon people.

By the time the Plan is done, I'm going to be a bona fide sexpert, and James Dean won't know what hit him. So I know I'm doing the right thing. I have to be.

NINETEEN

FRIDAY NIGHT IS here way too fast and I haven't had enough time to research. I haven't even started *Wings of Passion*, and suddenly I'm in Andrew's kitchen and the Plan is about to actually happen. I might throw up.

There's a plate of crackers and hummus in front of us on the counter, but I can barely touch it.

"Are you sure you guys don't want to come?" his mom asks, fastening an earring. They're about to leave for the symphony, which is about an hour away in Burlington, so they'll be gone for most of the night. "We could probably get some extra tickets. Rob is friends with the first violinist."

"No, you guys go." Andrew pops a cracker into his mouth.

This is the least I've ever felt like eating in my life.

I've brought my backpack with me, and inside are the educational sex books and a bunch of condoms I grabbed from the nurse's office in school when no one was looking. I had to fake a stomachache to get close enough to the counter. Now I can feel the weight of the books against my back.

"We'll just stay here," I say, my voice coming out squeaky. Andrew gives me a look. I know I'm acting suspicious, and we need our parents to leave. I clear my throat and eat a cracker to keep from speaking further. It tastes dry and salty in my mouth. "Probably just gonna watch a movie," I say, forgetting I'm trying not to speak and choking a little on the cracker. "You know, just normal stuff. Man, this cracker is dry."

He kicks me and narrows his eyes.

"Okay, well, we'll be home late," my mom says, coming over to us. She kisses the top of my head loudly, and then moves over to kiss the top of his.

"But don't have anyone over," his mom says, pulling on her coat. "We won't be home *that* late."

"Have fun. Be good," my dad says, waving. Then finally they're all out the door.

And we're alone.

Andrew and I linger by the hummus and crackers for a few minutes, neither of us speaking. I can hear the *tick . . . tick . . . tick* of the clock in the living room and the quiet buzz of the refrigerator. I reach for another cracker, eager for something to do, and bite into it. The crunch echoes loudly in the room, practically ricocheting off the walls.

And then I begin to giggle, quietly at first because I'm trying to hold it in.

"Really?" Andrew asks. "I thought we were done with this." But he begins to laugh too, and before I can help it, I snort, spraying bits of cracker out of my mouth and across the countertop. "Gross!" He's laughing harder now.

I open my mouth and stick my tongue out, showing him the rest of the chewed cracker.

"You look like a baby bird," he says.

"Oh, should I feed some to you?" I drop my head down so the mushy cracker in my mouth is dangerously close to falling out and onto him.

"No!" He jumps up and away from me, putting his arms up in a cross to ward me off, as if I'm a vampire.

"Fine," I say, swallowing the cracker.

He grins at me. "Really admirable seduction technique though. I can hardly resist you."

My smile drops as I remember why we're here. We stare at each other for a minute and I don't know what to do. I clear my throat. "Should we . . . get started?"

"Oh," he says, suddenly jumpy. He runs a hand through his hair, and it calms me down a bit. It makes me feel better that he's nervous too, even though he's the one who's done this a million times.

"Yeah," he says. "Let's go upstairs. I've got it all set up."

"What did you set up?" I ask, surprised. I follow him up the stairs, and when we get to his room, I'm comforted by its familiarity. There's his old navy blue carpet, frayed at the edges. There's the pillow I sewed for him in home economics back in sixth grade, misshapen and bright pink because I knew it would embarrass him. The smell of his room is just the same as always, like cut grass and pine and something earthier, the musky smell of *boy*, and it calms my nerves. He's just Andrew.

The only thing that's different now is his bed. The usually rumpled sheets have been straightened—maybe even washed—

and the blankets that always form a messy pile on the floor have been folded neatly and put away. And on top of the bed he's sprinkled a bunch of flowers.

"They're just from one of the vases downstairs," he says, scratching his nose. "No big deal."

"No, it's really nice," I say, feeling warm and cozy inside.

He claps his hands together and turns toward the dresser by his bedside. "First things first." He opens the top drawer and pulls out two bottles of watermelon Breezer, handing me one. "Sorry it's not cold, but I had to keep them hidden up here. Mom's been snooping a lot since the party."

"Thanks," I say, twisting off the top. "I thought you hated my stupid watermelon drinks."

"They're not so bad. I just like giving you a hard time." He sits down on the edge of the bed and I join him. We clink our bottles together. I feel slightly light-headed. I've been on his bed so many times, but this doesn't feel like sitting on Andrew's bed. This feels like sitting on the bed of a *boy*, and it's terrifying. I take a long sip of my drink and swallow it too quickly, sputtering a bit. Andrew pats me on the back.

"So, um. How should we do this?" I take another sip. "Do we need to take off our clothes? I guess our pants at least, but maybe not our shirts." I feel jittery, like I've had twenty cups of coffee. "I brought some . . . condoms from the nurse's office, but I don't know if they're the right size. Does that matter? Or is it more of a 'one size fits all' thing? Do you have a condom that you want to use instead?" I realize I'm rambling, but I can't stop.

"We can use the ones you brought," he says. "Or, I mean—

one of the ones you brought." He clears his throat. "It'll be fine."

"Okay, so we should put it on," I say, taking a deep uncomfortable breath. "You should probably do it, because I don't know how." I finish the rest of my drink in one go and put the bottle down on the floor. He sets his beside it.

"Hey," he says. "Slow down. Are you sure you want to do this?"

"I'm sure," I say, smiling weakly. "Oh!" I jump up and grab my backpack. "I forgot. I brought some books. For reference." I unzip the bag and pull out *The Art of Love* and *Wings of Passion*, setting them both down on the mattress. Andrew picks up *Wings of Passion*, smirking at the illustration on the cover. He leafs through it and begins reading aloud from one of the pages.

"'Maryanne had made love in the sky before, but never with a pilot quite like Captain Reynolds. Their lovemaking was fast and intense, full of a passion she had never known. He was hard and throb—'"

"Hey!" I scramble to grab the book back from him, feeling my ears go hot. "I thought it might be helpful to read. This one's better though." I crack open *The Art of Love*, flipping through the pictures inside. "It's got a bunch of positions and tips, like a how-to guide." I find the table of contents and run my thumb down the page until I get to the chapter I want. Then I show it to Andrew.

"I think we should try this one," I say, pointing to the first drawing. "It seems like the easiest. We can work our way up to numbers two and four maybe, but I don't know. They look kind of . . . scary."

He takes the book from my hands and folds it closed, setting it aside on the bedside table. "We don't need a book. Okay?"

"Oh," I say. "I guess it's all intuitive. I mean, animals learn to do it, right?" I think for a second. "Do you think animals watch other animals first so they know what to do? Or do you think they just know?"

"I think they just know," he says. "And we will too." He takes my hand.

"Okay," I say. "So what do you usually do with girls? Show me the first step."

"C'mere." He uses our clasped hands to pull me closer to him, close enough I can feel the heat radiating off his body. His fingers thread through mine, rough and familiar. "We can be natural about this." His voice is a whisper. "No steps. No planning. No books."

I nod, unable to speak or breathe.

"Just tell me if you want me to stop, and I will." He lifts his other hand to my face, resting it lightly against my cheek, and then tucks a strand of hair behind my ear. I lean in to his palm, getting used to the feel of him in this new way. He leans closer to me and I close my eyes, my lips parting slightly. My heart is thudding so loudly I'm sure he can hear it.

And then his lips touch mine, soft and tentative, and I inhale in surprise. I press back, leaning into him, and his hand on my cheek moves back into my hair, behind my head, pulling me even closer. He tastes familiar in a way I didn't expect, and I open my mouth to taste more, feeling his tongue glide against mine, deepening the kiss. I feel unexpectedly at ease, my nerves draining out of me as I melt and swirl, dizzy and light-headed. His fingers untangle from mine and he brings his hand up my arm, brushing his fingertips up and down my skin in soft patterns. I place my hand on his chest, realizing fleetingly I've never touched him there. This is new uncharted territory. He feels strong and sturdy, a contrast to the soft knit of his sweater.

He leans into me and I feel myself fall back, lying slowly down onto the bedspread, on top of the flowers. He settles his body onto mine, sinking me into the mattress, and I shift so we line up perfectly, touching everywhere. He gasps, pulling his lips from mine for a moment, and begins planting soft kisses on my cheek and over my neck. I giggle as I feel his tongue lick a sensitive spot below my ear, and he pulls away. I open my eyes for the first time, really looking at him, feeling dazed as he comes into focus, his green eyes soft and slightly glazed.

"Ticklish?" he whispers, and I nod. He smiles. "I never knew you were ticklish there."

"Me neither," I whisper back, and he leans down to capture my lips with his once more. I move my hands tentatively down to the bottom hem of his sweater and then reach inside, touching the soft skin of his stomach. There's a trail of hair leading from his belly button down below his belt, something I've noticed briefly over the last few years but have tried not to look at. Now I take my time, running my fingers through it, feeling the hard muscle of his stomach underneath. He leans away from me and pulls off his sweater and then his shirt, throwing them somewhere onto the floor, and I study the muscles of his arms, taking my hand from his stomach to touch the triangle of freckles on his shoulder.

He raises himself up onto his arms so he can study my face. I bite my lip, self-conscious that he's looking at me so closely, studying me as if I'm a girl, a *real* girl, one that he wants to be with. He moves his hand to the hem of my shirt, holding tentatively on to the fabric there.

"Can I?" He pulls it up slightly to reveal a strip of my stomach.

"Oh, right," I say, flustered. I pull the T-shirt over my head, tossing it onto the floor to join his discarded clothes, and lie back down. I'm wearing my own bra this time—not one of Danielle's—so it fits much better, although there's definitely less cleavage.

"So what next?" I ask, my voice hoarse, as if I've just woken up from a nap. "I've never . . . no one's ever seen . . ." I stumble over the words. "I've never taken my bra off with Dean."

"Do you want me to?" he asks, his voice low and strained. He reaches a tentative hand up to the fabric of my strap, running it between his fingers. He pulls the strap down, letting it fall past my shoulder. "Tell me to stop."

"I don't want you to stop," I whisper, and he reaches underneath me for the clasp. He fiddles with it for a minute, unable to get it open, and I reach back and do it for him, pulling the bra away before I have a chance to talk myself out of it. He smiles and leans down to kiss me again, covering my body with his. The feeling of skin against skin is electrifying.

"Keely," he whispers, pulling me tighter against him. He reaches a hand up to touch my chest, slow and gentle, and I find that I don't mind it, find myself actually enjoying it. I reach for the clasp of his belt buckle with tentative fingers and slowly pull out the leather strap. He moves his hands off me and reaches down to help, unzipping his jeans. He has to sit up away from me to pull them off, and they get stuck around his feet.

Once they're off, he drops them onto the floor and comes

back over to me in just his boxers. They're dark green and covered with little four-leaf clovers, and I notice with a thrill of—what, fear? Anxiety? Excitement?—that there's a tent in the front.

He reaches for the button of my jeans, and I gasp in surprise as I feel the pressure of his fingers through the fabric.

"Still okay?" he whispers, holding his fingers there on the button, not moving. I nod, kissing him softly on the side of the mouth. I lay my hand over his and help him move the button aside, sucking in a nervous breath as he pulls down the zipper. I feel strangely as if I'm in a dream, as if we're two people outside of ourselves. He pulls my pants slowly down my legs. When he sees my underwear, he grins.

"Polar bears?"

I flush, biting my lip to keep from laughing. He tosses my pants onto the floor and kisses me again, lying back on top of me and settling in. I'm acutely aware that all that separates us are two thin layers of cotton, and my mind is reeling. I can feel the hardness of him pressed against me, and I press into it, making him gasp. He pulls his face away from mine and gazes at me, bringing a hand up to cradle the side of my face.

"Keely," he whispers again, his voice so soft I can barely make it out. "You drive me crazy." He moves his hand from my cheek and trails his fingertips down my neck, and then to the delicate skin of my collarbone. I shiver, my eyes fluttering closed of their own volition. We're on the brink, standing on the edge of the cliff, about to jump. And once we've jumped, there's no turning back. I know what we've done has already changed everything, but maybe the strings could still be untangled. But not if we keep going—not after this.

"Do you have the condom?" I whisper, my voice catching.

"It's in your bag, right?"

I pull away from him and scramble for the backpack, which is on the floor on the other side of the bed. My hands are shaking so much I have trouble with the zipper, but finally I get the little square package out and hand it to him. I feel slightly dizzy, the room sliding in and out of focus as I try to get my bearings.

"Okay, so," I whisper. I don't know why I'm whispering, considering we're all alone in the house, but it seems like speaking in a normal voice would interrupt something. "I guess you should open it. Or no, actually maybe I should try to put it on you. Good teaching moment, right? Do you think Dean would be into that? That would look—"

"I don't think it matters." His voice is strained.

"He might be impressed if I knew how to—"

Andrew kisses me again, lying over me, and I kiss him back, forgetting about the condom for a moment at the feel of his lips and tongue. "Keely," he says, and I feel the word against my lips. "Let's just . . ." He doesn't finish, instead brushing fluttering kisses over my jaw. He pulls away and looks at me, his face barely an inch from mine. "I'll put it on," he says.

I nod, unable to speak.

"Are you sure about this?" His voice is scratchy and low. "I need you to tell me that you're sure."

I nod again, surprised how much I want him to continue. I ache in a way I didn't expect. Now we've come this far, it's hard to stop. I want to go through with things—feel suddenly there's a small piece of me missing.

It's so different from how I felt when I was in this same position with Dean. I remember the anxiety that flooded me then, how my brain was moving in a million different directions and I couldn't get it to slow down. It feels slowed down now—calm and sure. It's probably because I'm comfortable with Andrew; he's not someone I'm trying to impress.

"I think with Dean, I felt—" I start to say, but Andrew pulls away from me, his forehead wrinkled.

"What about Dean now?" He runs a hand over his face and sits up, leaning away from me on the bed.

"I was just going to say," I feel my voice waver with emotion, "I'm not as nervous as I was with Dean. I mean, I'm still nervous obviously, but Dean was like . . . another level. You're different." I laugh awkwardly, expecting him to laugh too, but he doesn't.

"Could you . . . just . . ." He turns back to me. "It really sucks you're talking about another guy right now."

"We're doing this because of another guy though. I can't not think about him." My voice feels unsteady. "I mean, Dean's the whole point, isn't he?"

"Okay," he says. "Yeah. But you keep bringing him up, and it's really hard to get . . . I can't just turn myself on and off like a light switch. It's more complicated than that." He runs a frustrated hand through his hair. "You're really messing with my head."

"Oh," I say, flustered. I hadn't thought of it that way, hadn't thought this could be anything but easy for him. Why is Andrew having a hard time? Is it because it's *me*? I feel a lurching horror at the thought. I lean up too, sitting beside him on the edge of the bed. "You could pretend I'm Cecilia or Abby or something," I say softly. "If that makes it easier for you."

"I don't want you to be—" he starts, but I keep going.

"I don't want to be doing this either, Drew. I just thought it made sense. And you agreed, right?" I feel tears stinging the corners of my eyes. I realize then I'm still naked from the top up and I cover myself with the blanket. "I know I'm not as hot as the girls you usually—"

"You're completely misinterpreting everything I'm saying."

"Then what are you saying?" I ask, letting out an irritated sigh. He's silent for a while, just looking at me, the expression in his eyes unreadable. He runs a hand through his hair and then wipes his face as if in exhaustion, and takes a deep breath.

"I'm . . ." he starts, then pauses again.

"What, Drew? If you don't want to do this, then just say it."

He sighs. "I don't think we should do this."

I feel something inside of me crumple.

"Okay. I'm sorry I asked."

I feel like I've been dumped in a bucket of cold water—all the warm, cozy feelings wash out of me, replaced by something icy and hard. I don't know how I let myself get so carried away. I shouldn't have asked Andrew for help in the first place—that much is obvious now—but besides that, how did I let myself start to enjoy it? This wasn't supposed to be *fun*; it was business. It was just practice. The biggest mistake was letting myself feel warm and cozy at all.

"I want to, Keely," he says, his voice pained. "It's not that. It's just, you're making this . . ." He drums his fingers on his bare leg and I look away. "I thought I could deal with you using me. But I can't."

I pale at his words. "I'm not . . ." I begin, stumbling over the words. "I'm not using you."

My phone rings from somewhere on the bed. I don't want to answer it, don't know how I could talk to anyone right now. He fishes around in the blankets for it and then sighs, handing it to me.

"Speaking of James Dean," he says, reading the words on the screen, his voice tight. I take the phone out of his hand, but I can't answer it. How could I possibly talk to Dean right now, sitting on Andrew's bed? My shirt is still somewhere on the floor, mixed in with his—and it suddenly hits me how *messed up* this whole thing is. Would Dean be mad if he knew? Or worse, would he not even care? I imagine the situation in reverse—Dean with a half-naked girl in his bed—and feel an unpleasant swoop in my stomach. But that's the whole point, isn't it? There have been lots of naked girls in Dean's bed and that's why I'm here.

"You can answer it," Andrew says. He reaches down to grab his T-shirt and pulls it over his head. The phone is still ringing.

I shake my head.

"It's fine," he says. "I'm gonna go." He turns to the door.

"Wait, this is your room," I say. He shrugs, and then turns around and shuffles through the door, closing it quietly behind him. I put the phone down on the bed and watch it vibrating, waiting for the ringing to stop. I wrap the comforter tighter around myself.

After a few minutes, I force myself to get up and pull on my clothes. All I want to do is to curl up in my bed and sleep—to be alone in my own room. But I can't leave things like this between us. I have to go downstairs and talk to him, even though I don't know what to say. I just want us to be friends again—to put this whole humiliating ordeal behind us. I steel myself and leave the room, padding quietly down the familiar stairs into the kitchen. He's not there. I peer into the living room and the dining room and see that he's gone. And then I see that his truck isn't in the driveway. So I pull on my shoes and coat and start the dark walk home.

TWENTY

I TEXT HIM once I get home.

> I'm sorry. Friends?

He takes a while to answer, and when he does, it's just one word.

> Friends

I can't help but think back to the day after Danielle and Chase hooked up, when she told him they could still be friends. I don't want to "still be friends" with Andrew after this. Not the fake way Danielle and Chase are.

I'm curious where he disappeared to, but I don't want to ask. It hits me suddenly he might be with a girl. He might have gone to her to finish what we started. The thought makes my stomach turn, even though I know I have no right to be upset.

I text my parents too, to say I'm not feeling well and decided to come home. I hear their key in the lock later in the night, the hushed whispers that mean they're trying not to wake me. My mom cracks open the door and I pretend to be asleep.

I spend all of Saturday on the couch, wallowing in my misery. Because my parents think I'm sick, they putter around me, trying to cheer me up with hot mugs of tea and plates of saltine crackers. And I do feel sick. Just not in the way they think.

I've been avoiding working on my final history project, so I decide to focus on that, spreading my books out on the coffee table and flipping through pages, but I can't seem to get anything done. It's hard to focus on school when I've already gotten into college and everything going on in my social life feels so much more immediate and combustible.

I try to read a chapter on the Fertile Crescent, words that sound oddly sexual and relevant to everything going on, and suddenly my mind is wandering over the events of last night, flashes of memory that make me light-headed.

I realize it's useless and turn on *House Hunters* instead. There's something comforting in the pointlessness of it; happy couples whose biggest problems are whether they can afford granite countertops or an extra bedroom for their cat.

I'm almost on hour four when I finally work up the courage to call Andrew. He doesn't answer.

I set my phone down on the coffee table and turn back to the TV, trying to focus, but I keep looking back at it, willing it to vibrate. And then it does, just a quick burst, indicating a text message. I reach for it eagerly and feel a little deflated when I see that it's from Dean, which is so completely backward.

DEAN

You playing hard to get?

ME

What?

DEAN

You never called me back

I suck in a sharp breath. He's right—I completely forgot he called last night, when I was still at Andrew's house. I can't believe I forgot to respond. I usually overanalyze our texts so much, but right now I don't really care. It feels like there are more important things.

But maybe this is a good thing. Danielle said I should play hard to get anyway. Even though my first instinct is to apologize, I think about what Danielle would say.

I was busy

I shut my eyes, clutching the phone in my hands but unable to look at it. He takes two commercial breaks to respond.

Wanna get pizza?

So it worked. Of course it worked. Danielle is a master. I look at the clock and see it's 5:30. I can't believe I wasted the entire day on the couch. My clothes feel sticky and my hair is matted to my forehead. My stomach rumbles. I have to get out of the house. I have to do something, anything to take my mind off my misery. And being with James Dean sounds like the only thing that could fully distract me.

ME

I always want to get pizza

DEAN

I can come pick you up

I text him my address and run upstairs to take a shower and pull on some clothes. My mom knocks on the door just as I'm zipping up my jeans.

"Feeling better?" Her eyes are soft with concern.

"Yeah." I rummage through my closet and find my birthday sweater before remembering it's covered in blue glaze. I push it away quickly so my mom won't see.

"Are you going somewhere?" She walks farther into the room and reaches an arm up as if to stop me. "I don't think that's a great idea."

"I'm just getting pizza," I say. "I haven't eaten all day."

"I could make you something here. We just picked up some fresh veggies from the farmers' market."

"It's okay. I want to go out."

She looks at me then, tilting her head and scrunching her nose. It's the look that means she's worried—a look that's special for me, that I've never seen her direct toward anyone else.

"Just come home early," she says with a sigh. "You need a good night's sleep."

Just a year ago, my mom would have insisted I stay in. But I know she's thinking about next year—how there are only three months until I leave for California and then we'll both be on our own. Three months until she and Dad won't be there to care for me when I'm sick. I know she's trying to prepare me for that; trying to prepare herself.

She reaches out and squeezes my arm. "Don't stay out too late."

The doorbell rings downstairs and I jump.

"Who are you getting pizza with?" she asks, turning to leave the room.

"Wait!" I say, my tone more panicked than I intended. "It's no one. I'll get it." I brush past her and run down the stairs. I can't believe I didn't think about my parents being here when I gave him my address.

But when I open the front door, it's not James Dean on the other side.

It's Andrew.

His hair is wet from the shower and he's in his favorite T-shirt, the one with WORLD'S OKAYEST GUITAR PLAYER written on the front. I feel paralyzed when I see him, and immediately the events of last night flash through my head—his naked chest, the look in his eyes when he took off my shirt, my bra, my pants. I can still feel him on top of me, can still feel the memory of his lips on mine.

I realize I've been staring and I try to find my voice.

"Hi." It comes out as a squeak.

"Can I come in?"

My mom comes up behind me. "Andrew! Of course you can come in. You know you never have to ask." She ushers him through the door, and we all walk into the den. Andrew and I take a seat on either end of the couch—as far away from each other as possible. My mom stands at the door, watching us.

"Mom, can we have a sec?" I ask.

"Of course. I'll be upstairs if you need me." She leaves the room, turning once to study us before she's gone.

"Hey," he says when we're alone.

"Hey," I say.

And then we both say it at the same time, our voices overlapping: "I'm sorry."

It feels good once it's out. Like I can finally breathe.

"Things aren't going to be weird between us, right?" I ask, fiddling with my hands, staring down at my fingers. I can barely look at him. Of course things are going to be weird. "You're my best friend. I hope I didn't ruin that."

"You didn't ruin anything," he says, from the other end of the couch.

"Good." I wish I believed him. "Okay, well."

"Well."

The silence hangs heavy over us like a thundercloud about to break. He picks up his phone and begins texting, the tip of his tongue peeking out the side of his mouth.

"Who are you texting?" I ask. "It looks important." I feel like I'm trying too hard to sound natural and easygoing; trying not to pry—which is ridiculous, because it's not like I'm his girlfriend or something. The Keely from a few days ago would have grabbed his phone out of his hands or read over his shoulder. But I don't know if I'll ever be able to get the Keely from a few days ago back. That girl is gone.

He looks up at me and shrugs. "Just a girl."

"Another girl, eh?" I say, trying to smile. Everything feels off.

"Yeah, another girl," he says back, his tone clipped. "Is that allowed?"

"Of course it's allowed. That's not what I meant."

I want to scream with frustration. This isn't how it's supposed to be.

There's a crunch of tires coming up the gravel driveway and then a honk sounds from outside. We both jump. James Dean. I completely forgot he was coming. *No no no no no.*

"Who is that?" He stands up.

"I have to go," I say, standing up too. "I'm really sorry. It's just—I didn't know you were coming over, so I made plans. You can stay here if you want. I'm not trying to kick you out. I just . . . have to go." I practically run out of the room and over to the front door. Andrew follows me.

"It's James Dean, isn't it?"

I wince and shut my eyes. "Yes." There's another honk outside, longer this time. "I'm sorry," I say, even though I'm not totally sure what I'm apologizing for.

"I want to meet him," Andrew says.

"What?"

"I think I deserve to meet him after all this. See what all the fuss is about."

"Andrew, no." I know they'll have to meet eventually at prom, but I don't want to push the experience any sooner. Especially when last night is so fresh in my mind.

"If he doesn't have the common decency to at least walk up and ring the doorbell . . ." he grumbles, heading to the door. I scamper after him.

"Andrew, wait!"

He whips the door open. And there's James Dean perched on a motorcycle in the middle of the driveway, looking like a cutout from a magazine. I guess I expected he'd borrow Cody's car again, but I shouldn't be surprised. He looks great on the bike—I'm just not sure how I feel about riding it. But I can't be a coward. The Keely I am for him—the Keely I've created—would jump at the chance to ride a motorcycle, just like she enjoys drinking whiskey. And there's a bit of a thrill in being that girl, the one who doesn't worry about everything that could go wrong. I don't want to let Dean down, but I don't want to let her down either. I want to be a Gryffindor too.

He raises a hand to greet me and gets off the bike, cocking his head to the side when he sees Andrew.

"Hey, man, what's up?" Andrew says, extending an arm to shake. "Andrew."

"Dean," Dean says back, bringing his arm up to match. They do a handshake all guys seem to know, full of snaps and bumps and manly aggression. "You're the Hitchcock guy?"

"I'm a little more than the Hitchcock guy," Andrew says, stuffing his hands into the pockets of his jeans.

Dean laughs. "Got it. Well we're gonna get going. It was nice to meet you, dude." He turns to me, nodding his head in the direction of the bike. "You wanna hop on?"

I glance back at the house, wondering if my mom is watching, knowing she'd kill me if she saw me get on the back of some guy's motorcycle.

"Do you have another helmet?" Andrew folds his arms.

"What?" Dean asks.

"She can't get on the bike without a helmet."

"Seriously, Andrew," I say, feeling my face flush. "You're not my dad."

"Her body, her temple," Dean says.

Andrew turns and walks over to the garage, reaching down

and pulling hard on the door handle. The door rolls up slowly and he goes inside, grabbing a helmet that's hanging from the rusty handlebars of a bicycle. It's white with bright green reflective racing stripes on the side. He hands it to me and I turn it over, inspecting the inside for spiders.

"Can you please just wear this?"

"*Drew*," I say, a warning in my tone. I glare at him but put the helmet on. To be honest, I'm kind of glad to have it. I just wish it didn't seem like he was forcing me.

Andrew reaches up to help me buckle it, pulling the straps tight under my chin.

"Good," he says, knocking the top of my head with his knuckles.

"All right, *thank God* that's settled," Dean says, grinning. He swings his leg back over the bike and turns it on. The engine roars to life and the bike shakes with the sound of the motor. I climb up behind him, slipping a little on the back of the seat. "Just wrap your arms around me," Dean says, looking back at me over his shoulder. "Here, so you don't fall."

He reaches around and takes both of my arms, wrapping them around him and clasping my hands together. I can feel the hard muscle of his stomach through his shirt and I run my hands over it, trying not to be obvious.

Andrew kicks at the gravel of the driveway. "Where you guys headed?"

There are only two pizza places in town, a place that sells cheap slices and always smells like old beer, and Giovanni's, the little Italian place we always go for my birthday. It's the kind of place with checkered tablecloths and melted candles, and I've always wanted to go there with a guy.

"We should get nice pizza," I say, "not slices."

"Cool, nice pizza it is." He nods toward Andrew. "See you later, dude."

Andrew raises an arm up to say goodbye. "Yeah, see you later," he says, giving us a thumbs-up.

Dean pulls the bike out of the driveway, spraying a cloud of gravel behind us.

TWENTY-ONE

THE RIDE IS bumpy and fast, and I hold on to Dean for dear life. The wind whips at my face, bringing tears to the corners of my eyes, and I bury my head in his back, against the leather of his jacket. The trees whip by in a blur on either side of the road. At each turn, the bike leans to the side and I scream, laughing and tightening my hold on Dean's waist. I'm so glad Andrew forced me to wear the helmet—though I'll never admit that to him.

When we get to the restaurant Dean pulls the bike up to the sidewalk and hops off. I climb off after him, my legs shaking and unsteady. I feel giddy, adrenaline coursing through me like I've just gotten off some amusement park ride. Who knew feeling out of control could actually be so *fun*? Still, I'm thankful to be back on solid ground again, and I relish the feel of the hard sidewalk beneath my feet. *I'm still alive.*

"High five, Prom Date," Dean says, holding his hand out to

me. I hit it with a satisfying smack. "You were a natural at that. You gonna drive us home?"

"*Can I?*" I ask, and then laugh in surprise.

Dean looks surprised too. "Easy, tiger. Maybe just around the parking lot."

I feel deflated for a second at the thought that his offer was just a joke. Of course he didn't think I would actually want to try driving. And the more I think about it, I realize it's a bad idea anyway. I would probably just kill us both.

We walk into Giovanni's, and it's dim and cozy from the flickering light of candles. Classic Italian music flows through the room, something cheesy with violins and accordions, and I have a flash of Dean and me as the dogs from *Lady and the Tramp*, our lips sliding together over one long slippery piece of spaghetti. I wonder if that's actually possible, if anybody in real life has ever tried. It seems like the kind of thing Andrew would find funny, and suddenly I'm thinking about my lips sliding toward Andrew's, and I push the thought from my head. I'm not supposed to be thinking about Andrew.

"Welcome to Giovanni's." A waitress appears. She looks about our age, and her gaze lingers on Dean just a little too long. It makes me nervous. "We have a corner booth open," she says. "You want that?"

"Sure, whatever." Dean shrugs. We follow her over to the corner.

"Thanks," I say, sliding into the booth. Dean slumps down across from me, dropping his helmet and bag down onto the seat next to him.

He looks at the waitress. "Can we get some wine?"

She flushes pink and fiddles with her hair. "Oh, um. Are you old enough?"

"C'mon," he says, cocking his head to the side.

Her voice wavers. "I'll need to see some ID."

"Sure." He pulls out his wallet and fishes through it, handing her his license. She looks at it for a second and then hands it back. Then she turns to me.

"And you?"

I freeze. What does he expect me to do?

"She lost hers on the ride here." He motions to his helmet on the seat. "We took the bike over and had a little spill. Her purse went everywhere. A bunch of her cards are missing. Gonna have to go back and look for them in the morning when it's not so dark."

"Oh, I'm sorry," she says, her eyes flicking over to me and then back to Dean.

"I promise she's old enough," he continues. "Just turned twenty-one a few weeks ago."

"April second?" I say, making up a date. The words come out as a question. I don't know how Dean is so good at lying.

"Okay, I guess that's all right," she says, finally relenting. "Just don't tell my manager. Which bottle do you want?"

"Red or white?" he asks me.

"Um," I say back, brilliantly. I don't know enough about wine to have a preference. I've had a few sips here and there, on holidays, but I've never had to order it. Dean seems so experienced, confident about so many things that are new and scary to me. It's confusing to feel so intimidated by him and so attracted to him at the same time.

I tell him to order red wine, because for some reason it feels more grown up.

"Great." He turns back to the waitress. "Your cheapest red."

I guess I can't fault him—we don't make very much at the video store and I have no idea how much wine actually costs.

"You got it," she says. "I'll be back with some menus."

"That was impressive," I say, once she's gone. "How did you come up with that? Do you have a fake ID?"

"My brother's old one," he says. "He's twenty-three. He reported it missing so I could have it."

He says it so casually, like it's no big deal. I look enough like my cousin Beth I could probably get away with using her ID, but the idea is terrifying.

The waitress comes back over with the bottle and two wineglasses, pouring a bit into one of the glasses and handing it to Dean.

"You like it?"

"Yeah, we're good," he says, not bothering to try a sip. She keeps pouring, filling up both of our glasses halfway, and then leaves the bottle on the table. He picks up his glass and I pick up my own. We clink them together.

"Cheers, Prom Date," he says, and I smile. I take a sip of the wine. It's bitter, but sweet, like juice that's gone bad. I don't hate it, but I don't particularly like it either. Still, it's way better than the whiskey.

Dean puts down his glass and leans back in the booth, folding his hands casually on the table. "So, I don't think your friend Andrew likes me very much."

I blush, taking another sip of wine. "He's just protective of me. We've known each other our whole lives. I think he doesn't like seeing me with a guy because he thinks I'm still a little kid." I feel my cheeks heat the second I've said it and take a sip to cover my embarrassment. I can*not* believe I just referred to myself as a little kid.

"I think he has a crush on you," Dean says, and I choke on my wine.

"It's not like that at all. We're just friends. He's like my brother." Those words have always come naturally to me, but now they don't sit right. I think back to what happened between us last night. *Brother* isn't the right word at all.

Dean sighs. "I don't think *you* have a crush on him. I just think *he* has a crush on you. He might be your brother, but you're not his sister." He takes a sip of wine. "I mean, I can't blame the guy. Look at you."

I reach up to smooth my hair behind my ears, feeling self-conscious. I still don't really understand what makes Dean say things like that, why he's asked me out at all. I can't figure out if we're on a date, or if this is just a part of the game—a big, expensive, complicated version of foreplay. I can't get my friends' advice out of my head. *A guy like James Dean doesn't want to date anyone.* They would knock any romantic notions out of my head so fast it would spin. We're probably only here because Dean still hasn't managed to sleep with me.

But I want them to be wrong. Maybe the Keely who drinks whiskey is a little bit real after all, and that's the girl who Dean is drawn to. I like that he brings her out of me. I just hope the little bit of her he sees is enough.

The waitress sets menus in front of us. Dean hands them

back to her without even looking. "Actually, we're all set. We'll get a large pizza. Pepperoni and mushroom. And can I get a side of barbecue sauce?"

"Sure," she says, taking the unopened menus from him. "Should be out soon." She smiles and then walks away before I have a chance to say anything. I'm annoyed Dean didn't ask me what I liked, didn't even let me look at the menu. He doesn't know I hate mushrooms—their squishy texture always reminds me of slugs.

"You're okay with the pizza, right?" he asks, too late to matter. I don't want to be difficult, so I smile and nod. I can always pick the mushrooms off. Dating is about compromise, right?

"It must be tough on Lover Boy to see you with me," Dean says, steering the conversation back to Andrew.

"I really don't think he likes me," I say, trying to explain it to him. "He has like ten different girlfriends a week."

Dean chuckles and leans forward in the booth. "Yeah, I know."

"What do you mean—you know?" I ask.

"He's with one of them right now." He nods, eyes focused on something behind me.

"What?" I whip around in my seat. Sure enough, Andrew is standing by the front door, speaking quietly to the hostess. And there's a girl with him—her hand draped lightly over his arm. I can see her black nail polish from here.

It's Danielle.

I feel my stomach drop, and I begin to cough. Wine sloshes out of my glass onto the tablecloth. What is he doing here? What is he doing with *her*?

He scans the room and when he catches my eye, he shrugs

and raises an arm up to say hello. At least he has the decency to look a little embarrassed. The hostess waves them toward us, to a table a few feet away from ours. When Danielle notices us, she stops short.

"Keely?"

"Well, isn't this a coincidence," Dean says, smirking and pouring some more wine into his glass.

"Yeah, sorry," Andrew says, bringing a hand up to his hair. "There aren't enough restaurants in this town. I didn't want to take Danielle to the questionable Chinese place or the dollar slices. You know." He shrugs, as if it's natural he and Danielle are here. Was she who he was texting back at the house?

"I remember you," Danielle says to Dean. "James Dean, was it?"

A pleased grin spreads across his face. "Close enough. You were at that party we had?" He leans toward her. "Were you the one in all the bras?"

"You're thinking of Ava." Danielle smirks. "I only wear one bra at a time. But that's personal." She fiddles with the strap of her dress, and my eyes are drawn upward to the gold necklace resting on her collarbone, and then down to the cleavage below.

"You're right," Dean says, smiling and raising his arms in surrender. "I shouldn't have asked." He takes a sip of his wine, and Danielle's eyes narrow.

She lowers her voice. "Wait, seriously, how did you guys get wine?"

"You can have some," Dean says, handing Danielle his glass. She takes a quick sip and hands it back to him so fast that the stain of red lipstick on the rim is the only proof it's happened at all.

"Maybe we should sit." Andrew glances behind him to the podium. The hostess is looking down at her phone, texting away obliviously. "It'd be less obvious."

He slides into the booth next to me, his leg brushing against the side of mine. I flinch at the contact and move my leg away. He reaches a hand out to the stem of my wineglass, trying to discreetly pull it toward him.

"Did I say you could have some?" I ask, swatting his hand away. I'm annoyed with him for coming here, for sitting down at our table and making himself at home.

And I don't like him with Danielle.

"*James Dean* said I could have some," Andrew says, taking a sip anyway. Danielle sits down on the other side of the booth.

"Actually, I have a water bottle in my bag," Dean says, rummaging through the pack next to him on the booth. "You guys can pour some in under the table and drink out of this. I've done it a million times."

"You're the absolute best," Danielle says. "Keely, hold on to this guy. Seriously." She reaches over toward the wine bottle and, looking around to make sure no one is watching, pulls it quickly under the table. A few moments later, she brings the bottle back up, placing it innocently on the tablecloth. Just as her hands leave the bottle, our waitress walks over, and Danielle snaps her hand back, bringing it up to examine her fingernails.

"Hey, two more?" She hands menus to Andrew and Danielle.

"No," I say, "they're sitting at a different—"

"Yeah, we can just sit here," Andrew says, taking the menu. "Thanks."

"Great!" the waitress says. "You guys drinking?"

"Not tonight." Danielle smiles sweetly. "Just water."

They order some food, and then when the waitress is gone, Danielle takes a long swig from the water bottle and hands it over to Andrew. He clinks it against her knuckles in a cheers before he drinks, and she smiles. I feel an uncomfortable swoop in my stomach and set down my glass, worried I'm going to drink too much before the food comes.

There's a quick buzzing in my purse, and I pull out my phone to see a text from Danielle.

> James Dean on a real date? Nice job. Didn't think you had it in you

I look up to see her reaching across the checkered tablecloth toward Andrew. A few unruly strands of honey-blond hair have fallen forward over his brow, and she lightly brushes them back into place. I have a quick flash of running my hands through that same hair last night, and flush with heat. Danielle whispers something close to him, and he laughs.

It feels like she's flirting with him just to torture me, just to throw everything in my face. But she doesn't know anything about what happened. She doesn't know about the Plan. I'm the one being ridiculous. I'm sitting across the booth from James Dean; I shouldn't care about hands in Andrew's hair—hers or mine.

I narrow my eyes and send her a text back.

> Yup, definitely have it in me

Then I text Andrew.

> What are you doing?? You don't even like her

"So, is this the first time you guys have ever been on a double date together?" Danielle asks, motioning to Andrew and me. "Actually, forget that. I don't want to know about this guy's dating history." She slaps him playfully on the arm. "Sophie's already told me too much."

"You couldn't handle it," he says to her.

"Whatever, Reed. I can handle anything."

"Is that a challenge?" he asks.

"You'll just have to find out."

I don't even know what they're talking about anymore. Their flirting feels so dumb and scripted. Party Andrew is out in full force. I bring my wineglass up to my lips and try to take a sip but realize it's empty.

ANDREW

Why do you think I don't like her?

ME

She's a hand grenade, remember?

ANDREW

That's what makes it exciting ˙⌣

"Keely, do you want some of my water?" Danielle asks, holding the wine in my direction. I grab it from her gratefully, taking a long swig. It burns the back of my throat.

"So, what's the deal with you two?" Dean asks, motioning a toned arm at Danielle and Andrew.

"Well, I mean, there's always sort of been a thing," Danielle says, reaching up to play with her necklace.

"Always?" I ask, because it's definitely not true.

"Remember when you gave me that stupid valentine in sixth grade?" Danielle asks, ignoring my question. She leans forward, eyes sparkling.

"Um." Andrew pauses, fiddling with the fork sitting on the folded napkin in front of him. There's an annoying *tap tap tap* sound as it hits the table. His cheeks are tinged pink. "I try not to remember that."

"It had one of those weird fighting turtles on it," she says.

"Ninja Turtles," Andrew corrects.

I think about the hours we spent on the couch in his basement watching reruns of the *Ninja Turtles* on TV; how we used cardboard paper towel rolls as weapons and ran around the room sparring with each other. I don't know how sixth-grade Andrew could have ever thought sending a Ninja Turtle–themed valentine to Danielle would be a good idea.

"Whatever," she says. "It said: 'I love you more than pizza.'"

"I can't believe you remember that," Andrew says, running a hand over the back of his neck. He looks a little sweaty, like he's just come down with a fever.

"Hard to forget something that embarrassing," she says. "You were such a nerd."

Why didn't he ask me for advice back then? It seems like something he would have checked in with me about. I could have told him the valentine was a terrible idea; that he should have given her something with glitter. I'm surprised he managed to keep this secret for so many years. What else don't I know about?

The waitress comes by with a basket of breadsticks, some butter, and dipping sauce, and puts it down on the table in front of us, leaving with a smile in Dean's direction. I grab one and rip into it, spraying crumbs over the tabletop.

"Anyway, you've liked me for years," Danielle says, cocking her head in Andrew's direction.

"Pretty confident of you," Dean says, taking a sip of his wine.

Danielle shrugs. "I'm a confident person."

"So I've gathered." His mouth curls up on one side. She imitates his expression, quirking her mouth into a matching smirk, hers artificial lipstick red. It strikes me suddenly how similar they are. It seems backward that I'm the one with Dean instead of her. But then it hits me—haven't I been imitating her this whole time? He's with Danielle and he doesn't even know it.

"I just don't know why it took you so many years to make a move," she says to Andrew.

"It wasn't that many years." He reaches over for the water bottle and takes a sip. I feel his leg brush against mine again under the table, and I move mine quickly away. It's getting exhausting trying not to touch him.

"Until junior year? That's a long time," Danielle says.

"But you're seniors," Dean says, stiffening. "You're about to graduate. Right?"

Danielle laughs. "Duh, James Dean. Don't freak out. You're not being pervy. Keely's eighteen."

"What happened junior year?" I pick up another breadstick and slather butter onto it, holding the knife stiffly in my hand.

"It doesn't matter," Andrew says. "It's weird we're talking about it."

"No, I want to talk about it." I bite into the bread, and even though it's slicked in butter, I have trouble swallowing it. I notice my knuckles turning white around the handle of the knife, and put it down.

"Ava was so mad at me after that party," Danielle says, reaching over for a breadstick of her own. "She said because she didn't have anyone to kiss at midnight, I was supposed to stay with her, and, like, sacrifice my own night. She was still hung up on Tim Loggins and was so mad he didn't show. It was the whole reason she'd thrown the party in the first place."

"What party?" I ask, feeling the back of my neck start to get damp with sweat.

"New Year's," Danielle says, biting into the breadstick, somehow managing not to spill any crumbs. "Don't you remember how mad she was? Just because I hooked up with someone and she didn't. Typical Ava. Always making everything about her."

Next to me, Andrew is bright red. He reaches a hand up to rub the back of his neck. I wonder if he feels as sweaty and uncomfortable as I do.

I know exactly what party she's referring to. Ava's parents were out of town for New Year's Eve. Someone got ahold of a bottle of peppermint schnapps and we were mixing it with chocolate fudge, and I felt such a sugar crash that I went to bed early, briefly waking up at midnight when I heard everybody cheering in the other room. I was sleeping on the twin bed in the guest room, and when I woke in the morning, Andrew was sprawled out asleep on the floor like a dog, wrapped in an extra blanket.

He hooked up with Danielle that night? How many other girls has he been with that I don't know about? I feel a sharp sting of betrayal at the thought, but I know it's silly. It just hurts he didn't want to tell me. He's told me about plenty of other girls. Why is this so different?

"But what are *you* guys up to?" Danielle motions toward Dean and me. Her words have begun to flow together, like a phrase of music, and I can tell the wine has gotten to her. "I heard you're going to the prom, James Dean."

"Looks like it," he says, taking a casual sip of his wine.

"Are you excited?"

"Sure," Dean says.

Danielle dips the end of a breadstick into the dish of sauce and brings it up to her lips, taking a bite and getting a bit of sauce on the edge of her lip.

"You enjoying that breadstick?" Dean asks with a low laugh.

"I love breadsticks," Danielle says. She wipes away the sauce from her lip with a long finger in a way that makes me certain she's had too much wine. "You know," she says, once her hands are clean, "Keely can't wait for prom, either. She loves breadsticks even more than I do."

Andrew clears his throat beside me. I turn to look at him and see that he's staring intently at the checkered tablecloth, his forehead wrinkled, the tips of his ears bright pink.

"Is that right?" Dean asks. "Could have fooled me."

I laugh, trying to pretend the joke hasn't made me uncomfortable. My phone buzzes again in my lap and I look down to see another text from Danielle.

James Dean loves stuffed crust and extra sausage

I cover the phone quickly, nervous Andrew can see what it says. Danielle laughs, and then types something else.

Careful, he might get alfredo all over you

I slam the phone facedown on the table and narrow my eyes

at Danielle. She looks back at me, mouthing "What?" with an innocent shrug of her shoulders.

"You know, I never went to my prom," Dean says, leaning back in the booth. "This will be my first."

"Aw, it'll be Keely's first time too!" Danielle says, and I slam my foot down on top of hers under the booth. "Ow!" She pulls her foot away.

"Our school doesn't have a junior prom," Andrew says, and I silently thank him for trying to rescue me. "So none of us have been yet. But it's not that big of a deal. "

"Whatever," Danielle says. "I've been three times. You just have to get asked by a senior."

"Why didn't you go to your prom?" I ask Dean, eager to latch on to a topic of conversation that isn't about my inexperience.

"Eh," he says, letting his lip curl up with the word. "It just wasn't my thing. I was into this girl in a punk band and they had a big show that night, so I went to that instead. It was way more epic anyway. Our prom was, like, in the gymnasium."

"Well, you're in for a treat, James Dean," Danielle says. "Our prom is badass. Did Keely tell you it's at the Walcott?"

"That big old hotel on the lake?" he asks. "That place is stuffy as hell."

"It's really pretty," I say, trying to get him excited. "I went there for brunch once and it's got these amazing high ceilings and old chandeliers. It looks a little bit like Hogwarts." I can see Dean's interest waning. "And there are secret passageways," I add, hoping that will get him. He raises an eyebrow.

"Secret passageways at a prom? Sounds dangerous." He reaches across the table and takes my hand, running his thumb over the sensitive skin of my palm, and suddenly I'm short of breath. "Who's going to stop us from sneaking away together?" His words send an excited flutter to my chest, but there's something uncomfortable there too.

"You guys should just rent a room upstairs for after," Danielle says. "That's what everyone is doing."

"I'm game," Dean says, a messy grin spreading across his face. "You think we should get a room?" His grip on my hand tightens slightly, and I feel unsteady, like his hand is holding me there in place.

"Yeah," I say, trying to smile, wondering why I have to try. "We should definitely get a room."

"Nice," he says. "I'll arrange everything."

I'll just have to tell my parents I'm sleeping over at Hannah's or something and hope they believe me.

"Who are you going to prom with?" Andrew asks suddenly, his attention focused on Danielle. His leg brushes against mine again as he shifts in his seat, and I inch away from him.

"What?" Danielle cocks her head to the side, clearly surprised.

"Are you going to prom with anyone yet?"

"I'm going alone." She takes a sip of the wine. "But I could be persuaded to change my mind." Leaning toward him, she lowers her voice. "Aren't you going with Abby Feliciano? That's what everyone's been saying."

"Not yet," he answers. "Haven't asked anyone."

"Is that so?" She breaks into a smile.

"You want to come with me?" he asks, leaning in to mimic her movements. I feel an unexpected lump in my throat, like I swallowed something too soon.

"C'mon, Reed. You have to try harder than that. You think I'd go with just anyone?"

He reaches over and takes her hand in both of his, cupping it between them. Then he brings it up to his mouth and places a gentle kiss on her wrist. Andrew has always been good at this. It's making me a little sick.

"Come with me," he says, his voice low and husky. "Danielle Oliver. I want you to come to the prom with me."

They stare at each other for a few seconds, and I have to look away, focus my gaze back on Dean, who's leaning back into the booth watching them with a lazy smile on his face.

"Well, all right," Danielle says, the corner of her mouth lifting up into a grin. "If you insist, Reed. No need to beg."

"Cool," he says, smiling wide.

"Cool," she says back, her smile matching his.

Just then, the waitress comes over with our food, placing one large mushroom and pepperoni pizza down in front of me and Dean, a Caesar salad in front of Danielle, and a plate of spaghetti in front of Andrew. I look at the spaghetti longingly, at the steaming pile of sauce and the piece of garlic bread wedged onto the side of the plate, the smell of it heavenly.

When Andrew sees our pizza, his eyebrows raise.

"You got mushrooms?" He reaches over me to grab the shaker of Parmesan cheese, and I hand him a few packets of red pepper automatically. "You hate mushrooms."

"I don't hate mushrooms," I say.

"You totally hate mushrooms," Danielle says. "I've eaten lunch with you like five hundred times." She leans toward Dean, bringing a hand up to her mouth as if to share a secret, though her voice is still loud and sloppy. "Collins eats like she's five years old."

"*Hate* is a strong word," I say, pulling a slice of pizza off the tray, wincing as the hot cheese burns my fingers. "Mushrooms aren't my favorite. But I'm not five years old."

Dean grabs a slice and folds it in half, dipping it into some barbecue sauce and biting into it like a sandwich.

I'm sorry I didn't ask your opinion, I want him to say. *I'm sorry I didn't ask what you wanted.*

"You can pick the mushrooms off," he says after swallowing. "It's no big deal."

Maybe he's right—I don't want to be the girl who makes a big deal about everything, who thrives on drama, who makes everything *difficult*. So I shrug and take a bite of pizza, trying not to wrinkle my nose when I feel the slimy mushroom between my teeth, trying not to think about how I am willingly eating fungus.

"See?" Dean says. "They're good, right? It takes seven full meals of something before your palate gets acquired to the taste. You just have to try more things." He leans conspiratorially over the table. "I can be your guide."

"They're okay," I say, not wanting to let him down. I do want to try new things and I want Dean to be the one who shows me how, but mushrooms will always be mushrooms.

"You're cute when you chew, you know that? Your nose crinkles." I bring my hand to cover my nose, embarrassed, but Dean pulls it aside. "Don't. Your nose is perfection."

I can't help the small burst of pride his compliment gives me, and suddenly I don't care about the mushrooms at all.

Beside me, Andrew clears his throat. "Should we get the check?"

"We just got our food," I say.

"What are we doing after this?" Danielle asks, piercing her salad with her fork.

"We could all go back to my place and hang out for a while," Dean says. "You guys want to come over? I'll just leave the bike. We can walk from here."

"I don't know," Andrew says. "It's kind of late."

"We should definitely go," Danielle says.

All three of them look at me, as if waiting for me to make the decision.

"Okay," I say. "I guess we could go for a little while."

TWENTY-TWO

A FEW HOURS and another bottle of wine later, we're sitting in the living room at Dean's house, grouped around the TV, where a seriously competitive game of *Mario Kart* is taking place. Dean and I are on one couch with Cody, all three of us leaning forward and staring intently at the screen, trying to win. Danielle is the only one who isn't playing. Instead she's sprawled out next to Andrew on the love seat, her legs in his lap.

Usually I can kill it at this game, but I feel like my fingers aren't quite connected to my brain, and I'm having a really hard time focusing on the race when I can see Danielle's long tan legs out of the corner of my eye like some commercial for shaving cream.

The wine combined with the circular movement of the cars on the screen has made me a little dizzy.

"How's your friend Ava?" Cody asks as his car careens off the edge of a cliff. He throws the controller on the couch and

THE BEST LAID PLANS

leans back, apparently giving up on the game. He looks over at Danielle. "Why didn't she come?"

"Who cares?" She sits up and throws an arm around Andrew's shoulder, trying to pull his attention away from the game and onto her. I can tell she's had a lot of wine. Her hair is thrown up in a sloppy ponytail and her cheeks are bright red.

"Ava's a cool chick," Cody says. "Plus she's a dime."

"Yeah," Danielle says. "If you're into purple hair."

Andrew is playing Princess Peach, and I watch as she shoots out a roadblock to my Toad, bumping him off the road. I turn to him and growl, but he's so far in the lead now there's no way I'm catching up. The cars careen around a turn and then Mario, Dean's character, zooms across the finish line first. The tinny music coming from the TV turns triumphant as the characters dance around on the screen in celebration.

"Yes!" Dean shouts, pumping a fist into the air. "Take that, fuckers!"

Andrew is hitting his controller against his palm and I see him roll his eyes. Dean jumps off the couch and drops his controller onto the floor, then he switches off the TV, turning to me.

"Keely, you want to come hang out in my room?"

The question catches me off guard. I glance over at Andrew. He's staring down at his controller.

"Um," I say. "What time is it?"

"It's only twelve thirty," Cody says in the casual way of a college boy who doesn't still live with his parents.

"Wait, really?" I jump off the couch. "I never told my mom where I was. I promised her I would come home early." I dig through my bag for my phone and pull it out, and sure enough

I have three voicemails. How could I have forgotten to check? "Gimme a sec," I say to the guys before turning to wander down the hall. There's no way I want Dean to hear me on a call with my mom.

She picks up after one ring.

"Hi, Mom," I say. "Yes, I'm with Andrew." I try to explain the situation to her, that we went over to a friend's place after pizza and lost track of time, but she rages on about my birthday party, about how I need to be more responsible. It's like she's trying to push me away before I've even left home. I sigh and promise her I'll come back, then end the call and head back into the living room.

"I'm so sorry, but I really have to go."

"I can take you back on the bike," Dean says. "We can walk back to Giovanni's."

"No way," Andrew says. "You've had like two bottles of wine."

"It's no big deal," Dean says. "I do it all the time."

"Oh, so you're a pro." Andrew's tone is flat and sarcastic. He turns to me. "I'll just drop you off. I haven't had anything to drink since the restaurant."

"Okay," I say, my voice hesitant.

He turns to Danielle. "And I can take you on the way."

"Oh, I can walk from here," she says.

"It's no problem though."

"Yeah, but it's only twelve thirty." She pouts. "I don't want to leave yet. Not all of us have curfews."

"It's not a curfew," I say. "She's just worried because I forgot to tell her where I was."

I know Danielle's parents don't care where she goes—that's the whole reason we were able to leave her house a few weeks ago to go to Dean's party. But I don't like the idea of her staying here alone with Dean, especially since they've both been drinking.

Apparently Andrew feels the same way.

"Just let me drive you home," he says.

"So you can kiss me good night?" She's smirking, leaning her body toward him.

He runs his hand through his hair. "Yeah," he says. "This was a date, wasn't it?"

"I don't kiss on the first date," Danielle says, but still she gets up and follows him to the door. "Bye, James Dean, bye, Cody."

"I'm really sorry," I say to Dean. "I wish I could stay."

"I wish you could too," he says, and then he pulls me into his arms and kisses me in front of everyone. I've never had an audience to a kiss before. It makes me feel powerful, like I'm finally a real girl—one that counts. But there's another part of me that can't help the embarrassment that washes over me as Dean pulls away.

I know it's because Andrew is watching.

Andrew's truck has only two real seats, with a little bench connecting them that's only really big enough for a child. Luckily, I'm pretty much child-sized, so we all fit up front—Andrew in the driver's seat, Danielle in the passenger seat, and me squished in between them.

It's uncomfortable, to say the least.

"Are you sure you're okay to drive?" I ask as Andrew slides his key in the ignition. Danielle turns on the radio and when a Beyoncé song comes on she blasts the music, singing along loudly, her voice raspy and off-key.

"I'm fine!" Andrew shouts so I can hear him. I turn the music down.

"Bitch!" Danielle says. She leaves it but continues mouthing the lyrics.

"I only had a few sips at the restaurant," he says. "I knew if I got drunk, I'd, well . . . I just knew it wasn't a good idea."

"Thanks," I say, because I know what he's implying—what he can't say in front of Danielle. He's worried if he drank he would have given something away, would have let something slip about the Plan he wouldn't be able to explain. "And thanks for taking me home."

"You're on the way," he says, and the casualness of it stings a little bit.

The night is warm, but the air streaming through the window is raising goose bumps on the bare skin of my arms. I feel awkward sitting in between the two of them. Like I'm intruding. This is the end of their date, the part where he drives her home and drops her off and tells her he had a nice time. Now I'm here, squished in between them, each side of me touching a side of them.

Nobody is talking, and so I wonder if they feel weird too. I'm thankful for the music playing on the radio, because it drowns out some of my anxious thoughts.

It only takes about five minutes to get to Danielle's house, and when Andrew pulls the truck to a stop in her driveway, I feel the awkwardness expanding—like the truck is a tank filling with water and we're slowly going to drown.

"You'll get inside okay?" Andrew asks. Danielle rummages through her bag for her keys, pulling out a key chain with a leopard-print heart. She pulls down the passenger-side mirror and checks out her reflection, using her thumb to wipe the skin around her eyes.

"My parents go to sleep at like nine thirty." She snaps the mirror shut and turns to us, smiling at Andrew and me with equal dazzle. "But just in case—do I smell like booze?"

She leans closer to me and breathes in my face and I cough. Her breath is sharp and tangy, the remnants of red wine. I start to nod but she leans past me toward Andrew. "You've been drinking too, Collins. You won't be able to smell it." And then she grabs the front of Andrew's shirt and pulls him even closer, so her mouth is only a few inches away from his. She breathes again. "All good?"

Andrew laughs and shakes his head. "You smell like a bar."

"Shut up, Reed," she says. "Like you've ever been in a bar." And still their mouths are only a few inches apart. She's leaning over me, her body pressed into mine like I'm not even there, and her hair is in my face. I move it out of the way so I can see them, even though seeing them is making it hard to breathe.

"Thanks for dinner," she says, and then kisses him squarely on the lips. It's not a real kiss, just a quick pressing of her lips to his, and it's over in a second—but it hits me in the chest. Before I can help it, I make a strangled sound and then feel my face turn a brilliant shade of red, because I'm horrified I've made any sound at all.

She pulls back and then seems to remember I'm sitting between them.

"Oh, sorry, Collins." She pulls her hair behind her shoulder so it's out of my face. "Forgot you were there." I turn to look at Andrew's face, to see if he's embarrassed or excited or sorry, but his expression is blank and unreadable. "All right," she says, opening the door to the truck and hopping out. "I'll see you kids later." And then she slams the door shut and we're alone.

He doesn't start the truck right away, and we sit silently beside each other, listening to the radio, which has changed to some local commercial for a grocery store, some silly song about fruits and vegetables. I focus intently on the words of the song, trying not to think about what just happened. I don't want to process my thoughts, don't want to think about the sharp pain in my chest, the way my breath felt strangled when I saw their lips touch. I've seen Andrew kiss so many girls, in way more intimate ways—tongues and teeth and hands—so this innocent peck on the lips shouldn't matter. It's just—this is the first time I've seen Andrew kiss a girl since he kissed me.

He drums his fingers on the steering wheel and then he reaches out and turns the key. The truck rumbles to life.

"Okay, let's get you home."

So he's not going to talk about it.

He looks behind him and backs the truck out of the driveway. I move into the passenger seat and buckle the seat belt—far enough away from him now so our arms are no longer touching.

"Why didn't you tell me about that New Year's party?" I ask suddenly, because I can't stand the silence between us.

"I don't need to tell you everything." His tone is clipped, his posture straight and tense.

"Why are you mad?" I ask, because I can tell. He runs a hand through his hair, further proving my point.

"I'm not mad," he says. "I just don't get why you care. That I didn't tell you."

"I don't care." I realize we're getting nowhere. We're going to keep spinning in circles unless one of us starts speaking the truth. "So you're a thing with Danielle now?" I turn to face him. Our eyes meet and I can't stand it, so I look away and down at my hands, picking at my nails. I don't ever paint them, but right now I wish I did, so I would have something to chip off.

"Yeah," he says.

"What about Abby?" I ask. "You're just done with her?"

"There was never anything with Abby."

"Okay then, Cecilia?"

"Cecilia knew it was coming."

"That still doesn't mean it's a very nice thing to do to someone."

"Because you're the expert on relationships." His words sting.

"Some of these girls might actually like you, you know. Have you ever actually liked any of them?"

"Oh they might actually like me?" His tone is sharp. "Thanks for the reassurance. It's good to know somebody might hook up with me because they want to—not just for practice."

I feel the guilt of last night suddenly and completely, the stupid, stupid Plan spreading back over us like a virus. Even if we've claimed that nothing has changed, there's no way we can go back to the way we were before. Our friendship is infected.

"That's not what I meant." I feel like I'm spinning out of control, like I need to find a handhold to steady myself but am grasping at air. "You're good with girls, Drew. It's not an insult. I just think—maybe you're *too* good with girls. I mean, Sophie Piznarski really liked you, and you dumped her out of nowhere. And now it's become this pattern—"

"That was freshman year. Are you seriously criticizing me for something like three years ago?"

"No!" I say. "But you haven't had another girlfriend. You just move on to a new girl anytime you see something better. You haven't dated anyone since."

"Neither have you," he says, throwing my words back at me. "Unless you're dating Dean. But I really don't think you see it that way." I feel my stomach clench at his words. "And why am I supposed to have a girlfriend? Why are you pushing me?"

"I'm not." I bring my hands up to rub my face. I don't know what I'm saying anymore. I don't want Andrew to have a girlfriend—especially not someone like Cecilia or Danielle—but somehow my words are coming out all wrong. "I just want you to stop acting like girls don't matter. It's insulting!"

"They know what they're getting into," he says, his voice rising. "And who are you to say they're not just as into hookups as I am? You can't shame girls for liking sex just because you don't."

His words feel like a slap in the face. I can feel the impact of them, red on my cheek.

We arrive at my house and he pulls the truck off the road and parks, but neither of us makes a move to get out. He takes a breath and lowers his voice back into a whisper. "And they're not stupid. They know what they're signing up for. Besides, I—"

"They know you don't like them? That you're just going to ditch them? How could they possibly know?"

"I tell them! I tell them all that I don't want anything serious."

I don't know why I'm pressing him. It's like I'm picking at a scab. "But why?"

"Because I'm already in love with someone!" His breath is ragged, like he's just run a marathon. He brings a hand up to his hair, pulling on the ends of it so it's sticking up wildly.

I feel stomach-punched at his words, like all the breath has been knocked out of me. How could he not tell me he was in love with someone? I thought we told each other everything. That's what best friends do. We're here for each other's weird shit. We handle it.

I guess I'm not as good at reading him as I've always thought. "Which one?" I ask, my voice soft.

"What?" He seems dazed and he's blinking at me like he's just noticed I'm there.

"Which girl?" I ask. "Who are you in love with?"

He scoffs, a short breathy sound that gets caught in the back of his throat. "It doesn't matter." All of the energy seems drained out of him.

"No, it does matter," I say. "I've always helped you with girls, haven't I?"

He laughs a little, leaning forward and resting his head in his hands. "I didn't mean to tell you this when you were drunk."

"I'm not drunk." I feel a little light-headed, but I haven't been drinking wine now for a few hours. And this conversation has certainly sobered me up. "Have you told her?"

"What?" he asks, lifting his head out of his hands.

"Have you told her you love her?"

"It's . . . complicated," he says, and there's a beat of silence as I think about what he's said. He turns his head slightly so he's facing me and rests his hand on mine, giving it a comforting squeeze. I feel my breath catch in my throat, unexpectedly pleased with the feeling of his palm on my skin. It feels like it did last night, back when he pulled me closer to him on the bed, told me to forget the rules.

"I . . ." I begin, but trail off, unsure of what to say. I shake my head, trying to wake myself up from the daze. "You should tell her. You can't just keep something like that bottled up. You'll burst."

"Okay," he says, taking a quick breath. "You're right."

"Will you tell me first?" I ask. "I want to know who it is." I pull my hand out from under his and tuck my hair behind my ears. Suddenly I remember what Dean told me earlier in the night: *I think he has a crush on you. He might be your brother, but you're not his sister.* I have a quick flash of last night, of the fluttering feeling in my chest when his lips first touched mine, of how badly I ached to go through with everything, how much it hurt when he walked out. But I push it away. I feel like everything is mixed up inside of me, and I can't get my thoughts in order. The thought that Andrew might have feelings for me is terrifying. Things weren't supposed to go this way. He's my best friend. We're just friends. That's it.

"Wait," I say, the words tumbling out of me. "Is it me? It's not me, is it?" I feel my face burning, immediately wanting to take back the words, but they're already out.

Andrew shifts away from me. He lets out a humorless laugh. "Are you fucking with me?"

"What?" I ask, taken aback. "No. I'm just making sure, I mean I'm just checking . . . sometimes friends end up liking each other and—"

"It's not you," he says, the words like an insult. "Don't worry."

I feel punctured, like a balloon inside me is slowly deflating.

"Okay," I say. "Okay." I need to say it again. I feel oddly hurt and disappointed. Obviously it's not me. He basically told me last night he couldn't keep it up when we were together.

"Okay, so who is it?" I ask. His eyes narrow slightly, and then he clears his throat. His answer is so obvious I don't know how it didn't occur to me, even though she was with us only a few minutes earlier, her cleavage pressed against my shoulder as she leaned over me to kiss him.

"Come on, Collins," he says. "I'm in love with Danielle."

TWENTY-THREE

I TURN AWAY so he can't see my face. I shouldn't be surprised, and I'm not, really. I should have known better. Andrew doesn't *love* me—why would he when he has a parade of beautiful girls at his disposal? And Danielle is the most beautiful, the most confident, the most powerful—everything Cecilia, Abby, Sophie, and all the rest of Andrew's castoffs have ever wanted to be. Why wouldn't he be drawn to that power?

I shake my head, trying to clear away the thoughts tumbling around inside. It's stupid to feel upset; I don't want Andrew in that way. I have James Dean. It's just that it felt nice for a moment to believe he could see me as one of those girls too, one of the girls like Danielle, who wears her skin like a fashionable coat instead of something that doesn't quite fit.

When Andrew first started dating Sophie Piznarski, he shared everything with me—that he thought she looked best in her sweater with the pink and blue stripes; how she hated spicy food but loved anything with peanut butter; how sometimes they made out on the couch in the living room while her parents worked late. He complained to me about having to attend her dance recitals, dragged me along to a few of them so we could whisper to each other behind a raised program.

And then after Sophie, I got used to hearing details about the girls he liked, watching as he walked hand in hand with a girl up the stairs, pulling her into a bedroom, or a bathroom, or a closet, their laughter loud and drunk and happy.

But he's kept Danielle from me. That means she's special. She wasn't someone to talk about the next morning over pancakes at Jan's. She was someone to keep tucked away, someone secret and meaningful.

"You're in love with her?" I ask, picking at a string that's come loose from the cushion of the seat. I look up at him and he looks away.

"Yeah."

"I had no idea."

"I know," he says. "I'm . . ." He pauses, running a hand through his hair so it's standing straight up, like he's been electrified. I feel just like that hair, shocked and alert, like I've been electrified too.

"You could have told me. I mean, before now. You didn't have to keep it a secret. I get it." I try to laugh, but it gets stuck in the back of my throat. "She's Danielle Oliver."

"Do you think . . ." He trails off.

I fill in the rest of his question in my head. *Do you think I have a chance? Do you think she likes me back? Do you think we'll still be friends after all of this?*

"Yeah." I open the door to the truck. "You'll be fine, Drew. Like I said, you should tell her. You're going to prom with her, right? That'll be the perfect time. You can do something big for her. Really make it count."

"Yeah."

I climb out of the truck and walk up the dark driveway and into the house. Then I watch through the window as his truck backs up and pulls away.

It looks like we're both getting the perfect prom, getting everything we want at just the right time, like the end of some teen movie. But if everything is so perfect, then why does it feel so wrong?

Hannah and I have plans to go prom dress shopping the next morning, so she picks me up in the Jeep and takes us on the long drive to the mall. She's promised to buy me a Cinnabon if I have a good attitude, so I'm trying to be cooperative, but I don't think I've worn a dress since I was the flower girl in my aunt's wedding in third grade. Secretly, I'm actually a little excited about everything, even though I have no idea what I'm doing. Luckily Hannah has dutifully taken on the role of my fairy godmother, picking out different styles and colors and holding them up in front of me, pleading with big eyes for me to try something on.

I still haven't told her about what happened with Andrew on Friday. I don't know if I'll ever be able to talk about it. I can give him that one thing, now that he's going to tell Danielle he loves her. I don't want to ruin that for him.

But I need to ask Hannah about them, need to turn the pebble over in my hands, examining it from all sides. We're together in one of the dressing rooms at Macy's, surrounded by so many puffy dresses it's giving me an aneurysm, when I finally break down and ask her.

"Did you know Andrew and Danielle hooked up?"

Hannah has a pink and white zebra-print monstrosity halfway over her head that I think she must have grabbed as a joke.

"I'm so sorry," she says through the fabric, and then she shimmies the dress down, reaching her arms through the sleeves. "Junior year at Ava's New Year's party." She turns away from me to look through the rack of dresses hanging beside her on the wall, like she's inspecting them. Like she's avoiding me.

"You knew?" I'm wearing a green dress that makes me look way too much like Tinkerbell because of my whole tiny blond thing. "How did you know before me? Does everyone else know?"

"You went to bed early that night," Hannah says, turning her back on the mirror to look at me fully. "Everyone saw them making out at midnight—typical Party Andrew. It was no big deal."

But it *was* a big deal. If it had been no big deal, we would have laughed about it together the next morning when he woke up at the foot of my bed, his hair sticking up at all angles, the imprint of the rug patterned into his right cheek.

Missed you last night, Collins, was all he said. And then he pulled the blankets off me so that I shrieked in the chilly morning air.

I shouldn't have been kept in the dark about it for a whole year.

"Why didn't you tell me?" I ask Hannah.

"I knew you wouldn't like it."

"You didn't have to protect me," I say. "I wouldn't have cared."

"You would have," she insists. "I know you don't like Danielle. You put up with her. You've always put up with her because she was my friend. But you don't like her. And I've always wanted you guys to get along. I've tried so hard to push you together, because I love you both, and I knew this would ruin that. This would be the thing that made it official, that turned you and Danielle antagonistic."

"It wouldn't have been like that," I say, protesting although I'm not sure I believe it.

"And you're protective of Andrew," she says. "Because he's yours."

"Hannah, he's not *mine*, that's—"

"And I knew it would hurt you that he went for her."

"He hooks up with girls all the time, Hannah."

"Yeah, but they don't matter to you like Danielle does. Even if it wasn't a big deal for him, I knew you would—"

"It *was* a big deal for him," I say, letting out a humorless laugh.

"It wasn't," Hannah insists. "That's why I didn't need to tell you. It would only have made things worse, like it is now—"

"He's in love with her," I say, letting the words finally tumble out of me.

"What?" Her face is pale.

"He told me last night."

"But that's not . . ." She brings a hand up to her hair and pulls it out of her face, back into a bun, like she means business. "That's not true."

"They're going to prom together," I say, as if that settles it.

"I thought . . ." She trails off again and I can see the wheels turning. "It doesn't make any sense."

"He's going to tell her he loves her at prom."

"But," Hannah says. She reaches behind her and unzips the zebra dress. "But they don't even know each other."

"Of course they know each other. We've been going to school together for like ten years."

Danielle moved to Prescott in fourth grade, a month after school had already started. Even at ten years old she had the same thick dark hair, high cheekbones, and commanding personality that promised more to come. Even then, everyone wanted to be along for the ride.

Andrew and I had been sitting together in the back of the bus when it pulled up to a new stop and Danielle got on. With a school as small as ours, new kids could never slip by unnoticed; they were an *event*, one of the few exciting things that ever happened. She hadn't looked nervous, hadn't shuffled around looking for a place to sit. Instead she'd walked up the steps, skinny legs under a bright turquoise skirt, hands looped through the straps of a fire-engine-red backpack, and *twirled*. I was fascinated—who was this girl who looked like she'd come off the set of some Disney Channel movie, whose clothes were as bright and bold as she was—who looked like she wanted to stand out, wanted attention the way I had always wanted to blend in? Danielle became the sun around which all of us rotated, and she'd done it within thirty seconds of stepping onto the school bus on that first day. But just like the sun, we could never get too close, could never stare too long or we'd get burned. Because Danielle could *burn*. That hadn't taken long to figure out.

Maybe Andrew had noticed her even then, had been fascinated by her like I had, but in a different way. Maybe he's been drawn to her sunlight for years, has always been rotating in her orbit.

"Of course they know each other," I repeat to Hannah.

"No," Hannah says, her voice insistent. "They don't. They only know, like . . . the polished versions of each other. But that's not really knowing someone. Party Andrew isn't really Andrew—you know that. You guys know each other without the bullshit. What Andrew and Danielle have is all bullshit."

"But isn't that what keeps it exciting?" I ask. "The not knowing?"

"Maybe it's exciting, at first," she says. "It's the thrill of the chase, the thrill that someone might like you back. Getting that attention from someone is a rush. But that's not love. Love is when your weirdness matches up with someone else's weirdness. When you're comfortable being exactly you." One of her hands falls to her neck, to the spot where Charlie's necklace used to be, and she drums her fingers softly, absently, against the hollow of her throat.

"Yeah," I say, turning back to the mirror. I feel weirdly like I might cry, which makes no sense at all. I take some deep breaths, turning away from Hannah so she can't see. I don't know what's wrong with me.

"Are you getting that dress?" Hannah asks. "You look amazing. What's Dean wearing?"

"I'm not sure," I answer. "We haven't talked about it."

The dress feels important all of a sudden, something I need to get right so that the rest of my night with Dean goes the right way too. But how am I supposed to know what Dean wants? I don't even know his favorite color.

TWENTY-FOUR

THE NEXT MORNING at school, I spend most of my energy Not Looking at Andrew, which is next to impossible because he seems to be everywhere. I've never noticed how much of my day I usually spend with him, how I'm always aware of him in my peripheral vision the way I'm aware of my feet and hands and nose.

Now I'm aware of his presence in a different way. Every time he comes into a room, I can feel myself tense, like the wires inside of me have been pulled tight and electric. When he walks into study hall and sits down at my table, I flinch. I force myself to look up at him and try to smile. I can be a normal, functioning human. I have to be, if I want my friend back.

"Hey," I say, tapping my pen against the top of my desk.

"Hey," he says back. He's wearing a dark green shirt that brings out the green in his eyes, and I shake my head, feeling stupid for noticing his eyes at all. Friends don't notice the color of their friends' eyes. Especially not the eyes of friends who are in love with Danielle Oliver.

"How was the rest of your weekend?" he asks.

"It was fine," I answer.

"I'm so tired."

"Monday sucks."

"Yeah."

Great, now we're talking like strangers.

Every time I look at him, the events of the weekend come tumbling back to me: the feel of his lips against mine, the condom in his hand, Danielle's fingers running through his hair at dinner, Danielle smirking at him, pouting her lips. *Danielle, Danielle, Danielle.*

He loves her. Right now, slumped at his desk and complaining about Mondays, he loves her. He'll love her when he raises his hand for attendance, when he walks down the hall on the way to lunch. It's a constant—an underlying buzz that will never go away. Danielle is part of him now. Isn't that what love is? Another person attaching themselves to your brain, eating away at your heart, your soul, consuming you entirely? Love is just a parasite.

I realize I'm staring at him and I look quickly away, pretending to rummage through my bag so I look busy. He turns away from me and starts drumming his pencil against the top of his desk.

I'm worried Danielle is going to turn him into Party Andrew forever, that she'll take the parts of him that make him unique and interesting and wonderful and ruin them, that she'll flatten him under her power. But I have to accept it. I have to let them be together if that's what he wants. It's just going to take a little while to get used to.

• • • • • •

"Did you and Andrew get in a fight?" Hannah asks me later on the way to lunch. "You guys have been acting so weird."

Andrew is behind us at the end of the hallway with Chase, and he hasn't called out to say hello to us, hasn't even acknowledged he's seen us. I feel guilty I haven't told Hannah I went through with the Plan, but I try to push it aside.

"We're fine."

"Is this about the Danielle thing?"

"It's just weird now," I say. "You won't tell her, will you? That he loves her?"

"Of course not!" Hannah says. "That's his situation." She peers back over her shoulder to where Andrew and Chase are laughing about something. "If Andrew's in love with Danielle, I don't know why he'd be friends with Chase."

It didn't occur to me until now that Andrew might have been upset at his party when Chase got with Danielle. He was so flustered when Danielle apologized to him at school. I guess Cecilia was his second choice that night. Someone else got the girl he wanted and then he got in trouble. But people don't just stop being friends with Chase Brosner, not even over a girl.

Well, he has the girl now. Or, almost. He just has to tell her.

Danielle and Ava are already at the lunch table, matching green cups of coca-kale-a in their hands.

"That was so fun Saturday night," Danielle says when Hannah and I sit down. "James Dean is très chic."

"You guys hung out on Saturday?" Ava asks. "Why didn't anyone tell me?"

"It was a double date," Danielle answers. "You would have been an odd number."

"I could have found a date. I'm not a leper."

"Hey, lepers can still find love," I say.

"*Lepers in Love*," Hannah says. "I would so watch that reality show."

"Sure, Ava. I'm sure you could have found ten dates," Danielle says. "That's your specialty." She rummages through her bag for her phone. "But not everything revolves around you. Maybe Collins and I wanted to hang out together."

A small mewl escapes from Ava's mouth, like she's an injured kitten, and she leans back in her chair, crossing her arms.

"It was last minute," I say, trying to make her feel better. "We kind of just bumped into each other."

"But Dean got us *wine*," Danielle says, her eyes twinkling. "We went to Giovanni's."

"Who were you on a date with?" I can tell Ava's warring between her frustration with Danielle and her curiosity. "One of Dean's friends? Wait, was it Cody?"

"Hey, guys." Andrew pulls out the chair next to mine and sits down. Danielle is texting on her phone and she barely spares him a glance. I know it's one of her tactics, one of the moves she tried to teach me when I first met Dean.

"How come you guys aren't eating outside?" Andrew asks. "It's so nice out."

Great. We're talking about the weather. Has it really come to that?

"We're trying to keep our coca-kale-a out of the sun," Ava answers. "It gets so gross when it's warm."

"It's gross when it's cold too," Hannah says.

"Fair enough," he says. He looks over at Danielle. "Hey, Danielle."

She sets down her phone. "Oh, hey, Drew."

"How was the rest of your weekend?"

"Uneventful."

I think about what Hannah said—how they don't actually know each other. In this moment, it seems kinda true. But then again, maybe they're nervous. Maybe Andrew feels uncomfortable he admitted his secret to me, that he knows I'm watching their interaction and I *know*.

Ava studies Andrew for a second and then looks at Danielle and then at me, glancing between all of us so fast she looks dizzy.

"Is this the guy you went on a date with?"

"I'm the guy," Andrew says.

Ava clicks her tongue. "Of course you are. I should have known." She stands and picks up her empty tray and cup of sludge. "Nobody tells me anything."

After school on Thursday I have work with Dean—the first time I've seen him since the double date from hell—and weirdly I'm kinda calm about it. It's a relief not to feel nervous every time I see him now, especially since I've become an anxious mess around Andrew.

Now that it's May, the weather is suddenly warmer, the air in the store heavy and stagnant. Summer is right around the corner, the end of the school year so close I can almost taste it.

Like everything else, the heat looks good on Dean. He has a fine sheen of sweat on his arms and forehead that makes him glisten.

"Does this place have any air-conditioning?" I ask, waving my arm in front of my face to cool off. I drop my backpack down on a chair in the break room and come back out, acutely aware of how sticky I am in all of the most unflattering places.

He smiles his aching, lopsided grin and shrugs.

"There's a fan in the back room, but personally I think you look pretty good all flushed." At his words, my face gets even hotter and I know it must look bright red. But I forget to feel self-conscious when he grabs my butt and pulls me forward into his heavy embrace. He kisses me, leaving his hand there and squeezing. I can't believe his hand on my butt feels normal now. I feel like I've come a million years from the girl who was nervous when his knee touched mine.

I let all of my worries fade away, let my mind melt into a puddle from the heat, from his kiss, my chest fluttering with practiced excitement. This is what I need more than anything. Why did I let myself get so anxious about Andrew?

"Did you have fun on Saturday?" I ask, pulling away.

"It was fine," he says.

Oh. Of course. Cue anxiety.

"Fine?"

"I mean, your friends are . . . just . . ." He trails off, not finishing his thought. Instead, he turns back to the counter and begins fiddling with some wires attached to the speakers. "I'm gonna find us an awesome soundtrack for today."

"My friends are just what?" I ask, my voice sounding sharper than I intended. He plugs his phone into the speakers and shuffles through it.

"I mean, they're just so . . . high school." He clicks a button, and blaring trumpets and violins fill the room, triumphant. "John Williams." He closes his eyes, letting the trumpets wash over him. "This guy has written, like, every single famous movie theme of all time. The man's a genius. He takes good movies and makes them *great*; makes them fucking memorable. This one's—"

"*Jurassic Park*," I say. "I know. And what's that supposed to mean? We *are* in high school." I don't like reminding him, but something about his tone is making me defensive.

"Rad," he says. "Here I am trying to teach you what you already know." Picking up his phone, he switches to another song, this one low and menacing. *Da dum. Da dum.*

"*Jaws*," I say automatically. He lets it play behind us, building and building.

"I mean, when I'm with you, I just want to be with *you*. But your friends are just so *involved*. They want to know things. They want to feel like they're a part of everything, when really it's none of their business. I mean, the first time you came over you brought a whole squad. That's what's high school about it." He taps on his phone and the music turns back into blaring horns. "If you don't know this one, it's just criminal. As store manager, I honestly don't think I could let you work here, if you can't name this—"

"It's obviously *Star Wars*," I say, shaking my head. "Okay, but your friends are involved. What about Cody?"

"But you don't see me bringing Cody along with us to dinner. I'm not gonna invite Cody in the room to watch us make out." He smirks. "Unless you're into that." He scrolls through his phone again.

"I'm not . . . I didn't," I stammer. The *Star Wars* theme still blasts triumphantly behind us. "You invited us all over after Giovanni's. I thought we were having fun."

"We were," he says. "I'm just saying, it doesn't have to be so complicated. Life isn't that dramatic. It's just life." He smiles, shaking his shoulders and arms like he's letting the tension out of them. "Just let John Williams soothe you. Close your eyes and listen to the master." He turns on the theme from *Schindler's List*, which feels out of place in our hot, sunshiny little store.

Maybe he's right and friends just complicate things. Andrew certainly has. Maybe it's better to keep friends and relationships separate, like food on a tray that can't spill over. One section for peas, another for mashed potatoes. Maybe that would keep my life from getting so messy.

TWENTY-FIVE

I NEVER THOUGHT I'd be thankful for finals, but suddenly it's the last two weeks of school and everyone is so busy that all of the drama gets pushed to the side. I finally force myself to finish my history project, and then spend every night for the rest of the week making flash cards and studying for Greek mythology and French.

By the time the last day of school arrives, I've forgotten to worry about it. But when I walk out of my last test of the day, I'm hit with a wave of sadness. It's funny how you can hate high school so much when it's happening, but start to miss it before you've even left. All of a sudden, I'm hyper-aware that everything I'm doing is for the last time. The last time I'll have to lean my shoulder into my locker door to get it unjammed, the last stale slice of cafeteria pizza, the last hours I'll spend staring out the window, counting down the minutes until it's all over. Somehow, even though every class seemed to last forever, the end has come way too fast.

It's been a Prescott tradition for as long as anyone can remember for all the seniors to meet at the lookout point by the lake to take pictures and then pile into limos to go to the prom. Usually prom is a little farther away, but the Walcott is only about twelve minutes down the road on the other side of the water. Still, we've still rented limos because we don't want to miss out on anything.

Danielle is having a party the last day of school—the night before prom—something she's coined "the last supper" because she wants to cook for everyone and, in her words, every party needs a good theme. She's invited the whole class, even Ryder and Simon Terst, who she's been mad at for weeks. Now that school is over, it's like all the arbitrary social boundary lines that have kept us all segregated don't even exist. My cousin Beth, who is seven years older than me, told me it would be this way: that just a few months after high school ended, we wouldn't care about who was popular, or who hooked up with who, or who we were supposed to hate. I didn't believe her at the time, but now I do. It already feels like high school was ages ago even as I'm still cleaning out my locker.

Just like we planned, Hannah and I get into her Jeep with the top down and scream as we race out of the parking lot. We put "Free Bird" on her stereo and blast it as loud as it'll go, rolling down the windows and laughing, pointing our middle fingers out to the sky. It's bittersweet to be here without Andrew. In the movie version of today—the one I planned in my head—the three of us were together, laughing and speeding away from Prescott, the same trio we were at the beginning of ninth grade now at the end of twelfth. But I saw him leave earlier with Danielle and I didn't even say goodbye.

We all go down to the lake in the afternoon, everyone lying out on brightly colored inner tubes and inflatable pizza slices. There's an ice chest full of beer hidden in the grass on the edge of the water, buried under a pile of beach towels so cops or parents or whoever else is around won't know we're drinking. The beach is crowded—practically everyone in our class is here, like we're all trying to suck up every last minute we have with one another, savor every last drop. The sun is high in the sky, casting a golden summer haze over everything, and the beauty of it makes me ache. I know it's never going to be just like this—like right now—ever again.

I'm lying on a pizza slice raft, taking a nap, when an excited shriek wakes me, a cold splash to my left. When I turn, I see Andrew and Danielle struggling to fit in the same inner tube. Her hair is in a wet knot on the top of her head, red bikini struggling to stay tied as she lunges onto his shoulders, trying to dunk him under. I can't seem to look away. They're both so beautiful, like they're in some bubblegum ChapStick ad in *Teen Vogue*, and the sight makes me a little sick. I wish they didn't look so much like they belonged together.

Andrew notices me looking and waves, shaking the water out of his hair like a dog. I wave back and his smile falters for a second and I know he's feeling the same way I am. We shouldn't be waving to each other across the lake, not today.

"Hey, Collins," Danielle says, shouting a little bit so I can hear her. "Do you think James Dean would buy us some booze? For tonight?"

I don't really want to get Dean involved, not when there are so many other available options; Andrew's cousin, for one, or whoever supplied the thirty rack of beer currently chilling in the cooler on the beach. But I know, for Danielle, it's some sort of test. She wants to see if I can; if I'll have the guts.

"I'll give you money," she calls across the water. "We need your help, Collins!" She loops a slippery arm around Andrew's neck, pulling him close. *We.* Like they're a unit.

"Yeah," I call back to them. "No problem."

• • • • • •

DANIELLE

Sooo did you ask James Dean for alcohol yet?

ME

Not yet

DANIELLE

Get some beer for the dudes. My parents have a margarita machine, so have him pick up some tequila and chasers too 😘

ME

I don't know, that's a lot to buy with a fake ID

DANIELLE

Just ask, Collins. If we don't have booze at the party it's on you

• • • • • •

ME

Hey

DEAN

What's up

ME

Can I ask you something?

DEAN

...

DEAN

What

ME

Danielle is having a party tonight and she needs alcohol

DEAN

That's not a question

ME

Do you think you could maybe get some for us?

ME

No pressure

ME

I'll pay you back

DEAN

How?

ME

...

DEAN

I'll see what I can do

• • • • • •

ANDREW

Hey

ME

Hey

ANDREW

Are you coming tonight? To the last supper?

ME

Yeah, you?

ANDREW

Do you want to go together?

ANDREW

I mean, carpool?

ME

I can't. I'm going to Dean's first

ME

to pick up alcohol

ANDREW

> Oh. Yeah I'm probably gonna stay over anyway, so carpooling won't really work

ANDREW

> Unless you wanted to spend the night too? Could give you a ride home

ME

> Yeah, we can spend the night

ME

> I mean, I know you're spending the night with Danielle. I just meant I'll be staying over too. On the couch

ANDREW

> Yeah, I got it

ME

> Ok see you there!

• • • • • •

When I get to Dean's house, he has a box waiting for me full of plastic handles, some tequila and something with a dragon on the label that looks like it might kill a grown man. He's sitting on the couch with Cody and they're playing *Mario Kart* again. It's like the world might end if they ever stop.

"Are you sure you don't want to come?" I ask him, trying to lift the box. It's way heavier than I imagined.

"Nah, you go ahead," he says. "You should come by after though."

"I don't know if I'll be able to get a ride." If all the contents of this box get consumed, there's no way anybody will be driving before tomorrow. And I don't want to walk across campus in the middle of the night.

"It's just the last supper concept is kinda weird," he says. "I feel kinda out of place going to your end-of-high-school stuff. You know, you could always skip it and we could drink this booze here." He's smiling in a way that makes me think he's joking and it's not a real offer. What's strange though is that I don't think I'd take him up on it if it were. For some reason, even though I've spent all of high school complaining about parties, I'm actually looking forward to this one. I think it's because it might be our last.

"It's not going to be anything weird," I say.

"I'll just see you tomorrow, okay?" he says. "For prom. That's gonna be the real party."

"Dean is so excited for prom he's practically peeing his pants," Cody says, and I can't tell whether he's being sarcastic. I get the sense that what he's saying is a little bit mean, but I can't be sure.

"Okay."

"It's two fifty for the booze," Dean says. I nod and dig through my wallet, handing him the money Danielle gave me. "I'll see you tomorrow night, okay?" he says. "You're not mad, right? You're still excited about prom?"

I pick up the box, straining as I head for the door. "Yeah," I tell him. "I'm still excited for prom."

TWENTY-SIX

THE PARTY IS already in full swing by the time I get there. The house is alive, vibrating with noise and energy, and it looks like everyone is here—all of the senior class and most of the juniors. The Olivers have the kind of house that's full of negative space—rooms that cost a fortune to decorate but no one ever actually uses. The staircase to the second floor wraps up from the foyer like a showpiece, the kind of stairs you'd expect a line of chorus girls to dance down in an old vaudeville show. Right now, it's crammed full of people.

There's a big poster board taped to the back wall with THE LAST SUPPER written across it in red paint. This is risky, because the paint doesn't seem totally dry, and every piece of furniture in this house probably costs more than a car. At the bottom of the poster in Sharpie, someone else has scrawled WHAT'S SUP? And another person: EAT MY DICK!

Below that is a folding table piled with food—trays of cookies and breads Danielle made, plus some suspicious-looking brownies she clearly didn't. There are electric tea candles everywhere, casting the party in a soft glow.

I carry the box of alcohol into the kitchen, my arms straining, trying to edge my way past groups of people who don't seem to see me or care to get out of the way. I scan the room and see Hannah dancing with a group of girls from her field hockey team. Before I can try to make my way over to them, Chase comes up to me, nodding his head toward the cardboard box full of bottles.

"Collins!" he says. "What did you bring me?"

I tilt the box toward him and he grins, pulling out a bottle of tequila.

"Looks like we didn't really need this," I say, motioning to all the people around us who are clearly already wasted.

"Dude, no, you're a god." He twists the bottle open and takes a swig, wiping his mouth with his hand.

"You're just drinking it straight?" I ask, wrinkling my nose in distaste.

"Believe me, I need this right now." He takes another quick swig and holds the bottle out to me. I set down the box.

"No thanks." I don't want my head to be too clouded, especially by something like tequila, which Ava has always said "makes her clothes fall off." "Hey, have you seen Andrew?"

Chase nods behind him. "He's with the lady of the house."

I look to where he's motioned and that's when I see them. Andrew is sitting on the couch in the TV room, Danielle perched on his lap. His hand is resting lightly on the thin strip of exposed skin between her shirt and her jean shorts.

"They look cozy," I say.

"They've been on top of each other all night," Chase says. "He's like her tumor." He takes another sip of tequila. Before I know what I'm doing, my hand reaches out and grasps the edge of the bottle.

"Can I have some of that actually? I changed my mind."

"Be my guest." He gives it to me. I pour it into a cup with a little margarita mix and then wince as I bring it to my lips. "It's not poison," Chase says.

"Actually, it sort of is." I take a sip, expecting to shudder in disgust like I did with the whiskey, but it's surprisingly good. Dangerously good. I suddenly understand why people sing upbeat, beachy songs about margaritas. I know I'm going to have to drink it really slowly or it will hit me fast.

I glance back and see Andrew tucking a lock of hair behind Danielle's ear and something clenches in my gut. I don't know what's wrong with me. My gut was perfectly fine before the stupid Plan.

"Hey, can I ask you something?" I turn to Chase suddenly. If there's ever going to be a time to get information out of him, it's now, when we're on the same side.

"Yeah, Collins, shoot," he says. "You've seen me ass naked, so at this point what's left to hide?"

"Did you write the notes?"

"What notes?"

I shake my head. "I mean that thing on the wall of the lounge. About Danielle."

"Fuck no," Chase says, and I believe him. "I would never be a dick like that."

"Okay, but then why did you tell everyone you slept with her?" I take another sip of my drink and feel the heat of it spreading down my chest, making me more confident. I don't know if maybe I've crossed a line and he'll get mad, but at this point, I don't really care anymore. Surprisingly, he just shrugs.

"I fucked up," he says. "I shouldn't have told Ryder. I've known the kid since kindergarten and I know he has a big mouth. But he's my best friend. When you finally get with the girl you like, aren't you allowed to tell your best friend?"

I think about all the personal things I've ever told Hannah, how upset I was learning that Andrew hooked up with Danielle and didn't tell me. How can I be mad at Chase for spilling a secret he was excited about when it's something we all do?

"You like her?" I glance over to the couch where she and Andrew are sitting. Of course he does.

"It's too late now," he says, following my gaze. "I blew it."

"Ryder blew it," I say. "You're right—she can't fault you for telling somebody. You're not the one who told the whole school. Why didn't you say something to him?"

"To Ryder? We're in the final sprint of high school. Just ride it out, Collins." He clinks his tequila bottle against my cup. "After next week, we'll never have to see any of these people ever again." Then he smiles and walk away, slinging his arm around Cecilia, who's just come into the room and is scowling in the direction of the couch. It strikes me that even though I've seen him naked, I don't really know Chase at all.

I make my way over to Hannah, and I can tell she's tipsy. Her cheeks are flushed pink, her bangs messy.

"Keely!" she shouts when she sees me, like it's been three years instead of three hours. "Happy last day of finals!" She's with Molly Moye, the two of them swaying back and forth to the beat of some old Ariana Grande song.

"What have you been drinking?" I like the feel of her next to me, warm and secure.

"All of it," she answers, bopping me on the nose.

"Are you excited for tomorrow?" Molly asks me. She holds her drink out in the direction of mine and I tap my cup against hers and take another long, tangy sip. I start to nod, about to say something about prom and how it's a moment and all of the other phrases I've been forcing through my head for the last week or so, but I realize all of a sudden that no—I'm actually not that excited for tomorrow. When I think of tomorrow night, I don't think of prom itself, of dancing with my friends, celebrating the end of school, the final few moments we'll still be together. All I can think about is the hotel room that Dean and I got for afterward, the moment when we'll both be undressed, right on the edge. The moment that I promised him.

Losing your virginity is supposed to be exciting, right? Tomorrow night is making my stomach swoop, but not like it's full of butterflies. More like it's full of gas. But I don't want to think too much about it right now, so I take another long sip of my margarita and I lie to Molly.

"I can't wait."

She lights up like a Christmas tree and loops her arm through Hannah's so we're all linked together, like a drunken daisy chain.

"Me too," she says.

"Me three," Hannah agrees.

"I'm going to miss you guys next year," Molly says, and maybe it's just the alcohol that's got us feeling all sentimental, because

I barely know Molly Moye. Well, that's not true. I know all of the facts about Molly: she's dating Edwin Chang, she's played field hockey since fifth grade, she's going to Dartmouth in the fall. But knowing these details about Molly's life doesn't mean I know what's going on inside her. And yet, when she says she's going to miss me, I understand what she means. Because I'm going to miss Molly too. She's part of my ecosystem. I'm used to her life orbiting mine, like she's always just on the edge of my vision. And I know after we graduate—after summer is over, when I go off to California, and Hannah leaves for New York, and Molly for New Hampshire, I'll probably never see Molly Moye again.

I wander around the house feeling slightly lost in the crowd of people, the sweaty mass of bodies. I'm already on my second margarita and the tequila is blurring them together, morphing them into strangers.

In the kitchen I find Danielle and Ava. I guess Danielle must have peeled herself off Andrew's lap. Where has he gone?

There's a cookie sheet on the counter and they've sprinkled tortilla chips and cheese on it, their fingers greasy. Because these are Danielle nachos, there are other ingredients too: black olives, jalapeños, sliced onions, and tomatoes. I can picture her cutting vegetables up before the party started, putting them in little bowls like my mom does.

"Collins!" Ava shouts when she sees me. "Come eat the last supper with us! We're making a feast." Ava operating an oven is probably a bad idea, but I'm happy she's moved from kaleories to nachos. Hopefully Danielle will keep her from burning the house down.

THE BEST LAID PLANS

"Where's Andrew?" I ask, grabbing a chip off the tray and bit-ing into it.

"Wait!" Ava shrieks. "They're not ready yet!"

"Let's make guacamole." Danielle grabs some avocados from the basket of fruit on the counter and then picks up a big knife.

"Don't!" Ava says. "You'll cut your hand off. I read an article about it on BuzzFeed—like hundreds of people are going to the hospital with guacamole-related injuries."

"Do you even know me at all." Danielle slices expertly into the skin of the avocado, sticking the knife into the pit and throw-ing it into the compost. "If I ever wound myself on an avocado, please finish me off."

"Have you guys seen Andrew?" I repeat.

"Not for a while." Danielle puts the tray of nachos into the oven. "Just wait until these start cooking and then he'll magi-cally appear. Guys can't resist melted cheese. It's science."

"I'm going to find him," I say, and turn on my heel, leaving them to deal with the oven.

Jason Ryder and Susie Palmer are pressed up against the wall in the back hallway, practically eating each other. I step around them to walk the rest of the way down the hall and then I'm at a screen door, the one that leads out to the porch. The night air is warm, the hum of crickets loud even over the music from the party.

I start to go outside, but then I freeze when I see Andrew. Because he isn't alone.

He's with Cecilia.

I close the screen, hiding myself behind the wall so I can watch them. She's sitting on the porch railing and Andrew is in front of her, standing so their faces are level. I think at first that they might kiss, but then I realize they're speaking, their voices soft. I have to strain to hear them.

"So you're just gonna pretend it didn't happen?" Cecilia sets her beer down on the railing next to her and flicks the metal tab on the top of it back and forth. "You've barely even looked at me all night."

He steps away and reaches a hand up to rub his neck. "I'm sorry. Danielle and I . . ."

"Yeah, I know," she snaps. "You're going to prom with her. So you're just done with me forever?"

"I thought it didn't mean anything," he says. "You said that. I wouldn't have—"

"I said that because I knew it's what you wanted me to say. God, Andrew, you just don't get it."

"Why would you lie about that? I didn't think it was—"

"I lied because I had to!" Her voice is raised now, sharp and strained. She runs a hand through her mass of blond curls, big and unruly from the humidity. "I knew you didn't like me. I knew you just wanted to get with me because you could, and I wanted to date you, but that's desperate, right? Feelings are such a turn-off." She lets out a harsh laugh. "So I took the parts of you I could get. You never would have gone for me if you'd known I liked you. That ruins it. Everyone knows you're a player."

"I'm not a player," Andrew says, and I want to shake him. She's telling him what I've been trying to tell him all along. He raises his beer to take a sip, but then shakes his head and sets it down on the railing, running his hand over his face.

"Oh, come on, Andrew!" I wonder how much she's had to drink, if she would have been brave enough to say these things to him sober. She picks her beer up off the railing and clutches it so hard between her fingers the can dents. Is she going to drink it or throw it in his face? "You think you're such a good guy, but good guys don't hook up with a girl and then move on the second they see someone better."

"I'm sorry," he says, his voice catching. "I just didn't think . . . I mean, I thought we were on the same page. I wouldn't have been so . . ." He trails off, struggling with his words. "I thought you knew."

"It's not my job to be the girl you hook up with while you're waiting for *the one*. I'm not here to entertain you until you find someone else."

"I'm sorry," he says again. "Really. I didn't think about it that way."

"Yeah, whatever," she says. "I should have listened to Susie. She kept telling me not to waste my time. But I thought maybe I could change you; that maybe I was special. Stupid, right?"

"Don't call yourself stupid when I'm the asshole," he says. The corner of her mouth twitches, like she's trying not to smile.

"You're a huge asshole," she says. But she raises her beer toward him and he clinks his can with hers, and I know she's forgiven him. Why is it so easy to forgive the people we have feelings for? I feel bad suddenly for the things I've said about Cecilia, the way I've joked about her with Andrew. I'm no better than she is.

"We're okay?" Andrew asks.

She smiles, tilting her head at him in a way that's clearly flirtatious—like even after all this, she's hoping deep down somewhere she still has a chance. Even if she knows better.

"You're getting off easy," she says. "If you had slept with me and then pulled this, I'd pour my beer on you."

"We could always remedy that," he says, grinning.

CAMERON LUND

Her words catch me off guard. *If you had slept with me—if*, like it's never happened. But that's impossible. They were hooking up for months, weren't they?

"Don't test me." She holds the beer up over his head, laughing, and he ducks out of the way, his smile matching hers.

"Do it. I'll get you another one. Promise." He looks up at her and then shuts his eyes, scrunching his nose in anticipation. Without hesitation, she pours the beer over his head, shrieking like she can feel the cold liquid down the back of her neck instead of his.

He shakes his head, beer sprinkling off his hair and onto her, and she screams and jumps off the railing onto the deck to get away. She's coming straight at me, so I run back into the house, not wanting either of them to find me spying. I can hear them both laughing still as I run back through the hallway, like they're the best of friends.

Danielle won't let Andrew get away with things like this. She's stronger than Cecilia. That's her superpower—always being able to say what she means to say when she means to say it. But even Danielle isn't completely fearless—she still hangs out with Ryder and flirts with Chase, like everything between them is completely okay. In that way, she's just like Cecilia, just like most girls: flirting because it's easier to flirt and forgive than to get mad, because as girls we've been trained our whole lives to give boys what they want, to say "sorry" when what we really want to say is "fuck you."

I can smell the nachos from the kitchen—burnt cheese, warm and smoky. But nobody is eating them. A crowd is gathering in the den, where something more interesting seems to be happening. And then I see it: Danielle holding an empty bottle of tequila, a wicked smile on her face.

"Who wants to play spin the bottle?" She shakes the bottle back and forth, taunting us.

"Come on," Ava says. "We're not in eighth grade anymore. We don't need a game to make out with each other." She tugs at her tank top, pulling it down so her boobs are dangerously close to making an appearance.

"Maybe *you* don't need a game to help you make out with someone, but not all of us are so . . . talented." Danielle raises an eyebrow and turns away from Ava, setting the bottle down on the floor. "Everyone get in here!"

Jason Ryder bounds down the stairs and into the room, whooping. "Fuck yeah!" There's a beer in his hand and a bit of it spills onto the floor. I see Susie creep down the stairs behind him. A trail of guys comes in from the garage, leaving their game of beer pong abandoned. Sophie Piznarski and Molly Moye, who have been whispering to each other in the corner, both nod their heads and come forward to join. I hear a noise behind me and see that Cecilia and Andrew have emerged from the back porch. His hair is dripping beer.

This is my nightmare. There isn't anyone in school I want to kiss. And I certainly don't want to watch as the bottle spins from Andrew to any of the girls he's hooked up with. Which would be worse? Cecilia? Sophie? Danielle?

Hannah comes up behind me and slings an arm over my shoulder.

"This is your favorite game, right?" She pulls away and sticks her tongue out to show she's kidding. She must have stopped drinking, because she seems a lot more collected than the last time I saw her, her cheeks less flushed. Or maybe we've just switched places. Maybe now I'm the drunk one. I try to laugh along with her, but mostly I just feel queasy. The room blurs slightly and I shake my head, trying to clear the tequila from my system.

"I don't think I'm going to play," I say, trying to back out of the circle.

"You're here," Andrew says, coming up next to me. His arm brushes against mine, and it's wet from when Cecilia dumped her beer on him. I shift slightly so we're not touching. "I've been looking for you." He's smiling and it kills me because I know it's a lie. Was he looking for me when Danielle was draped over him in the living room? When Cecilia was flirting with him out on the porch? It's a line he's always used on girls at parties, and now he's using it on me. I turn my head away and don't respond to him.

"Hey, Chase, come play!" Danielle shouts. "Brosner, get your ass in here!" And because she's ordered it, Chase appears, ambling over to us, his hands full of nachos. *Why does she want him to play?*

Danielle takes a seat and everyone follows her lead, spreading out into a big circle on the wood floor. Somehow I find myself sitting too.

"Ava! You're the pro." She hands the bottle to Ava, who sets it down gently in the middle of the circle.

"Alcohol please," Ava says, holding her empty palm out. Chase hands her another bottle of tequila, this one only halfway gone, and she takes a showy sip, smacking her lips and shaking her head, shuddering as she swallows. "Thanks, Chase." She pats him gently on the cheek, letting her fingers stay there for just a little too long. Then she reaches out and gives the bottle a spin. We all watch it, moving our heads around and around, back and forth, the possibilities and combinations running through our minds.

It lands on Jason Ryder. Everyone cheers and Ryder raises an arm up to fist pump, spilling a little beer on his shirt in the process. Next to him, Susie's forehead creases a little, but the smile stays on her face. We all know that the rules of high school mean she can't act like she cares.

"Aw, no fun," Ava says, pouting. "We've already made out."

But she leans forward and kisses him anyway. Ryder pulls away with a smack, and then reaches a hand up to squeeze her boob. Everyone cheers, and I force a laugh, even though I don't think it's funny, even though I see the frown on Ava's face for a fraction of a second. I wonder if the other girls in the circle know it's wrong too, if they're all forcing laughs because the guys are laughing, if they're cheering because it's *Ava* and that makes it okay.

And then Ava is laughing too.

"Not in front of everyone, Ryder," she says, sitting back down on her side of the circle. "Behave."

Now it's Ryder's turn. The bottle is spinning, spinning, spinning, and I pray it won't land on me. The thought of Jason Ryder's tongue in my mouth makes me want to vomit.

The bottle stops on Chase.

Everyone goes wild.

"No fucking way!" Ryder says. "Guys don't have to kiss each other." He motions to Susie. "Susie is right here. I'll kiss her."

"Jason," Danielle says, reaching into the circle and picking up the bottle, like by holding it she has the power to speak. "My house. My rules. And I say you have to kiss Chase."

I see the twinkle in her eye. She's loving this. This is her pay-back to Ryder for what he just did to Ava and for what he said to Danielle in the senior lounge. It's her payback to Chase for a lot more. "Come on, boys, we don't have all night." She smirks and taps the bottle against her open palm. Tap. Tap. Tap.

"This game is fucking stupid," Ryder says. "I don't need a game to get with girls." He stands up. "I'm getting another beer."

"Does that mean you're out, Jason?" Danielle asks, her voice saccharine sweet. He walks into the kitchen and raises a hand in the air, flipping her off without turning around. "So touchy," she says.

"Do I get to spin?" Chase holds his palm out to Danielle. She looks at him for a moment, sighs, and then places the bottle into his open palm.

"Use it for good, Brosner."

"I'll just kiss you instead." He turns the bottle so it points in her direction. "You're the one I want it to land on."

"Those aren't the rules." She turns the bottle back at him. "Spin."

"Dani," he says, his voice soft.

"Spin."

He sighs and reaches forward, giving the bottle a spin. It lands on Danielle, of course. Because that's the way things work for Chase. She rolls her eyes and leans over the circle toward him.

"All right, Brosner, fair is fair. Lay one on me."

He smiles and grabs the back of her head, gently pulling her toward him. She keeps her lips pressed tightly together as his inch closer. Still, I see her break into a smile right before they touch, like she can't help it, like maybe she wanted to kiss him all along.

I glance over at Andrew, hoping he doesn't look too upset, but he's barely even watching. He's staring down at the floor, drawing a pattern in the wood with his thumb. He must feel my gaze on him, because he looks up and over to me.

Are you okay? I ask him telepathically. *Is this hard to watch?*

This game sucks, he says back.

Danielle places the bottle down on the floor and spins, and we all watch as it rotates back and forth. I take a long swig of tequila. At this point, the margarita mix isn't necessary, because the tequila alone has started to taste pretty good, sort of sweet and tangy at the same time. When I set down the handle and look back at everyone, I notice that the bottle on the floor is pointing right at Andrew.

Everyone in the circle cheers, and Danielle crawls toward him, using her finger to motion him forward. They meet halfway and his hands slide through her hair like they belong there, and then they're kissing. I saw them kiss before, in the car, but not like this. Not since I knew he loved her. I realize I'm still holding the bottle of tequila, and hand it back to the person next to me.

Then it's Andrew's turn to spin, and I feel like I can't breathe. I don't want it to land on me, because I don't want to kiss him in front of anyone, in front of everyone. But I don't want the bottle to land on anyone else either. I don't want to think about what that means.

"Reed's already kissed every girl in the circle!" Simon says.

"Not everyone," Andrew says.

"Not Collins!" Edwin says, and I wince. Andrew's ears redden, but he's laughing and the bottle is spinning, spinning, spinning. Someone hands me the tequila and I take a sip, letting my eyes blur, letting my throat burn and my stomach fill with heat.

Andrew looks over at me for a brief second, our eyes meeting quickly, before he turns back to the bottle, and I wonder what he's thinking; if he's worried about the bottle landing on me.

The bottle rolls to a stop and I feel suddenly like I'm about to cry.

It's pointing at Hannah.

I raise a hand up to my mouth to try to cover the sound that's escaped from me. Somehow I haven't considered this possibility. Somehow it's the worst one. I know it shouldn't matter. This is a game, so it doesn't count. My breath is coming out in short spurts, and I want to tell them I don't feel well, tell them to stop, tell them they're making me dizzy. But what right do I have? We all knew the rules of the game when we sat down to play. I'll just embarrass myself if I say anything, only make Danielle think I have feelings I don't have.

I stare down at the floor, trying not to watch, fixing my gaze on an imperfection in the wood, a long scuff mark where someone must have dragged a chair or a table. Everyone is clapping and cheering, but I can barely hear them. I glance up, because I can't resist, because we're always drawn to the things we're most repulsed by.

Andrew and Hannah aren't kissing. They're both looking at me.

"What are you waiting for?" Danielle asks. "Kissy kissy."

"I can't," Hannah says. I feel relief flood into me, relief that has no right to be there.

"We can't," Andrew repeats.

"Don't be stupid," Danielle says. "Everyone else has kissed. You could've already been done by now."

He glances quickly back and forth from me to Hannah to Danielle, and back to me.

"Just do it!" Simon shouts.

"I don't want to, okay?" Hannah says, her voice getting sharper. "Can't we just mutually decide to bow out of this round? He's your prom date anyway. It's too weird."

Danielle turns to Andrew. "As your prom date, I give you permission."

"It's not going to happen," he says.

I know they're acting this way for my sake and I'm grateful to them, but it also makes me nervous. Did they see the panic I was trying so hard to hide?

"Fine." Danielle folds her arms and sits back with a pout. "Fine. New rules. Whatever. Hannah, just give your kiss to someone else."

"Hey," Ava says, "that's not fair. I wouldn't have kissed Ryder if I didn't have to."

"Stop pretending you don't like him," Danielle snaps, and Ava looks away. "All right, Hannah. Who do you want to make Andrew kiss?"

"Pick Chase!" Cecilia says. "Pick Edwin!" *Pick me*, I know she's thinking.

But of course Hannah will pick Danielle. She knows Andrew is in love with her—the secret I wasn't supposed to tell. That's why Danielle is changing the rules in the first place. Because she knows Hannah will pick her too.

Hannah picks up the bottle, holding it tentatively between her hands. Then she turns it around so it points at me.

"Keely."

TWENTY-SEVEN

"WHAT?" I ASK, feeling my breath catch in my throat. "That's not—"

"Keely hasn't had a turn yet," Hannah says to the room.

What is she thinking? She knows Andrew and I are tiptoeing around each other, trying to pretend everything is still normal. But then I realize—she doesn't know. I still haven't told her I went through with the Plan. She doesn't know Andrew and I have already kissed, have already done a whole lot more. She's wanted us to be together for so long. Of course she'd jump at this chance. She probably thinks she's a genius.

I glare at her.

"Well?" Danielle says, motioning between Andrew and me. "We're all waiting."

"Right," Andrew says. He brushes his hands off on his shorts and then moves closer to me. He's actually going to do it. I feel my pulse quicken, my heart in my throat. My mouth is dry and I reach my tongue out to wet my lips, tasting tequila on them, the sting of lime. This won't be so bad. It'll be over in a few seconds. That's all it will take—all people will expect. Just a few seconds, his lips against mine in a peck, and then it will be done. Except a part of me doesn't want it to be over that fast. A part of me wants more than a few seconds, more than a few minutes, to sink into him, to melt against him. I shake my head and push that part far away.

"Okay," I say, letting out a shaky breath.

"Okay," he says back, threading his hand through my hair. I wonder if any part of him wants this too. I can't let my emotions show on my face, just in case no part of him wants me at all.

Out of the corner of my eye, I see Sophie Piznarski get up and leave the room, and Cecilia lean forward to watch, her hands pressed so hard into the floor they're turning white. But then all I can see is him, green eyes focused on mine. And then I can't see anything at all as my eyes close and our lips touch. It's just as I remember it. I didn't realize you could grow familiar with someone's kisses after only kissing them once—but that's what it is: familiar. He tastes like home. I never knew home had a taste, a smell, could feel like someone's lips on mine—slightly chapped and dusted with salt. All I can hear is the rush of blood in my ears—if anyone is clapping or cheering, I can't tell.

It ends just as quickly as it began, and as I pull away, my eyes flutter open and I remember where we are: surrounded by people, surrounded by the girls of Andrew's past, the girls of Andrew's present. I look away from him, trying to focus my eyes on anyone, on anything else.

"Collins, your turn to spin!" Danielle says. She hands the bottle to me and I take it with shaky hands, my heart still beating wildly in my chest. I feel slightly out of my body, like everything is happening to someone else and not to me. I sit back down, and the circle parts to make room for Andrew and Hannah on either side of me. Hannah squeezes my knee and I look over at her and she breaks into a big smile, clearly pleased with herself.

"Spin, Collins," Danielle says again. She's drumming her black fingernails against the wood floor.

I feel dizzy as I lean forward and place the bottle down. I don't want to spin—I'm already too confused, too disoriented, and kissing Ryder or Chase or Simon or anyone will only cloud my head more. I want to think about what's just happened with Andrew, to figure out what it means. If it means anything at all.

"Spin!" Ava shouts, her tone light and gleeful. I turn my head too quickly to look at her, and she blurs—two Avas in one, four boobs bouncing as she claps her hands together. She raises her arms up to cheer and a trail of light and color follows the motion. I have to shake my head to clear it away.

"Spin!" somebody else says, and then a chant starts: *spin, spin, spin.*

I lurch forward and raise a wobbly hand to my mouth.

"I don't feel well," I say. "I'm gonna be sick." I trip as I try to get onto my feet, my sock slipping on the polished wood floor.

"Ouch, Reed!" somebody taunts. "How rank is your breath?"

I run down the hall to the bathroom and slam the door before anyone can come after me, shutting out the sound of the laughter and jeers from the other room. Leaning over the sink, I run some cold water and splash it over my face, then rest my head against the mirror, the cold glass making me feel better. Maybe I can hide in here, my face on the glass, until everyone moves on, keeps drinking, and forgets I was ever here in the first place. Would anyone even notice?

There's a soft knock on the door.

"Collins?" It's Andrew, voice muffled. "Are you okay?"

I don't answer.

"Can I come in?"

There's a long pause as I consider if I can handle lifting my forehead off the mirror. I don't know if I want to be near him.

"I'm fine," I say, my voice raspy. "I just didn't feel like playing anymore."

"Because I'm a horrible kisser?" I can hear the playful note in his voice. "I know for a fact that's not true. I have sources." There are some shuffling sounds outside, the tapping of his fingers against the door. "Maybe I'm such a good kisser you were overwhelmed with bloodlust and you had to get out of there. It's—"

"Bloodlust is a thirst for blood." I pull my head off the mirror. "I don't want to kill you."

I open the door a crack and see him grinning on the other side. He comes in and shuts the door, sitting down next to me on the edge of the Jacuzzi tub. Even though it's the downstairs bathroom, the one right next to the guest room, it's still huge, twice the size of my parents' bathroom. Next to the sink, there's a framed photograph of Danielle from middle school, standing proudly next to a horse. I turn away from her stare.

We sit in silence on the edge of the tub. Somehow it was easier to talk to him through the door, to remember how to be his friend when I couldn't see him. Now that he's next to me, his left leg against my right, the slight smell of him—his sweat, his shampoo, the beer that's now drying in his hair—is making me dizzy.

"Is this how it's going to be?" I ask finally. I pick at a thread hanging from my shorts. "I was always so proud of us because we'd managed to stay friends after growing up. But maybe we just have to accept the fact that it doesn't work."

"Of course it works," he says. "It's been working for years. Just because we kissed in a stupid game, it doesn't mean we can't—"

"It wasn't just that stupid game," I say. "It was everything else. It was the Plan. It was you seeing me naked, touching my boobs." Saying it out loud, I burst into unexpected laughter. Andrew starts laughing too, and I feel something ease inside of me.

"They're nice boobs," he says, and I swat him. His eyes widen and he loses balance, falling backward into the empty tub. I yelp as he pulls me with him so that I land hard on his stomach, bumping my elbow against the porcelain.

"Ow!" I hold up my elbow where I know a bruise is going to form. But I can feel him shaking with laughter beneath me, and so I'm laughing too. It all feels so natural again, like the old days.

"Can we just stay here the rest of the night?" I ask. "I don't want to go back out there."

"Deal," he says, leaning back into the empty tub and rearranging himself so we fit sort of comfortably. He sits back against one end and brings his legs inside, bent at the knee. I sit back against the other end, so that we're facing each other. The tub's nozzle is right next to my neck and I have to tilt my head to the left to avoid it. He folds his arms behind his neck and closes his eyes, pretending like we're in a real hot tub.

"Comfy?" I ask.

He nods with his eyes closed. "Remember when we used to take baths together? How did we ever fit?"

"You weren't a hundred feet tall back then."

"You're still the same size," he says, and then breaks into a grin. "Most places."

"Shut up." I push him with my bent knee.

"Hey, we should turn the water on. Pretend it's ten years ago. Hot tub time machine."

"What?" I ask, even though I've heard him.

"Let's fill up the tub."

"We're in our clothes," I say, knowing as I say it that I've started blushing.

"So? Live a little. I have to wash my hair anyway."

"Yeah, you stink."

"Cecilia dumped a beer on me."

"You probably deserved it."

"Yeah, I did," he says. Then he unbends his leg and reaches a foot up to the faucet, using it to turn on the water. It shoots down onto my shoulder.

"Turn it off!" I shriek. "It's cold!" I scramble to get out of the stream, but the more I move, the more I slip, water spraying everywhere.

"It'll warm up in a sec," he says, and I reach a hand under the faucet to splash him. But even as I do, I feel the stream of water turn deliciously warm. "See?" he says when I splash him again. He wipes the water off his face and runs a wet hand through his hair. I give up and lean back against the wall of the tub, finding myself enjoying the feel of the warm water as it streams down onto my neck and shoulders. Slowly the tub fills up around us, and my shorts grow heavy and uncomfortable.

Andrew's gray T-shirt gets darker as it dampens, sticking to him like a second skin. I look down at my own T-shirt, hoping it won't stick to me in the same way, and I pull at the bottom hem, lifting it away from the shape of my body so he can't see.

"Fuck it," Andrew says, and he reaches down and pulls his

shirt off, throwing it onto the tile floor, where it lands with a wet smack. "Much better."

"Drew!" I say, scolding him, though something in me tightens at the sight of his bare chest again, at the trail of hair that connects his belly button with the waist of his shorts. His hair is wet and sticking up at all angles, and droplets of water are stuck in his eyelashes like snowflakes.

"What?" He raises his hands out of the water to motion to his bare chest. "This is just like a bathing suit. No biggie."

"Right," I say, trying to take a deep breath, remembering too easily the kiss we shared earlier. "I'm not taking mine off."

"Fine," he says, flicking at the water with his thumb. "I'm not expecting you to."

"Fine," I say.

"Fine."

And then I do, my hands reaching for the hem of my shirt like they don't belong to me, like they're someone else's hands and they're not under my control. I peel my shirt up and over my head and set it down on the side of the tub. My bra is gray cotton and might be a little see-through, but I try not to think about it. He's staring at me, and I'm staring back, the air between us thick.

He reaches down into the water and undoes the button of his wet shorts, and I mirror him, reaching down to undo mine. We peel them off at the same time, and the water sloshes out of the tub. I lean forward, trying to shimmy out of the heavy, wet fabric. He leans forward too and lifts his knees, his legs on either side of me, holding me in place. His shorts are still half off, but he's stopped undressing, because now the front of him is pressed up against the front of me, and our faces are less than a foot apart, and I'm not thinking or breathing. The heat of the bathwater is making my head spin and I feel dizzy again, but not in an unpleasant way, like before. Not like I'm going to be sick. No, it feels like the moment on the top of the roller coaster, the moment before you fall, the moment that you're weightless.

Then he closes the space between our lips and kisses me, his wet chest pressed against mine, slippery and warm and delicious. The water is still coming out of the faucet behind me, the sound of it rushing like the blood in my ears. He reaches a hand up into my wet hair and pulls me even closer to him, biting my bottom lip, the feel of it sending a chill through me despite the heat of the bath.

All I can think is *more more more*. I need to get closer to him. I want to be as close to him as possible, to become a part of him, to sear together like two atomic particles.

And then there's a loud banging on the bathroom door.

I'm jolted into awareness, my eyes opening so fast there are stars behind them. Andrew's eyes are open too and his breathing is ragged. He leans into me, trying to capture my lips again.

"Just ignore it," he says.

The banging continues, loud and insistent.

I shake my head, trying to get my bearings, to come back into my body. And then the weight of it all crashes down on me — everything I've been trying not to think about.

"Keely, are you in there?" It's Hannah's voice at the door.

I reach behind me and turn off the faucet, and when the roar of it is gone, the silence is deafening. I shake my head again and try to back away from him, but his knees are still holding me in place, and we're tangled together in his shorts. I remember what he said to me earlier: *I've been looking for you*. The same line he's used on every girl at every party. He said it to Cecilia on my birthday, and then took her into the bathroom, into the shower. I can't believe I fell for it, not when I've got his script memorized. I've always felt bad for the girls who have fallen for Party Andrew. And now I'm one of them.

"Let me go," I say, trying to get away from him. Water sloshes over the tub and onto the tile floor. He moves his knees, leaning back against his side of the tub and pulling his shorts back on the rest of the way. "This is all one of your moves, isn't it?"

He runs a hand through his hair and shakes his head, water spraying in all directions.

"What are you talking about?"

"How many girls have you taken a bath with?"

"Keely!" Hannah's voice is still calling from the other side of the door, high and strained, and I can tell from the pitch of it that something's wrong. I try to stand up, but the floor of the bathtub is slippery and I wobble, putting my hands out on either side for balance.

"I can't believe after everything, you're trying to get with me."

"I'm not trying to get with you," he says.

I know I'm as much to blame for this as he is, but it's too hard to think about. It's like what he said to me a few months ago, about how it's easier to feel nothing than to get hurt. Maybe that's why he hasn't told Danielle the truth, why he's using me as a distraction.

"I have to go," I say, climbing out of the tub. I put my wet shirt back over my head and it's freezing cold, clammy on my skin.

"Wait," he says, and I stop for a second, my hand on the doorknob. But I can't turn around. Hannah is still pounding on the door, so I open it. I'm surprised to see that she's crying. Trails of mascara run down her cheeks and her breath is coming out in little gasps.

"What's wrong?" I pull her into a hug, forgetting my clothes are soaking wet, that Andrew is standing behind me, still in the tub, shirtless. Hannah doesn't seem to notice.

"He's back for the summer," she says, reaching a hand up to her eyes. "He's here at the party."

"Who?" I ask, though it should be obvious. There's only one person who can make Hannah so fragile, so easy to rip apart, like a paper doll version of herself.

"It's Charlie," she says. "Charlie is here."

TWENTY-EIGHT

"WHERE IS HE?" I pull out of Hannah's hug to scan the room behind her. I was already upset before this, but now I'm feeling murderous. And Charlie is the perfect target.

"I don't know." She wipes at her cheeks. "I just saw him for a second and I ran. I didn't want him to see me cry." Her voice is coming out in little hiccups. "He can't see me like this."

I feel Andrew's presence behind me and then his hand is on the wet fabric of my back.

"Are you guys okay?" he asks, and I shake away from his reach.

"We're fine," I say, moving closer to Hannah. I can't be near him. Hannah looks back and forth between the two of us, her eyes widening, and I see her take in our wet hair for the first time, the fact that Andrew isn't wearing a shirt.

"Wait, what's going on?" she asks.

"Come on, we should get you home," I say, "before Charlie comes over here."

"Keely," Andrew says, reaching out to stop us. "You were

going to stay over, right? I can take you guys home tomorrow."

"I can't stay here." I turn away from him. Suddenly I feel just as fragile as Hannah, like a paper doll myself. I don't know whether it's the tequila that's still making me so dizzy, so unsteady, or whether I'm just reeling from the nearness of him. There are little droplets of water running down his chest and my eyes follow one as it trails down his skin and disappears beneath the waistband of his shorts. "And put on a shirt." I grab Hannah and pull her down the hallway, leaving him behind us.

There's no one sober enough to drive, so Hannah and I decide to walk. The air is warm enough, even at this time of night, and I'd rather walk a few miles in my wet clothes than spend any more time at this party, with Andrew and Danielle and Charlie, the Death Eater. Besides, it feels good to move, like with each step the tequila is leaving my body, clearing my head.

We've barely made it past the driveway when Hannah pounces.

"Okay, so what the hell was that back there? Why wasn't Andrew wearing a shirt?"

"I don't know what you're talking about." I'm not sure why I can't tell her. The Plan was her idea to begin with. Really, I should have told her the moment I asked him. It's just that now it's too late. And talking about Andrew out loud—about all the things that have happened and almost happened between us— makes me afraid of what I might say. I start walking faster, like there's a chance I can outrun my problems. Hannah speeds up too.

"Come on, Keely. I'm not an idiot." Her tears have stopped and she looks fierce, wild. If there's one good thing that could

CAMERON LUND

come of tonight, of my mistake with Andrew, it's that Charlie
seems to be gone from Hannah's mind. We're the perfect distraction. "Were you guys hooking up?"

"No!" I say, the word rushing out of me. It just feels easier
to deny everything than to have to think about it. But I can't
do that to Hannah. "I mean, I don't know. Yeah, we were . . .
kissing. We kissed, okay? It all happened so fast." I throw my
hands up in the air, wishing I could take back the past few
hours. Or even better, the past few months. "But it doesn't matter anyway. It was stupid. He's in love with Danielle, and I *know*
that, but I still fell for it. We always knew he was a player, right?
I just never thought he would play *me*." I'm practically running
now, and Hannah is running right alongside me.

"Hey, slow down!" She reaches an arm out to me. I stop suddenly and she almost collides into my back. "He's not trying to
play you. Andrew would never do that to you." She puts a hand
on my shoulder and I whip away from her.

"How do you know?"

"Because he loves you."

The words make it even harder to breathe. "Stop."

I can't handle any of this right now. A wave of nausea rolls
from my stomach up through my chest and I clench my teeth
together until it passes. She continues on.

"Come on, Keely." Her voice is soft. I feel bad that she's comforting me when just a few minutes ago she was the one in tears.
"That boy would do anything for you."

I know I have to tell her about the Plan, why everything is so
messed up. Then she'll know why she's wrong.

There's a sliver of light on the horizon and the sky around us
is hazy and blue, almost morning. There's a bird chirping some-

288

where, but I can't tell what kind it is. I've forgotten all of the birdcalls we learned in kindergarten. I wonder how long it will take me to forget everything else.

I sigh and turn to Hannah. "This wasn't the first time, okay?"

"I know," she says. Not what I was expecting.

"What?"

"You're my best friends and you guys have been acting so weird around each other lately. It's not like I haven't noticed. You can barely be in the same room together. Of course something is going on."

"I lied to Dean, remember? About being a virgin?" I feel a sharp pain in my head and I reach a hand up and press it against my forehead, wishing for the millionth time I didn't drink 20,000 margaritas. I can feel the tequila churning in my stomach.

"Of course I remember," she says. "Keely, did you sleep with Andrew?"

"It was that thing you said at lunch that day," I say, the words spilling out of me. "That Andrew was such an expert, that he knew what he was doing. He could help me practice—"

"So you've been practicing with him?" she asks, and I can't help but notice Hannah seems a little excited, her eyes glittering.

"Hannah, stop," I say. "This isn't good news."

"No, this is great news!" Now she's full-on smiling.

"No, we're not friends anymore, okay?" It feels freeing to finally say it to someone. I didn't realize how much I needed to talk about this with her, how heartbroken I've been to lose him. "He never wanted to . . . practice . . . with me in the first place. We didn't even go all the way, because he couldn't do it. He just . . . left."

We turn off Danielle's street and into town, past the EVmU campus and onto Main Street. I'm struck by the sudden fear that we'll run into Dean, that he's stopped playing *Mario Kart* and has decided to come into town to go to the bars. I can't see him right now. Not when I'm feeling like this.

"That doesn't make any sense," she says. "That's not what was supposed to happen."

"You can't just meddle in other people's lives, okay?" I say, harsher than I intended, and her face goes white. Her mouth turns down and she shuts her eyes for a second and I can tell that I've hurt her.

"I didn't realize all of this was *my* fault." Her eyes narrow.

"You've been trying to get us together for years," I say. "If you had just stayed out of it, then none of this would have happened."

We walk by Jan's, the windows still dark. It hurts that I'll never have a pancake breakfast with Andrew here again. The smell of something baking wafts in the air around us and it makes me sick.

"I didn't force you to do anything," Hannah says.

"Yeah, but look how happy you were that I did!"

"I was joking, okay?" she says with a humorless laugh. "When I told you to practice with Andrew. I never thought you'd take it seriously."

"You weren't joking!" I say, my voice gaining volume. "You can't backtrack on that just because it didn't go how you planned."

"I wasn't planning anything," she says, but the catch in her voice says otherwise.

"You wanted us to fall in love and instead it ruined us. And so now you're saying it was all a joke. Well, sorry your plan didn't work out. Some of us know better than to fall in love with players. This isn't like you and Charlie."

Her face goes bright red, like I've slapped her, and I sort of have. Hannah turns to me and her voice is venom. "If you don't think you're in love with Andrew, you're delusional."

"He's my best friend," I say, my usual line, the line that used to come so naturally but now always feels like a lie.

"Yeah, so?" she says. "He's your best friend and you're in love with him and it's destroying you. If you just tell him, everything can go back to normal. What are you so scared of?"

"I have to go," I say, speeding up my walk and hoping she won't follow. I need to get away from her. I need to be alone.

"Go where?" she asks, but she's not running after me.

The truth is I *am* scared. I'm scared of tomorrow night, of the future, of who will be there and who will disappear with high school, like those birdcalls we learned in kindergarten. But mostly, I'm scared Hannah is right. Because if I'm in love with Andrew, *if I'm in love with Andrew,* it means I'm completely screwed. Because even if I'm in love with Andrew, he's still in love with Danielle.

TWENTY-NINE

IT TURNS OUT the only thing worse than getting ready for prom is getting ready for prom alone. Hannah and I were supposed to get dressed together, but she ignored me earlier when I texted to go over details, so I guess we're not talking.

I'm standing in front of the mirror with an eyelash curler, staring at it like it's a weapon of torture. The events from last night keep flashing through my head like some twisted movie reel of my greatest mistakes—playing spin the bottle, taking a bath with Andrew, fighting with Hannah. I know I said some messed-up things to her about Charlie, but I can't remember them. I can only remember the way the color drained from her face, the sick feeling in my stomach when she told me I was delusional. When she told me I was in love with Andrew.

I push everything from my mind and try my luck with the eyelash curler. I know I should have texted Danielle or Ava—someone would have taken me under her wing for today, but Hannah is probably with them. Besides, I can't handle watching

Danielle get ready, listening to her excited chatter about her stupid night with Andrew. But as I wrangle with the eyelash curler and all the rest of it, I wish more than ever I had Hannah here to fairy-godmother me; that I hadn't pushed her away.

My mom swoops in to save me. I never realized she actually knew how to do any of this because she's always so dressed down and mellow. But maybe part of being a woman is learning how to put on this armor. She paints my lips a dark red, sweeps my hair to one side, soft waves down my back. Hannah made me buy the green dress from the mall, and I guess it doesn't look as ridiculous as I thought. When I check the mirror, I don't even recognize myself. For the first time, I think I understand what Dean sees in me.

"You look beautiful," my mom says when she's all done. And I smile, because I actually agree.

Dean said he would meet me at the lake, so my parents drive me there for pictures. I ask them to stay in the car, but I know they won't. This is probably even more meaningful to them than it is to me. My mom needs these pictures for when I'm in California.

When we get there, everyone is standing around in little groups, giddy with excitement and nerves. I scan the parking lot for Dean, but I don't see him, and I'm struck by the horrible thought that maybe he won't show up. I can feel all of my earlier confidence fading away as I look around, searching for somebody to stand with so I'm not the girl all alone with her parents. I wish for the millionth time that I hadn't pushed Hannah away last night because more than anything I want her here with me. I want to tell her I'm sorry, to ask her about Charlie and make sure she's okay.

"Oh, there's Diane and Robert," my mom says, pointing toward where Andrew's parents are standing. "Let's go say hi."

I try to dig my heels into the ground to keep her from dragging me over there, because the thought of seeing Andrew after last night is excruciating. When I do see him, standing with his parents, my breath catches. He's in a navy blue suit, his hair combed flat to his head. I miss the way it usually flops down into his eyes. He spins around and puts a leg up on the fence post for a silly picture and I hear his mom's voice as we approach.

"Can't we at least get one serious picture?"

"Mom," he says. "Just wait until Danielle gets here." At the mention of her name, I feel something sharp in my chest.

"I just want one nice picture of my son in a suit," she says. He shakes his head, laughing as she snaps furiously with the camera. And then he turns and looks right at me and I stop walking, like I've run into an invisible brick wall. The smile is frozen on his face, his eyes are dancing, and they're so green, and I can't help but think back to last night when there were drops of water in his eyelashes like morning dew on grass. My parents keep walking, meeting up with his, greeting each other with hugs and handshakes, but I'm barely registering it because I can't move, can't stop looking at him, can't breathe. All I can think about, looking into his eyes, is how badly I want to kiss him. I want to be right back in that bathtub, his skin slick against mine, his hands threading through my hair, pulling me tight against him, so tight that it's like we're made out of the same particles.

And I realize Hannah is right. Hannah is so, so right, has always been right. I'm in love with him.

But I don't want to be just like Cecilia, just like so many other girls who fell for him the same way and were tossed aside. I don't want to just be the girl he made out with in a bathtub at a party after too many margaritas, the girl who fell for his stupid lines even though she knew better. Because I'm not in love with Party Andrew. I'm just in love with Andrew. My best friend.

But that doesn't make it any easier.

He must realize I'm having trouble moving, because he walks toward me, closing the distance between us.

"Hey."

"Hi," I say, suddenly shy.

"You look . . ." he says, but then doesn't finish the sentence. I want him to say that I'm beautiful, but I know if he does it'll just be another line.

"Thanks," I say instead, like he already has.

"We need a picture of you two for the fridge!" My mom waves her camera. "Get together." Our parents surge forward and push us into each other, smoothing down the waves in my hair, picking imaginary lint off his suit jacket so that we look perfect.

"Drew, put your arm around her," my dad says. "What are you scared of?"

"Look how grown up you both are," Andrew's mom says, her voice going misty.

"You're both so beautiful," my mom says.

It's weird to me how our parents have no idea what's going on between us. Once, they knew everything about our lives, and now there's so much right under the surface they'll never understand. My dad is so clueless he can casually tell Andrew to put his arm around me, not realizing Andrew's arm around me is both the best and the worst thing in the entire world.

Andrew looks at me and then back at our parents and then dutifully obeys, placing his arm gently around my waist, his hand just barely resting against the fabric on my hip. I think of how many times he's slung his arm over my shoulder in the past, leaning on me at parties, pulling me tightly against him like it's no big deal. I think of the hammock in his backyard, all the times we lay there together, letting gravity pull us practically on top of each other. Touching him now shouldn't matter, shouldn't be a problem, but his hand on my hip is hot and heavy and it's all I can think about.

Our parents take about a million photos, and then we pull away as fast as possible so we're not touching. I wonder for a heartbreaking moment if we'll ever touch again. I can't be around him, not if it's going to feel like this.

I glance toward the parking lot. Danielle is here now, with Ava, and she looks like someone you'd want to paint, her gown the color of red wine with a slit practically up to her neck. Ryder is behind them, not very discreetly drinking out of a flask. Even though he and Ava are here together, they're Not Together as dates; Ava wanted to go stag. Chase walks up to them then, his arm around Cecilia.

When your school is small, in the end it's all just one big game of spin the bottle.

I start to move toward the group, but Andrew holds out a hand to stop me.

"Wait," he says. "Before we . . . I mean." He lowers his voice so our parents can't hear, but they're not paying much attention anyway, too busy looking through the pictures in the digital camera. "About last night," he says. "I didn't mean to . . . I mean, I *did* mean to, I wanted to, I just . . ."

"Don't worry about it," I say. "I was about eighty percent made of tequila by that point, so—"

"I know," he says. His voice is so quiet, and he's leaning close to me so our parents can't hear, and it hurts because his lips are only about three inches away from mine. It's funny how something can be so close but actually so far away. "I shouldn't have kissed you."

"I kissed you back," I say, my voice catching.

"But you were drunk."

"So were you." It's like we're talking in circles. "Let's just forget it happened, okay? All of it." And then I walk away from him and over to the parking lot. When I turn around, I'm surprised to see he hasn't followed. He's just standing there, scuffing one of his nice shoes into the grass. Then he nods and moves past me right to Danielle. She smiles when she sees him and wraps her arms around his neck, pulling him into her body so they're plastered together. It feels a bit like someone is stabbing me repeatedly with a blunt knife.

There's the rumbling of an engine and then a motorcycle peels into the parking lot, and *thank God*, it's Dean. He looks good—better than good. It's like he's straight out of an action movie in his black tuxedo. He's not James Dean anymore. He's James Bond.

I make my way over to him just as he's stepping off the bike, and I can feel his eyes sizing me up, his gaze slowly traveling down the length of my body, lingering in all the places that are a bit more exposed than usual.

"You clean up nice, Prom Date." He tries to reach for me, to kiss me in front of everyone, but I back away from him because I know my parents are watching.

"Thanks for coming," I say, relieved.

"I wouldn't miss my first prom," he says, and then he takes

my hand, lacing his fingers through mine. I wait for the usual fluttering in my stomach, the shortness of breath that always accompanies his touch, but it's not there. I don't feel anything at all.

I realize then that my crush is gone, surely and completely. The feelings I had for him feel silly all of a sudden—how could I have been so into Dean when Andrew was right in front of me the whole time?

My parents come over and introduce themselves, and Dean is charming as always. I should have known he would be. Somehow, he calms them down about the motorcycle, promises my mom he would never let me ride it, even manages to make her laugh. Once they're not looking, he leans into me, whispering into my ear.

"That's a nice dress. I can't wait to take it off you."

I turn and slap him playfully on the chest, but inside I feel like I'm about to split into a million different pieces.

Hannah's Jeep pulls into the parking lot then, and I feel a pang of guilt that I'm not with her, that I was too proud, too stubborn to admit she was right. Hannah didn't have a date, and now she's coming here alone. I'm the worst friend.

But then the doors open and I feel my stomach clench, because she isn't alone. She's with *Charlie*.

They walk over to us, and Hannah can't meet my eyes, like she knows she's done something wrong and she's afraid I'm going to fault her for it.

"Collins," Charlie says, holding out a fist like he expects me to bump it. I don't. He moves his fist toward Dean instead. "Hey, man. I'm Charlie."

Dean smirks. "The famous Charlie." They bump fists and then

launch into a discussion of Being Old and In College.

The parents corral us into a big group so they can take a picture, and then it's time to go. We pile into our limo—all the parents waving and crying and telling us to be safe, and I know I'm supposed to be having fun, but everything feels so twisted.

The second the doors close, Ava pulls out a full bottle of champagne from her bag like she's Mary Poppins.

"Who wants some bubbly?" She hands the bottle to Ryder to open, shrieking when the cork pops. Everyone collectively relaxes, way too willing to drink away a little of the awkwardness.

The limo drives us around the edge of the lake and I look out the window at the water. It's almost sunset now, and the light is catching on the surface in that golden way that reminds me of summer camp, of the feeling at the end of August when you know everything is ending.

Dean's hand is draped casually over my leg like it belongs there. He and Ryder are laughing about something, passing the flask back and forth between them, but I'm not listening. All I can think about is how his hand feels on my skin, how the first time he ever laid his hand there it had electrified me, but now I feel nothing. He leans in and kisses the sensitive skin around my ear, and his breath smells like whiskey, making me shiver. I can't help but look a few seats to my left to where Andrew is sitting with Danielle, their faces practically connected.

Hannah and Charlie are across the bench from me and when Ava hands Hannah the bottle of champagne, Charlie reaches up to run his hand over Hannah's thick braid, pulling lightly like he never lost the right to touch her. That one little movement makes me so mad. Hannah takes a sip of the champagne and then she hands it to me. Our eyes meet and I tilt my head to the side, trying to tell her with my expression everything that's so messed up about this situation. How could she have been so right about Andrew but so wrong about this?

Andrew laughs about something and then kisses the inside of Danielle's wrist. It's like a ripple effect around the car. Cecilia wraps her arms around Chase's bicep and snuggles her nose into the collar of his shirt, and I feel myself leaning closer to Dean, letting his hand crawl higher up my knee. I hate that I'm reacting the same way as Cecilia—that we're both just two girls Andrew's cast aside.

"I'm excited for tonight," I whisper into Dean's ear, because I'm trying to convince myself I am. If Andrew can have meaningless hookups, so can I. I don't have to like Dean to sleep with him. I can sleep with him because he's hot, and it's prom, and everything is perfect. Why would I waste a moment like this one?

"Me too." His eyes light up like he wasn't sure until right this second that I'd follow through.

We pull up to the Walcott and everyone piles out. The whole place is strung with twinkle lights crisscrossing over the ceiling like the sky is enchanted. The walls inside the ballroom are hung with giant cardboard waves painted in blue glitter, and there's a bubble machine at the entrance. "It's so whimsical!" Ava squeals when she sees it, and then she's twirling and we all follow her in.

There's a buffet table, large platters of chicken and salad and risotto no one is touching, and a bowl of punch that—if teen movies are to be believed—I should stay far away from. Sophie Piznarski is at a table scattered with cookies and brownies, and she's holding a basket of muffins, offering it to everyone who walks by. It's like student council forgot we'd all be too nervous to eat. But maybe that's just me. Andrew will probably eat three whole chickens and still be hungry.

Sophie holds the basket out to us. "Don't forget to vote for King and Queen!"

"Can you actually vote in a monarchy?" I ask, and Hannah laughs and then her face hardens again like she's not sure if she's allowed to think I'm funny right now.

Danielle makes us stop at the table, her laser-beam eyes making it clear who we're supposed to vote for. I write down Hannah's name, a silent apology that she can't see. The guys keep walking and sit down at one of the tables on the edge of the dance floor. And it is so weird to see Andrew and Dean together.

"Did you make these?" Danielle asks, picking up a cookie.

"No, they're from Green Mountain," Sophie answers, and Danielle drops the cookie back into the basket. Sophie frowns. "You don't have to eat one."

I reach into the basket and pull out a blueberry muffin to be polite, but I know I'm too anxious to eat it.

"I'm saving up for Taco Bell later." Ava wobbles on her heels. "If I drink any more coca-kale-a, I think I might puke."

"She only needs to fit into her dress long enough for Ryder to take it off her," Danielle says.

Sophie sets down the muffin basket. "Wait, are you guys are going to . . . you know?"

"Gross," Ava says.

Danielle raises an eyebrow. "Yeah, I'd say odds are in his favor."

"Okay, can I tell you guys something though?" Ava lowers her voice to a conspiratorial whisper. "Ryder is actually kinda the worst in bed. It's like he just copies all this awful stuff from porn and doesn't care if I'm even into it."

"You watch porn?" I ask. I was too scared to even google sex tips on my phone. Maybe I should have gone to Ava for advice all along.

"Everyone watches porn," Ava says. "Sometimes you have to get things done yourself."

"I don't," Sophie counters.

"Well, someone should tell Ryder to stop with all the teeth," Ava says. "Vampires are only hot in movies."

We all laugh, but I can't help wondering why Ava hasn't said anything to him. But I guess I'm doing the same thing with Dean. Why is it so much harder to be honest about what we want when we're naked?

"Who are you here with?" Danielle asks Sophie, as if she doesn't already know. Prescott is too small for mystery.

"Jarrod Price," Sophie says. "You're here with Andrew, right?"

"Yeah." Danielle breaks off a piece of a chocolate muffin and pops it into her mouth. "No hard feelings?" She's speaking to Sophie but her eyes flick over to me for just a second. I look away.

"My thing with Andrew was ages ago," Sophie says, then turns her gaze on me. "You're with that guy Dean, right? He's so cute."

"So cute!" Ava repeats, pronouncing the word *cayooot*, like it has two syllables.

"You're so lucky." Sophie is looking over my shoulder to where the boys are, and I turn around to see. There's no denying how good Dean looks under the flashing lights. He's taken off his suit jacket and has rolled up the sleeves of his white button-down so that we can all see the tan skin of his arms. I know how it must look to Sophie. Why she thinks I'm lucky.

"Thanks," I say, trying to feel excited. Mostly I just have a stomachache. I put the muffin down.

"She's going to get even *luckier* later," Danielle says, breaking into a wicked smile. She has a glint in her eye I know means she's up to something.

"Come on, Danielle," Hannah says, a warning in her voice that gives me hope she won't hate me forever.

Danielle ignores her and leans closer to Sophie. "Not everyone gets to lose it at the Walcott."

Apparently, I'm supposed to keep all her secrets, but she can't keep mine.

"No way!" Sophie squeals, clapping her hands over her mouth. "Keely, this is so exciting. You're going to have the best night. Prom night is kind of perfect. Maybe not as perfect as your wedding night, but the next best thing, right? Do you love him?"

Love him? The question is so ridiculous I almost laugh. But Sophie isn't kidding. She's looking at me with big, sincere blue eyes. When I don't answer right away, she blinks and clears her throat.

"I didn't mean to put you on the spot. It's fine if you don't, I just—"

"No, it's okay," I say, trying to smile. "I don't love him. I just want . . ."

What? I just want to get it over with? I just want to take my mind off things, to forget about Andrew for a while, to use Dean as a distraction? I wish I knew what I wanted. Wouldn't that make everything so much easier? I wish I loved him. If I loved Dean, then maybe I could forget for a second that Andrew loves Danielle.

"It's just the right time, isn't it?" I say, the best answer I can give.

"I wouldn't know," Sophie says. "I'm waiting for marriage."

"What?" I ask. "You're still—"

"A virgin?" Sophie finishes. "Yeah. It's no big deal. I'm just not ready yet. I'd rather wait until I know someone loves me, you know? The guys at this school aren't worth it."

"But what about Andrew?" I glance over my shoulder again and see that Andrew and Chase have started dancing, jumping up and down in that silly way guys do when they're showing off. Andrew notices me looking and waves a hand in our direction, at me or maybe at Sophie or Danielle, motioning for us to come join them. The genuine glee on his face makes my chest ache.

"Andrew didn't love me," Sophie says. "You should know that better than anyone."

"Of course he did," I say. But we both know it isn't true. I think back to all the times he complained to me about her. Andrew and Sophie had been all wrong for each other. Maybe Sophie knew it all along. I haven't given her enough credit.

"It's fine, Keely," Sophie says, smiling. "He wasn't the one. Actually, he was a pretty bad boyfriend. I always thought, I mean, we broke up because he just wouldn't—" She stops suddenly, turning to look at Danielle. "Never mind, sorry. I shouldn't be bashing your date like this." She stands up and grabs the handle of the muffin basket. "I'll just keep handing out these muffins and you can forget I even said anything."

"He just wouldn't what?" Danielle asks. She's not one to let statements hang unsaid in the air. Sophie sighs and looks back at me.

"He wouldn't stop talking about you, Keely. It was exhausting."

"We're just friends," I say immediately, the line coming naturally. But her words ignite something in me and suddenly I feel like I'm a hot wire.

"Yeah," Sophie says. She picks up a blueberry muffin, ripping a bite off the top. Grainy sugar crumbs sprinkle down onto the surface of the table. "I get that now."

THIRTY

WE HEAD OVER to the table to dump our purses and then grab the guys, pulling the rest of them out onto the dance floor. The song is upbeat and happy and despite everything going on, the fact that everybody in the circle is probably mad at somebody else, none of it matters. This might be the last time we're all together, one big messed-up group, and I think we're all feeling the pull of time.

The song changes to something slow and we break apart to dance with our dates. I wrap my arms around Dean's neck and feel his skin, damp and sticky. He passes me the flask and I take a quick sip. I'm so used to the taste of whiskey at this point I almost like it. Or maybe I'm just trying to convince myself I do.

A fast song starts up and we're all together again and I throw my arms up in the air and I'm spinning and dizzy and happy. The music slows and we all put our arms around each other so that we're rocking back and forth in one big circle. And then before I know what's happening, Chase has snaked an arm around

Danielle's shoulders and they're dancing alone. I expect her to pull away from him—after all, hasn't she been pulling away from him every day since my birthday?—but she doesn't. She's laughing and pulling him closer.

It's like we've all been waiting to follow her lead, because as soon as she accepts Chase's dance, we break apart in different directions. Hannah lunges for Dean, pulling him into her, and before I can change my mind, I reach for Andrew. I nod my head in thanks to Hannah, knowing she's doing me this favor on purpose. She nods back, and in that moment I know that she *knows*. I don't have to tell her she's right.

"Hey," I say, placing my hands on his shoulders.

"Hey," he says, and wraps his arms around my lower back. I'm trying to keep a respectable distance between us because everyone is watching, but he moves closer, so I'm forced to wrap my arms around his neck. We're touching all the way from our hips to our chests. I know it's wrong to be this close, that I'm only torturing myself, but it feels right to be fitted together like this, like we're matching puzzle pieces. I rest my head on his chest and wish I were tall enough to brush my lips against the soft skin of his neck. He smells familiar, like cut grass, the same way he smelled when he was over me on his bed, his body covering mine. The music is playing soft and slow around us, but I can barely hear it. All I can hear is my heart beating, the blood rushing in my ears. I know if I pull my head back just slightly, I could kiss him. I keep my head locked on his shoulder so I won't be tempted. I feel suddenly like I'm about to cry. It was so much easier before I realized I loved him. I want to rewind the last few hours and become that girl again.

"Are you having fun?" The sound of his voice is close enough to tickle my ear. I nod my head and bury my nose into his chest. I'm worried he can sense how I feel, that he can read the truth of it on my face.

"I'm going to miss you," I say, pulling away from him far enough that we can see each other.

"Collins," he says softly, reaching a hand up to my cheek. He must notice my eyes are watering. "Are you okay?" His expression makes me want to tell him everything.

"I . . ." The words catch in my throat. I know they're too powerful, that even though they're just words, their meaning will change everything. They're words that can't be unsaid. Besides, what would be the point?

"Keely," he says, his thumb brushing lightly against the sensitive skin of my cheek. It's strange to hear my first name from him, and the sound of it feels intimate and personal, like he's seeing me naked.

"Drew, I—" I start to speak but the music changes to something fast and wild and the thumping beat feels like a slap. I remember suddenly where we are, the people surrounding us. It feels like I've been dunked into the cold water of the lake.

"Did that make you jealous?" Danielle asks Andrew, grinning and pulling on his arm. "If I tell you Chase is a better dancer than you, will you be mad?" Before Andrew can answer, Ava comes flying at us, tripping on her heels and using me as support so she doesn't fall.

"Want some champagne?" She holds up a new full bottle. I don't know where she found it and how she hasn't gotten in trouble yet.

An arm circles my waist and I turn to see Dean behind me. I let myself lean against him, nervous about what he might have seen between Andrew and me. I wonder if Dean can tell how I feel. If he even cares.

"Ava, put that bottle away," Danielle hisses. "You're a mess. Where did you even get that?"

Ava takes a long sip. "I pulled it out of your ass."

Just then the music cuts out and a voice comes over the speakers. "If everyone could take their seats, we're going to start the crowning in a few minutes."

Our principal, Mr. Harrison, is on a raised platform at the other end of the ballroom, holding a stack of white envelopes. We all head to our seats. I end up between Dean and Charlie, so I lean as close as I can to Dean and completely ignore Charlie when he asks me if I can hand him a soda. Andrew is across from me with Danielle, so I focus instead on watching Ava and Ryder, who are taking turns with the flask.

"Can you guys hear me?" Mr. Harrison asks. There's an unenthusiastic murmuring from the crowd.

"Oh, just get on with it," Danielle hisses, taking a sip of her soda. She sets it down on the table and brings a hand up to smooth down her hair. She doesn't need to. She still looks perfect.

"You seem pretty confident," Ava whispers in the loud way people do when they're tipsy.

"I am," Danielle says. "I mean, it's kind of obvious." She pauses for a second and then looks around at all of us. "No offense."

"Oh, it's obvious?" Ava asks, her voice rising a few decibels. Ava has never been good at keeping quiet, and now that she's had a few glasses of champagne, she's projecting in her full musical theater voice. She folds her arms in front of her, raising her boobs up in the process, so they're dangerously close to spilling out of her strapless gown. "I'm glad it's so obvious to you. Wouldn't want any of the rest of us to get our hopes up."

Mr. Harrison's voice comes again, amplified across the ballroom. "All right, so prom court is only open to senior Prescott students. Apologies to all of you underclassmen. You'll get your shot later."

"Oh please, Ava," Danielle says. She motions a hand toward Ava's cleavage. "You shouldn't go up onstage anyway, because you'll just flash everyone. I'm saving you the humiliation. Like usual."

"Come on, guys," Hannah whispers. "It's just stupid prom. This isn't the Nobel Peace Prize."

Ava's face remains stony, her gaze fixed on Danielle across the table. Her eyes are glistening slightly in the corners, matching the sparkling glitter on her eyelids. She takes a quick breath, and when she speaks, her voice is high and strained.

"Well, I don't think they'd give Prom Queen to someone who tastes like rotten fish."

Danielle's head snaps around and her eyes bulge. "What did you just say to me?"

Ava's bottom lip quivers, but she stares unblinkingly back at Danielle. Andrew is looking straight ahead, back rigid, eyes on the stage. His ears are pink.

Mr. Harrison speaks again. "Can I get a big round of applause for the folks at the Walcott for helping out with this event?" There's a smattering of weak applause. "And for the prom committee for all their dedicated work. You guys rock! It really does look like we're under the sea."

Dean leans close to me, nudging his shoulder against mine, and whispers in my ear. "Now do you get why it's so high school?"

He laughs. "What do you think—*Heathers* or *Mean Girls*? I guess it depends what decade you're into."

"Not everything has to be a movie reference," I spit, more aggressively than I mean to. I *love* movie references. But sometimes it feels like they're all Dean has.

"I said," Ava starts, "I don't think they'd give Prom Queen to someone who—"

"I heard what you said," Danielle snaps. "I just want to know why you said it. Why the *fuck* would you say that to me?" Her voice is rising in volume, and at the curse word a few people at the next table look over. She sighs and lowers her voice. "I think you've had too much to drink."

"Oh look, you're telling me what to do again," Ava says. "Surprise, surprise, surprise."

"Can you just cool it?" Danielle hisses. "You're totally out of line."

Ava raises her hand up in a salute. "Yes, Your Majesty."

Dean snorts next to me and covers his mouth, fighting off a laugh.

Mr. Harrison speaks again, and I turn back to the stage. "All right, so let me bring up the head of your prom committee. She's got a few announcements to make for you guys, so hold tight. Sophie Piznarski!"

As Sophie walks up the steps and takes the microphone, I can't help flashing back to what she told us earlier. I can't believe I didn't know Sophie is a virgin too.

Ava is speaking again. "Am I allowed to take another sip of my drink?" She holds up her glass, tilting it forward so some of the liquid threatens to spill out and onto the table. "Or is that against your rules?"

"Do what you want," Danielle snaps. "You're already a train wreck."

Ava sets her glass down with a *thunk*. Her expression looks hurt, eyes big and droopy like a puppy that's just been kicked. Her bottom lip quivers again, like she's holding back tears. And then she takes a breath, pressing her lips together in a hard line. Her eyes narrow, hurt flashing into anger. "I wrote everything."

Danielle doesn't move, doesn't give any indication she's heard Ava at all. But then I see her hand, the one resting on the table, clench into a fist. She turns to Ava slowly. "I need to talk to you. I need to talk to you *outside* so there won't be any witnesses when I kill you." She stands up, her knees knocking against the table, and grabs Ava by the arm.

"Ow!" Ava whines, trying to shake off Danielle's hand, which has settled clawlike into the skin of her arm. They disappear through the side door. I look up at Hannah, hoping she'll know what to do.

"I think she might really kill her," I say. "Should we . . ."

She follows my gaze over to the door and then we both jump up and follow them. When we get outside, we almost run over Susie Palmer, who's leaning against the wall, smoking. I know she's probably hiding—from Ryder and Ava; from the fact that she was his first choice last night and now she's not. It's easier to hide than to act like you don't care.

"They went down to the dock," she says, motioning with her cigarette.

"Thanks," Hannah says, and we head in the direction she pointed.

The light shining from the windows of the Walcott makes it difficult to see anything beyond, but I can just make out the shape of the lake, spread out huge and dark in front of us. We walk across the grass and over to a set of steps leading down to a wooden dock. I can hear Ava and Danielle before I can see them, their voices high and shrill. We walk closer and their fuzzy dark outlines come into view.

Hannah holds out an arm to stop me. "We should let them fight it out. They have a lot to resolve."

"Did you know it was Ava?"

Hannah sighs. "I didn't know for sure, but I guessed."

I don't know why it never occurred to me. I was so fixated on the guys, so sure that these ugly words were from them. But Ryder doesn't have the finesse or the subtlety for a pain like this one—when guys hurt you they want the credit. Girls are best at the cuts beneath the surface, the bites you don't see coming until you're dragged underwater. And Ava has been taking those bites from Danielle for too long—it was only a matter of time before she bit back. Still, it breaks my heart to see their friendship turned into something so ugly. Danielle and Ava were each other's everything once, and now they've ended up like this. I can't let that happen with Hannah.

"I'm sorry about Charlie. What I said." Hannah has always supported me—has always been such a wonderful, beautiful friend. I need to be the same for her.

"You're right though," Hannah says. Her voice is shaky. "I know I shouldn't, but . . . I still have feelings for him. He stopped by my house this morning and said he wanted to take me to prom and I just couldn't say no. I'm so *weak*."

"You're not weak. You're in love."

"Sometimes I think it's the same thing."

And then because Hannah is being so honest, I know I have

to be too. "Turns out you were right too. About Andrew." Even though saying it makes me sad, Hannah's face lights up like I've given her the best news. I guess I just need to let her be happy about it.

We stop at the edge of the dock, but Danielle and Ava don't notice us.

Ava is crying, one hand waving angrily in the air, the other holding up her dress. "All I ever did was try to be your friend—for eight years—I tried so hard, and you just knocked me down." Her voice is shaky with tears.

"My *friend*, Ava?" Danielle says. "If you had a problem with me, you should have told me. Real friends talk shit to your face and not behind your back."

"Real friends don't talk shit at all, Danielle. That's what you don't get. You're so mean to me. All the time. You stopped being my friend years ago. You've just become such . . . such a *bitch*!"

"Oh, so I'm a bitch now too? Why don't you write that on a note." Danielle digs through her champagne-sequined purse and pulls out a pen, throwing it at Ava. "Let's see . . . I'm a bitch, a slut, what next? Come on, Ava. There's no way to win, is there? You're a slut if you do, a tease if you *almost* do, a prude if you don't, and a bitch if you stand up for yourself. I'm sick of the name-calling. We should have each other's backs."

Ava clicks her tongue against her teeth and laughs. "Seriously? You've been calling me a slut for years."

Danielle crosses her arms. "I don't use that word."

Ava raises her voice in an impression of Danielle. "Oh, Ava, what do you know about being a virgin? Oh, Ava, are you gonna fuck Ryder again? Stop humping everything that moves, Ava. You're embarrassing yourself."

"You're embarrassing yourself now."

"I don't care anymore." Ava's voice is strained, like she's fighting to speak and breathe at the same time. "I just couldn't get through to you. You don't see me as your equal. I'm not just your stupid sidekick. Sometimes it's *my* story. Not yours."

"Oh please," Danielle says. "Don't martyr yourself. If you felt like a stupid sidekick, you could have done something about it."

"I did!" Ava shrieks. "I wrote those freaking notes!"

"And how did you think that would change things? What, you thought calling me a slut would miraculously make things better for you? You're just making guys like Ryder think they're right. You don't get power by knocking other girls down."

Ava shrieks, a high animal sound, like someone has just stepped on her tail. "You're such a hypocrite! That's totally how *you* get your power. You've always gotten off on knocking me down. You're like a social vampire." She wipes at her cheeks. Her hair has come down from its chignon, and there are bobby pins sticking out at weird angles around the base of her neck. She starts yanking them out and throwing them onto the ground. "I like Chase. I've liked him for years. You *knew* that. But then suddenly you decided *you* had to have him, and that was more important. You slept with him at that stupid party, and you didn't even like him! You dropped him right after you finally got what you wanted. How do you think that made me feel?"

Danielle sighed. "I didn't . . . drop him because I was done with him. I dropped him because he was done with me. He fucked me and then told everybody about it! And then I'm supposed to wait around for him to tell me *he's* done? Please don't tell me all of this"—she motions back and forth between herself and Ava—"is about Chase, because he's not worth it."

"It's not about Chase," Ava says. "It's about you taking something you knew I wanted because you knew you could. And you're doing it all over again with Andrew! You're only here with him because of Keely." I flinch at her words.

Ava pulls out the final bobby pin and her hair tumbles over her shoulders in purple waves. She throws the pin at Danielle. "I'm surprised you never fucked Charlie. Hannah would have flipped and you would have loved it."

Danielle lunges at her, grabbing hold of the necklace around Ava's neck, and as she pulls away, beads fly everywhere— scattering and rolling across the dock in all directions. Ava grabs a strap of Danielle's gown, pulling and ripping so that it tears, and Danielle shrieks.

"Stop!" I say, and Hannah and I rush toward them. We grab on to their arms, trying to pull them off each other. Ava turns to me and her eyes are wild, like she's gone mad. Her blue, glittery makeup has smeared down the side of her temples, and there are mascara tracks down her cheeks.

"I don't need your help!" she wails. She shrugs my hands off, and I grab her again, trying to keep her steady, keep her calm, but she's howling and flailing like a woman possessed. I try to grab for her but she's tottering on her heels, and then suddenly she's falling backward, tipping slowly away from me. Her arm shoots forward, reaching for something to hold, finding only air. And then she's gone, over the side of the dock and into the water.

There's a loud splash.

Danielle stops grappling with Hannah and turns. "Oh, *come on*," she says. "I'll get her." And then she jumps in after Ava.

"I'll go get a teacher," I say, turning away from the lake and back toward the Walcott. I begin moving toward the other end of the dock, but I hear a gasp from behind me and turn back to the lake. Danielle and Ava have just burst through the surface, and Hannah is on her knees, pulling them up. The water is deep enough that only their heads are exposed, but it looks like they can stand. Hannah grabs Ava by the shoulders and Danielle hoists her from below up and onto the dock, where she sputters and coughs. Then Hannah grabs Danielle.

"Hannah!" A voice shouts from the top of the steps, and the figure of a girl appears, her silhouette dark against the bright windows. "Hannah!" she calls again, running down the steps toward us. As she gets closer I see that it's Susie Palmer, her pale skin luminescent in the moonlight. She freezes when she sees the group of us, Danielle and Ava lying on the wet dock, their dresses like a puddle of melted ice cream. "Um, Hannah?" she says when she gets to us. "They're looking for you inside. They called your name and no one could find you. You're supposed to go dance with Chase."

"What?" Hannah asks, confused. The front of her gown is wet where she pulled Ava from the water. Her braid is falling out, her bangs flattened to her forehead. I can tell she's still buzzing from what's happened and doesn't understand what's going on. But I know. It's obvious, should have been obvious all along.

"You're Prom Queen."

THIRTY-ONE

SOMEHOW EVERYTHING has gone to shit.

After Chase and Hannah's dance as King and Queen, after Danielle and Ava finally come back inside, leaving the floor so wet that Edwin Chang slips and falls, I find myself tired out, sitting back at the table and not really in the mood to dance. It's getting late. Some of the cardboard waves have fallen off the walls, and one of the bubble machines has malfunctioned.

Dean is with Ryder somewhere, probably outside smoking, and I can't be bothered to look for him. I sigh and stand up, heading over to get more punch. At this point, who cares if it's spiked?

"Shitty prom, huh?" Chase says, coming up behind me.

"Yeah." I scoop myself a cup of punch and then scoop one for him. "How's Cecilia?"

He takes a sip of punch, leaving a thin red stain on his upper lip. "She's nice," he says, his voice flat.

"And that's the problem?"

THE BEST LAID PLANS

"I'm not really into nice."

We both turn and look over to where Danielle and Ava are still being cleaned up and dried off by the chaperones.

"Where's your date?" Chase asks.

"Who knows," I say, taking another sip of punch. For some reason, I feel like being honest.

"You don't like him that much," Chase says, not a question.

"It's nice to have someone to come with."

"What do you mean?" Chase takes another sip. "You could have come with any of us."

"As a friend," I say. "I mean, it's not like any of you guys ever . . . hit on me. I'm not a real girl. I don't count."

"Come on, Collins, you're hot." He says it so casually, catching me off guard.

"What?"

"That's really why you think no guys ever hit on you?"

"Well, yeah," I say. "I mean, you guys talk about all your weird bodily functions in front of me, so clearly you're not—"

"No guys ever hit on you because you were with Reed." I stiffen at his words. If only Chase knew how much I wish what he was saying were true.

"I'm not *with* Reed," I say, running a frustrated hand through my hair. "You know he's with Danielle. And like five million other girls." My voice comes out in a hiss and I hate how jealous I sound. It was never supposed to be like this.

Chase just shakes his head. "Nah, I mean, I know you guys aren't dating, but you go together. You're a pair. Nobody wanted to get in the way of that. Besides, he's territorial as shit."

"What?" I set my cup of punch down on the table and a bit

of it splashes over the edge of the plastic rim, leaving a little red stain on the cheap white tablecloth.

"This one time in sixth grade, Ryder said something about how you were 'growing up nicely.'" He motions his hands in front of his chest to indicate Ryder's real meaning. "Andrew punched him."

I remember that, remember Andrew getting suspended for three days. He told me Ryder had pushed him first, an easy story to believe.

"That's why Ryder always made a show of treating you like one of the guys," Chase continues. "That's why we all did, I guess. We all like Reed, so you were off-limits." He downs the rest of his punch in one gulp and tosses the empty cup into the trash can beside us.

I can't help the pressure that starts building in my chest, like I'm slowly expanding from the inside out, filling up with air. Chase's words are repeating in my head. *You go together. You're a pair. You were off-limits.* It has to mean something, doesn't it? Why would Andrew warn other guys away from me if he didn't have feelings, if some small part of him didn't want me for himself?

I scan the crowd behind Chase's head, looking for Andrew, but he's not there. I turn around to look at the tables behind us, scanning all the seats quickly for a sandy-colored head, but he's nowhere.

Could Andrew actually like me back?

"Looks like you found a date anyway though," Chase says. "It just took a dude who doesn't go to Prescott to scoop you up, someone who doesn't know the rules."

I pick my cup of punch back off the table and notice that my hand is shaking. "And what are the rules?"

Chase grins. "It's the guy code." He leans toward me and lowers his voice like he's letting me in on a secret. "Never ditch your bros for a ho . . . *sorry*," he says when I wince at the word. "Never let a guy get in a fight alone, and *never* go after another guy's sister. You might not be his real sister, but in terms of the code, you definitely count."

And there it is. *Sister.* The word crashes down on me; the balloon in my chest pops and deflates. Of course that's what Chase meant. He's still grinning at me, like he's proud that he's let me in on the code, like I should feel special and not like my entire world has shattered into a million different pieces, my hope exploding like the Death Star.

I crush the empty plastic cup in my hand and throw it into the trash can.

"I have to go," I say, suddenly filled with anger, like my veins are crackling with electricity. It all makes sense. I might have met a guy earlier, might not have stayed a virgin for so long if Andrew hadn't gotten in the way. And it's not because he's been jealous, because he loves me back. It's just because I'm like his sister.

"I would have hit on you, you know," Chase says. "Just for the record. You're totally cute." And then he smiles and heads over to Danielle and Ava, throwing his arms around both of them.

My hands are shaking. I need to find Andrew. I move to the edge of the room, pushing through crowds of people. The whole world is whirling color, shapes moving together in and out of focus, and it feels like I'm drunk. But it's just the energy spreading through me like fire, blurring the edges of my vision. I can't remember ever being so alert.

And then I see him coming out of the men's bathroom and I'm struck by how much I want to hit him or kiss him or both, anything to just be touching him, to release some of this energy into him so that he can feel just as alive as I do.

I charge in his direction. When he notices me, his face breaks into an easy smile, but it soon disappears when I fly at him.

"You told guys not to hit on me?"

"What?" His forehead wrinkles and his hand immediately goes up into his hair like I knew it would, like it always does.

"What gives you the right, Drew? All this time I thought nobody liked me because of *me*, and all along it was because of *you*. All these parties you've been getting with girls and I've had to go sleep on the couch by myself, and I was so lonely and left out because everyone else was hooking up and getting boyfriends and having sex and I thought something was wrong with me, when it was all your fault!"

"Collins, what are you talking about?" he asks, leaning into me with his voice lowered. I'm vaguely aware we're still in the ballroom, surrounded by people. Abby Feliciano is standing a few feet to our left, texting something on her phone, and when I look at her, she giggles and looks away. But I don't care.

"You're such a hypocrite!" I hit him on the shoulder. "You're allowed to sleep with every girl on the planet and I'm not allowed to get with anyone? Is it because I'm a girl, Drew? I'm just a delicate freaking flower you have to look after? I don't need you to protect me. I never stopped girls from getting with you. I was the best wingman!"

The Wingman and the Cockblock. We're like a depressing superhero duo of doom.

"I know you're not a delicate flower," he says, reaching out to me. He puts a hand on my shoulder and I shrug it off. "Clearly. Come on, Collins, I just didn't want you to get your heart broken."

"My heart isn't your problem," I say, and my voice cracks, because of course I want it to be. "You should have let me get my heart broken. That's just a part of life, isn't it? You can't keep me locked away in a tower like freaking Rapunzel!" He takes a step toward me and I take a step back, needing to get away from him before I do something stupid. "You're not my brother or my boyfriend."

"Keely, I didn't mean . . . I just know these guys and I hear the way they talk and I didn't want that for you. You deserve better. You deserve someone who loves you." His voice is soft and kind and it kills me.

"Well, how am I supposed to find that if you won't let anyone near me?"

"You found someone anyway, didn't you?" he says. "Where's your date?"

"I don't know," I answer. He could be standing right behind me at this point and I wouldn't notice. My entire focus is on this conversation, on this fight. "Did you tell him to stay away too?"

"Of course he's missing." Andrew sighs. He shoves his hands into his pockets. "Typical."

"Why do you hate him?" I'm yelling now, and I can see that Abby has completely given up on her text, watching us with rapt attention.

"I don't hate him," he says, and then shakes his head, pulling his hands out of his pockets. "Actually, you know what, I do hate him. I have every right to. You *used* me to get with him. You fucking said his name while we were hooking up. You're the hypocrite, Collins. You get mad at me for using girls, for hooking up with girls when it doesn't mean anything, but you're the master at using people. You didn't even care about my feelings."

"You never care about anyone's feelings!" I say, throwing my hands into the air. "You've been sleeping with girls for years, throwing them away the second something better comes along."

"No I haven't!" he shouts.

"Are you kidding? You've—"

"I haven't been sleeping with anyone!" He looks quickly behind him and then takes my arm and pulls me farther into the corner, out of earshot.

"What are you talking about?" I say, pulling my arm out of his grip.

"I haven't . . ." He pauses, and his voice is so quiet I can barely hear him over the thumping of the music. "I haven't slept . . . with anyone. Ever."

"That's not . . ." *That's not true*, I want to say. But—he never slept with Cecilia, she said so herself, never slept with Sophie, because she's waiting until marriage.

"You're a virgin?" I ask, feeling as small as my voice.

"Yeah."

It all makes sense now—why he's been acting so cagey around me. It's because, this whole time, he's been scared I'll find out the truth.

"You lied to me," I say. "I thought . . . you let me believe you were some sort of expert. I never would have . . ."

"Come on, Collins, that's not fair. What was I supposed to say? You came to me and you were so vulnerable and I just wanted to help you. I just felt bad—"

"You felt bad for me," I say, the words hitting me like a punch to the gut. Could I be any more pathetic? "You could have told me the truth. I feel like such an idiot. I asked for your help, I wanted your advice, and you didn't know anything either."

"It's not easy for guys to just . . . admit they don't know anything. I never lied to you, I just didn't correct you when you assumed—"

"You made it pretty easy to assume!" I think of all the times he's told me about his hookups, how I never once asked for clarification on what the term meant; how convenient that must have been for him. Hooking up can mean so many different things: making out on a dance floor, a hand job at the movie theater, going almost all the way in someone's bed but changing your mind.

"There are expectations when you're a guy," Andrew says. "There's pressure. Guys talk shit. And you've always had these ideas about me—Party Andrew. Everybody has these ideas about me now, and I can't just . . . I'm all fucking talk, okay? Is that what you want to hear? If people want to believe I'm some big player, I'm not going to correct anybody. You can't just admit to other dudes that it hasn't happened yet. That you want sex to be special. Nobody buys that."

"But I'm not just anybody," I say. "I'm *somebody*. I'm your most important somebody."

I'm not though; I realize as soon as I say it. "So you haven't slept with Danielle." It's a statement, not a question. He doesn't answer, and I let the word hanging between us unsaid come to the surface: "Yet."

He rubs the back of his neck and doesn't answer, but he doesn't need to.

"Why?" I ask.

"What?"

"You've had plenty of opportunities. Why did you let Chase get there first?"

He takes a long time to answer, like even now the words are hard for him to admit. "It's not a race, Collins."

"Are you sure?" Because that's how it's felt so far—like high school is one big competition and I'm the one losing.

Just then, I feel a heavy arm on my shoulder, the familiar smell of aftershave and tobacco that once made me so giddy, and I know that it's Dean. Andrew's expression hardens and he stands up a little bit straighter, and I bristle, because there it is in action: there's the overprotective brother.

"What are you two fighting about now?" Dean asks, and the question makes me sad. Andrew and I have disintegrated so much—our friendship is so strained—that Dean assumes we're probably fighting about something. And even though Dean is the reason for it, it's my fault really. I was the one who couldn't be honest with myself, who couldn't be honest with Dean. I was the one who decided to risk my friendship with Andrew instead of telling Dean the truth. I'm the one who messed everything up.

"We're not fighting," Andrew says. Even though he's admitted his secret to me, I can tell he still doesn't want anyone to know.

"Oh thank God," Dean says, his tone flat and sarcastic. He nuzzles his face into my neck, tickling my skin with his nose. "It's getting pretty boring here. You want to head up to the room?"

I know I should answer Dean, but I can't look away from Andrew. His cheeks are red from our fight, and he's breathing hard. His hair is sticking up in all directions, and he looks, suddenly, so young, like the little boy I used to tell everything to.

And all I want to do is comfort him, even though I'm the reason he's upset in the first place. I want to leave everything behind—leave this ballroom, leave Dean, leave Prescott, and just be with him, just hold on to him and never let him go. But it's too late for that.

I know suddenly what his grand gesture is going to be. I know why he and Danielle got a room tonight. He's going to tell her he loves her and then he's going to sleep with her for the first time. His first time.

So I have to let him go.

I turn around and face Dean, placing my hands on either side of his chin and pulling his face toward mine. Then I kiss him like there's nobody else around—like we're already up in the room. I kiss him like it's a promise. When I pull back, I can see his pupils have dilated.

"Yeah, let's head up to the room," I say, my voice scratchy.

He begins to lead me away and I let him, following him toward the exit. I don't want to look back at Andrew, but I can't help it and at the last second I turn and look behind me, afraid of what I'll see on his face.

But he isn't there anymore. I don't know when he left. Maybe it was a long time ago.

THIRTY-TWO

THE ROOM IS beautiful. It's everything you'd expect in an old hotel—dark wooden beams crisscrossing the ceiling, a red carpet and plush armchair, a fireplace with a coat of arms over it like we're no longer in Vermont but in some European castle far, far away. Best of all (though it doesn't feel that way right now) there's a giant four-poster bed.

Dean heads directly for the bed, pulling me with him. The sheets feel like they're made of butter, like you could melt into them. It's like we're in a movie—this is exactly the moment I wanted it to be. It's exactly the right time.

I feel like I'm going to throw up.

Dean kisses me and I kiss him back but then pull away and slide a few feet away from him, so there's a respectable space between us on the bed.

"Thanks for coming with me tonight," I say, because I need to fill the silence.

"No problem," he says. Then he breaks into a smile and I can see the joke forming behind his eyes. "I'll come with you all night."

I try to laugh, but I feel a bit dizzy and the sound doesn't come out quite right. I can still hear the thumping bass of the music coming from downstairs, but everything is muffled. Dean reaches over and takes my hand in his and I remember when that feeling, his skin on mine, was the most wonderful feeling in the world. I want that feeling back.

"Are you having a good time?" I ask, trying to stall.

"I'm having a good time now," he says. "Now that we're alone." He tucks a strand of hair behind my ear, resting his warm palm against my cheek. "This is what prom is about, isn't it? You and me? It's not about that other shit. That other shit is what we have to deal with to get to this."

"That other shit—those are my friends."

"Are they, Keely? Are you sure? You're better than that."

Sometimes it feels like Dean is telling me things he *wants* to be true, not things that actually are. What makes me any better than the other girls at school? *Why me, Dean?* Is it just because I'm a challenge?

An image flashes through my mind of Andrew and Danielle dancing downstairs, wrapped up in each other, his hands gripping her like he's scared she'll float away. That's what Andrew wants. So this is what I want. It has to be.

And maybe it's better like this. I wanted to get my first time out of the way with someone I didn't have feelings for. Now here we are. The girls who have it right are the ones like Ava—who sleep with whoever they want just because they want to. *You can't shame girls for liking sex just because you don't*, Andrew said to me once. And he's wrong, because I can like casual sex too. So what if he's about to have a moment, if he waited for the girl he loves? I've waited long enough.

Dean uses our clasped hands to pull me closer on the bed and I let him, leaning over to kiss him like it's everything that I want. His breath tastes like champagne and risotto, and the smell of his aftershave wraps me up. I'm trying to find the feeling I once had while kissing him—trying to find the swoop in my stomach. But it isn't there. His tongue is just a tongue—slimy and wet. The stubble on his face feels scratchy against my cheek.

It's funny how things work out, how everything flipped upside down and in the end I still got what I wanted: sex with a guy that didn't have to mean anything at all. It turns out the Plan wasn't such a bad idea after all; I just had the wrong guy in mind to do it.

Dean deepens the kiss and pulls me against him, threading his hand through my hair and pulling just a bit, just enough that I know he's into this. My eyes are closed and I let myself pretend for just a moment that he's Andrew instead, let myself envision the honey color of his hair, his smattering of freckles, his green eyes. I haven't kissed Andrew since I realized I love him, and I get light-headed at the thought of it.

Dean moves his hand down the side of my neck and then to the zipper at my back, trying to get it loose. I reach back and help him, because I want this too. I slide down the zipper and then stand up so he can peel the green dress off me. We leave it in a pool on the floor. Dean unbuttons and takes off his shirt and undershirt, and then I'm looking right at the tan muscles of his chest and they're mine if I want them, and I do. I run my hands down him, and he sucks in a sharp breath as I reach the V of muscle above his belt. He's so beautiful—his dark eyelashes, the hard edges of his cheekbones. I could cry because I should want this so much—anyone would want this.

I wonder if Andrew and Danielle have left the ballroom yet, if they've wandered up to their own room, their own four-poster bed. I can see him now—pulling her down the hallway, both of them giddy and laughing. He's pushing her up against the wall because he can't wait until they get to the room. Andrew always did like kissing girls against the wall. I've seen him do it so many times at so many parties, so why wouldn't he be doing that now?

I can see him fumbling with the key to the room, Danielle clucking impatiently, then taking it herself, opening the door and pulling him into the dark, stripping off the layers of his clothes until he's all skin.

I reach for Dean's belt buckle and work it open and then he lifts his hips and pulls down his pants, kicking them into some corner of the room. Once they're off and we're in just our underwear, he rolls his body onto mine and lies down, pressing me into the mattress.

My mind flashes to the last time I was in this position, a boy on top of me pressing me into a mattress strewn with flowers; how I felt more alive than I ever expected to feel with a boy who was just a friend, only a friend.

Dean reaches out toward my underwear and I pull away from him.

"Let me get a condom." I sit up, feeling light-headed at the rush of it, and bend over to find my purse.

"You brought a condom?" he asks.

I reach into my purse and rummage around, cursing myself for not cleaning the junk out of it before I took it to prom. It's still littered with old tissues, gum wrappers, and ticket stubs from movies I went to see months ago, and somehow the condom has gotten lost in the mess.

"If you can't find it, no biggie," Dean says. "I've got a bunch."

"I've got it." I dump the purse upside down onto the bed, and everything tumbles out, a tube of lipstick that my mom made me bring, my phone, a cracked pair of sunglasses, and the little square wrapper. I reach out for it but my hand stops on something else—a white cardboard square, rough around the edges. I flip it over and my breath hitches. It's a card, one I don't remember getting, one I must have been carrying around in my bag and never noticed. It has a Ninja Turtle drawn on it in Sharpie, a bunch of silly cartoon hearts. And then, in Andrew's scratchy writing: *Happy Birthday. I love you more than pizza.*

It's just like the valentine he sent to Danielle so many years ago, back in middle school. The one she didn't understand. What is this doing here? When did he slip it into my bag? Why hasn't he said anything? Did he make this for *me*?

"Did you find it?" Dean asks, coming up behind me and resting his head on my shoulder. "What are you looking at?"

"It's nothing," I say, closing my hand around the card. I don't want him to see it, because even if I don't understand it, it's wonderful and private and mine.

I love you more than pizza.

It doesn't add up—none of it makes sense. Danielle doesn't like Ninja Turtles, or pizza, or climbing trees, or riding her bike. She doesn't like skating on the lake in the winter, sledding down the big hill at turbo speed. She's not the one Andrew calls when he's upset, not the one he lies with in the hammock in his backyard, looking up at the stars. Maybe she's the one he kissed at a New Year's party, but she's not the one he made sure to spend the night with, not the one whose room he ended up in. The pieces don't fit. I can't forget the way he looked at me when he told me he was in love, the way he held my hand, how I thought for that brief moment that maybe he was going to say my name.

"I have to go," I say, stuffing everything back into my bag. I stand up and step into the circle that my dress has made on the floor, pulling it up and over me so quickly that I'm already dressed before Dean makes a move to stop me. If there's a chance—if there's one small chance Andrew could love me back, how can I possibly go through tonight without finding out?

"What the fuck?" Dean says, springing off the bed.

"I have to go," I repeat, heading toward the door.

"You can't just leave," he says. "You promised."

"Well, I changed my mind," I say.

"You can't do that," he says.

"Actually," I say, hand on the doorknob, "I can do whatever the hell I want."

"That's bullshit," he says.

"This whole thing is bullshit," I say, the truth of it making me laugh. "You and your pretentious shirts, and your motorcycle, and your movie references. It's like you're not even a real person. You're just trying so hard to be this cool guy. Well, I don't want someone cool! I want . . ." I think back to what Hannah said to me in the dressing room. "I want someone whose weirdness matches my weirdness!" I throw open the door and then stop suddenly, filled with the need to tell him the truth. "And just for the record, I *am* a virgin."

And then I'm running out of the room and to the elevator. Because I need to find him. I need to ask him about this card—need to find out if it's a mistake, if it's a joke, if it means nothing at all. I've been so in my head, so close to the situation that I haven't been able to grasp the cold, hard truth until now. Because the truth is: *I don't want to have sex with Dean.*

As soon as I think it, I feel suddenly free, like a heavy weight has been lifted off my shoulders and I might just float away. I always thought Dean was out of my league, that I had to pretend to be a better version of myself to impress him. But the realization that comes to me suddenly makes me laugh with relief: Dean isn't too good for me. *I'm* too good for *Dean.* I don't want a guy I can't be myself with; who made me so insecure I felt like I had to tell a lie.

And I can still be the adventurous Keely—the one who breaks the rules, who drinks whiskey and rides on the backs of motorcycles—without him. I just have to let go, to learn to take a risk, to tell Andrew how I feel before it's too late.

It's not a race, Andrew said, and he's right.

Except right now, as I careen out of the elevator and run through the lobby to find him, it kind of is.

THIRTY-THREE

I DIAL ANDREW'S number, but he doesn't answer. Either he's still in the ballroom and the music is too loud, or he's with Danielle and he's ignoring me. When I run through the double oak doors, past the fallen cardboard waves and the broken bubble machine, I realize the ballroom is mostly empty. I might be too late.

There are a few teachers standing over by the DJ booth, helping put everything away, some couples sitting down at the tables, their shoes in their hands. Abby Feliciano is on the side of the stage, crying about something. Jarrod Price is at the buffet table, picking at a tray of chicken. But that's it. I don't see any of my friends.

I check my phone. It's 11:30. It makes sense that most people would have left.

I turn around and head back to the lobby, calling Andrew once more for good measure as I approach the front desk. Again, he doesn't answer.

"I need some information about one of the guests here," I say to the concierge.

He's a middle-aged guy, purple bags under his eyes, and he looks at me with a blank, uninterested expression. "We don't give out any information about guests."

"I just need the room number," I explain. "My friends are staying in one of the rooms and I can't find them."

"Are you a relative?"

"No, but—" I say, and he stops me.

"Then I can't give you anything."

"I'm basically a relative," I say, knowing he won't understand, that he doesn't know the intricacies of the Reed and Collins families: our history. "It's an emergency," I say again. "Please."

"A prom emergency?" he asks, raising an eyebrow and looking me up and down.

This isn't how this is supposed to work. In movies, once you realize you're in love, you just hop in a taxi and race through traffic and get to the airport right in time—the power of true love and all that. I'm not supposed to be held up by a concierge. What if I don't get ahold of him at all? Or worse, what if I find him and it doesn't go the way I'm hoping, *praying*, that it does? I know he might love Danielle, that he might still want to be with her and I could be interrupting. But our friendship has already been ruined. If there's any chance at all he might feel the same way that I do, I have to tell him. It's what a Gryffindor would do.

I spin away, heading back in the direction of the elevators. Fine. If no one will tell me any of the information I need, I'll just have to find him myself.

The elevator doors *ding* open in front of me. There are twelve floors—twelve shiny gold buttons taunting me. He could be on any of them. I curse myself for not checking ahead of time where they were staying, for trying to act like I didn't care, as if asking any questions might give away my feelings. The elevator gets impatient with me and the doors close again and then reopen, reminding me I'm supposed to push a button or get the hell out. I sigh and go back into the hallway. If only there were some way to get him to leave the room—to force him to come back downstairs and away from Danielle. But there's not really anything that could possibly pull any teenage boy away from sex, especially sex with Danielle Oliver; probably only threat of death or fire.

And then it hits me, the idea so absurd I almost choke.

I look up at the wall in front of me, the beautiful filigreed wallpaper, the dark wooden beams crisscrossing just below the ceiling, and there it is, a little red box above my head with a white lever, black words printed across it: PULL DOWN IN CASE OF EMERGENCY. In case of emergency. Probably not what they had in mind, but an emergency all the same.

So I pull down.

The air around me shifts and stills, and I stop breathing, listening only to the steady beating of my heart in my chest—and then like a sleeping dragon roused from its slumber, the building roars to life. All around me alarms start wailing, high pitched and screeching, and when I run back into the lobby, everything is chaos.

"Everyone outside!" the concierge is shouting. "This is not a drill."

All the teachers have come back out of the ballroom, ushering students outside through the lobby. Jarrod Price runs by me with the entire tray full of chicken. Mr. Harrison looks pale, his face drawn, and I feel a rush of guilt that I'm the one who did this.

Sophie Piznarski is by the concierge desk, holding her shoes in one hand, and when she notices me, she hurls herself toward me. "Keely! What's happening? Is there a real fire?"

"Have you seen Andrew?" I ask her, which I realize is not a sensible response.

"What?" she asks, and suddenly her voice is high and wavering like she might cry. "Is he okay?"

"There's no fire," I say quickly, scanning the area behind her. People are rushing down the main staircase. Jason Ryder slides down the banister, laughing, and I can tell he's drunk. Ava is with him, wearing his suit jacket over her bra, her purple hair all over the place.

"I have to go," I say to Sophie, booking it over to Ava. "There's no fire!" I call out again behind my back, hoping she'll calm down. "Ava!" I almost crash into her.

"Everybody outside!" Mr. Harrison says, herding us toward the front doors. The crowd around us is growing and we get pushed through. The night air is warm and wet and things feel calmer now that the sound of the siren has muffled. I scan everywhere for Andrew but there are too many people and it's too dark.

We spot Chase standing in the crowd and head over to him.

"Dude!" Ryder says. "Prom was so lit it caught on fire!"

"Were you smoking in your room?" Chase says, and Ryder grins.

"Is everyone okay?" Ava shouts.

"Everyone's fine," I shout back. "I pulled the alarm."

They all gawk at me.

"What?" Chase asks. "Why?"

"Collins doesn't break rules," Ryder sputters to Chase, talking about me like I'm not even here.

"Where's Danielle?" I turn to Ava. "Do you know what room she was in?"

"Is she trapped?" Ava asks, her eyes going big.

"She's fine!" I say. "There's no fire." The crowd around us is growing and I know Andrew has to be out here somewhere, but I can't see him through the mass of bodies. "What room were Danielle and Andrew in?"

"I can't remember," Ava says. "I can text her and . . ." She pulls open her purse and starts to dig through and then stops mid-sentence. "I forgot our phones broke when we fell in the lake. Sorry."

"509," Chase says all of a sudden.

"What?" I turn my attention back to him.

"Room 509, fifth floor," he says. "She told me earlier. When we were dancing." He looks slightly guilty. "It was like . . . almost like she wanted me to remember the room. She said it was her favorite number."

"509 isn't her favorite number," Ava says.

"509 isn't anyone's favorite number," I say.

And then Ava puts her hands on her hips. "Come on, guys, really? Danielle told you her room number because she wanted you to come hang out. Danielle and Andrew don't even like each other. You're all such idiots." She flips some purple hair behind her shoulder.

We all look at each other for a few seconds and a wave of understanding passes through us. For the first time everything

CAMERON LUND

is so clear, all the pieces finally fit into their rightful places.

"I have to go back inside," I say, motioning toward the door. "I have to find Andrew."

And then I turn around and run back through the front doors.

"She's running back into a burning building for him!" Ava shouts behind me. "It's true love!"

And then I hear Chase. "There's no fire." And then Ryder. "Where's that other dude?"

I push my way past the two gangly teenage bellhops who are trying to guard the front doors.

"You're not allowed back in the building!" one of them shouts as I pass, but I ignore him and keep running. Now I know where I have to go. Stairs. Five flights up. The concierge is in the middle of the lobby, directing people toward the doors, and when he sees me run past, we lock eyes and *he knows* I'm the one who pulled the alarm. It's like he doesn't know I'm Keely Collins, that pulling alarms isn't in my nature. He thinks I'm someone else, someone wilder and freer and more alive, and I kind of like it.

I run as fast as I can toward the back stairwell, already feeling a cramp in my side. I hear footsteps behind me and turn, expecting to see the concierge, but I'm surprised to see Chase right behind me.

"I can't let you be the only hero," he says, grinning. "Maybe now she'll forgive me."

We tumble together through a swinging door.

"Wait," I say. "We should split up. I take these stairs and you take the ones on the other side." He nods and heads in the other direction, saluting before he disappears back through the swinging door. "Go get your girl!" I call after him.

Then I begin to climb. This is slower going, because the stairs are old and twisty. Finally I make it to the fifth floor, and I push open the door into the hallway. It's empty—only flashing lights and blaring alarms. I let myself lean against the wall for a minute to catch my breath. If he's not on five, I should just go back outside. I'll find him eventually, once the alarm shuts off and the chaos dies down. I heave myself off the wall and head back to the stairs.

Then there he is at the other end of the hallway.

"Collins!" he shouts over the sound of the siren. "We have to get out of here!"

"Where's Danielle?" I ask, expecting her to come around the corner behind him.

"She went outside," he says. "I came up here to find you. Ava said you went back to the fifth floor. There's a fire!" He lunges forward to grab my hand, like he'll be able to pull me to safety.

"It's okay!" I shout back. I let him take my hand and I link our fingers together. "There's no fire!"

"What?" he asks, and I'm not sure if he can't hear me or if he's just confused about what I said.

"There's no fire!" I repeat. "I pulled the alarm."

He's still running down the hallway toward the back stairwell, pulling me along behind him. And then he stops suddenly and I crash into his back.

"You pulled the alarm? Why the hell would you p—"

"You came back for me," I interrupt.

"Of course I came back for you," he says.

And then before he can finish, before I can think it through, I kiss him. It must catch him off guard because it takes about three seconds before he reacts, but then he kisses me back, pulling me tight against his chest, wrapping his arms around me. The sirens must still be wailing but I can't hear them because all I can hear is the heavy thudding of my heart. I take a few steps forward, pushing him until his back hits the wall, and then I press him into it. He brings a hand up into my hair and pulls me closer. We kiss for what feels like forever, and I don't mind, because I could probably keep on kissing him for the rest of my life. When we have to part for air, I pull back and see his eyes flutter open.

"What are you doing?" he asks. Our faces are so close together now that we don't have to shout anymore. I can hear him over the alarm, can feel his lips brush against mine as he asks the question. "Why did you pull the alarm?"

"I needed to find you," I say, tightening my hold around his waist, like now that I have him, I won't let him go. "I've been looking for you."

He grins and I feel his smile against mine. "That's my line."

"I know," I say. "But it's true. I was with Dean and—"

At the sound of Dean's name, Andrew's head jerks up and away from me, looking in both directions down the hallway. "Did he hurt you? Where is he?"

"It's fine," I say. "Everything's fine. But I was with him and I just . . . I wanted it to be you. I really wanted him to be you. I think, I mean, the thing is . . ." I can't believe how hard it is to get the words out, even now.

"Say it," he says, and he kisses me again quickly, the hope sparkling in his eyes giving me courage. "Come on, Keely, say it."

"Iloveyoumorethanpizza," I say, the words tumbling out of me so quickly they blend together. "I love you more than pizza,"

I repeat, slower this time. "I got your note. Is it true?" I feel like I can't breathe.

"Are you kidding?" he says. "Keely, I'm so stupidly in love with you." He leans closer to me so our noses are touching. "I've been in love with you since middle school."

For the first time in my life, I feel really and truly alive. I kiss him again, and it's just the two of us, the only two people in the entire world. But after a minute, I pull away, remembering that's not true.

"But you love Danielle," I say. "You told me. You gave her that valentine."

"Do you know how many times you've turned me down?" he asks, shaking his head. "How many times I started to tell you the truth and you made some joke as if dating me was the most ridiculous thing in the world?" I want to disagree with him, but I know it's true. "So I started saying it before you could say it first. If I could convince myself it was true—if I could agree it was ridiculous, then maybe I could get over you."

"I'm glad you didn't," I say.

"I made that valentine for you, you know, back in middle school. I was going to tell you how I felt. But then you made another stupid comment like you didn't like me, and I chickened out. I gave it to Danielle because that's what everyone else was doing."

"I'm so sorry," I say. "I've been such an idiot."

"Yeah," he says. "You have." He's grinning and I whack him on the shoulder. "But so have I." He reaches up and tucks a strand of hair behind my ear. "When you asked me who I was in love with, I thought you knew it was you. I thought you were trying to tell me you loved me back. But then you turned me down again, and I couldn't handle it. I told you it was Danielle, because it was easy. I knew you would hate it. And then I felt so stupid and I didn't know how to fix it. I wrote you that card on your birthday, and you never even said anything."

"I didn't see it!" I say.

"I should have just said something to you," he says. "Could have saved us so much time."

"You're right. We're both idiots."

I kiss him again.

"You're sure there's no fire?" he asks.

"No fire."

"Good." He grabs my waist and flips us so that my back is against the wall, then presses me into it, covering my body with his.

"Hey!" A voice shouts from down the hall, and Andrew pulls away from me to turn and look. I miss the feel of his lips on mine immediately, and I wonder if every time we're not kissing for the rest of my life I'll be missing him. "Hey, there she is!" It's the concierge from the front desk, running toward us. And with him is Andrew's uncle Leroy, dressed in his full fireman uniform.

Before I can think about it, I grab Andrew's hand and start running down the other end of the hallway, pulling him along behind me. I throw open the door to the back stairwell and we barrel through it and keep running, trying hard not to fall down the stairs and kill ourselves. When we get down to the main level we keep running, turning random corners, tearing down hallways until we've lost them. There are so many doors that I wonder if even the concierge knows every hidden nook and cranny. The alarm is still blaring around us, lights flashing.

"In here!" Andrew says, taking a sharp left and then opening a door to a storage room under the stairs. I follow him in and then he shuts the door behind us and immediately, the sound of the siren is cut off. It's dark in here, almost pitch-black, and I should be worried about spiders or rats or something, but I'm not. Because Andrew's arms are around me and then we're kissing again and he loves me and that's all that matters.

"I'm so losing my job for this," Andrew says, his smile against mine.

"It's worth it," I whisper.

"Oh, it's so worth it." He kisses me again and I reach up and undo his tie just enough so that I can pull open the buttons of his shirt. He reaches behind me and I can feel him struggling with the zipper of my prom dress. I help guide his hand and pull the zipper down, rolling the dress off my body. Reaching out, I undo his belt and then he zips down his fly, the sound of it loud in the quiet room. I can't see him but I can feel him, can feel his hands as they slide my underwear down over my hips, as they touch me in a place that's never been touched before. I gasp as he moves his fingers there, reaching my own hands into his boxers and touching him.

I realize suddenly that this is what it's supposed to feel like—this ache between my legs, this urgent need in my chest, the feeling in my stomach like bubbling champagne. This was how I never felt with Dean, upstairs in that beautiful suite, on the canopy bed, where everything was supposed to be perfect.

I reach into my purse and pull out the condom—the one I had planned to use earlier. Fumbling, I hand it to him in the dark and listen as he rips it open and slides it on.

"Are you sure?" he asks, his whisper tickling my ear.

"Yes," I say, and I am. I'm suddenly so sure that I might die if he doesn't continue.

"I love you so much," he whispers against my mouth.

"I love you too," I whisper back.

And so I lose my virginity on prom night, and it isn't perfect, because how could I expect it to be? Here's what I've realized about moments: you can't plan for them. The best ones are always the ones that take you by surprise.

THIRTY-FOUR

SO WHAT I DIDN'T know is that pulling a fire alarm is a misdemeanor, which means it goes on my record and I could actually go to jail.

Luckily that doesn't happen.

What happens is this: Andrew and I come out of the cupboard eventually and are taken down to the station. Andrew's uncle calls his parents, who then call my parents, and soon they're all at the police station with me, pulled out of bed in pajamas and bathrobes and all with something to say. My parents have never been so mad at me (not just about the alarm, but also the hotel room, and the whiskey, and the whole resisting arrest thing), and when they eventually tire of yelling, Andrew's parents step in and take over. In the end, I'm fined seven hundred dollars, which I'll be working for months at the video store to pay back. I *would* say that spending all summer with Dean is the worst thing I could possibly imagine, but it beats jail. Barely.

Andrew is thrilled by the fact that I'm officially a criminal. When I wake up the morning after prom, his truck is waiting in my driveway. I'm supposed to be grounded until graduation, but my parents give me five minutes to talk to him. Secretly, I think the exception is because of how excited they are that we're together; I have to keep reminding my mom we're too young for her to make jokes about our babies.

When I open the door to his truck, I'm struck immediately by the smell of pizza. He's wearing his glasses—which I *love*—and when I see him I'm suddenly shy, remembering everything that happened between us. What's funny is I don't really feel any different after having sex with Andrew. It turns out losing your virginity is kind of like having a birthday. No one can tell just by looking at you if you're seventeen or eighteen, if you've slept with one person or ten or no one at all. I thought having sex would magically change me, but Andrew didn't turn me into the girl I am now. I did that all on my own.

"I brought you breakfast," Andrew says, holding a pizza box in my direction.

"It's morning," I say back. But I climb in beside him and open the box, toasting my slice of pepperoni against his.

"Should I have asked for mushrooms?" he asks. "I heard you like those now."

"Shut up." I shove him with my shoulder.

He's grinning and adorable. "You know, I never would have guessed that between us, you'd be the felon."

"You still have time," I say, my grin matching his. "Don't count yourself out."

"You're right. I've got way too much time this summer to get up to no good now that I'm out a job."

"But you didn't pull the alarm! Your uncle can't blame you for what I did."

"I'm an accessory to the crime, remember?"

"Speaking of accessories," I say with a wicked smile, "any chance you can get your hands on a fireman uniform?"

"If you wanted me to do a sexy fireman dance for you, you should have thought of it before you pissed off the whole Prescott fire department." He picks a pepperoni off his slice and pops it into his mouth. "I've been thinking of telling my parents I'm not a vegan, actually. It seems like the right time, you know, while everyone's so mad at you."

I laugh, leaning over to kiss him. "I guess love makes you do crazy things." At the word *love*, his smile gets even wider and I see his cheeks redden. It still doesn't feel real. We love each other. He's mine and I'm his. That's worth seven hundred dollars.

Graduation comes a week later, out on the field at school, under a big white tent. Hannah, Andrew, and I go together, piled into Hannah's Jeep with the old wrappers and the trash bags, just like always. I was worried things might be weird now between the three of us, now that two of us are dating—but the thing is, as Hannah puts it, nothing has changed at all. "You and Andrew have been dating since sixth grade," she told me, waving my concerns away when I asked.

Hannah is officially back together with Charlie, which doesn't make me happy, but I know it's my job as her best friend to support her no matter what. He'll probably break her heart again. I'll just have to be there for her when he does.

When we get to the field, we mingle with the parents for a bit, taking so many pictures it feels like prom all over again. But

I don't mind it now; this is something to remember. Right now, I'm the happiest I've ever been.

I want to check the mirror before the ceremony starts, so I head into the school, through the multipurpose room and into the women's bathrooms. The school is empty and quiet—quieter than I've ever heard it, and it strikes me that this might be the very last time I'll ever be inside this building, seeing this shiny linoleum floor, the blue and white tiles on the walls.

I'll never come back here, not if I can help it. But it still feels sad in a way.

I push open the swinging bathroom door and then stop, surprised. Danielle is sitting on the ledge of the sink, her face smudged with mascara. When she sees me, she hastily reaches a hand up to wipe away tears.

"Sorry," I say, letting the bathroom door bump me on the butt. I hesitate for a second, trying to decide if I should leave her alone or step farther into the room.

"In or out, Collins?" she asks, her voice dry.

I take a few hesitant steps forward. "Are you okay?"

"Obviously not."

I turn back around. "Look, if you don't want to talk to me, I'll just leave you alone." I open the door and begin to walk out.

"No," she says, her voice small. "Wait." It's unsettling to hear her sound so vulnerable, like a little girl, like someone who doesn't have full control of every situation. I close the door again.

"I'm gonna miss this place," she says.

"I can't wait to leave," I say, but I know what she means. High school always seemed kinder to Danielle, everyone rooting for her, always on her side. But maybe high school was just as hard for her. Maybe she was just better at dealing with it.

"Did you know it was Ava?" she asks, fiddling with the tassel on the front of her graduation cap. "Writing the notes." I shuffle over to her and climb up next to her on the sink, feeling water seep into the bottom of my robe. It surprises me that she's still so upset about what Ava did—not because it's silly to be, but because Danielle has always seemed so strong.

"I would have told you."

"You wouldn't have told me," she says, her tone emotionless. I realize she's right. I wouldn't have wanted to get involved. Maybe I would have told Hannah instead, hoping that Hannah would do the right thing.

"Would you have believed me?" I ask.

"Probably not," she answers. "You've never liked me much."

"That's not true," I say, feeling defensive.

She looks at me pointedly. "It's not a big deal. I've never liked you much either."

Her words should hurt, but somehow instead of feeling insulted, I'm relieved. It's nice to get it out in the open, to be able to stop pretending. "It's nothing against you," she says. "You just don't like any of the same things that I like. I can feel you rolling your eyes at me every time I talk. You think just because I like doing my hair and makeup, and looking nice, and flirting with boys that I'm dumb." She doesn't sound angry or aggressive—just very matter-of-fact.

"I don't think you're dumb," I say. "I think you're . . . intimidating." I pause before the word, nervous that she'll laugh or throw it back in my face.

"It's just so high school," Danielle says. "Isn't it?"

"What?"

"Pretending to like the people we hang out with. Hanging

out with people we don't like because we're supposed to."

"Well, there aren't very many people at school to choose from."

"But I like Sophie way more than I like you," she says. "No offense. But for some reason I hang out with you way more. Because there are four of us. That's just the way it is. I don't even know how it started. Hannah, I guess. And Andrew. They liked you, so I had to like you. But all you did was act like you were so much cooler than me, because you could skateboard and liked old movies and were friends with the guys. And then, oh wow, this hot college guy liked you, and that just made you even cooler. What makes you so special?"

"But," I protest, finding her hard to believe. "But you're Danielle fucking Oliver. You're cooler than everyone!"

She laughs, hiccupping a little bit. Even like this, even while crying and feeling sorry for herself, she still looks amazing. "I know," she says, licking her thumb and wiping the mascara away from under her eyes. "You know," she says, studying the smudges on her fingers, "I think this is the first real conversation we've ever had."

"Some friends," I say, laughing.

"I thought it could have been you," she says, "writing the notes."

"What?" I ask, my voice rising. "I wouldn't have."

"Yeah. But then I realized you're a terrible liar. You couldn't have gotten away with it."

I laugh and flick some water at her.

"Hey! I'm in fancy graduation robes here!" But she's laughing too, the mood between us light. It's like we've spent all of high school in a bubble that's finally burst. Now is the time to ask, if I ever want answers.

"So did you even like Andrew?" Even though he's mine now, even though I'm sure of it—my chest still feels tight. I realize that this is what love is—this constant ache for the rest of my life that someone or something could take him away.

"Course not," she says. "I've liked Chase for like ten years, Collins. I thought that was obvious." She takes her graduation cap off and studies herself in the mirror, bringing her hands up to flatten the stray wispy pieces around her forehead. "Andrew was so jealous of your college boy he was about to explode. So I knew we could help each other out. I'm a manipulative bitch, remember?"

"You're not a bitch," I say, meaning it.

Our eyes meet in the mirror and she smiles. "Do you think we'll stay friends after we graduate?"

"No." It feels freeing to finally speak the truth. "And that's okay."

She sighs. I know she's thinking about Ava.

"You guys will make up," I say.

"I know I need to be nicer to her." She stares down at her hands, her fingernails still shiny and black. "I think maybe we're meanest to the people we love the most because we want to believe they'll love us no matter what."

Before I think about what I'm doing, I take her hand and squeeze. "Ava still loves you. Just give it some time."

"Thanks." She smiles, and it's a real one—the kind that shines through her eyes.

"We should go back out there," I say. "Face our future and all that."

We get up off the sink and leave the bathroom together, still hand in hand, heading back out to the field to see everyone.

When we reach the big white tent with all the chairs, she squeezes one more time and then lets go, veering off to where Chase and Ava are standing. Chase throws an arm around Danielle, pulling her close, and I see the flash of hurt on Ava's face before she breaks into a resigned smile. I hope they make up eventually, but maybe they won't. Maybe some friendships are meant just for high school. Maybe Danielle and Ava no longer fit together, no longer speak the same language.

I wave to them and then head over to Andrew and Hannah, pulling them into a tight hug, just the three of us.

"I'll miss this," I say as the graduation march begins.

I know it's not the end, not just yet. We still have all summer before we're pulled in different directions. Andrew and I have two months before we have to go long-distance. But we'll never be the exact same as we are right now. We'll never have eighteen-years-old, summer-before-college ever again, when we're free and optimistic, when we're all in love for the first time and the world is spread out before us, untouched and shimmering.

I don't know what the future holds. I don't know if Andrew and I will stay together forever, if he'll always be my best friend, my favorite person, my most important somebody. I hope so. I hope I'll be eating pizza with him until we're too old to chew. But I know I can't plan it all out right now. I can't look for answers in a book, can't map everything out before it happens.

Sometimes life isn't perfect. It isn't a movie. I can't direct it, can't edit out the scenes that I don't like. Life is messy and complicated and full of misunderstandings. And that's okay. Whatever happens, I can't wait.

I'm so ready.

ACKNOWLEDGMENTS

As a kid, when I imagined the ideal writer version of myself, it looked like this: me, alone in a cabin somewhere, on an island, or a beach, or on top of a mountain surrounded by trees. And while part of that has come true (I have written on several different islands), the truth is that writing is not something you do alone; there are so many people who have helped and cheered me along every step of the way.

First, I must thank my parents, who have always been supportive of my love of the arts (whether that meant driving me to rehearsals, plying me with piles of books each Christmas, or encouraging me to write on weekend mornings instead of watching cartoons). I'm thankful that the words "I'm bored" were always met with suggestions of how to fill my time with art and music. Thank you for understanding that I was never going to take a typical path and for cultivating my creativity. To my dad for inspiring in me a love of stories by reading to me each night before bed. To my mom, who, when I was feeling down about my music, said "I think you should be a writer" and changed the course of my life.

A huge thank-you to Shirin Yim Bridges. I started your class with an idea for a story, and now I get to share it with the world.

To my original writers group and the rest of the Richmond gang: Amanda, Jessica, Sara, Joey, Irene, Remi, and Erich. Thank you not only for your brilliant writing expertise, but for letting me text you endlessly about my anxieties, and in general for your magical unicorn friendship.

To the other writers who read my first drafts and helped me shape this story: Cassia, Cady, Jenn, Julie, and Marjorie. You've been with Keely and Andrew since the beginning. And to the rest of Shirin's Army, thanks for your company and support and late-night glasses of cognac.

Thank you to Jody Gehrman, Sabrina Lotfi, and Renée Price for your beta reads and your enthusiastic championing. You *fairy-godmothered* this book and got her ready for prom.

I am incredibly lucky to have so many amazing friends. To the Doobs—with a friend like you, I play the right part. To my magical book club, thank you for being hilarious, intelligent, feminist queens who are always ready with a Harry Potter reference. Endless love to 4th Floor South, the Gauchos, and the whole Bae Area crew! You're all my family and I am so thankful to have so much laughter in my life. If high school me—who was lonely and insecure and afraid of the future—could have seen you all coming, she would have been so proud. I know we will all stay friends forever and I can't wait to eat pizza with you until we're too old to chew. If this book sells well, I promise to buy the commune.

And of course, thank you to my amazing agent, Taylor

Haggerty, and the rest of the Root Literary team (special shout-out to Melanie Figueroa for picking me out of the slush!). Thanks to my incredible editor, Julie Rosenberg, and to everyone else at Razorbill, for believing in this book and making my dreams come true. Thank you to Heather Baror-Shapiro for bringing this book abroad, and to Mary Pender-Coplan for film. Thanks to my designer, Maggie Edkins, and my illustrator, Carolina Melis, for my beautiful cover. To the marketing and publicity teams at Penguin for everything you're doing to share my story.

Last, but certainly not least, thank you to the readers. Without you this would all be meaningless.

TURN THE PAGE FOR A PEEK AT CAMERON LUND'S NEXT BOOK!

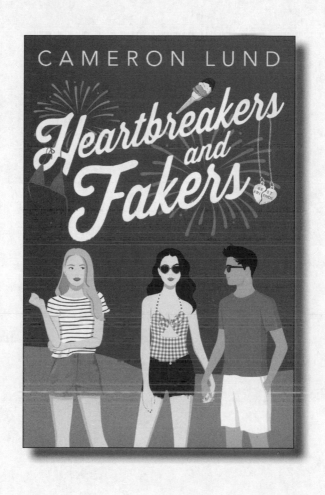

NOW

IT TAKES ME A SECOND to realize I'm not in Jordan's bed.

My head is pounding—a throbbing ache at my temples—and before I pry open my eyes, I'm struck by how bright the light is on the other side of my lids. I reach a hand out, expecting to feel Jordan's warmth beside me, envisioning his smile, the crooked tooth that only makes him cuter. I've been waiting half my life to wake up next to Jordan Parker.

Instead, my hand touches what feels like grass, wet with morning dew. That's when I open my eyes. Because I'm not in bed at all. I'm on a lawn chair in Jordan's yard.

I scramble to sit up, and as I do, a wave of nausea rolls through me, my stomach twisting. I'm not sure whether it's from the alcohol still coursing through my system, seeping out my pores like sweat, or whether it's from the knowledge that Jordan and I did not sleep together last night, in any sense of the term. That somehow I ended up on this chair and I can't exactly remember how I got here.

I stumble to my feet, noticing then that my shoes are missing, the hot pink high-tops Olivia and I bought together last week. We'd wanted to match. When you match with somebody, it proves to the rest of the world you're important; you're part of something. And everyone wants to be part of Olivia.

Now both my shoes are gone, one foot totally bare, the other covered in a slimy wet sock. My knees are bruised, but I don't remember falling. Actually, I don't remember much of anything. Dinner with Olivia and Katie at the place downtown with the endless breadsticks and the waiter that never cards; piña coladas and margaritas and daiquiris, because the best drinks are the kind you can take pictures with, that make it look like you're on vacation and make everyone else on Instagram jealous.

I remember leaving dinner, arms thrown around each other's shoulders, laughing so hard in the Uber it felt like I might pee. Then later, dancing to Lana Del Rey in Olivia's room, helping her apply the perfect smoky eye. The feel of Jordan's arms around me when we got to his house, the way his cheek felt scratchy against mine; the smell of him, something earthy and exciting, a thrilling reminder of our plan for later.

But the rest of it is a blur. How did I get out here on the lawn? And why didn't anyone bring me inside?

I pull my phone out of my pocket—thank god I haven't lost it too—and check the time. It's nine a.m., which isn't as late as I'd usually sleep after a party, but isn't that early either. I must have been out here for hours. I don't have any texts, which is unusual. In the mornings, my phone is typically buzzing like crazy—conversations happening on every app about the night before. *Did you see Brett and Darlene making out? How drunk was Katie? You looked so hot last night. Love ya, babe. Love ya love ya love ya.* But right now, it's quiet, the screen darker than it's been since sixth grade, back when I was still Pukey Penelope. Back before Olivia discovered me.

I can't help the buzzing fear that something is wrong. Because if everything were normal, I wouldn't be out here. There's something I can't remember, something I'm pretty sure involves Olivia. I can feel it in my gut. And I'm scared of what she might say.

Olivia has always had a way of telling the truth to your face and making it sound like a kindness, her dazzling smile tricking you into thinking she's on your side. *Maybe next time, don't be such a sloppy mess. Girls like us are better than that.* It's just I'm not usually on the receiving end of it—not since we became best friends. These were comments meant for Katie, who's always a little too eager and embarrassing; for Myriah, who cries in school over bad grades; for Romina, who always ditches us to hang out with the guys. No, I'm always on Olivia's good side, the one she laughs about it with later.

But maybe I'm overreacting. I probably told my friends I was heading home and then couldn't get a ride or something. I bet this chair just seemed like the best option at the time. When I go inside, everything will be totally normal. Olivia will be asleep on the L-shaped couch with Katie, grumbling and hungover, but happy to see me. *I knew you wouldn't disappear before breakfast sandwiches!* she'll say, laughing and unpacking the eggs and cheese and muffins we bought yesterday to prepare for today's hangovers. Jordan will be upstairs in his room, the bed with the fresh sheets he washed just for us, because last night was meant to be special. Our first time.

Jordan and I officially started dating last December, but I've been in love with him for years. He finally asked me to be his girlfriend right before winter break, and then Olivia was dating Jordan's best friend, Kai, by Christmas. I love that we got boyfriends at the same time, and even though Kai is one of the most annoying people on the planet, I deal with him for Olivia's sake.

Last night was supposed to be perfect—the final night of our junior year, the first day of summer, officially seniors, the ones in charge of everything.

Now I'm not so sure.

I'm still in my junior class shirt, the one we all wore to school yesterday so everybody could sign them. Some of the signatures are smudged now, the Sharpie running from the wet grass. My hair is still in its twin braids, same as Olivia's, hers blonde to my brunette. I don't want to see my face. I'm sure it's a disaster. I really went for it—full contour, highlight, brows. I wanted to look like the kind of girl Jordan would be proud of. I'll have to run to the downstairs bathroom to clean up before I see him.

Raising a hand to shield my eyes, I turn toward the house. Sun roasts the back of my neck, the heat of it making me dizzy. I squelch through the damp grass in my sock to the sliding glass door that opens up to the TV room and try to pull it open, but it's locked. Peering inside, I see Katie asleep on the couch in a position that can't be comfortable, one foot on the floor, an arm thrown above her head. I knock on the window, and she startles awake. When she sees me, a wave of emotions passes over her face—first a smile, then a grimace, finally settling on confusion, her eyebrows knitted together, frown lines on her forehead that are sure to cause wrinkles. It makes me nervous. It makes me even more sure something is wrong.

She stands up from the couch, coming over to me, dodging piles of trash—cans, red cups, spilled chip bags—that have become a maze on the floor. Katie's got these unruly black curls that are almost bigger than she is, and right now, they've tripled in size from her night on the couch. She unlocks the sliding door and pulls it open, just barely, not enough that I can fit inside.

"Penny," she says, almost a whisper. "What are you still doing here?"

"What do you mean?" I say. "Come on, Katie. Open the door."

She glances behind her. "I really think you should go."

"But this is my boyfriend's house." Even right now—even feeling like this—I can't help the little burst of pride that blooms inside me as I say it. Katie claims to have a boyfriend too—a guy named Matt she met at summer camp and never stops talking about—but none of us have ever seen a picture, so we're not sure he's real. "You can't block me from Jordan's house, Katie. That doesn't make any sense."

Katie presses her lips together in a tight line. "I'm trying to help you." And there it is again—the buzzing in my chest. Something went horribly wrong last night, and Katie knows what it is.

"I guess I spent the night on the lawn?" I try to put a smile in my voice. If I can pretend this whole thing is funny, then maybe everything will be okay.

"I thought you went home," she says. "After everything that happened."

"Katie, what happened?" My stomach clenches. The nausea is worse now, and I'm sweating in earnest, the sun on the back of my neck unrelenting.

"Penny, you should leave."

This isn't how things work with Katie and me. I'm usually the one in control, the one on the better side of the door.

My brother once told me that popularity wasn't real, that I should stop worrying about something that doesn't matter. But he's a guy, so of course he doesn't get it. I told him I could rank every girl in our class in order. Olivia is number one, obviously. I'm number two, and Katie is number three. Darlene is number fifteen, because even though she's weird, people still hang out with her to buy weed. Sarah Kozlowski, who doesn't wash her blue hair—who pricked her finger once in biology so she could study her own blood under the microscope—is number fifty-six. Dead last. It's not something that's ever really talked about; everybody just knows. It's important to know your place in the world. It gives you a road map of how to act— who to be friends with, who you're allowed to date, who you need to avoid at all costs.

"Katie," I say again. "Please let me into the house."

"Fine." She sighs heavily and pulls open the door wide enough for me to squeeze by. Inside, the hot summer air is trapped with the stale stench of trash and sweat. There are other people in the room, I realize. Danny Scott is asleep on the other side of the couch, and Romina and Myriah are curled up on an air mattress in the corner.

"Thanks," I say to Katie. "I'm gonna get cleaned up. I feel like roadkill."

"You *look* like roadkill," she says back, which I should have expected. She shakes her head, pausing before she adds, "Are you okay?"

"I'm fine. I love the fresh air." I know I sound ridiculous, but

I can't make any of this a big deal. Not if I want the story to go away.

I'm about to walk into the downstairs bathroom when I'm stopped in my tracks by a familiar voice. "What the hell are you doing here?"

Olivia has just appeared at the top of the stairs and she's looking at me like I'm the enemy. Her blonde hair is out of her braids—so that we no longer match—and her skin is fresh and dewy; Olivia's hangovers don't show on her face. She's still in the same junior T-shirt as I am, and I can see my message for her there, right over her left boob: *love you forever*. I want to read it to her, make her remember I'm the girl that put it there only yesterday.

"Hey, Liv," I say, forcing out a laugh. "You'll never believe where I slept last night."

"I don't care where you slept." She folds her arms, looking down at me with a sneer.

"Oh . . . okay," I say, still hesitant. "Should we start breakfast?" We've made breakfast sandwiches at every sleepover since middle school, and even though our sleepovers have now turned into parties, we would never let the habit die. Maybe right now the sandwiches will make everything better—will smooth over whatever went down last night.

"So you're just gonna pretend you don't remember?" Olivia puts her hands on her hips, and I know that eggs will not magically fix anything.

"I *don't* remember, Olivia. I mean, I remember parts of last night, but if we got in a fight or something, I'm sure it wasn't a big deal." My voice is really wavering now, and my nose starts to itch as I hold in the tears. Katie sits down on the end of the couch, watching us with big eyes. The others are waking up now too—Danny yawning and pulling out his phone, Romina and Myriah laughing quietly, whispers back and forth like the hiss of snakes. I can't cry, not in front of an audience.

"How convenient for you," Olivia says.

I rack my brain, trying to think of anything I could have said to offend her. But everything yesterday was so *fun*. It wasn't a real school day—the teachers dismissed us early because we were all so hyped up on summer. We gathered in the field to sign each other's shirts, but Danny had sneak-attack pelted us with water balloons, and soon it was all-out war—Olivia and I teaming up on Jordan and Kai and dropping balloons on them from the second-story stairwell. Then we'd gone home and dried off and gotten ready to go out, laughing and dancing around in her room. Olivia had been excited about Jordan and me. She'd looked up silly sex tips online—the ridiculous ones from *Cosmo* that I swear no one has ever tried in real life. We'd read one that suggested throwing a handful of pepper into the guy's face while in the act and died laughing so hard Olivia fell off the bed. I'd brought a little pepper shaker to the party with me as a joke and when I showed her later, she'd screamed.

Whatever happened to ruin all that must have been bad.

"If I said anything that hurt your feelings," I say, "I'm sorry."

"You're sorry," Olivia repeats, her voice flat. "Well, that changes everything."

"Where's Jordan?" I start walking up the stairs, pulling off my sock when it squelches into the carpet. Whatever went down between Olivia and me, I know Jordan will take my side. I need him to tell me that everything is going to be okay.

"Why would you care?" Olivia laughs, but there's no humor in it, and suddenly I'm terrified. Is this all about Jordan?

"Liv, what are you talking about?" My voice catches, and I have to clear my throat. "I love Jordan."

She steps to the side, blocking me from passing. Jordan's room is across the hall at the top of the stairs. I can see the bumper stickers on the door: KEEP TAHOE BLUE, BOB MARLEY, SANTA CRUZ BEACH BOARDWALK.

"Oh really? Did you think about him at all last night?" she asks. "No, wait, you can't remember anything."

"You don't live here," I say, dread pooling in my stomach at her words. "Let me talk to him."

She pauses and then smiles. "Okay. Let's talk to him. That sounds fun."

She steps aside, and I walk past her and up to the door. I push it open and then there he is, lying on the bed, a sheet twisted around his bare torso, dappled sunlight shining through slits in the closed blinds. He's beautiful—tan skin and clean, hard lines. I'm not the only one obsessed with Jordan—we're all half in love with him. I'm just the lucky one who actually got him.

"Jordan," I say, coming into the room and sitting down on the edge of the bed. I glance behind me and see Olivia hovering in the doorway, watching. There's a peal of laughter from downstairs, someone telling someone else to shut up. I want to close the door. I want Olivia to leave. But I want to fix things with her, so I don't say anything.

"Jordan," I say again, tapping him lightly on the shoulder. He groans, shuffling around under the sheet, and then jerks awake, his eyes flashing back and forth between Olivia and me before settling firmly on my face.

"Penny," he says in a gust of air. "What are you still doing here? I thought you went home last night."

"No, I . . ." I trail off, not wanting to fill him in on the rest of the details. I'm holding my breath, waiting for something else to go wrong. "I'm so sorry about last night . . . if something happened." I don't know what I'm apologizing for, but it seems like the right thing to do.

"Penny doesn't remember anything," Olivia says, taking steps into the room. "She has *amnesia.*"

"I just drank too much." I turn back to her, the tang of the piña coladas, margaritas, and daiquiris still sharp and sweet in the back of my throat.

"You were a mess." Jordan sits up, and the sheet falls down around his waist.

"I know," I say. "I know, and I'm sorry." *Are we okay? Do you still love me?* That's what I really want to ask. Jordan has always been too good for me, our relationship so tenuous.

"Come on, Penny," Jordan says. He reaches out like he's going to take my hand for a second and then pulls back, clearly mad at himself for doing it. "This is seriously unfair. You do something fucked up, but you don't remember it, so then you don't have to feel guilty?" His words cause a flare in my stomach, the feeling like I've lost control of my car on the freeway.

"What happened, Jordan?" I'm trying to keep my voice steady. "I love you." How can I make him believe it? I repeat the words in my mind, like I'll be able to imprint them on Jordan's heart. *I love you, I love you, I love you.*

Olivia sits down next to me on the bed. "Well, maybe you should have thought about that before you made out with my boyfriend."

"What?" For a second I think Olivia must be joking. It's a well-known fact that Olivia's boyfriend, Kai, and I don't get along.

And besides that—I would never do anything to hurt Olivia.

But then there's a flash of memory—I'm leaning into Kai, my hands in his hair, a feeling of want pooling in my stomach. I instinctively shake my head to make the image go away. It's not a full memory, not exactly, just a flicker of feeling. It's like what we learned last year about Plato's cave; I can't see the image, just a shadow of the image reflected onto the wall.

"Do you need me to repeat it?" Olivia asks.

"Jordan." I turn to him. "I didn't. I wouldn't do anything with Kai. I don't even *like* Kai."

"Olivia walked in on you guys kissing," he says. "In the laundry room."

And I know it's true. I can see the basket of folded clothes upturned on the floor, can feel my back pressed against the washing machine, can remember leaning in to kiss him, trying to convince him I wasn't that drunk, him pulling away. It's all there in my memories—a horrible movie reel of terrible decisions.

No no no no no. It doesn't make any sense. Last night was supposed to be special. I'd been planning it for weeks. Why would I ruin that? Why would I ruin that with Olivia's *boyfriend*?

"I'm . . . sorry," I say, my voice weak. I know *sorry* doesn't cover it. I know there isn't anything I could actually say to make this better. I'm the worst person in the entire world.

I remember lying with Olivia on her bed last night before the party, the conversation drifting from Jordan and the questionable *Cosmo* sex advice over to Kai. "I just can't figure him out right now," she'd said, unsure. "I feel like we're drifting apart."

"What if you stuck an ice cube down his pants?" I'd suggested with wiggling eyebrows, referencing one of the stupider tips we'd read.

"Yeah, that'll win him over." She'd laughed and then we'd moved on, like the conversation hadn't even happened. And I'd made everything so much worse. She'd been upset about things with Kai and instead of being a good friend, I'd *kissed* him.

"I think you should probably leave," Jordan says now. "I don't really want to do this anymore."

"Do this like . . . this conversation?" I ask softly. "Or, like . . . *us*?"

"I mean, I don't think we should be together."

I feel bile rise at the back of my throat, tears stinging the corner of my eyes. I have to get out of here before anything gets any worse. I can't cry in front of everyone. Worse—I can't throw up. Pukey Penelope will *not* be making another appearance. I've worked so hard for this, to be here in Jordan Parker's bedroom, best friends with Olivia Anderson, finally a girl everyone else wants to be—a girl with friends who make her feel like she matters.

There's no way they'll still want to be friends with me. I wouldn't want to be friends with me.

"Did anything happen last night with you and Olivia?" I ask Jordan, working at a hole in his sheet with my fingernail. It's the question that's been nagging at me, a sliver of unease in the back of my mind. It's the way her hand is still on his shoulder, how she's sitting on his bed like she belongs there. This problem with Jordan is fixable—I know I can get him back, so long as Olivia hasn't gotten to him. In a competition against Olivia, anyone would lose.

"Anything going on with me or Jordan is none of your business," Olivia answers. "You lost the privilege to know anything about us when you stuck your tongue in Kai's mouth."

"I'm sorry," I say, even though I know it's not enough. "I don't know why I kissed him. It doesn't make sense. I love you guys." I shake my head, trying to clear the memory away, like if I can forget it happened, everyone else will too. I know that's why I couldn't remember it when I woke up. It was self-preservation.

My mind flashes again to the way Kai's hair felt between my fingers, his hands on my back before he pulled them away. I wish I could make this all his fault, but I know it's not. He'd tried to stop me, but I'd kissed him. And I'd *liked* it. That's the worst part.

Because besides the horrible fact that he's with Olivia, there's also this: Kai ruined my life in elementary school. And yeah, maybe we grew up and were forced to hang out, but I've never quite gotten over it.

According to chaos theory, a butterfly flapping its wings can cause a tornado all the way across the world, events flowing outward like ripples on the surface of a lake. All of this started when Kai moved to our town from Hawaii in fifth grade—Pukey Penelope, my friendship with Olivia, falling for Jordan; all the moments of my life built one upon the other.

And this right now? This is the freaking tornado.

"I have to go." I stumble out of the room and down the stairs, holding my breath so the tears don't fall.

I can hear Olivia's footsteps behind me. "Yeah, get out!" Her voice is sharp as a knife, her words twisting in my gut. Katie's eyes are wide, mouth hanging open. Romina has her phone pointed in my direction, and I see the light that means she's recording. Soon my misery will be posted all over social media. Soon the whole school will know what I did.

I pull open the screen door and race out into the yard,

Olivia right behind me. The sprinklers are on, and I run through them, the cold water shocking me awake. My bare feet squelch through the grass and then I'm on the blacktop, tar burning hot from the sun, and running down the driveway. It's not until I'm out onto the street, around the corner, where I know Olivia can't see, that I start to cry.